LOST

BOOK 1

ADRIANA PRIDEMORE

This book is 100% created by a human. The author (a human, albeit a goofy human) wrote all of the fictional insanity that is contained within this work.

Now for the technical/legal stuff:

ISBN: 979-8-9909128-6-1 (print)

ISBN: 979-8-9909128-7-8 (ebook)

Library of Congress Control Number: 2026912909

Cover art: Miblart

Printed in the United States of America

To my husband, who fell in love with this story from the moment I started writing it and has bugged me to finish it ever since. Thank you, Frank, for the encouragement and for the nagging.

Contents

The Arazi Empire
Zmajev Provence
Znanje
Doseg
Zatvor
Imperial City
Uscar Provence
Mirath Bay
Dalasi
Siewek
Sinir River
Arazi Sea
Javaj
Bay of Riba
Koric
Sinir
Arazi Warship/ dragon battle
N
W
E
S
Kraj
Junzi
Najanz
Ka River
Northgate
Shipwreck
Azgin Su River
Wenzake Village
Southgate
Ka Petra
The Walking Corpse
Holy Mountain
Fishing Hut
Ka Provence
Garach

Intruder

Some debts can never be repaid, but Ro was determined to try, even if it took her life. Not that guarding the side gate was likely to get her killed. It led from the courtyard to the kitchen garden, and no one but the kitchen staff ever used it. It was, quite literally, the dullest assignment in the duty roster, and yet, Ro was determined. She sighed and shifted from one foot to the other, trying to ease the stiffness creeping into her back.

"Day's almost over, girl."

Ro glanced at Beck. Her fellow guard leaned against the wall on the other side of the gate. He had one knee bent with his foot braced against the wall behind him.

"You know, you wouldn't get so sore if you'd relax once in a while." Beck scratched the stubble on his chin. "It's not like anything ever happens on Koric. This island is about as eventful as a brothel in a graveyard."

"I take my duty seriously."

"Nothing wrong with taking it seriously, but you don't need to stay so stiff that it breaks yer spine."

She turned back to survey the courtyard. The fading sunset bathed everything in a soft pink glow. Ro rolled her shoulders and rubbed the back of her neck. Maybe she was standing too stiffly; her neck was starting to tingle. She sighed again and readjusted her stance.

Beck chuckled and shook his head. "You're young yet. You'll learn."

Ro waited for the jibe against her gender, but it didn't come. Being the only woman in the House Guard of Koric had left her the butt of endless jokes from the rest of the Guard. She didn't like it, but being in the Guard seemed like the best way to repay Queen Abeth.

A scrabbling sound above them made them both turn and stare up. A couple of loose pebbles rolled off the top of the high wall behind them. Ro and Beck exchanged a look. As one, they reached up and slid their swords free from their shoulder harnesses. Beck moved forward and placed a ready hand on the gate latch. He glanced back at Ro. She nodded. He shoved the gate open.

It banged back against the stone of the garden wall. Beck stepped into the garden. Ro stayed back, glancing between the top of the wall and the gateway.

After a moment, Beck reappeared. "Nothing there." He sheathed his sword. "Must have been a bird."

Ro frowned, staring at the top of the wall. Her neck was still tingling. She rubbed at it absently. "Are you sure?"

Beck gestured toward the gate. "Go look for yourself."

Ro didn't hesitate. She walked into the garden and looked around. Light poured out of the open kitchen doorway on the far wall, and faint sounds of dinner preparations floated across the rows of well-tended vegetables. She glanced around the garden. Shadows crowded close in the fading light. Nothing moved except the leaves waving in the breeze. She turned to scan the tops of the garden walls. At first, there was no sign of movement, but then something caught her eye, a shadow amongst the shadows.

She squinted, trying to see if there was something there or if it had been a trick of the fading light. Then she heard the scrabbling sound again.

She dodged back through the gate. "I heard it again!"

"Yep." Beck watched the wall.

A gray furry face with bright yellow eyes appeared, looking down at them from the top of the stone wall. It disappeared just as fast.

"It's just an animal," Beck laughed and stalked over to pull the garden gate shut.

"But what was it?" Ro stepped back, stretching up on her toes to get a better look.

"Animals come and go." Beck shrugged as he leaned back against the wall again.

"I've never seen an animal like that on Koric." Ro rubbed her neck. A couple more pebbles tumbled off the top of the wall closer to the King's Tower, which dominated the southwestern corner of the courtyard. "Something just doesn't feel right."

"So, go chase it down." Beck pushed off the wall and walked over to where she stood. He peered up at the wall. "I'll stay here."

Ro glanced at him, wondering if he was teasing her or if he was serious.

Seeing her suspicious look, Beck said, "Part of being a good House Guard is following your instincts." When she still hesitated, he gave her a shove. "Go. I'll keep our post here."

Ro moved along the wall, listening and watching for any sign of movement. The sound was intermittent at best, but it was definitely moving toward the King's Tower. She heard it again at the base of the tower next to one of the finchberry bushes that grew wild all over the grounds of the castle.

Ro stopped and squinted into the shadows. The scraping sound grew louder as some of the long grass growing close to the wall shifted. Ro crept closer and waited for the little animal to pop out, thinking maybe she could catch it.

She rolled her shoulders, trying to get the tingling in her neck to ease. As she watched, a gloved hand shoved the grass aside. Ro raised her sword to strike the intruder. At that moment, a very blonde head appeared.

"Leema!"

"Ro?" Leema froze, looking up. "Uh... what are you doing here?"

Scowling, Ro slid her sword back into her harness and reached down to pull Leema to her feet. "You can't keep sneaking out like this." Ro glanced around to see if Beck had seen the youngest princess crawling through the shrubbery, but the finchberry bush blocked his view.

Leema dusted the dirt off her borrowed boy's tunic and pulled twigs from her hair. "Don't tell, all right?"

"Have I ever?" Ro glanced toward Beck again, but he was staring off toward the other end of the courtyard. She turned back to inspect the weeds where Leema appeared. "How do you find these places?"

"I saw a cat using it yesterday. It's a drain." Leema shook some dirt out of her shirt.

"We'll have to seal it up like the others."

Leema slid a mutinous glance at her. "You could leave me one bolt hole, you know."

Before Ro could answer, they heard a scrabbling sound. The girls looked up. They could see the furry body outlined against the twilight sky. It was halfway up the side of the King's Tower.

Leema squinted. "What's that?"

"I don't know."

"Why is it climbing the tower? There's nothing up there it could want. It can't be looking for food." Leema gestured back toward the garden. "There's plenty down here."

"I'm gonna try and catch it." Ro trotted toward the door at the base of the tower. "You better get changed before your sisters catch you," Ro said over her shoulder as she reached the door. She yanked it open and nearly collided with Princess Brenith and Princess Aritha.

"Ro!" Brenith gasped as she staggered back.

"Pardon me, Highness!" Ro ducked a quick bow and tried to slip around them.

"Have you no respect at all?" Aritha snapped, flicking her golden hair off her shoulder and glaring at Ro.

Ro stepped back and pressed her lips together. Aritha's venomous attitude always rankled.

"Sorry, Ro. We didn't mean to get in your way."

"Get in her way?" Aritha braced her hands on her hips. "What about her getting in our way?"

"Aritha, enough." Brenith sighed, frowning at her older sister. She turned to Ro. "Mother sent us to find Leema. Have you seen her?"

"Yes." Ro was careful not to mention what Leema had been doing or the state she had been in. "She was in the courtyard earlier."

"Thank you." Brenith moved to the side, pulling her sister with her.

"Highness." Ro bowed again, then dashed up the stairs.

Behind her, she could hear Aritha berating Brenith. "Why do you treat her like she's our sister? She's not, no matter what mother says."

Aritha's words chased Ro up the stairs. Aritha was right. She wasn't part of the royal family, and yet she was bound to the queen by something stronger. Ro owed the queen her life, her blood, everything, but even that would never be enough to repay her debt to Queen Abeth. She had thought about nothing else. Every night for the past twelve years, she had climbed to the top of the King's Tower. It was as far as she could get from the memory of being chained to the wall in the Zatvor mine. Someday, somehow, she would repay Abeth.

Ro reached the heavy oak door at the top of the stairs. Carefully, she pushed it open and stepped out onto the battlement. She scanned the horizon. The sea seemed empty, not a single sail. Only glittering waves. Echoes of laughter from the town below drifted on the gentle breeze. The last of the sun's light had faded, and now, only the moon was left glowing in the twilight. Far to the southwest, she could see smoke from the Holy Mountain writhing into the sky. It looked like a clawed demon, reaching for the moon.

Ro shivered. As she reached up and rubbed at the back of her still-tingling neck, she caught a glimpse of her arm. Her uniform seemed red as blood in the dim light. Shaking off the eerie feeling of dread, Ro paced the perimeter of the tower but found no trace of the furry animal.

Standing on her toes, she tried to see over the edge, but she was too short. She wedged herself between the merlons and stared down the side of the tower. Below her, on the ledge of a window, she could see a furry tail protruding.

Ro squirmed her way back off the wall and ran back to the stairway door. Gliding down the spiral in short, quick steps, Ro reached the landing that led to the queen's chambers. The tingling in the back of her neck increased.

Ro scanned the hallway. Her gaze pierced every shadow. Her uneasiness grew, but she still saw nothing. Her gaze was drawn to the window, but the owner of the tail was no longer sitting on the ledge. Ro frowned and stepped closer.

"Krr." The sound came from below the window. A small shadow detached from the wall and darted up onto the sill.

She caught a glimpse of it just as it cleared the window casing. It was small and furry with a long bushy tail. Ro sprang forward. She poked her head out of the window just in time to see the ringed tail disappear around the corner of the ledge.

"Now where's it going?" Ro frowned as she pulled her head back in and closed the window, latching it. The tingling in her neck intensified. Ro clenched her jaw and turned to scan the hall. Although she didn't see anything, this time, she knew something was there.

Assassin

Keeping her back to the wall, Ro edged toward the queen's chambers. Her eyes continued to search the shadows until she reached Abeth's door. Ro fumbled behind her for the handle. The tingling had spread to her entire back now. Turning the knob, she shoved the door open with her heel and stepped backward into the room. She pushed the door closed and flipped the latch to lock it.

"Ro?" Queen Abeth rose from her seat by the fire. "Is everything all right?"

"No." Ro rotated slowly, scanning every part of the room. The tingling had spread to her legs and arms. She didn't like it. Ro searched around the room, moving curtains and checking under the bed. "You feel anything?"

"Like what?" Abeth stepped closer. "Ro, what's wrong?"

She rubbed the back of her neck. The tingling was nearly unbearable. "You don't feel that?"

"Feel what?" Abeth stepped closer and laid a hand on her arm. "Are you ill?"

Ro shook her head in confusion as she backed away from the queen toward the door. The closer she got, the more the tingle burned. "Something is..." Ro spun and yanked the door open.

Standing framed in the door was a huge man with a sword in his hand. Black shaggy hair stuck out below his leather helmet. A jagged scar ran down his face, bisecting his drooping mustache. Without a sound, the man lunged.

Ro stumbled backward to avoid his strike.

"Ro!" Abeth screamed.

Ro tried to get control of her feet while she reached up to draw her sword. She barely got it out in time to block another swipe of the man's blade. The blow was powerful enough to knock her backward.

Abeth ran to the window. Throwing it open, she screamed for the guards.

Ro positioned herself between the intruder and Abeth. Shouts echoed through the tower as the guards thundered up the stairs, spurring the man into action. First a feign, then a quick swipe. Ro countered. The tingling seemed to pull her the right way just before he moved.

They danced back and forth. Swipe. Thrust. Dodge. Feign. Swipe. He was so fast. Ro felt like she was fighting in syrup, but she always managed to block his cuts.

Once again, he feigned and swiped upward. At the last second, he twisted and changed the direction of his swing, bringing the blade across.

Ro yelped in surprise and tripped sideways, barely avoiding his strike.

"Ro!" Abeth cried.

Ro tried to get her feet under her as he raised his sword for another strike, but she lost her footing. She slipped on the rug, fell backward, and bounced off the bed, ricocheting forward. As her knees hit the floor, her sword buried itself in the ribs of the intruder just as he moved to bring his sword straight down toward her head. Ro gasped in surprise. The intruder looked down to where her blade protruded from his chest. He was just as surprised as she was. Slowly, he dropped to his knees.

Ro froze. The intruder held her gaze. Blood bubbled out of his chest as the light faded from his eyes. She watched him pant his last breaths. There was a sickening, slurping sound as her blade slid out of his flesh as he toppled over and was still.

The door burst open. The House Guards rushed through the opening but stumbled to a stop. They stared at Ro, who was on her knees beside the intruder's body. Her bloody sword hung from her loose fingers.

High Marshal Taus shoved his way into the room. He looked at Ro. He looked at the body. He looked at Abeth. Then he shouted at the frozen guards. "All right, move it! There's been an intruder. I want a full search of the entire castle. Check the rest of the family. Move!"

At the sound of his voice, the men snapped out of their shock and scrambled to obey. As soon as the room was clear, Taus turned toward Ro. She was still staring at the man she had killed. He glanced at Abeth. "You all right?"

The queen nodded and came forward slowly. Taus knelt and watched Ro. He was careful to stay out of sword reach.

"Ro?" he called quietly. "Rohamina." When she didn't move, he called again. "Tiny?"

She looked up at him. Her face was pale, and the blue of her eyes was almost white. She let her sword clatter to the floor and threw herself at Taus. He caught her and held her tight, but she didn't cry.

"It's all right, Tiny." Taus hugged her tighter.

Now that it was over, fear and realization overwhelmed her. She had never dreamed that when she had asked to join the House Guard three years ago, she would have to kill. Koric was not a violent place.

He looked at Abeth over Ro's head. "What happened?"

"I don't know." Abeth shook her head. "She came in saying that something was wrong. That she could feel it. She searched the whole room, went back to the door, and there he was."

Ro turned slightly and looked at the dead man. "I killed him."

Abeth covered her mouth. "Oh, Ro!"

"Yes, you did." Taus held her away from him so he could see her face.

"I killed a man."

Taus sighed and squeezed her shoulders. "Was he going to kill you?"

Ro shrugged, then slowly nodded without taking her eyes off the dead man.

"Was he going to kill Abeth?" She nodded again, still staring at the body. A puddle of blood was forming under it. Taus turned her so she would look at him.

"Was there any way this could have come out differently with you and the queen alive in the end?"

Ro looked at the queen and then at the body. "No."

"Then you did what you should have."

"Taus, she's only a child."

"Age doesn't matter to duty." His gruff answer pulled Ro's shoulders back. "This is what it means to guard the royal family. You can't just play at swords in the practice yard."

Ro's spine stiffened, although her chin began to quiver.

"Are you still determined to be a Guard? The red of your uniform represents blood. Blood that will be shed to protect the family and Koric. Do you still want to wear it?"

"Taus, please." Abeth stepped forward. He held up his hand to stop her.

Ro stared at Taus. Her lower lip quivered. She then looked down at the body at her feet. The puddle of blood was dark against the white rug. She could still hear the sickening sound of her sword piercing his flesh.

Taus was right; she had been playing at swords. The Guard was real. Death was real. She glanced up at the queen. Abeth's face was covered in anguished tears. Abeth had saved her from a lifetime chained to a wall in that mine, lost and forgotten. It seemed only right that her life be dedicated to protecting Abeth. It would never be enough to pay the debt, but it would be a start. She looked back at Taus.

"I am a Guard." Her chin quivered a little, but her eyes were returning to the pale blue they normally were.

"Very well, then join your fellow guards and find out how this man got in."

"Aye, sir." Ro snapped to attention, snatched up her sword, and dashed out the door.

Taus released his breath in a whoosh, then shouted after her, "Ro! Clean your sword!"

"Are you sure that was best?" Abeth brushed a hand across her cheek, cleaning the tears away.

"First blood always scares the piss out of them. She has to see it with logic, or it'll eat away at her."

"But she's only a child."

"She's old enough to know what's done is done." He glanced toward the door. "Did you see her eyes?"

"She was afraid."

"No, that's not it." Taus shook his head. "They turned almost white. I've seen her eyes do that before on the practice field. There is something more to that girl than what we can see."

"She said she felt something when she came in. She seemed quite disturbed by it."

"I'm going to have to keep a closer eye on her from now on." Taus knelt beside the body and rolled the man onto his back. "As for this fellow..." Taus searched the body, finding multiple weapons. "He came for a fight." He searched a little more but then froze.

"What's wrong?" Abeth asked, wrapping her arms around her waist.

"He has a tattoo. See here?" He pointed to the small spiral with a diagonal line through it just behind the man's left ear.

"What is that?" Abeth peered at the symbol.

"It's an assassin's mark."

"Assassin!" The queen stumbled backward from the body. "For me? Why?"

"I don't know." Taus sighed as he stood, shaking his head. "I'll lock down the port for now. We'll have to be vigilant. There may be others since this one didn't accomplish his mission."

Summons

Queen Abeth traced the top of the merlon with one hand as she stared out toward the sea. Ro stood near the stairwell door with her thumbs hooked in her belt and looked past the queen. The mountains across the sea to the northwest stood silent, black, and ominous. Ro let her eyes drift over the glowing sheep meadows of Koric, the yellow grain fields that looked gray in the moonlight, and the dark silhouettes of the town riddled with tiny lights, twinkling in the taverns and houses.

After the assassin's attack nearly three months ago, Taus had closed Koric's ports and searched every ship. Koric's soldiers had searched every house, barn, and shop within twenty miles of the city, but nothing out of the ordinary had been found. No one knew anything about the assassin. The island had settled back into its natural, quiet rhythm for three months, until yesterday, when an Imperial warship arrived to deliver a message. Since then, the queen had become pensive.

After dinner, the queen had come to the King's Tower to think, so Ro stood guard. High Marshal Taus had insisted that someone be with the queen constantly since that night, and Ro was happy to volunteer.

"My Queen, you sent for me?" Ro jumped at the sudden appearance of Taus at her elbow. She hadn't heard him coming.

"Yes, High Marshal."

"High Marshal? You never call me that." Taus stepped up beside Abeth. The gray in his hair glowed white in the moonlight. "What's wrong?"

Abeth stared out at the sea. "Everything is changing."

"That can be said of any day." Taus turned to watch the sea too. They stood silently, shoulder to shoulder.

The queen handed a rolled parchment to Taus. He held it so that he could read by the moonlight.

"We have been summoned to the Imperial City." Abeth sighed. "The Arazi's son has reached the age of majority. If we do not report to the Imperial City in thirty days for the swearing ceremony, then Koric will be branded an outlaw province. Every member of the family must attend or be branded a traitor."

Taus looked up from his perusal of the edict. "That seems a bit harsh. Koric has always been loyal to the Arazi."

She snorted. "Of course we have! If it was the Emperor Fonus Arazi IX who had sent the invitation, there would be no talk of branding anyone a traitor, but he is in the east with the Border War. This is from the Empress, and she is not made from the same stuff as our illustrious Emperor. I didn't see much of her when I was in the palace, but I heard a lot of unpleasant rumors about her politics. I'm afraid that we must take these threats very seriously."

"So, you're saying that because of some hussy's politics we have to pile the whole family onto a ship and scamper over to the Imperial City just to reassure the Arazi's brat?"

"Beware of your words, Taus." Abeth glanced around nervously, making Ro tense.

"No one can hear us up here." Taus waved a dismissive hand, and Ro relaxed again.

"I don't want to take the whole family. What if something happens?" Abeth's voice wavered. "Dragon attacks have become more frequent in the last few years. There are rumors of unrest in the north."

Taus turned and leaned his back against the wall. He read the edict again. "It won't be the safest voyage."

"No, it won't." Abeth sighed and looked out to sea again. She paced along the wall. "Did I ever tell you that all those years ago, when I was in the Imperial City, I met the Arazi's great-grandmother?"

"Ha!" Taus pushed away from the wall. "She must've been a thousand years old!"

"Nearly." Abeth couldn't help but smile. "She read my future."

"Lots of dark, handsome strangers showing up on your doorstep?" Taus laughed.

"Hardly!" Abeth scoffed. "She gave me a warning. She said that one day, I would be on a ship and my children would flee."

Taus crossed his arms. "Well, what does that mean?"

Abeth whirled to face him. "I don't know! It can't be good!"

"And you believed her?"

"I had no reason not to." Abeth's voice cracked. "I think that day has finally come."

"Now," Taus walked over to her, "don't go getting upset."

"Oh, Taus, what if something happens to my children! I've already lost my husband, I can't lose them too." Abeth stifled a sob. "What if a dragon attacks? Or worse?"

Taus laid his hands on her shoulders. "You can't let the 'what ifs' eat you up like this. We will get through this. We'll take precautions. Have I ever failed you?" Abeth shook her head as she sniffled. "And I never will. Don't put too much faith in a senile old bat's ravings, all right?"

"All right." Abeth nodded and dried her tears. "Thank you, Taus. You are a dear friend."

"Right." He squeezed her shoulders once and let go. "I'll make preparations." He turned and headed for the stairs, giving Ro a meaningful glance as he passed, but she wasn't sure what he wanted her to do.

Abeth returned her gaze to the horizon. Sea birds dipped and spiraled on the air currents before diving into the water.

"Ro?"

"My Queen?"

"Come here," Abeth said over her shoulder.

Ro moved up beside her and waited.

Abeth turned and gazed at Ro. "You've grown into a beautiful woman." She reached up and tugged on Ro's short midnight hair. "No matter how much you try to look like a boy."

Ro shifted uncomfortably. She wasn't trying to look like a boy. It was just easier to fight without long hair getting in the way.

"You've changed so much from the tiny, fragile girl I found in the Zatvor mine."

"I've tried to make you proud," Ro muttered.

"You have!" Abeth shook her head. "I've heard nothing but good about you. You're well-liked by the other guards. Your dedication to the safety of this family has become legendary amongst the Koric people. Everyone is talking about the guard that saved the queen."

Ro shook her head. "I'm just doing my duty."

"I know." Abeth smiled. "You've inspired quite a few young girls, you know. We may have more women applying to the Guard in a few years." Her smile faltered. "I'm sorry that I have failed you."

Ro reared back. "You haven't failed me! You saved me from a life of misery. You gave me a home."

"You deserve more than that. You deserve to know where you belong."

"I belong here with you!"

"You do, but," Abeth sighed, "I won't always be around."

Ro clenched her fists. "Yes, you will."

Abeth shook her head and turned away. "Everyone dies eventually."

Ro slipped around in front of her.

"Is this about what you told Taus? About what the Arazi's great-grandmother said?"

Abeth's brow wrinkled.

"You don't know what she meant. *She* probably didn't even know. She was probably just playing games at your expense."

Abeth sighed. "Ro, it wasn't like that."

"No? I remember what the Court was like."

"You remember?" Abeth stared at her in surprise.

"When Yana brought me from the mine into the palace, we had to wait with the Court until The Arazi could see us." Ro scowled as she remembered. "They amused themselves by insulting us."

"Ro, I'm sorry." Abeth reached out a hand to Ro. "All these years, and I never knew."

"You can't trust anyone like that." Ro turned away, staring out to sea.

"Rohamina, the only flower that grows in Zatvor. Yana named you well," Abeth whispered, then took a deep breath. "I want you to stay here on Koric when we go."

Ro spun back to her. "No!"

"You'll be safe here."

"No. You are not leaving me behind. Not when I can be there to protect you! What if there is another assassin?"

"I don't want you on that ship. I don't want you in that city again, Ro." Abeth shook her head. "I don't want to lose you. You have become like a daughter to me."

"And you are like a mother to me, but I'm not letting you leave me behind."

"We never found out why you were in that mine. What if they put you back in? I don't want to take that chance." Abeth blinked rapidly. "You must stay here."

"If you haven't found out who I am by now, then how could anyone in the Imperial City know? They probably don't even remember me. I swore to protect this family from any threat. I can't do that if I'm not with you." Ro shook with determination. "If you try to leave without me, I'll follow."

Abeth reached forward and engulfed her in a hug. Ro fiercely returned the embrace. Abeth leaned back and framed Ro's face with her hands. "All right. I won't try to stop you from coming. Just promise me that you will do everything you can to be safe."

"I promise to keep you and your children safe regardless of the cost."

"Oh, Ro." More tears slipped down Abeth's cheeks. She tried to smile. "Whoever your parents were, they would be so proud of you."

After a moment, Abeth stepped back and took a deep breath. She tugged her sleeves down and smoothed her skirt. "I hope you've gotten better at sailing."

"I doubt it," Ro snorted.

Attack at Sea

THE CREAKING OF THE *Maiden's Crown* sounded eerie as it echoed in the dense fog. Ro planted her feet against the swaying of the deck. Her stomach rolled again. She glanced around. The fog had become so thick that she could barely see more than a few feet. The guards and sailors who lined the railings were only vague shadows in the grayness. Even the glow from the lamps was nearly swallowed by the haze.

Ro could no longer see the lights of the *Seabird,* the other ship in the Koric delegation. Taus had insisted on spreading the family out between the two ships. Ro wondered how Abeth and her son, Sebastian, were doing on the other ship.

There was barely a breeze to fill the sails, so the mist swirled and clung, making everything damp. Somehow, this fog seemed unnatural. Ro shivered. It had boiled up from behind the ships and engulfed them just before the evening bell. Every hand had been called out to stand watch. They were still far from land, but it paid to be cautious.

Mist, disturbed by movement from behind her, swirled across the back of Ro's neck. Leema appeared silently at Ro's side. Ro liked Leema. She was three years younger than Ro and had always been kind. She was a glowing, golden-haired child, but there was nothing about her that could be called princess-like. Her attitude had more in common with the rough and tumble boys of the city alleys than her sisters' ladylike qualities. Maybe that's why Ro got along with her so well. For years, Leema spent every spare moment pestering Ro to teach her everything she learned in the Guard.

"This is creepy," Leema whispered.

"Shh," the sailor next to her hissed. The captain had called for silence so that any change in the sound of the water or wind could warn of danger.

Leema leaned over the bulwark and looked at the water sliding past in the ship's wake. Seeing her hanging over the railing made Ro feel queasy.

A low rumble sounded from the port quarter. Leema straightened up and turned. Ro looked too. Slowly, like an undulating snake, the line of sailors from the starboard side moved toward the noise. Everyone was listening intently, trying to identify the sound.

Ro's neck began to tingle. "Oh no."

Leema glanced back at her. The tingle blazed through her body just as the fog whooshed aside, revealing the figurehead of another ship not more than a few feet away from the *Maiden's Crown*. It was headed straight for them.

Sailors screamed and ran from the port quarter railing. Someone rang the alarm bell. Just before the other ship rammed into the *Maiden's Crown,* Ro grabbed Leema and hauled her down against the bulwark.

Splinters of deck planking exploded through the air, raining down on and around the ship. The *Maiden's Crown* rocked dangerously, knocking everyone off their feet. The enemy ship had lodged itself into the *Maiden's Crown* on impact. The aft mast creaked and swayed. Chaos broke loose as the rigging snapped.

Battle cries sounded from the other ship as fire arrows lit up the fog. The glowing projectiles whistled through the air. Some hit the deck, blooming into flowers of bright flame. Many of the arrows found human targets, sending them screaming into the water.

Ro hauled Leema to her feet and pulled her away along the deck, trying to get her as far from the other ship as possible. As they neared the hatchway leading below deck, Aritha and Brenith dashed up to Ro.

"What's going on?" Aritha screamed.

"We're under attack!" Leema shouted as she ducked away from some swinging rigging.

Ro glanced upward. The sail attached to that rigging was slipping off the yard arm.

"We have to move!" She pointed up at the slipping sail. Leema was already running. Ro reached out and grabbed Aritha and Brenith and shoved them toward the bow just as yards of heavy canvas crashed to the deck.

Ro squinted, trying to make sense of the pandemonium near the stern. She could hear more than she could see. Screams and the sounds of clashing steel echoed through the fog. In places, the gray mist glowed orange from the fires.

"What do we do?" Brenith yanked on Ro's sleeve.

"Stay here. Stay together." Ro drew her sword and waited. She would protect the girls at all costs. She had promised. Her gaze swept to the side. Somewhere out there was the *Seabird*. Surely, they could hear the sounds of battle and would come to help.

Then, just as if they had heard her, a bell sounded through the fog.

"It's the *Seabird*!" Leema bounced up and down.

The tingle in Ro's back suddenly erupted. A heartbeat later in the direction the bell had clanged, the fog blazed fiery red. A screeching roar sliced through the night. The girls covered their ears and cowered down onto the deck. A vicious hot wind buffeted what was left of the *Maiden's Crown,* parting the fog for just a moment.

Ro looked up in time to see firelight reflect off the scaled monster as it flew overhead.

"Dragon," she whispered. All of a sudden, it came together in her head. The dragon, the red blaze, and the hot wind. The dragon had attacked the *Seabird!*

Ro leapt to her feet and rushed to the railing. "Abeth! Taus!"

"Ro, we have to go!" Leema appeared at her side, yanking on her arm. "The guards! Ro! They said we're sinking. Ro!"

"Abeth!" Ro stared into the fog. Searching desperately for some sign that they had survived. Ro prayed for an answer, but all she could hear was the screams of battle behind her.

"Ro!" Leema punched her in the arm to get her attention. "Come on!"

Two men in red uniforms rushed out of the gray and grabbed the girls. Leema turned immediately, but Ro began to fight, trying to stay at the railing.

"The queen is out there! Let me go!"

"Ro! Let's go!" Beck growled in her ear as he fought to pull her from the railing. "Ro! If you get in the launch, we can go look for them!"

His words penetrated her brain. She stopped fighting. Beck pushed her toward the other railing, where Captain Marin and the other guards were lowering the launch. The men worked quickly, and the small boat splashed down safely. One by one, the girls were sent over the side and into the launch. When Beck, the three princesses, Ro, Captain Marin, and three sailors were safely in the boat, they pushed away from the already sinking ship. Behind them, another launch was being lowered.

The dragon screeched again, and the refugees in the boat covered their ears, ducking low. Red fire burst down on the *Maiden's Crown* and the second ship. The screams of sailors burning alive filled the air. The fire reached the powder store of the *Maiden's Crown*, and what was left of the broken ship exploded. Hot wind blasted across the water toward the small boat, pushing it sideways. Moments later, a second explosion rocked the enemy ship. Smoke and fire billowed upward as splintery debris shot outward. One piece skewered the man rowing next to Marin. He screamed and toppled into the water.

The waves caused by the explosions rose and rocked the launch, tipping it. Guards shouted, and the girls screamed as the boat flipped.

Ro flailed in the dark water. She broke the surface, only to be pushed back under by a wave. The weight of her sword hampered her efforts as she kicked toward the surface. She gained the air and thumped against the overturned launch. Ro grabbed for it, desperately trying to find something to hold onto. All around her, she heard shouts and thrashing water, but the darkness and the fog made it impossible to see anything.

"Ro!" Leema shouted from off to her left.

"Here! Leema! Here!"

"Leema!" Brenith's voice broke through the din.

"Here! Come this way!" Ro felt Leema bump against her as she reached the launch.

"Ro?" Marin called. "Aritha?"

"Here!" Ro shouted just as the dragon screeched above them. The air glowed red. Ro pulled Leema and Brenith under the water until the glow faded. Without the boat to keep her at the surface, the weight of her sword pulled her down again. She grabbed for Leema's hand.

The young princess hauled her to the surface.

"Get under the boat!" Marin ordered. "Use it as a shelter until the dragon goes."

Quickly, Ro took a breath, ducked beneath the water, and came up under the overturned boat.

"Where's Aritha?" Brenith spat water out as she surfaced.

"I'll find her. Ro, stay with them!" Marin ducked under the surface.

Ro felt along the inside of the boat for handholds for the girls. She grabbed onto one of the oar locks and pulled herself up. Her arms cramped from trying to pull her head above the water while her sodden clothes and sword grew heavier. She kicked her feet to help her stay above the surface.

Aritha splashed into the cavern made by the launch. Marin's head popped up next to her just as another head broke the surface. It was Beck.

"Where are the others?" Beck coughed.

"I couldn't find them." Marin's voice sounded strained.

They heard the dragon screech again as it flew over their hiding spot.

"Ro, Beck, you have to dump your swords." Marin grabbed the rim of the boat.

Beck spat out seawater. "What about the dragon?"

"Your sword won't make a difference. It'll burn you before you can use it." Marin spat out the water that washed over his face. "The weight of it will drown you first. Lose your boots and armor too. Anything heavy."

"We'll be defenseless."

Leema coughed. "Better that than drowning."

Ro started to pull the laces free on her jerkin. With one hand, Marin helped pull the buckles open on her sword harness.

"Fine," Beck growled and unbuckled his harness with Leema's help.

"Ladies, you need to shed as many of your skirts as you can," Marin said as he worked at his own harness. "Miles of wet cloth will pull you down too."

"I'm not taking off my clothes!" Aritha smacked the water, sending droplets everywhere.

"Not all of them, just most of them." Brenith tried to calm her sister. "The underskirts."

The six survivors quickly shed what weight they could, letting it sink into the abyss.

"What now?" Brenith asked through chattering teeth.

"Now we wait." Marin readjusted his hold on the launch. "We should drift away from the battle for a while, and when it's safe, we'll try and flip the boat back over and look for survivors."

A grim silence settled as they each prayed there would be survivors.

Set Adrift

IT WAS SO QUIET and so very dark and cold. Ro could hear the slapping and sloshing of the water against the launch and the labored breathing of her exhausted fellow castaways, but she couldn't see them. The tingling she had felt just before the enemy ship attacked had finally subsided to one small, annoying spot on the back of her neck.

Ro tried to still her chattering teeth long enough to speak. "M-M-Marin-n?"

"Yeah?" His voice was hoarse.

"I th-think it's s-safe."

"Why?"

"I f-feel it-t." Ro shivered. She wasn't sure if Marin would believe her. Rumors about her ability to sense danger had been circulating through the Guard since the night of the assassin.

Marin sighed. "Right."

There was a splash as Marin ducked beneath the surface. Ro waited for another splash to warn her that he had returned, but she only heard the slapping of sea water against the launch.

"Is he coming back?" Aritha cried.

"Yes," Beck growled.

Water sloshed over Ro's head as Marin's head bobbed up next to her.

"It's safe." He coughed and spat. "We need to flip the boat."

"How?" Leema asked.

"Maybe," Marin hesitated, "maybe we can climb on top and get it rocking."

"When it flips, it'll be full of water." Beck floated closer.

"We'll have to get someone in it to start bailing before it sinks." Marin didn't sound too confident.

"Wait, are you saying that if we flip the boat, it may sink?" Aritha's screech echoed in the tiny space.

"Yeah," Marin hedged, "it might."

"Then I say we don't do it." Aritha splashed. "What happens to us if it sinks? At least we have something to hang onto right now!"

"If we don't get out of this water soon," Beck snarled, "we'll freeze!"

Aritha was near panic. "But we'll freeze if the boat sinks."

Marin was silent for a moment. Ro didn't like the idea of freezing, but drowning was just as bad.

"All right, let's take a vote." Marin spat out some water. "Flip the boat. Yea or nay. I vote Yea. Beck?"

"Yea."

"Aritha?"

"Nay"

"Leema?"

"Yea."

"Brenith?"

"Nay. Better some boat than no boat."

"Ro?" Ro hated being the last vote when she really didn't know which decision was best. But Marin was the Captain of the Guard, and she trusted his judgment.

"Ro?"

"Yea."

"Right, let's flip it." Marin snapped into action. "Leema, you're the lightest. Be ready to climb in and start bailing. Beck and I will get on the ends and help guide the turn. Aritha, Brenith, Ro, we'll get you on top, then start rocking. You'll have to move together. It should flip pretty fast, so be ready to swim."

"This is the worst idea ever." Aritha splashed way more than necessary as they each ducked out from under the launch.

It was only marginally brighter once they were out from under the boat, just enough to see the outline of the hull. It was unnerving. Marin was still shouting directions to everyone as they moved into position. The top of the upside-down boat was only a foot or so above the water, but the wood was slick. Aritha tried to climb on top of the boat on her own but fell back into the water.

"Hold on. Hold on." Marin sighed as he swam back toward the sound of the flailing and cursing princess. "Aritha! Stop splashing! Damn it!" Once she calmed down, he hauled her back to the launch and grabbed the side.

"Ro. You first." He pulled her around in front of him. He clutched the oar lock for leverage. "Bend your knee." He cupped his hand around her foot. "On the count of three, straighten your leg and grab for the keel."

"All right."

"One. Two." They bobbed in the water for a moment as he counted. "Three." He hefted her up. She straightened her leg, forcing him under the water. Ro shot out of the water and slammed onto the boat. Frantically, she grabbed for the raised ridge of the keel and hauled herself up. Marin bobbed to the surface and shook the water out of his eyes.

"Brenith, you're next." Marin repeated the instructions to Brenith and hefted her up. This time, it went easier because Ro grabbed Brenith's hand and pulled her up.

"Aritha. You're up." Once again, Marin hefted while Brenith and Ro pulled. The girls straddled the boat like they were on horseback.

"You all right?" Ro called down to Marin. He was breathing hard. Each time he'd shoved a girl upward, it'd pushed him under the water.

"Yeah, just give me a minute to rest."

Ro shivered as the sea air caught her wet clothes. She turned and searched the horizon. An orange glow showed through the darkness. She tapped Brenith on the shoulder. "Look."

"That must be the ships," Brenith whispered. "I hope Mother is all right and Sebastian..."

"And Taus," Ro murmured.

"Beck, you ready?" Marin called. The other guard only grunted.

"Girls? We're ready if you want to start rocking."

It took a couple of tries to get synchronized, but finally, they were rocking together. The launch, however, barely moved even with the men at each end pushing and turning.

"Wait. Wait!" Ro shouted. "Hold on, let me try something else. We aren't getting enough leverage."

The girls stopped rocking and waited while Ro slowly pulled her feet under her and balanced carefully as she knelt and turned to the side.

"Marin? Beck? If you come back around the side and grab the keel when it rocks your way and throw your weight with the rocking, I think I can grab the side and throw my weight back at the same time."

"Right," Beck shouted. "On your mark, Ro!"

"All right, go ahead," Ro said to Aritha and Brenith. The girls started to rock. Ro's fingers cramped as she tried to hold onto the keel. From either end of the boat, loud splashing started.

The boat rocked high, and Ro threw herself forward. She grabbed the lip of the gunwale and yanked backwards with all her weight. The boat flipped. Ro, Aritha, and Brenith toppled into the sea. Ro gasped as water rushed in over her head. She thrashed and kicked her way to the surface. Coughing and spluttering, she heard everyone shouting at once.

"Leema! Get in there!"

"Beck! Help her!"

"Hurry! Bail!"

"I am bailing!"

"Aritha! Swim!"

"Brenith!"

"Ro! Where are you?"

Ro swam toward the chaos and bumped into the side of the boat.

"Ro!"

"I'm here!" she coughed. Water splashed her in the face as Leema threw it out of the boat with cupped hands. Marin worked his way along the side until he was next to Ro.

"You all right?"

"Yeah."

He patted her on the back. "Good work."

"Hurry up, Leema!" Aritha whined.

"I'm going as fast as I can!" Leema threw more water. "I can't see anything!"

"Argh! Did you just throw water at me?"

"Aritha!" Brenith snapped. "Leave her alone!"

"She did that on purpose!"

"Well, you deserved it," Brenith muttered.

"What did you say?"

"Ladies, please, this isn't helping." Marin's annoyance edged into his voice. "Beck, you wanna help Brenith into the boat? We'll balance it." He elbowed Ro, and they reached up and grabbed the lip to steady it.

"Why does she get in first?" Aritha whined.

The boat rocked as Brenith climbed in. The sounds of bailing became frenzied as both girls threw water.

"Ro, go around and steady it on that side. Aritha. Your turn."

Ro worked her way around the boat hand over hand.

"Do it!" Beck shouted as soon as he felt Ro next to him. The boat rocked as Aritha climbed in.

"You have to help bail, Aritha!"

"I'm tired," the eldest princess whined.

"So are we!" Brenith snapped.

"Think I might stay down here where it's peaceful for a while," Beck muttered to Ro.

Ro grunted in agreement.

"It's only about ankle deep now, Marin," Leema puffed.

"You're up next, kid." Beck reached over to help Ro up. Ro bobbed and heaved herself over the side of the boat. "Marin? You next. I'm the heaviest."

Ro leaned toward the side Beck was on as Marin hauled himself over the edge. The launch rocked dangerously. Aritha screamed.

"Oh, shut it!" Leema huffed.

Ro moved next to Marin to help balance the boat as Beck tried to clamber up. It took two tries, but he finally flopped into the boat with a splash. As the boat rocked wildly, everyone froze, clutching any handhold they could find. Finally, it settled. Leema and Brenith started bailing again. The others joined in, and after a while, only the bottom of the boat was still sloshing with seawater. Exhaustion and cold had taken their toll. One by one, they stopped trying to throw water out and collapsed.

Survivors

Ro woke suddenly. Her limbs were stiff and ached from the cold. She struggled to sit up and noticed the sky was lighter, but the fog still clung to the sea. Debris floated all around the launch, but there was no sign of the *Maiden's Crown,* the *Seabird,* or the ship that had rammed them.

"Marin." Ro nudged him with her foot.

He coughed and sat up with a groan. "What is it?"

"Look." She pointed toward the floating pieces. He reached over and shook Beck awake. Ro turned to rouse Leema, Brenith, and Aritha.

"Keep your eyes open." Marin scanned the debris. "Look for anything that could help us. Water barrels, food, oars, anything."

Beck looked from one side of the boat to the other. "Weapons?"

"Or survivors." Ro's voice cracked.

As the debris floated closer, they grabbed each piece and checked it. Beck kept a couple of pieces that could be used as oars, but the majority was completely useless.

Then they found the bodies. Some were whole, but most were only pieces of men, burnt and torn. Their flesh molted from the seawater and fire. The smell of scorched meat drifted across the water. Aritha couldn't stand the sight. She hid her face against the hull and cried. Brenith vomited until there were only dry heaves left. Leema said nothing, but tears ran down her cheeks. Ro, Marin, and Beck just kept searching. They had seen death before.

Ro's neck started to tingle. "Marin." She grabbed his arm. "Something's wrong."

He watched her for a moment, then glanced at Beck. He was staring at Ro too. "Where?"

"I don't know." She cast about, looking for what could be causing the feeling. There was nothing but bodies and chunks of ship. One of the bodies dipped below the surface.

"What was that?" Leema pointed to a patch of swirling water.

Beck peered at the waves. "I didn't see anything."

Behind them, something splashed. They all turned, but nothing was there.

The tingling spread across Ro's back. "Marin!"

"Where? There's nothing here!"

Another splash. This time, they turned in time to see another body disappear.

"Gods, no." Beck's face paled. "Please."

"What is it? Beck?" Leema backed away from the side of the boat.

"Shh." He leaned forward and whispered, "Leviathan."

Leema stared at him with her jaw slack. She shook her head and started to tremble.

"Not a word," he breathed. Beck glanced at the others. "No sudden movements."

Marin slowly reached down and picked up the plank that Beck had kept as an oar. He held it like a club and scanned the water.

The sinuous beast scavenged more of the dead. Ro's tutors had taught her about leviathans. They were long, snake-like sea creatures, carnivorous beasts with long spiked teeth and poisonous spines that preyed on sailors. They mainly stayed in the deep ocean, but they had been seen more in recent decades in the Arazi Sea. They had even been known to snatch fishermen from the shores. Never in her life did Ro think she would actually see one.

The launch drifted slowly toward a large clump of debris. Ro couldn't tell what it was from this distance, but the tingling grew as they neared it. She reached out and grabbed Marin's arm. He looked where she pointed.

The clump was a good-sized chunk of the ship. It looked like someone had managed to take shelter on it. He wasn't from Koric. What was left of his clothing was unfamiliar. Burns covered most of his body, and he was missing part of his leg. They were only a few feet away when the man moved. He raised his head and saw them.

The tingling became a roar.

The man started yelling and beating the water, trying to get his makeshift raft to move.

"No! No! No!" Beck hissed as the boat thumped against the raft.

The screaming man launched himself toward Beck, grabbing the front of his shirt. As Beck struggled to get free, the launch tipped and they both toppled into the water.

"Beck!" Marin lunged for the spot where they had disappeared.

Leema and Ro threw their weight against the opposite gunwale, trying to keep the little boat balanced. Behind them, the leviathan splashed. The boat rocked sideways as the beast brushed against it.

Beck's upper body erupted from the water, flailing toward the boat. Marin reached for him. He managed to grab Beck's hand. The boat rocked again as Beck was dragged back under the water. Marin toppled in after him. Ro lunged and caught the back of his shirt. Leema and Brenith grabbed Ro to keep her from falling in too.

Together, they hauled Marin back into the boat. Ro and Marin landed in a heap. Ro tried to shift out from under him but couldn't move his weight. Brenith wrapped her arms around Leema as their eyes scanned the water but saw nothing. Beck didn't resurface.

Marin curled up in the bottom of the boat, holding his leg. The launch rocked sideways again. Aritha whimpered. Brenith shushed her. Ro looked down at Marin. He had a death grip on his thigh just above his knee. He squeezed his eyes shut. His face was red from holding back the scream. In that moment, Ro knew. He had been stung by the leviathan. He was going to die.

The beast bumped into the launch again. Marin was sweating, tendons stood out from his neck as he clenched his jaw. His feverish eyes opened. They were filled with terror. He grasped Ro's forearm and held on for dear life. It felt like he was going to break her arm. Ro's chin quivered against the pain and fear. She brushed the hair from Marin's face, trying to soothe him.

She looked from Marin to where the princesses were huddled together, clinging to one another. Aritha had her face buried in Brenith's lap, and Brenith had wrapped her arms around Leema. They hugged each other tighter each time the beast knocked into the boat.

Eventually, the sun rose and burned off the last of the fog. The launch drifted away from the debris field, and the leviathan returned to scavenging the dead.

Eventually, Marin's grip eased, and Ro realized that he had passed out. Leema and Brenith helped Ro move Marin out of the remaining seawater to a dry spot in the bow.

"He's going to die, isn't he?" Aritha asked. She was sitting as far from Marin as she could.

"Yes." Brenith reached out and smoothed his hair. "Leviathan stings are always fatal."

"What are we going to do?" Leema's voice was barely a whisper.

"Ro?" Brenith looked at her across Marin's sleeping form.

Ro shook her head. "I don't know."

"You're a guard. You're supposed to protect us!" Aritha glared at her. "Surely, you know what to do?"

Ro gazed down at Marin, thinking, *Don't leave me! I'm not a leader. I don't know how to do anything!*

Leema reached out and squeezed Ro's arm. Ro raised her eyes to find Leema gazing at her with complete faith. "I'm sure you'll think of something."

Ro looked away and stared at the waves, wondering what Taus would do. "We drift, or we paddle, but I don't know which way." She gestured around the boat. The sea stretched on for miles in all directions. "I need a reference point, like the Holy Mountain's smoke or anything, but there's nothing." Ro shrugged. "We'll have to wait until night. If the fog stays away, we'll use the stars." She had stared at them every night from the King's Tower. She should be able to get some direction from them. "You should all get some sleep. I'll sit with Marin."

For the rest of the day, the launch drifted. Ro kept watch, praying the leviathan would stay away. She tried to soothe Marin. His unconscious state became a fitful sleep. Sweat beaded on his face. Ro glanced at the dozing princesses. They were huddled together in the stern of the tiny boat, trying to stay out of the water that still sloshed by their feet. When Marin died, she would be the only one left to protect them.

"Abeth, I know I promised, but..." She stared out to sea, wishing by some miracle that Taus or Abeth would appear on a shining ship to save them, but they were more than likely dead. "Taus—" Ro felt tears slip down her cheeks. She felt so helpless and alone.

Marin moaned, pulling her attention back to his pale form. She had trained with Marin and Beck daily for the last ten years. Now she would never hear Beck's growly voice or hear his nasty laugh ever again. And Marin, if it wasn't for Marin, they would all be dead. He had always been so sensible. He had risen through the ranks of the Guard because of his ability to think and act quickly and correctly. She reached down and brushed away some of the sweat. If only he would wake up and tell her what to do.

"Marin, I don't know how to do anything." She glanced at the girls again. "How am I supposed to keep them safe? What am I going to do?"

Ro shivered. Her shirt was still damp. She squinted up at the sun. At least it was shining. Maybe it would dry her off. She stared at the discarded plank. Marin must have dropped it when he'd tried to save Beck. She was relieved that it would not be necessary to hang over the side of the launch in order to paddle with her hands. The thought of what else might be lurking under the water, ready to bite, had her scooting as far from the sides as she could get.

Her stomach rolled from the constant rocking. The cook from the *Maiden's Crown* had given her a powder to put in everything she ate or drank. He had poked her in the stomach and winked. *'It'll keep it in yer belly.'* He had been right, but the powder was wearing off, and the cook was gone. Ro rubbed her face and pulled her knees to her chest. She needed to keep busy somehow to keep her mind off her grief. That's how she had survived the mine. That's how she'd survive this.

Ro squinted up at the sun again. It seemed like it was making a path straight overhead. Which made sense considering it was high summer, but she would have to watch longer to see which way it was headed. Then maybe she could pick a direction. Ro sighed. How close were they to Koric? How far had they drifted? The Imperial City was to the northeast, but that was too far. They would die from thirst long before they reached it. Was Koric still directly north of them? Ka lay to the south, but was it closer than Koric? The drift of the tides might make it impossible to get back home. Ro sighed again and wished for miracles.

Marin moaned. Ro moved back next to him. He turned and buried his head in her lap. She smoothed his hair and let the tears slide down her cheeks, feeling completely lost and alone.

Washed Ashore

"RO?" A GENTLE HAND shook her shoulder.

Ro woke with a gasp and looked around. "What's wrong?"

Leema and Brenith were kneeling in front of her, but Aritha was asleep.

"I'm sorry, Ro," Leema whispered, turning her gaze to Marin.

Ro looked down to where his head was still cradled in her lap. He wasn't moving. She felt for his heartbeat. Marin was gone. Ro's chin began to quiver.

Brenith grasped Ro's hand. "I'm sorry, Ro."

Ro couldn't speak. She just stared at Marin.

"What are we going to do now?" Leema asked Brenith.

Ro gazed at her fallen captain. "He should have a proper burial."

Brenith rubbed the back of Ro's hand. "We don't know when, or if, we'll reach land."

"Brenith!" Leema gasped.

"She's right. We don't know. He can't stay on board all that time." Ro's voice was quiet and scratchy from unshed tears. "We'll have to let him go."

"I'm so sorry, Ro." Brenith squeezed her hand again.

Ro shrugged.

Carefully, she lifted Marin's head and moved. Brenith and Leema shifted backward. With shaking hands, she reached forward and began to search her friend's body.

"What are you doing?" Leema rocked forward onto all fours to watch Ro.

"If he has anything in his pockets that will help keep us alive," Ro's voice had lost all inflection, "it doesn't need to go with him."

She found a small knife, a few coins, and a locket on a cord around his neck. Anything else he may have been carrying must have gone to the abyss already, just like all of Ro's supplies. Carefully, she removed the locket and tied it around her neck. She couldn't bring herself to look inside it just yet. She sat back on her heels.

"Aritha!" Leema scrambled across the boat and shook her other sister. "Wake up."

"Stop shaking me!" Aritha shoved Leema's hand away. She sat up and took in their long faces. "What's happened?"

Brenith didn't look up. "Marin is gone."

"Gone! What do you mean gone? He can't be! What are we supposed to do now?"

"Please. Just stop." Leema glared at her. "We have to let him go."

The boat rocked as Aritha tried to stand. "Let him go, what does that mean?"

"It means he must be given to the sea." Ro turned, her blue eyes had turned to ice. "He can't stay with us."

Leema stared at Ro. She had never seen that look in her eyes before. Aritha snapped her teeth together as if she had been slapped.

Ro's gaze softened as she looked at Brenith. "Would you say something, please?"

"Of course." The girls bowed their heads as Brenith asked the gods for safe passage for their fallen protector.

"May he be honored in death for the deeds of his life," Leema added when Brenith fell silent.

"May he be honored," Ro repeated. Then, together, the girls hefted and shifted Marin's limp body to the edge of the boat. Aritha and Leema balanced against the opposite side as Ro and Brenith rolled him into the sea. The launch tipped wildly as Marin disappeared into the waves.

Ro knelt at the side of the boat for the longest time, staring into the water. Brenith moved up beside her and put her arm around Ro's shoulders.

Ro moved away from Brenith.

"So, now what?" Aritha crawled back to the dry spot in the stern and began to finger-comb her long blonde hair. "Do we still have to wait for the stars to figure out our direction?"

Ro stared up at the sky. The boat seemed to be drifting at an angle to the sun's path. "We're drifting south."

"What?" Aritha stopped fussing with her hair. "South? We can't be going south!"

"Why not?" Leema looked up at the sun.

"Why not? Because the Imperial City is in the northeast, idiot."

"Aritha." Brenith frowned at her sister.

Leema splashed Aritha. "Don't call me an idiot!"

"If we are floating south," Aritha flicked water back at Leema, "then we are going the wrong way."

Brenith sighed. "I don't think that we have much of a choice which way we float, Aritha."

"If we are headed south, then we should be able to see the smoke from the Holy Mountain, right?" Ro stood up, making everyone look at her. She gazed toward what she thought was the west.

Leema shifted around, held her hand over her eyes, and searched the horizon.

"Not necessarily." Brenith also looked to where they thought the mountain was.

"I could always see the smoke from the King's Tower. We had just rounded Shepard's Point when the fog came up. If we are drifting south, we could be just east of Jardarwa." Ro still gazed west.

"You can only see the smoke from the Tower because it's so tall." Aritha continued to untangle her hair. "You can't see it from Shepard's Point. Don't you know anything?"

"Leave her alone, Aritha!" Leema splashed water at her older sister again.

"Stop splashing me!"

"Ladies!" Brenith sighed and turned to Ro. "We could very well be west of Koric by now. We would have to paddle across and against the current to reach Koric, but if we paddle with the current, it should take us south, right? We should reach Ka Province?"

"Ka!" Aritha whined. "I don't want to go to Ka Provence! They're savages! Do you know what they'll do to us?"

"Aritha! It doesn't matter what you want. The boat is drifting with the tide. We have no supplies and no way of paddling, except this hunk of wood." Brenith picked up the splintery plank and shook it at her sister. "We're going to Ka!"

"Fine, but don't blame me if you get raped or eaten by cannibals." Aritha flipped her hair over her shoulder and stared off into the distance.

"Oh, seriously." Brenith turned back to Ro. "It is wilder country than we are used to, but I'm sure that there must be someone who could help us get to the Imperial City."

Ro shrugged. She really didn't know anything about Ka Province. Her tutors had only told her that it was a 'widely unpopulated land, steeped in superstition with a backward culture'.

"Sounds like fun," Leema chirped. Ro looked down at her. The sixteen-year-old grinned up at her, blinking in the glare of the midday sun. She held her hand up to shield her eyes, but it wasn't helping any.

Brenith handed the plank to Ro and moved to the opposite end of the boat from Aritha. Ro looked at the plank, wondering how she was going to paddle without making them go in a circle.

"I'll steer." Leema popped up, making the launch teeter. Ro crouched and grabbed for the side of the boat to keep from falling. Leema bounced to the stern and pushed Aritha. "Move. I need to reach the tiller."

Her sister made a disgusted, unladylike noise and crawled toward the middle of the boat. Ro settled onto the bench in the middle of the launch and then started to paddle. The plank was jagged and not the best shape for effective paddling, but Ro tried her best. She put all her muscle into pulling the little boat through the water. It was good to have something to do. Splinters dug into her palms. A couple of times, she had to stop and pull a sliver from under her nail.

Hours ticked by. Stroke after stroke, Ro kept them moving. Her shoulders ached. Her legs were beginning to cramp. Her lungs were burning. Finally, she had to stop and rest. The plank felt heavy where it lay on her legs.

"Why did you stop?" Aritha shifted from her nap. "Are we near land?"

Ro glared at her as she panted.

Brenith moved up next to her. "I'll take over, Ro."

Ro hissed in pain as she uncurled her cramped fingers from the plank. Her palms were raw and red. She plunged them into the seawater that sloshed in the bottom of the boat. The cold temperature felt good, but the salt stung each and every cut. Shaking the water from her aching hands, she crawled into the bow. Her arms were shaking. She collapsed against the hull, curled her hands against her chest, and closed her eyes against the glare of the sun. She desperately wanted water as she listened to the sound of Brenith paddling.

Ro shifted against the hull. Opening her eyes, she was surprised to find the sky was filled with stars.

"Did you sleep well?" Brenith said from beside her.

Ro looked over to find Brenith curled next to her in the bow. Leema was now rowing, and Aritha was doing what looked like steering. She sat next to the tiller with only her elbow holding the lever steady. Her head was braced in her hand as she stared off into the night sky.

"I didn't realize that I'd fallen asleep." Ro rubbed her eyes and winced. Her hands still felt cramped. "How long have I been out?"

"A few hours." Brenith yawned and settled back into the bow. "Hard to say really."

Ro sat up and looked around. She was so stiff. The sea glittered in the starlight. A chilly breeze skimmed along the surface, whipping Leema's blonde hair into her face as she rowed. She shook it out of her eyes then kept rowing.

Ro stared up at the stars. She could see the three bright stars that formed a straight line. It was the constellation that she always looked for from the King's Tower. It pointed directly downward to the Holy Mountain.

"What are you looking at?" Leema puffed. Her rowing was slow and unsteady.

Ro pointed. "The King's Spear."

"I never understood that story." Leema pulled a couple of strokes, rested, then pulled another stroke.

"It's a stupid story," Aritha mumbled.

"I always liked it. The idea that one of the Great Kings wanted to protect the world from demons makes me feel watched over," Brenith said from the darkness.

Ro continued to watch the twinkling stars.

"There is no magic spear that's going to fall from the heavens and kill demons," Aritha griped.

"What do you know about it?" Leema stopped paddling and turned to her sister.

"More than you."

"Come on. I'll paddle." Ro pushed herself up and stretched. She crawled stiffly to the bench where Leema sat. The youngest princess took Ro's place in the bow and snuggled next to her sister.

"Make sure you have us going that way." Ro pointed to a spot just to the left of where the bow was already headed.

"Yes. Yes." Aritha sighed. The bow's direction was slowly corrected.

Ro's shoulders did not appreciate the second shift of rowing. The stiffness worked out slowly as she pulled stroke after stroke, but the muscles ached. Ro paddled in silence. She thought that the girls had all fallen asleep, but then Leema's quiet voice whispered out of the shadows.

"Why did that man attack Beck? We could have helped him."

Brenith cuddled her sister closer. "He was out of his mind from his wounds."

"Why did that dragon come?" Leema sounded very young at that moment.

Ro pulled a couple of strokes before Aritha's voice floated out of the darkness behind Ro. "There have been more dragon sightings in the past few years. In the past, the dragons stayed behind the mountains in the far north and rarely ventured to the sea, but now there are reports from Zmajev of burnt villages on the fringes of the mountains and scorched crop land."

It was the first time that Ro had ever heard Aritha sound competent. It was a strange change from her normal whining.

"Have you ever seen one before?" Leema, for once, was in awe of her older sister.

"No. This was my first." The eldest princess sounded diminished. "There are stories from before the formation of the Arazi Empire about dragons ravaging the world. About people trying to control the dragons."

"What happened?" Ro puffed as she pulled another stroke.

"There was a war. I don't really remember the details." Aritha shrugged. "It's just another stupid story."

"I wonder why they are coming back." Leema shifted, trying to find a comfortable position.

Ro shrugged. "Maybe they're hungry."

"There's better pickings on land," Aritha snorted.

"Maybe it was after the leviathan," Leema offered.

"Maybe."

The girls went quiet again. Ro pulled stroke after stroke.

"Ro?" Leema's voice was almost too quiet to hear. "Do you think Sebastian and Mother made it off the *Seabird*?"

Ro didn't want to lie to her. "I hope so."

After that, Leema didn't speak again. Ro just kept paddling stroke after stroke, far into the night until Brenith relieved her. Ro curled next to Leema and slept. When she woke, the early light of predawn was spreading across the sky. Leema was at the paddle again. She was obviously getting too exhausted to keep up the pace. Her strokes were erratic, and her head kept drooping forward. Ro crawled over and took the plank from her fingers. The young girl gave her a halfhearted smile. Too tired to crawl to the front of the boat, she laid down right where she was and instantly fell asleep.

Ro took a moment to scan the horizon. Not much had changed: sea, sea, and more sea. Ro sighed and started to paddle.

"I don't see why you are trying to keep up this pace. I understand why we were paddling at night; we needed the stars for reference, but why not just sleep during the day?" Aritha yawned and stretched. She was still manning the tiller. Ro doubted that she had taken a turn paddling.

Ro shrugged. "The more we paddle, the sooner we make land."

"Ah yes, Ka. Can't wait to get there."

"Better than starving and dying of thirst in a boat," Ro grunted.

"You sound like Taus."

Ro would have said thank you, but the lump in her throat blocked her words. Ro leaned into the strokes, pulling with all her might. Her shoulders screamed in protest, but it eased the lump.

Dawn broke across the undulating waves, gilding them in golds and pinks. Ro kept rowing. As the morning waned, the wind picked up, and the clouds rolled in. The waves became bigger and bigger. Dropping between the swells made the boat bounce and jump. Ro was glad they had nothing to eat; her stomach wouldn't have been able to keep it down anyway. The girls were tossed and rolled from side to side as the launch bucked in the churning waves. Ro fought to maintain her seat as the boat rocked wildly.

"Brenith! Help!" Aritha strained to hold the tiller, but the lever was still swinging out of control. Brenith clawed her way along the gunwale to lend her strength to Aritha's.

Leema pointed. "Birds!"

"There must be land close!" Brenith yelled over the roaring storm.

Ro grabbed the side of the boat and looked for land. She glimpsed it as the boat rode to the top of the wave. It disappeared again as the launch slammed down into the trough. A wave of white foam sloshed over the side. Ro coughed and spat out the salty water.

"Rocks!" Leema screamed.

Ro's head whipped around in time to see the dark shapes burst out of the foam off to the right. "Hold on!"

The boat's side smashed into the rock, knocking the girls to the bottom of the launch. They scrambled back up, holding tight to the side of the boat. The launch smashed into another rock. This time, the wooden side splintered.

"Leema!" Ro launched herself forward and grabbed the girl as she washed out the side of the broken boat, sucking Ro with her.

She heard the screams of the other two girls as the water engulfed them. Leema and Ro were pulled first one way, then another. Ro kicked for the surface, hauling Leema with her. They sucked in air as soon as they felt it, only to be knocked into a rock. Ro kept her grip on Leema's tunic by sheer terror.

The swell pulled them back and up, rising high into the air. Ro caught a glimpse of the beach. Uneven bits of broken rock riddled the shore. Leema clutched Ro's arm as the wave crested. The two girls were thrown forward. Ro's left foot scraped against underwater outcroppings as the wave propelled them toward the beach. The girls slammed into the shore. Ro lost her breath as the air was forced from her body.

The backwash tried to suck them out to sea, but she clawed at the rocks, fighting against the force of the water. She pulled Leema farther up the beach as another breaker crashed over them.

They fought wave after wave, crawling a little farther up the rocks each time until the water only reached their feet. Ro lay still, panting with one hand clutching Leema's tunic and the other wedged in the rocks. Leema still had her hands wrapped around Ro's arm. Leema's coughing was the last thing Ro heard as she succumbed to oblivion.

Now What?

RO SHIVERED AS COLD air skimmed across her back. She winced at the rocks poking her in the chest. She moaned and slowly pushed herself up onto her knees. Her head was pounding, and her mouth felt thick and dry. Every part of her hurt.

As Ro untangled her cramped fingers from Leema's soaking wet tunic, the young princess groaned. Ro checked Leema's limp form. All her bones were intact. Except for bruises and a few scrapes, she didn't seem to have any other injuries.

A cold wind swept across the beach. Ro shivered, rubbed her gummy eyes, and gazed around. Behind her stretched the angry waves of the Arazi Sea. She looked up the beach to find black rocky cliffs covered in clumps of dark green grass. Although not very tall, the jagged formations were imposing. The air smelled of salt, fish, and pungent plants. There was nothing welcoming about the shoreline.

Ro tried to stand but winced and remembered her left foot hitting the rocks as the waves threw them toward shore. She sat back down, sending stones skittering down the beach, and examined her foot. Her stocking had been ripped to shreds, and there were bloody scrapes all along the side and bottom of her foot. She sighed, wishing she had kept her boots. Ro looked out to where the waves crashed against the rocks.

Bits of the launch were scattered across the beach. Farther down, she could see Aritha and Brenith.

Ro limped across the loose rocks, sliding and slipping as the jumble of stones gave way under each step. Finally, she reached the girls. She knelt to check each one. They were both unconscious but alive. Aritha was bleeding from a few cuts in her scalp, and Brenith had scrapes down her leg, *but they were alive.* Ro closed her eyes and offered a silent thank you to the gods, then looked around again. She rubbed her wrist across her runny nose and shivered. Water and shelter. They needed both badly. A little way up the cliff was a stone hut built into the rock. It looked tumbled down and abandoned.

She reached down and pulled Brenith's limp body into a sitting position. Ro knew it was going to be a painful trek back up the beach. She closed her eyes for a moment and blew out a breath. Ro lifted Brenith up onto her shoulder with a grunt and pushed to her feet. The cuts on her left foot blazed pain up her leg as she slowly made her way back up the rocks to the hut.

She lowered Brenith to the ground next to the hut's wall. She knelt beside her for a few breaths, then struggled back to her feet. Panting, Ro stared back to where Aritha lay, then looked to Leema. Leema was closer. Ro limped down the beach and pulled the young girl up onto her shoulder.

"At. Least. You're. Lighter." She huffed as she staggered up the rocks. Ro dropped to her knees and, as gently as she could, slid Leema off her shoulder. Ro slid sideways, landing on her rear. She held her foot as she tried to catch her breath. Closing her eyes, she tried to swallow. She desperately wanted water; her tongue felt a mile wide.

Ro sat still for a few moments, debating whether to leave Aritha where she was. The eldest princess had never been nice to her. In fact, Aritha had been horrible to her since the day that Ro had arrived on Koric. She sat debating until her breath was almost even.

Ro's vengeful side lost the debate. She pushed to her knees and staggered back down to Aritha. Every step was agony as she hauled the unconscious harridan back to the hut. Without ceremony, Ro dumped Aritha on the grass and collapsed beside her.

For the longest time, Ro lay still, watching the birds circle overhead. Each breath seemed like too much effort. She knew she needed to get up and find water. It just seemed like more effort than it was worth.

Move it, soldier! Taus' voice echoed in her head. *Sittin' on your backside ain't gonna get anything done!*

Ro sat up. She crawled over Aritha and pulled herself up the side of the hut. Step by agonizing step, she moved around the building until she found a door. It was barely attached by its hinges and had stood open so long that the grass had grown up around it, preventing it from ever being shut again. Carefully, she stepped into the dimness. The only light came from the countless holes in the walls and ceiling.

It was a fishing hut. Bits of netting were piled in the corner. Some hung from the wall. Most of the strings were rotten. A thick layer of dust permeated the entire hut. There was a broken chair against the back wall and a barrel sitting under a big hole in the roof.

Ro limped toward the barrel. It was brimming with water. Relief made Ro giddy as she cupped her hands and scooped up the cold liquid. She had swallowed several mouthfuls before the thought that the water might be tainted crossed her mind. Ro froze and stared hard at the water. Nothing moved or grew in the barrel. She shrugged and took a few more swallows.

When her tongue felt like it was normal-sized again, she began to search the hut. There was no food, but there was an old, mouse-eaten blanket that smelled like rotten fish. Under one of the piles of netting, Ro found a dented metal cup.

Ro knocked it against the nearest wall beam. Years of caked-on dirt busted loose and fell out, filling the air with dust. Ro coughed as she reached in and chipped out the remaining dirt with her fingernail, then rinsed it out with some water. When it was as clean as she could get it, she dipped it into the water barrel.

Trying not to slosh out too much, Ro limped back out to where the princesses still lay. Ro crouched in front of Leema, trying to keep her weight off her left foot. She lifted Leema's head and held the cup to her mouth. Water drizzled across her parched lips for a moment before she began to swallow.

Leema coughed and opened her eyes.

Ro flashed her a quick grin. "Welcome back."

The young girl pushed up into a sitting position and took the cup. She gulped down the rest of the water before looking around.

"My sisters?"

"They're here." Ro took the cup and stood. She hissed as her foot took her weight.

"You hurt?"

Ro shrugged. "My foot."

Leema scrambled to her feet and took the cup from Ro.

"Where's the water?"

"In the barrel in the hut." Ro sank to the ground, glad to let her do the running.

Leema made two quick trips to the barrel, bringing water to her sisters. They revived slowly.

"You seem none the worse for wear," Aritha griped, holding her head as Leema moved amongst them.

Leema smiled and fluttered her lashes at her sibling. "It's because I'm not old."

"Leema, run down to the shore and get some of the seawater. We need to wash out our wounds," Brenith said without looking up from the gash in her leg.

"Are you sure? Shouldn't we use the fresh water?"

"The salt will help clean the wound, and I don't want to waste the fresh water."

Leema marched off toward the shore. Brenith tore a length of cloth off the bottom of her ragged skirt. When Leema returned, she slowly poured the seawater over the scratches on her sister's leg while Brenith scrubbed at it. Blood washed onto the grass as she cleaned the wound. Leema left for the shore again as Brenith used her torn bit of skirt as a bandage.

Aritha put up her hand when Leema came back. "You are not pouring that on my head."

Leema leaned to pour. "Let me do it, Aritha."

"No." Aritha shoved her sister's hand away, nearly spilling the cup.

"Either you clean out the cuts on your head now," Brenith's face was blank as she stared her sister down, "or we hold you down and slice them open later when they become infected."

"Fine." Aritha threw away the rock she had been fiddling with and crossed her arms.

Leema poured the water while scrubbing her sister's scalp.

Aritha squealed and screeched the whole time. "Not so rough!"

"Oh, be quiet." Leema finished emptying the cup onto her sister's head. "All right, Ro." She turned to Ro. "You're next."

Ro waited for her to return with the water. She braced her left ankle on her right knee and pulled off her shredded stocking. The scrapes weren't bad, but they weren't good either. Once the youngest princess returned, they cleaned out the bits of sand and rock from Ro's cuts. Ro looked around for a moment, debating how to protect her foot. She shrugged, pulled her other stocking off, and slid it onto her injured foot.

"Now what?" Aritha carefully felt the scratches on her head.

Brenith looked at Ro. "No food in the hut?"

"No food."

"We need food!" Aritha leaned forward.

"There were some old nets in there. Can we fish?" Leema sat down next to Ro.

"Maybe."

"Anything to start a fire?" Brenith asked.

"I didn't see anything."

Aritha sat back. "I'm not eating raw fish."

Ro pointed up the hill behind the fisherman's hut. "I'll go see what's up there." She creaked to her feet and began to limp her way up the hill.

"Leema, go help her," Brenith said quietly.

The girl dashed up the hill, almost knocking Ro over when she tripped on her skirt.

"I wish we could wear pants like you," Leema grumbled as she jerked her skirt out of the way.

Ro said nothing as she dropped to all fours to make it up a steep bit. The climb was higher than it seemed. Both girls were panting by the time they reached the top of the cliff.

Leema shielded her eyes and stared out to sea. Ro turned and surveyed the land. Grass-covered rock gave way to what looked like a moor. Patches of green and brown grass were interspersed with pools of dark water. Way in the distance, Ro could see the dark shadows of trees.

"There's a forest."

"Where?" Leema turned to see where Ro was pointing. "That's a long way."

"Hmm." Ro nodded. "No settlements."

"Someone had to have lived around here. Otherwise, why build a fishing hut?" Leema stared down at the hut.

Ro looked at Leema, then back down the hill to the hut, then back at Leema.

"Let's check up there." Ro hobbled toward where the hill dropped down and twisted around an outcropping. Leema bounded down the hill ahead of her and disappeared around the rock.

Ro limped faster. She didn't like losing sight of the young princess.

"There's a cottage!" Leema popped back into view with a grin as Ro caught up with her.

The building itself looked to be in no better shape than the fishing hut. Bits of the wall were crumbling, and there were gaping holes in spots. An overgrown, broken rock wall surrounded the house but did nothing to keep the stray chickens in.

Ro and Leema approached the dwelling slowly. Ro fingered Marin's small knife where it was tied to her belt. Leema knocked on the door. "Anyone home?"

"Who's there?" An old voice screeched, making Leema jump.

"We need help. We were shipwrecked."

"Shipwrecked!" the voice moaned. Movement sounded from within, then the door slowly creaked open just enough for a wrinkled eye to peep out.

"Aye, you look wrecked." The eye looked them over. "But are you here to take what Fisp has?"

"I'm sorry," Leema cocked her head, "what?"

"You have manners. Must not be here to take Fisp's things." The door opened wider, and a crumpled old woman peered up at them. "You're girls?"

Leema curtsied. "Yes, Grandmother."

The old woman pushed past them. Ro winced as she stumbled backward. The woman was thin and hunched. She was wrapped in several layers of ragged clothing. Fisp waddled to the stone wall, looking this way and that. "There more?"

"Yes, our two sisters." Leema followed the woman to the wall. "They are down by the fisherman's hut."

"The hut?" She appeared confused for a moment, then she nodded sadly. "Ah, the hut. Belonged to my Dal."

"Dal?" Leema prodded.

"My mate. Lost at sea. So long ago. Took his nets and boat. Didn't come back."

"I'm sorry." Leema patted her on the shoulder. The crone smelled like rotting flesh. Leema wrinkled her nose.

"Why?" Fisp snapped. "You didn't drown him. Did you?" She turned and peered at Leema.

"No, Grandmother."

"Get your sisters." Fisp waddled back to the cottage without looking back.

Leema looked to Ro. There was nothing else to do. Ro shrugged and nodded, so Leema ran back toward the cliff.

Hospitality

ARITHA WRINKLED HER NOSE as she stepped inside the dark cottage. Brenith poked her in the ribs before she could make a rude comment. Aritha frowned at her sister but kept her silence.

Ro was kneeling before the hearth, trying to clear enough space to kindle a fire. Dust and ancient ash clogged the firebox and had overgrown the surrounding hearth. A grimy pot hung on a hook, but it looked like Fisp hadn't used it in a while. Ro unhooked it and started to clear the ashes into it.

Leema pushed in behind Brenith and made her way across the cluttered floor to where Fisp was rummaging through jars on a corner shelf.

"Grandmother, I've brought my sisters."

The old woman turned and eyed the newcomers with suspicion. "Look wrecked too."

Aritha smoothed her skirt self-consciously.

Brenith curtsied. "Thank you for your hospitality."

The old woman began to cackle.

"What's so funny?" Aritha crossed her arms.

"Never been curtsied to so much in my life!"

Ro smiled as she raked more ashes into the pot. Leema tried to hide her own smile as she moved over to help Ro. She carried the pot outside and let the wind have the ashes. It took five trips, but eventually the fireplace was clean enough for a fire to actually burn.

Ro layered chunks of peat moss from a pile next to the hearth into the firebox. She rummaged through the debris around the hearth until she found flint and struck a spark. The room glowed suddenly as the flames caught the moss.

She glanced around. The cottage was only a single room. A rumpled pallet lay in the corner, and a crooked table with two chairs stood near the opposite wall. Fisp was still fussing with jars from the only shelves in the room.

"Ah!" Fisp held up a potato.

Brenith and Leema exchanged a glance.

"Is that all you have?" Aritha stared at the potato.

"Nope." Fisp waddled across the room.

Leema glanced at Ro. "Perhaps we could catch some fish."

"Nah, too late in the day. Fishin' is for mornings." Fisp pulled a knife off the mantle, waddled to the table, and began to chop the potato into tiny pieces.

"Leema, if you would run and wash the pot." Brenith shooed her sister out the door.

Fisp hollered after her. "There's water in the barrel!"

"Can we help?" Brenith offered.

"Suppose so." Fisp peered at her through the dimness. "But I'm thinkin' yer the ones that need the help."

"Indeed, we do."

"I tell ya what. There's a crock for washin' out there. Ya girls get yerselves cleaned up. It'll take up the time while ya wait for the stew."

"Thank you, Grandmother."

"Name's Fisp. Ain't a grandmother." The old woman turned away from Brenith, mumbling to herself.

Aritha was the first out the door. She took a deep gulp of fresh air. "How can she live like that? It reeks in there! She reeks!"

Brenith stood for a moment, looking up at the sky. Dark and ominous storm clouds were building over the sea. "She's old, Aritha, and alone.

It can't be easy for her." Brenith led the way around the crumbling building, looking for the crock.

"How hard is it to take a bath!"

Brenith stopped and stared at the tiny crock sitting on a splintery old table under a wooden awning. Under the edge of the awning stood a rain barrel that was half full.

"Does that answer your question?"

"She takes a bath with that?"

Brenith didn't answer. She just stepped forward and filled the crock from the barrel. A dirty rag was tucked under the crock. Brenith picked it up doubtfully and stared at it. With a resigned sigh, she dunked it in the water and started to scrub the salty dirt from her skin.

Aritha shook her head. "I am not using that nasty rag to wash."

"That's all there is," Brenith sighed.

"I can't believe this is happening to me! We were supposed to be dining at the Imperial Palace! Now we are forced to live like savages!"

Her younger sister stopped washing and turned away from the table. She slapped the wet rag onto Aritha's chest.

"When you find a different way, let me know." She stomped back toward the house.

"Hey, you see the water barrel?" Leema asked as she came around the corner. Brenith pointed and kept walking.

"What's the matter with her?"

"How should I know?" Aritha was holding up the rag with two fingers.

"What are you doing?" Leema watched her scowl at the rag as she filled the pot from the barrel.

"We are supposed to clean up with this."

Leema shrugged. "Better than not cleaning up at all."

"Why are you always so cheery?" Aritha splashed the rag into the crock.

"You'd rather I act like you?" Her sister tossed over her shoulder as she walked back to the house.

Aritha sighed in disgust and started to scrape the salty dirt from her arm.

When Leema entered the room, she found Ro standing in front of Fisp with her arms crossed. Leema crossed to the fireplace and hooked the pot onto the swing arm.

Fisp waddled away from the guard. "I don't need help."

"I'm not offering help." Ro limped after her. "I'm offering payment for shelter."

Leema watched the old woman sway from side to side. It was obvious she wanted whatever Ro was offering but couldn't bring herself to take it.

"I offer shelter." Fisk gathered the chopped potatoes into a pile.

Ro leaned on the table, resting her weight on her right foot. "And we accept. Allow us to offer gratitude." Fisp picked up a handful of potatoes and waddled to the fire.

Outside, thunder rumbled. Aritha appeared in the door, breathing hard. She jumped when thunder sounded again, earning an odd look from Leema.

"Talk tomorrow." Fisp returned and picked up more potatoes. The old woman was getting more and more agitated.

"Ro," Brenith laid a hand on Ro's arm, "let it go."

Ro shrugged and limped outside. She followed the worn path around the corner of the house and found the crock. Quickly, she washed away the sweat and grime from the past two days. It would have been nice to have soap. As she washed her neck, her fingers brushed against the cord of Marin's locket. Carefully, she laid the rag down and stared at the locket. Marin had a wife. Ro had met her once when she had come to the barracks.

"I'll return it to her, Marin," Ro vowed. Lightning flashed, illuminating the cliffs. Seconds later, thunder cracked, making the ground vibrate. Ro finished scrubbing and hobbled back around the cottage. She hadn't reached the door before the sky opened up and dumped on the cliffs. Ro stopped in the doorway and tried to wring out some of the water that had soaked her shirt and pants. She shook most of the water from her hair, then swung the door closed.

The cottage was not as warm as it could have been or as dry. The holes in the walls let the heat out, and the roof let the rain in. Aritha retreated to the pallet and sat hugging her knees. Leema stirred the pot of soup while dodging a steady drip from a hole above the hearth. Brenith sat at the rickety table with Fisp.

"My Dal loved the rain," the old woman mumbled. "Used to say it brought the fish."

"How long has he been gone?" Brenith asked quietly.

"Long and long." Fisp shook her head. "Only me now."

"Are there no other cottages or a village?"

"All gone." Fisp heaved herself up and tottered over to the fire. "Village to the far south over the moor, but too far to market." Thunder cracked again as she took the spoon from Leema and tasted the soup.

"What about the forest?" Ro asked, watching Fisp spoon the thin soup into the only two bowls she owned. Fisp handed one to Leema and waddled across the floor to Aritha.

"There, you eat that up." She patted Aritha on the head and turned back to Ro. "The forest?"

Aritha groaned but devoured the first meal she'd had in two days. Fisp scratched her belly as she thought. Leema spooned more soup into her already empty bowl and handed it to Brenith.

"Thank you." Her sister took the bowl graciously.

"Heard some strange stories about that place."

"Strange?" Leema found a dry spot near the fire and sat down. Aritha set her empty bowl down beside her on the floor.

"Terrible things in that forest." Fisp waddled over and picked up the bowl. "Bandits and thieves." She returned to the fire. "And the Sellemeh a Salladeh."

"What's that?" Leema's eyes were huge.

"People of the Water. Not men. Frightening things. They live in the water. Snatch travelers." Fisp filled her bowl and settled into her chair again with a grunt.

"Another stupid story," Aritha scoffed.

"Are there settlements in the forest?" Brenith ignored Aritha and carried her empty bowl to the hearth.

"Here and there. No paths. These cliffs run up to the forest, getting higher as you get closer."

Brenith filled her bowl and handed it to Ro.

"Used to be a road around it on the sea side. Forest shoved it into the sea. Nothing in that forest but death." The old woman's chuckle was drowned out by the thunder.

Recouping

IN THE MORNING BEFORE dawn, Aritha complained so loudly about the smoke billowing back into the cottage that Ro climbed up onto the soaking roof and cleaned the chimney before the others were awake.

Ro and Leema started the task of repairing Fisp's cottage. Ro patched the roof while Leema carried rocks from the shore to fill in the holes in her walls. Ro shoved another daub of mud around the patch she had made. It was the last hole in the roof. The cottage was almost weather-proof now.

Brenith set herself the task of repairing the fishing nets. However, after half a day of fixing the holes and then attempting unsuccessfully to catch anything, she gave the nets over to Leema. Not more than an hour later, the youngest princess came back with several fish.

Brenith eyed her younger sister. "Just how much time did you spend sneaking off to go fishing instead of studying?"

Leema sent her a dazzling smile.

Fisp laughed at the grinning princess proudly holding her string of fish and clapped her ancient hands. "Come on, girl, I'll show you how to dry them!"

However, Aritha refused to touch anything in Fisp's grimy hut until Brenith threatened her with no food. Finally, she agreed to sweep out the cottage, but Brenith found her sitting at the table a short time later. "What are you doing?"

"Resting."

Brenith braced her hands on her hips. "There are things that need to be done."

"I am not a servant." Aritha crossed her arms.

"I am ashamed to call you my sister," Brenith muttered, "and my older sister at that. This woman has opened her home to us. We are alive only because of her goodwill. The least you can do is help with some chores!"

Aritha's eyes popped open wide. "But I—"

"You are the eldest. You should be the first one to offer help! Mother would..." Brenith covered her face as she choked to a stop.

"I'm sorry, Brenith." Aritha stood and put her arms around her younger sister. "It's just... I don't know how to do anything."

Brenith sniffled, and Aritha wiped the tears from Brenith's cheeks with her sleeve.

"I'm not like you or Leema. She's always sneaking off to run with the boys, and you are always helping the cook or the healers." Aritha shrugged. "All I've ever done is learn to dance, sing, and follow politics so I can marry well for Koric. I am useless outside of the Court."

"You're not useless." Brenith sniffled again. "I could teach you."

"Thank you. You are a good sister." Brenith smiled at the compliment. "Can you teach me to wash our clothes? I'm tired of stinking!"

Brenith nodded and led her sister outside to find Fisp and ask about soap.

With too much patience, Brenith explained several times how clothes were washed. Once she was sure that Aritha understood, she left her to wash the blankets first. Fisp gave up a tiny portion of soap that she had been hoarding. Aritha demanded more.

"I can't make any more!" Fisp wailed.

"Well, why not?"

"Ain't got no fat." Fisp hugged the jar to her bony chest. "Huntin's pretty thin 'round here!" Fisp waddled away as if she thought Aritha might wrest away her precious stash.

Aritha stamped her foot. "Oh, for love of the gods!"

Once she had cleaned and dried the blankets. She found the girls, one by one, and traded them a blanket for their skirts and tunics. It took most of the day to wash, dry, and return each girl's clothes in sequence. Finally, it was Fisp's turn.

"Come on, Fisp." Aritha doggedly followed the old woman around. "I already have the wash water. If I wash your clothes now, you won't have to give up any more soap."

Fisp hobbled faster. "Go away!"

"Fisp!" Aritha growled, "Don't make me dump water on you."

"You're horrid!"

"Fisp?" Brenith gasped when the old woman dodged behind her as she came around the side of the house. "Aritha! What are you trying to do?"

Aritha crossed her arms. "She won't let me wash her clothes."

"Fisp?" Brenith turned to the old woman.

"Tell her to go away!"

"Aritha is only trying to help."

"She's tryin' to take Fisp's clothes!"

"She just wants to wash them. She will give them back." Brenith laid a hand on the old woman's shoulder. "Honestly, she will give them back."

Fisp peered at her suspiciously, and then, reluctantly, Fisp let Aritha lead her back to the cottage.

Ro turned away from the scene to watch the sea. It surprised her that there had been no ships. She had seen not a single sail in three days. Ro watched as Leema climbed up the hill from the fisherman's hut with two fish swinging on her string. "You're getting good at that."

"Yeah," Leema held up the fish and squinted at them. She dropped her arm again and stared out to sea. "Seen anyone?"

"Nope."

"Are we just going to stay here?"

Ro shook her head. "We can't. We have to answer the Empress' summons. I just don't know how to get from here to there."

"If there are no ships, then maybe we can catch a ride with someone in that village Fisp mentioned."

"She said it was to the south." Ro pointed. "The opposite way we need to go." Ro sighed. "We'll probably have to walk if we can't flag down a ship."

"I only remember a little of Ka geography. There's a city on the Ka River. Maybe we could get passage there." Leema turned and looked toward the forest in the distance. "But I think that we would have to go through that to get to it."

Ro looked at the hazy trees in the distance, muttering, "Bandits, thieves, and Sellemeh a Salladeh."

"Do you think those stories Fisp told were real?"

"Dragons are real," Ro shrugged as they walked to the cottage, "so why not water people?"

"I don't know if I want to see Sellemeh a Salladeh." Leema kicked at a clump of grass. "Seeing a dragon was bad enough."

When Ro and Leema reached the cottage, they could hear Fisp moaning.

"Oh, quit complaining," Aritha's voice floated out through the door. "Be happy you'll have clean clothes soon."

"I'm freezing!" Fisp whined. Leema giggled and slipped around the side of the cottage to dress out her fish.

Ro stepped inside. Fisp was sitting at the table, wrapped in a blanket, watching Aritha shake out her wet clothes.

She caught sight of Ro and grabbed for her hand. "She's trying to freeze me to death!"

"I am not!" Aritha sighed.

"Fisp, why are there no ships passing here?" Ro looked down at the old woman.

"Nothing here."

"But not even sails pass." She sat down at the table.

"Too close to Jardarwa." The old woman shrugged and pulled the blanket closer.

"I don't understand."

"The Holy Mountain is on Jardarwa."

"I know that. What does that have to do with ships?"

"Ka avoids the Holy Mountain. Men shouldn't fiddle with Death. It's unnatural to bring people back from the dead."

"They only resurrect spirits for a short time. They don't bring people back to life." Aritha turned Fisp's clothes so the fire could dry the other side.

The old woman sniffed. "It's still unnatural."

"So, they just avoid this end of the province?"

Lightning crackled across the sky, illuminating the inside of the cottage. Seconds later, thunder shook the walls. Leema burst through the door, holding her cleaned fish. Brenith rushed in behind her and closed the door.

"There were more villages and things, but they always had bad luck. Like my Dal. The closer you are to Jardarwa, the worse yer luck."

Resurrection

LIGHTING FLASHED ACROSS THE sky. The air crackled and buzzed. Porsa, apprentice to High Priest Voc of Jardarwa, flinched. He did not want to be here. The flames from the fire in front of him scorched his face as he leaned in close. His hand shook as he reached out. He just wanted to get this over with. Porsa cringed as thunder vibrated the mountain top.

Lightning fizzed again, turning the midnight air pink and making the hair stand up on his arms. He *really* didn't want to do this. Porsa bit his lip and took a breath. Just as he was about to sprinkle what he hoped was the right herbs into the fire, thunder cracked. He jumped, and instead of a sprinkling, he dumped the entire concoction into the flames. Panic filled his eyes.

"Oh, n-n-no!"

It was supposed to be a little in the flames and a little on the body while speaking the incantation. He lunged forward and tried to flick some of the burning herbs onto the body lying next to the fire. Thankfully, some landed on the corpse, but so did some stray embers. Porsa scrambled to slap out the smoldering flames. Suddenly remembering that he was supposed to speak the incantation, he sputtered a few words. He cursed his stutter, took a breath, and started again.

Sizzles of lightning and cracks of thunder shocked him into silence more than once before he was done, but finally he managed to complete the ritual. He sprinkled the second mixture on the fire and on the body. Relieved that he had gotten that part right, he sat back and stared at the corpse.

Nothing happened.

He waited a few moments more. Surely something was supposed to happen.

Porsa's shoulders slumped. He had failed. He should have known better. He should have gone back to the citadel when the High Priest had been killed, but he didn't want to be punished. It didn't matter now. He had failed anyway.

The ground trembled. A great whoosh of wind blasted down onto the fire. Porsa fell to the ground as air rushed down onto the top of the mountain. Porsa jammed his eyes closed and dug his fingers into the rocky soil. He gritted his teeth against the force that held him against the ground. The mountain shuddered again as if repulsed by what had just taken place. Logs from the fire vibrated and rolled away, plunging the clearing into near darkness.

"I-I'm s-sorry!" Porsa cried.

The downward pressure stopped as quickly as it had started. Porsa let out a relieved breath, but then the mountain shook again. The ground heaved like it was trying to push something out from deep within the earth. Porsa curled into a ball, whimpering. Then it all stopped. Slowly, Porsa lifted his head. Lightning still flashed, periodically illuminating the area. Remnants of the fire glowed eerily.

Porsa waited for another flash of lightning to see where the body lay. Thunder grumbled in the distance as he slowly crawled forward. He couldn't see enough by the lightning alone, so he tried to rebuild the fire by rolling some of the hotter logs back into a pile. Porsa finally managed to produce enough light to see the corpse.

For long moments, he watched. He blinked a few times and continued to stare at the corpse. He crawled forward, trying to tell if it moved, but it was too dark to see. He crept a little closer. Slowly, he laid his head against the corpse's chest. He couldn't hear a heartbeat. All he could hear was the thunder rumbling above.

Porsa sat back on his heels. Just then, the body sucked in a breath and arched off the ground. Porsa skittered backward.

The now-living man slammed back down onto the ground, coughing. He sucked in another breath and coughed again. He thrashed against the ground as his body struggled to remember how to live.

Porsa just stared; he had no idea what to do. Voc had only told him the ritual. He had repeated it over and over again as he lay dying on the side of the trail, but he'd never told Porsa what would happen afterward.

The man slowly caught the rhythm of how to breathe again and calmed down. Porsa crept forward. He jumped back again when the man tried to move his arms.

"S-s-steady on." Porsa reached out to stop the man from trying to move.

"Where am I?" he croaked, unused to his new vocal cords. "My voice!"

"P-please," Porsa took a breath, "s-stay c-c-calm."

The man tried to roll on his side.

"W-what's your n-name?" The apprentice prayed he had called the right spirit back.

"Bazin." His eyes were wide and wild. "Am I alive?"

"Yes."

Bazin started to laugh. Porsa shivered; it was an awful laugh, giddy and terrifying, almost hysterical. Tears glittered in the firelight as they slid down Bazin's temples.

"Why?" he finally managed to ask.

"A j-job."

"Right." His laughter died away. "Who are you? Why does my voice sound wrong?" Bazin shifted, trying to understand what he was feeling. "I don't feel right."

"I-I'm P-P-Porsa. Your v-v-v-v…" Porsa stopped and tried again. "Your v-v-v-v-v…"

Bazin closed his eyes. "Take a breath."

Porsa sucked in air and blew it out slowly. "Your v-voice and body are d-different bec-c-ause you have been dead for th-three months."

"Three months!" Bazin tried to rise, but his body wouldn't cooperate.

"W-we had to f-find a d-different body."

"Whose body?"

"A c-cobbler's son. W-was stabbed in a t-tavern brawl."

"I'm in a cobbler!"

Porsa nodded.

"Three months!" Bazin tried again to move.

"W-we fixed the stab w-w-wound," Porsa offered helpfully.

Bazin stared at Porsa. "Are you a High Priest of the Holy Mountain?"

Porsa shook his head.

"Then how..." Bazin took in the shadowy gray of Porsa's robes and suddenly understood. "You're an apprentice!" The skinny youth nodded quickly. "How did—? I thought only the High Priests could resurrect."

"He d-died. Horse k-k-kicked him in the head."

"A horse? Then how— Were you trained in resurrection?" Porsa shook his head again. "So, if you aren't trained, how do you know you did it right?"

"My m-master t-taught me."

"Before or after the horse kicked him?"

"After."

"Oh Vunkah!"

At the time, Porsa hadn't thought it was a good idea either. "He had t-to t-tell m-me. He w-was d-dying."

Bazin finally managed to get one arm to move. It flopped up onto his chest. He let his head roll to the side and peered into the darkness. They seemed to be alone in the chill of the night.

"Where are the others?" Bazin looked back at Porsa.

"O-others?"

"Yes!" Bazin glared at the apprentice. "Resurrections are usually inside a temple and with a lot more priests. And there usually isn't a body."

"Ah... w-well... there's... um..." Porsa didn't really want to admit that his master was working outside of the Order's knowledge.

"Spit it out!"

"My m-master was p-paid to resurrect you." Porsa blurted in a rush, then gave a sigh of relief. "You are t-to k-k-kill a g-girl."

"What did you say?" Bazin went very still.

"They arranged that you w-w-will have t-two m-moons to k-k-kill her, or your spirit goes b-back to the und-derworld. If she d-dies, you get to s-stay in this b-body."

"What girl?"

"The f-f-female g-guard from K-Koric." Porsa shrugged. He had no idea who she was.

"Female guard?" Bazin stared hard at the skinny apprentice. He thrashed, trying to get his new body to move. One leg hitched its way up until his knee was bent. One by one, he forced his new limbs to move.

With jerking movements, he regained his feet. Porsa skittered back from him. He was terrified to ask, but he had to know the man's decision.

"Are you g-going to f-f-fullf-f-ill the c-contract?"

Bazin snorted as he turned and staggered awkwardly into the darkness.

Porsa stared after him. "W-was th-that a yes?"

The shaking apprentice started to gather up his scattered supplies. He couldn't leave them on the mountain, and it was a good excuse not to follow Bazin. He knew that he should, but that man scared him.

"W-w-why me?"

"Why you, Porsa?" A voice from the darkness echoed across the remains of the camp.

Porsa froze, clutching a satchel of herbs to his chest. His eyes searched the darkness.

"Porsa, where is your master?" a second voice asked.

"Porsa, what have you done?" another voice joined in.

From the darkness, several robed figures in white drifted into the dying firelight. Porsa stared at the Holy Brothers. Blood drained from his face as he realized there was no Master Voc to protect him from the wrath of the Order.

"Oh n-no."

Hedonism

BAZIN STUMBLED DOWN THE mountain in the dark. His legs still weren't entirely working. This body just didn't feel right. For one, he was shorter. He had liked being tall. There was something to be said for towering over enemies. He scowled and wondered if his legs didn't work properly because his resurrection had been done by a stuttering, idiotic apprentice.

"Just my luck." Bazin stumbled to a stop as a horrible thought occurred to him. He looked down and felt between his legs. "That better work, or I'm killing that scrawny little bastard."

Ahead, Bazin could make out the lights of the small scattering of buildings that surrounded the base of the Holy Mountain. The last time that he had been to Jardarwa, there had been a lively little tavern near the docks. Mostly sailors and townsfolk frequented The Walking Corpse. The Holy Brothers had tried to get the name changed, but the locals wouldn't have it. If they had to live next to the Gates of the Underworld, they would deal with it in their own way.

Bazin staggered forward as he thought about what the apprentice had said. He was to kill the female guard on Koric. He stopped. *That girl. The one that skewered me.* He felt her sword slide between his ribs as if it had just happened. He shivered.

Two moon cycles to kill. Sixty days to take revenge on that little bitch who sent him into torment. Three months of pain. Three months of torture. It had felt like years. Every pain he had caused in life, every death, had been inflicted on him again and again.

He shuddered as he remembered his own continuous screaming for redemption and forgiveness. He had pleaded and vowed never to take another life, never to cause another pain, if only he could be set free. Now, here he was. Free. Alive again, but only so long as he killed again. A cruel trap.

He shook his head and stumbled forward. He was alive and free of torment, at least for now, and he was going to enjoy it. Two moon cycles to kill the Koric girl gave him plenty of time. Koric was only a few days away by ship. Nip over, kill her, and nip back. But first, he wanted to know if all of his body parts worked. A man had to have priorities. He had been dead for three months, and this was a new body.

With any luck, he could even find a mirror to see what he looked like now. A cobbler's son. That could mean anything. He hoped he wasn't hideous. He reached up to feel his cheekbone. The scar that ran across his face and upper lip was gone. The skin was smooth. This was not his body. He didn't fit in this skin. His gut twisted as the realization shook Bazin to his core. He lurched forward, drawn on by the thought of strong ale to help him forget.

Light from The Walking Corpse spilled out onto the boardwalk. The door had been propped open to let in some of the night air. Smoke from the patrons' pipes wafted through the door. The noise of laughter and friendly arguments from within was comforting. With every step, the salty air cleared Bazin's head a little more, and his legs worked a little better. Just before he stepped through, he remembered Porsa saying that he—no, his body's former occupant—had been stabbed in a tavern brawl. If he walked through the door and he was supposed to be dead, what would happen then?

"Darin?" a voice from behind him exclaimed. He was engulfed in a bear hug from a round man who smelled of bread and flour.

"Uh..." *Guess that answers that.*

"I knew you'd make it!" The baker was young but not a child. "I told Cara you'd be back!" He danced them around, then finally let Bazin go.

"Cara?"

"Yeah, don't you remember the girl you were fighting over?" The baker slapped him on the shoulder. "Just like you to get stabbed and not even remember why."

Bazin smiled as if he shared the joke, but thought, *Great, I'm in the body of an idiot.*

"Come on." The baker threw an arm around his shoulders and pulled him inside. "I wanna celebrate."

Bazin let himself be dragged up to the bar. The tavern was just as he had remembered it. Smokey and overly warm, filled with half-drunk locals and completely drunk sailors. Barely-contained serving maids served more than ale and pies. Bazin grinned.

The baker ordered a round, shouting, "Darin's back. Told you a little knife wound wouldn't keep him down!"

"Darin's dead!" shouted a voice that sounded like falling rocks. Most of the room went quiet.

"He's not." The baker pointed. "Look here."

There always has to be that one friend, Bazin shook his head and downed a long gulp of ale.

"I say he's dead." The owner of the rocky voice pushed his way through the crowd as the rest of the room fell silent. His face matched his voice: pockmarked with broken teeth.

"Looks alive to me," a woman said.

Bazin turned to find the owner of the hot, buttery voice. One of the tavern maids was leaning against the other side of the bar. Bazin looked her up and down. Her ample wares were about to overflow her lacings, and her eyes were asking for help to make it happen.

"Hey, Cara," the baker slapped Bazin on the shoulder again, "look who's alive and kicking."

"Not for long," she smirked and pointed behind them. Bazin turned in time to receive the punch aimed at his face. Ale sloshed out of his tankard as his head snapped backward.

Bazin shook his head. Darin's jaw was not as hard as Bazin's had been. Cara rescued his tankard before the next blow landed. She moved out of range and downed a couple of swallows. Bazin took the second punch in the nose. The baker jumped forward, trying to land his own punch on the snarling attacker. Patrons started to jeer and roar encouragement.

Bazin rubbed his nose with the back of his hand and stared at his blood. He frowned. *This is a great start with a new body.* The pockmarked bastard swung at him again. He reared back to avoid the punch. *Time to see what this body's got.*

He balled up his fist and, with a quick jab to the ribs, knocked his assailant sideways. The patrons roared again, this time cheering for Bazin. They didn't really care who won. They just liked the entertainment, especially if it wasn't any of them getting beaten.

Bazin landed a few more punches, but his arms were tiring. This cobbler's son was not in shape. His opponent came back at him with a hard upper cut. Bazin staggered backward over a table and landed in the lap of a sailor who was laughing so hard at the fight that he started to cough. He dumped Bazin on the floor and laughed harder.

"Stop breaking my tables!" bellowed the owner of The Walking Corpse.

The baker made a reappearance. He grabbed the man from behind and spun him around, but the punch he had intended never landed because the pockmarked man swung as he turned. The baker woofed as the blow to his belly knocked the wind out of him.

Bazin staggered up from the floor. He tried to blink away the fog from his eyes. He wasn't sure if it was the lack of muscles or maybe it was that he had been dead recently, but he seemed to be losing this fight. He really didn't know how to take that revelation. Bazin the Assassin did not lose fights.

His opponent grabbed him by the front of his shirt with one hand and pummeled him in the face over and over again. Bazin's head rocked backward with each punch. He couldn't get his arms up to protect his face. He was nearing the blackout point when the baker smashed a chair across the brute's back.

The pockmarked man let go of Bazin as he dropped to his knees from the blow. Bazin followed him to the floor. The baker swung what was left of the chair, hitting the big man in the side and knocking him sideways. Bazin frowned at the pockmarked man who lay groaning about a foot away.

A cheer went up from the crowd. It was a good end to the fight. Bazin could feel his face starting to swell.

"Up ya get." Cara slid her hands under Bazin's armpits and lifted him from the floor. The baker pranced around the room, accepting congratulations and pounding his chest.

Bazin wobbled on his knees and peered at Cara. "I used to be a better fighter than this."

"Oh, I know, love, let's get you fixed up." Cara helped him stagger to the back of the tavern. She deposited him on a bench near the kitchen door, set a tankard in front of him, then went into the kitchen.

Bazin drained the tankard, feeling depressed and defeated. Cara returned with a bowl of water, a rag, and a second tankard. She handed him the second ale and sat on his lap.

"I really was better," Bazin moaned as she cleaned the blood away from his eyes and nose.

"I believe you."

He drained the tankard. "It's just I've been dead."

"You're alive now," she giggled, wiggling on his lap.

"Yes, I am." He grinned and buried his face in her chest.

Porsa's First Confession

PORSA LOOKED UP FROM where he knelt in the center of the highly polished marble floor. "T-t-truly! I...I h-have only f-f-followed the orders of m-m-m-y m-m-master!" Porsa wailed as the white-robed brothers formed a circle around him.

One silver-haired priest, Master Farin, asked. "And what did your master tell you to do?"

Porsa gazed around the circle of priests, wondering if he would find sympathy with any of them. The flickering torches along the walls cast undulating shadows on their accusing faces.

"In m-m-my defense, I w-w-was taught to obey my m-master in all things."

"That is what we teach." The kindly priest, Master Thosin, nodded.

"Master V-Voc received a c-c-contract," Porsa's nerves were not helping his stutter, "for a r-r-resurrection."

"That is not so unusual." Master Thosin gestured for him to continue.

"B-but he t-t-told me to k-k-keep s-silent about it."

"Why?" a priest behind Porsa demanded. "We have undertaken many contracts."

"Go on, Porsa," Master Thosin urged.

The apprentice swallowed, then continued. "He t-took payment, and he had m-me s-steal a b-body."

"A body!" the priest behind Porsa gasped. The other priests murmured their disapproval.

"Porsa, you know that resurrections are in spirit only." Master Thosin frowned. "Why would you steal a body?"

"It is n-not my place to q-q-question m-my master!" Porsa wailed again, causing the priests to mutter and grumble. Thosin glanced around and shushed them.

"Porsa, please continue," Master Thosin said gently. "Once your master had the body, he took you outside the citadel?" Porsa nodded. "Then what happened?"

"On th-the w-way up the m-m-mountain, a f-furry animal j-jumped out of th-the t-trees and spooked the horse, and it k-k-kicked him in the head."

"Did that blow kill Master Voc?"

"N-no." Porsa trembled. "He was d-dying and t-told me I had to c-c-complete the r-r-ritual."

"If he was dying, why complete the contract?" The priest behind Porsa scoffed.

Porsa shook his head. He hadn't thought to ask. Master Voc had beaten into him the importance of obeying him in all things. It was only now occurring to him that he could have chosen not to perform the ritual.

"What did he tell you to do?" Thosin prompted.

Porsa stared up at him. He didn't want to try and repeat the incantation; it had been hard enough the first time.

Master Farin insisted, "Porsa, you must tell us exactly what you did."

The apprentice began the painstaking task of telling the exact steps of the ritual. He confessed about the accident with too much of the herbal mixture landing in the fire, and about the many times that he'd had to start over again because the lightning had scared him. Sweat covered his brow as he labored to get the words out.

The ring of priests listened quietly, but tension permeated the air. Master Thosin exchanged worried glances with his brothers as Porsa spoke.

When Porsa had finished, Master Farin murmured, "This shouldn't even be possible!"

"Blasphemy," another whispered.

"Where did Master Voc come by this incantation?" Master Thosin asked.

Porsa shook his head. "I d-don't know."

"Porsa, let me understand this correctly. Master Voc wished to resurrect the assassin, Bazin, giving him two moon cycles to kill this girl. If he succeeds, his spirit may stay; if he fails, he is to return to the Underworld?"

Porsa didn't even try to speak; he only nodded.

Master Thosin looked around the circle of Holy Brothers, then shook his head. "I'm sorry, Porsa, but the words of the incantation you spoke meant something else."

Porsa stared up at him in horror. "I-I-I t-t-tried. I f-f-f-f-followed M-M-Master's inst-tructions!"

"I believe you, Porsa. But he may not have explained it correctly considering he was injured at the time." Master Thosin shook his head again. "The incantation you recited calls Bazin's spirit to remain only if the girl is alive. If she dies, he returns to the Underworld."

"Oh n-no!" Porsa's eyes grew huge. He crumpled into a ball on the floor, covering his head with his hands. He knew no good could come from this. He hadn't wanted to do it in the first place. *Oh, why did my father sell me?*

"Porsa?" Master Thosin stared down at the apprentice. "Who commissioned the contract with Master Voc?"

Porsa raised his head. "H-he w-w-wouldn't t-tell me, but I h-heard h-him t-t-t-talking."

"And?" The priest behind Porsa had become impatient.

"D-D-Drugi M-M-Moc."

"Drugi Moc?" Thosin's eyebrows rose.

A murmur of disbelief and anger swept the room, followed by vehement protests.

"The Dragon Priests must not be allowed to interfere with Life and Death in this way."

"Sacrilege!"

"Only the Holy Brothers speak to the dead!"

"Brothers," Thosin held his hands up, "please!"

"We must not allow that misguided cult to tamper with our Holy Edict!"

"They have broken the Circle! It is the fundamental belief of our Order, Life comes full circle to Death, which begins again in new Life as the Goddess dictates, not because it is forced into a stolen body!"

"This is treachery!"

"They cannot be allowed to claim sovereignty over the spirits like this!"

"My Brothers, please! We must remain calm in this time of crisis." Master Thosin looked around the room at each of the other priests. "Two spirits now hang in the balance; the very sanctity of our Order is at stake. Porsa, who is this girl the assassin was to kill?"

"M-Master V-Voc d-didn't s-say." Porsa groaned. "J-just that she w-was a f-female g-g-guard from K-Koric."

"And where is this Bazin now?"

"I d-don't know," Porsa mumbled from the floor without getting up. "He left."

"You must find him!" Thosin glared down at Porsa.

Porsa moaned as he pushed up from the cold marble floor.

"You must explain the correct terms of his resurrection. Then, you and he must find this girl and ensure her survival. They must both return here to the Citadel before any damage is done to the Circle."

The apprentice stared up at Thosin with pleading eyes, begging to be left out of the whole thing.

"I am sorry, Porsa, but your actions have consequences. You should have informed the Order of Master Voc's defection from the Path. You owe recompense for your mistake." The old man looked up at his fellow priests. "We must also take action, my brothers. The Arazi must be informed of the Drugi Moc's meddling. We must send a delegation to the Imperial City."

The circle of Holy Brothers nodded their agreement. Breaking the circle, Master Thosin stepped forward and stooped to help Porsa rise.

"You must go quickly. Do you understand what you must do?" He gazed into Porsa's pained countenance. "You must find Bazin and explain, then find the girl, and bring them both here. We must save her. We cannot allow her to die for a mistake. This is your debt to pay, Porsa, not hers."

Porsa nodded, resigned to his fate.

Master Thosin turned to the other priests and snapped, "Search Voc's chambers. I want to know where he learned this spell. Tear the Citadel apart if you have to but find it."

Porsa's Second Confession

BAZIN FELT A WARM, furry weight tickling his bare chest. He moaned and tried to return to sleep, but the furry thing dug in its claws.

"Argh!" His eyes popped open as the little points dug into his skin. The brightness of the room played havoc with his throbbing head. He slammed his eyes shut again and slowly opened them a slit.

"Krrr." A furry yellow-eyed face, not more than an inch away from Bazin's nose, peered at him suspiciously. The claws flexed a little and dug in again. "Krrr?"

"Dinko?" Bazin gaped in disbelief. At the sound of his name, the fuzzy lemur did a tiny dance in a circle on Bazin's chest. He stopped and peered into Bazin's face again with his nose twitching, trying to catch his scent.

"It's me, Din. It's Bazin." He unearthed his arm from under Cara's ample chest and scratched Dinko's ears. "Ah, Din, I missed you."

The lemur purred and pushed against his master's hand. He stopped and peered into Bazin's face again.

"I know I don't look right." He held up his hand and stared at it as he turned it one way then another. "This is my new body." He sighed and let his hand drop. "Guess we'll both have to get used to it."

The lemur sat back and curled his bushy tail around his feet. He carefully scanned every inch of Bazin's new face as if he were memorizing it.

"How did you find me?" The lemur stared hard and long into Bazin's eyes. The image of Bazin's death shimmered in his mind. He shuddered as he watched the girl spit him on her sword. Then the image was replaced by the Holy Mountain Citadel. "You came to the Gates of the Underworld after I died?"

"Krrr." Dinko did his little dance again.

"But how did you know?" Bazin narrowed his eyes and searched the lemur's face.

A soft knock drew Dinko's attention to the door. Bazin lifted his head as it eased open.

"S-s-sorry to d-disturb you," a trembling voice whispered from the door, "but I n-n-need to speak with you."

"Krrr."

Bazin glanced over at the face sticking around the edge of the door.

"Not you again." Bazin flopped back onto the pillow. His head hurt. "It's barely sunrise. Go away."

"I have t-to t-tell you," Porsa shoved the door open and slipped inside Cara's room. "I m-made a m-m-mistake."

"Don't worry about it." Bazin waved dismissively. "Turns out all my pieces and parts work just fine."

Porsa glanced at the very naked Cara, who still slept snuggled up to Bazin's side. Porsa's mouth moved, but he couldn't get a word out. Brothers weren't allowed to associate with naked women.

"Hey!" Bazin snapped his fingers, and Porsa blinked.

"Krrr."

Porsa glanced at the lemur still sitting on Bazin's chest. It seemed to be laughing at him.

"I-I got the s-spell wrong," he finally managed to sputter.

"What?" Bazin sat up like a shot. Dinko lightly leapt to the foot of the bed, and Cara moaned but snuggled back into the pillow.

Porsa stepped back quickly. "M-M-Master V-V-Voc t-told me wrong."

"Wrong how?" Bazin glared at the apprentice.

"Krrr." Dinko's tail bristled.

"What he t-told me t-to do was the wrong inc-cantation." Porsa looked from Bazin to the lemur. "You h-have to k-keep her alive."

Bazin stared at Porsa for a long time. "Alive?"

Porsa nodded. "Or you go b-back."

"She dies, I die?"

Porsa swallowed hard and nodded again.

Dinko turned and looked at his master. "Krrr?"

Bazin scrubbed his bruised face and winced. He sighed. "Kill her or I die again."

"Krr?" Dinko lifted one paw.

"That bitch of a guard who killed me." The lemur cocked his head, and the image of the black-haired girl in red shimmered into Bazin's mind. "Yep, that one."

Porsa frowned as he listened to only one side of their conversation.

"Krrr." Dinko flattened his ears and shifted unhappily on the blankets.

"Believe me, I don't want to go back either." Bazin rubbed at the fresh scar on his ribs. It itched as if it was still healing. It was strange to have a scar from a fight that he hadn't actually been in.

"Krrr." Dinko looked at Porsa and then back at Bazin.

Bazin flung an eloquent hand toward Porsa.

Dinko sighed heavily, then glared at the apprentice. "Krrr."

"I know. Nothing's ever easy," Bazin complained as he untangled himself from the blankets and Cara.

"I s-said I was s-sorry." Porsa glared back at the lemur as he fiddled with the strap of the satchel hanging from his shoulder.

"Krrr."

Bazin smirked at the lemur's comment, but he didn't share the joke with Porsa as he started scavenging his clothes. "Am I still under the time limit? Two moon cycles?"

"I-I think s-so."

Bazin stopped and glared at Porsa. "You think so? You don't know?"

"M-Master Thosin w-wasn't sure." Porsa huffed, "Th-there's m-more."

"Of course there is," Bazin growled as he picked up Cara's bodice off the floor. He tossed it aside and glared at Porsa. "Well?"

Porsa took a deep breath and tried to deliver the rest of the bad news as Bazin found his pants.

"The Holy B-Brothers have d-d-decided to s-send m-me to help you f-find her and then b-bring you b-b-both b-back to the Holy M-mountain."

"Why?" Bazin stopped pulling on his pants and stared at the apprentice.

"Th-they want to f-fix m-my m-mistake. Th-they s-said I have to p-pay my d-debt."

"Krrr." The lemur shifted restlessly on the bed.

"What does that mean for me? Does that mean I go back to the Underworld?"

Porsa shrugged. "I d-don't know."

Bazin and Dinko exchanged a long look. Porsa frowned, wondering what they had said to one another.

Bazin blew out a long breath through his nose and finished pulling on his pants. He buckled his belt with a sigh. "I don't see that I have a choice right now." He sat down to pull on his boots.

"Krrr." The lemur glanced at his belt.

"Don't start." He frowned at Dinko. "I'm going to need a lot more than just a sword. This body is in no shape to fight or defend anyone."

Porsa cringed a little as he looked at the bruises and cuts from whatever Bazin had been doing last night. He glanced at Cara's sleeping form, and his eyes widened. Maybe that's why Brothers weren't allowed to associate with naked women.

"You got a name?" Bazin asked as he pulled on his tunic.

The apprentice pulled his gaze away from Cara. "P-Porsa."

"Porsa. Right." Bazin laced up his tunic. "Can you get us passage to Koric?"

"She's n-not on K-Koric."

"Krrr." Dinko sprang up onto Bazin's shoulder and tilted his head at Porsa.

"Lovely." Bazin tilted his head and stared at Porsa too. "You got any idea where she is then?"

"Ah," the apprentice shivered a little at the twin stares, "th-the Holy B-Brothers s-said K-Koric just s-sent a d-d-delegation to the Imperial City."

"Fine. Let's find a ship." Bazin gestured toward the door.

"B-b-but—" Porsa held up his hand.

Bazin glared at him. "But what?"

Porsa sighed, steeling himself for a long explanation. "There w-was a d-dragon."

Bazin let out a rueful laugh. "Of course there was."

"The b-b-brothers resurrected a recently d-d-deceased g-g-guard n-named B-Beck."

Bazin crossed his arms and asked, "Was he from the Koric delegation?" Porsa nodded. "And he didn't survive the dragon?" Porsa shook his head. "What of the girl?"

"B-Beck said she w-was ad-drift in a l-launch."

"Adrift in a launch." Bazin nodded, glaring at Porsa. "Adrift where? I don't have time to scour the entire sea!"

"Krrr."

"Their b-b-best g-g-guess is that she is f-f-floating t-toward K-Ka."

"Best guess?" Bazin stamped down the urge to strangle Porsa.

"Krrr." Dinko flexed his claws.

"Did this dead guard at least know where the dragon attacked them?" Porsa nodded again but with a little less conviction.

"Come on," Bazin said as he stalked out the door, "we need to find someone who knows the tides."

Being Practical

"What have you done to your skirt?" Brenith stared at Leema's legs.

"Do you like it?" The young princess grinned and pulled the sides of her new pants out so her sister could really see her handiwork. She had worked all morning on cutting and resewing her skirt into a somewhat comfortable pair of pants. At first, they had been too much like a skirt, wide and open all the way to her ankles. With a little ingenious use of some cord from the fishing net, she had managed to pull the material tight around her calves. She had formed a crisscross lacing from her ankles to her knees, but the top was still baggy around her thighs. "It's done wonders for my fishing!"

"They aren't very ladylike." Brenith didn't know what else to say.

"Good!" Leema picked up her string of fish and stomped off.

Brenith sighed and followed her sister up the hill. She hiked up her skirt to avoid stumbling, but she couldn't catch up to her little sister. Brenith stopped to catch her breath and shook her own skirt into place before continuing to the cottage.

"Did you see what Leema did to her skirt?" Aritha met her at the stone wall with her arms crossed. "She looks like a boy!"

"I think she's being practical." Ro's voice floated down from the roof of Fisp's cottage. She was fixing a hole in the roof that she had missed during the first repair. The rain had almost doused the fire last night.

"Practical? She is the daughter of the Queen of Koric! A Princess!" Aritha jammed her hands on her hips and yelled up at Ro. "She should not look like a boy!"

Ro poked her head over the edge of the roof. "She is a shipwrecked girl who is making the best of her situation." As she turned back to her work, she muttered, "Which is more than I can say for some."

"What did you say?" Aritha glared at the spot where Ro had been a moment ago.

Ro didn't bother answering.

Aritha rounded on Brenith. "You can't possibly agree with this."

"I'm not sure." Brenith gazed after her younger sister. "Part of me thinks we should maintain our dignity, but Aritha, look at us." She gestured to her bedraggled gown. "We are lost. Maybe Leema has the right of it."

"I am not wearing pants!" Aritha stomped out the gate and down the hill. Brenith watched her go and sighed again.

"You're right, you know." Ro stuck her head out over the edge of the roof and stared down at Brenith with icy blue eyes. "We are lost, but we can't stay lost forever. We must answer the Arazi's summons. We can't let the Empress brand Koric as traitors. A couple more days of preparation and helping Fisp, then we should be on our way."

"I know." A tear slipped down Brenith's cheek. "I just don't know what to do."

"Perhaps you should follow Leema's example. It's a long journey between here and the Imperial City. We're not going to have an easy time of it. Dignity won't keep us alive."

"You are cruelly honest, Rohamina."

Ro's eyes became darker blue. "I'm sorry, Princess."

Brenith sighed and followed the path around the building to where Leema was cleaning her catch. She paused to watch her younger sister, who, with a few quick movements, skinned and filleted the fish. Ro was right. Leema had adapted to their situation with cheerful gusto. Leema's enthusiasm could be attributed to the fact that she was only sixteen and still saw everything as an adventure, but perhaps it was more than that.

"Leema?" She stepped forward, determined to do better. "I'm sorry. I shouldn't have insulted your work. You have been very good at adapting to our situation."

Her sister didn't turn. "Thank you."

"I mean it, Lee, and I would be honored if you would help me." She held out her skirt, not really sure how to ask her to make pants.

"You really mean it?" Leema put the knife down and stared at her sister. "You wanna wear pants?"

"Yes," Brenith nodded, "Ro is right. We have a long journey ahead of us, and we need to be practical about it."

"You know, if we are going to be practical, then we need to find Ro some shoes." Leema picked her knife up and started on the next fish. "She can't walk miles upon miles with one scraped foot and one without even a stocking."

"I guess I hadn't noticed. She does limp." Brenith glanced up at the roof. "She's been doing so much work and never complained."

"Ro never complains." Leema finished that fish and started on another one.

"I feel terrible. I should have seen."

"I tried to make her some sandals from the fish skins, but they just fall apart." Leema stabbed the fish in frustration. "I wish she could fit in one of our shoes, but mine are too small and yours are too big. Of course, our shoes are not suited for travel either. I doubt they will last long, but they are better than nothing. We have to come up with something for her before we leave."

"Perhaps we could just wrap her feet in cloth somehow?"

"Cloth from where?" Leema snorted.

In her mind, Brenith ran through all the things that Fisp had around the cottage. Nothing seemed suitable for shoes.

"It would just get wet anyway, and that couldn't be good." Leema stacked the fish filets to the side.

Out of the corner of her eye, Brenith caught movement. Her head whipped to the side, searching for the cause. Her eyes darted over the rocky landscape for a while. Finally, she saw it again. It was a rabbit.

"Leema," Brenith grabbed her sister's arm, "look!"

Leema followed her gaze. "Is that a rabbit?"

"Yes." She glanced back at Leema. "Oh, Lee, we could have something besides fish."

"I don't know how to catch a rabbit."

"Maybe Fisp does or Ro?"

"Wait. Stay here and watch it. Don't let it out of your sight." Leema turned and sprinted away. She leapt over the stone wall and kept running.

Brenith didn't watch her go; she just stared at the rabbit. It hopped aimlessly from one clump of grass to another. It vanished suddenly at one point. Brenith ran a little way forward but stopped as it appeared again.

"Come on, Leema," she whispered.

Minutes crept by with agonizing slowness as Brenith stared. Her vision clouded after a while, forcing her to blink rapidly to clear it. She heard Leema returning.

"I'm back," Leema whispered. She slowly untangled the fishing net from her fist.

"You think fishing for rabbits will be like fishing for fish?" Brenith asked under her breath.

Leema shrugged and crept toward the furry animal. She had crossed about half the distance between Brenith and the rabbit when it noticed her. The rabbit flinched and froze. Leema froze too. It stared at the princess with its nose twitching rapidly. The rabbit finally decided she was a threat and darted away. Leema sprinted after the fuzzy critter. It dodged this way then that, trying to shake her from its trail. The rabbit was fast, but Leema had longer legs.

"Hurry! Leema! Catch it!" Brenith yelled. The rabbit dodged again. "Oh no! That way!"

"What's going on?" Ro shouted from the roof, then she saw Leema and a furry blob zigzagging back and forth across the top of the hill. The princess held the fishing net out to one side, ready to throw it at the perfect time.

The chase went on forever. Finally, Leema flung the net and threw herself forward onto the ground where it landed. Ro strained to see if she had caught the rabbit. Then a shriek pierced the air. It sounded like a child screaming. Leema gathered the edges of the net carefully as she stood, trying not to let the rabbit out. The screeching continued.

Fisp waddled across the rocky hill behind the house toward Leema. She passed Brenith, who was covering her ears. The crying wailed on. Finally, Fisp reached Leema.

"Why is it making that sound?" Leema yelled at the old woman.

"Doesn't want to die." Fisp shrugged as she reached for the net. Leema let the old woman have it. Fisp spun the net up and then smashed it into the ground. The shrieking stopped. Leema covered her mouth with both hands.

"Dinner," cackled the old crone as she waddled past Brenith, who was on her knees, retching into the grass.

Fisp stopped by the table where Leema's fish lay and picked up the knife. The young girl approached slowly.

"Wanna learn?" Fisp asked over her shoulder as she began to gut the rabbit.

"I guess," Leema croaked.

Ro joined them at the table. Her stomach churned a little at the sight, but it was one of those survival skills that she would need soon. So she watched, concentrating to remember all the steps. Fisp showed Leema and Ro how to gut and skin the rabbit, and how to cut the meat with very little waste.

When she had finished, she had a pile of hide, a stack of meat on the bones, and a few globs of fat. Fisp giggled to herself. She scooped the meat into Ro's hands, gathered up the pile of fat, then waddled to the house. Ro followed her.

"I'm not sure I can eat that." Brenith stepped up next to Leema as they watched Fisp disappear.

"It's no different than fish." Leema shrugged, but her tone was bland.

Brenith shuddered. "Fish don't scream."

"That you know of," Leema said absently. She picked up her own kills and stared at the fillets. "I better dry these. Then we can work on your skirt."

Brenith watched her sister's retreating form. "I don't think I like being practical."

Foraging and Fighting

"YOU KNOW, THIS ISN'T all that bad," Brenith mused as she bent, swayed, and practiced walking.

"I tried to tell you." Leema shrugged as she wrapped the remaining thread around her fingers. It had taken hours to unravel the bottom of her sister's skirt to get enough thread and then to re-sew Brenith's skirt into pants.

"You think we can get Aritha to re-sew hers?" Brenith experimented with running in place.

Leema snorted. "Not likely!"

"Brenith!" Aritha snapped when she found them behind the house. "What can you be thinking?" She marched past Ro and Fisp, who were working on the stretched rabbit hide. Fisp chuckled under her breath.

Brenith turned to face her older sister. "I'm being practical."

"Practical! You are showing way too much to be practical!"

Brenith looked down at her new pants. They covered her from waist to ankle. Nothing was showing except the tops of her feet, and those were crisscrossed by her shoelaces.

"Civilized ladies do not show the shape of their legs!" Aritha regarded her sisters in horror. "You will remake those... pants into proper skirts again immediately. Both of you!"

"Is that what I sounded like?" Brenith glanced at Leema, who nodded cheerfully. "Ah. I apologize."

Leema shrugged. "Forgotten already."

"You will do as I say. I am the eldest and without mother—"

"Mother is gone!" Leema snapped.

Aritha blanched at the raw anger in Leema's voice.

"You don't know that!" Brenith whirled on her sister. "She may have survived just like we did!"

Leema blinked at Brenith, clenching her jaw, and then resumed fussing with the thread.

Brenith turned back to Aritha. "If you want to make it back to your precious Court, you'd better start thinking, Aritha. Look around you! There are miles of wilderness that we have to walk through. Are you going to keep up in that?" Brenith pointed at Aritha's skirt.

"I will not arrive at the Imperial City looking like a boy!" Her older sister turned on her heel in a swirl of fabric and marched back to the house. Aritha snarled at Ro as she passed, "I blame you!"

"What did I do?" Ro watched her disappear around the rock wall.

"Ya wear pants." Fisp shrugged without looking up from the rabbit pelt.

"That's hardly my fault. This is my uniform. I am a soldier, a House Guard of Koric."

"And yer outshining her royal high and mighty."

"I don't mean to outshine her. I'm just trying to protect them all." Ro swung a leg over the rickety bench Fisp was sitting on and took over trimming the hide.

Fisp sat back to rest. "She's just angry 'cause she's lost and feeling helpless."

Ro laughed without humor. "So am I."

"Ah, but ya don't show it."

"I don't know about that."

"Ya know more than ya think." Fisp chuckled, taking the hide from Ro. "There's somethin' special about ya, child." She gave a broken-tooth grin as she inspected the hide.

"Are you going to make shoes for Ro?" Leema asked as she joined them.

Ro pulled her feet under her self-consciously. The scrapes on her foot were healing. She barely limped now, but sharp rocks or prickly stickers were another matter. It was one of the things still weighing on her mind about leaving. With no shoes, her ability to protect the princesses was greatly diminished. At least, until she grew some callouses.

"Nope." Fisp twisted the hide into a circle and held it up to Leema. "Satchel to carry yer food."

"A satchel?" Brenith asked, glancing at Ro's feet.

"Got to have somewhere to carry all the fish ya been dryin'. It'll be mostly waterproof, and the fur will keep away most of the bugs." Fisp pulled out the fishnet cord that Ro had unraveled for her. Brenith and Leema exchanged a glance as Fisp started to thread a fishbone needle. It was larger than the one that Leema had used for their skirts.

"Ah, but what about Ro?" Brenith was uneasy about leaving without shoes for their only protector.

"Not enough there for shoes," Fisp snorted.

"Fisp's shown me what to do with the hides. If we find more rabbits..." Ro shrugged.

"But Ro—" Brenith reached toward her.

"It's fine, Highness, I am more worried that the only weapon we have is Marin's knife."

Brenith stopped cold. She had not thought about weapons.

"Can't we make a spear or something? A bow and arrows?" Brenith gestured helplessly.

"No suitable materials." Ro stared up at her with those icy blue eyes again.

"Come on, Bren," Leema pulled Brenith away, "we need to convince Aritha about her skirt."

Once they were past the corner of the stone cottage, Brenith stopped Leema. "Have you noticed Ro's eyes?"

Leema glanced back to make sure they were alone. "You mean how sometimes they are darker blue and sometimes icy blue?"

"Yes."

Leema nodded. "I've seen it before."

"There is something about her sometimes..." Brenith shivered, trying to shake off her fears.

"It doesn't change who she is." Leema frowned. "She's still our friend."

Brenith nodded. "You're right. Come on. We have a sister to argue with."

"Right." Leema wrinkled her nose. "How about you fight with her, and I'll go down to the tide pool I found yesterday and see if I can find some more of those mussels."

Brenith frowned. "Coward."

"Nope," Leema grinned as she skipped around the rocks leading to the beach, "Just being strategic."

"Strategic." Brenith gave a very unladylike snort and went searching for Aritha.

***

Leema reached into the tidal pool and, using Marin's knife, she popped the suction seal under another mussel shell. She tossed it up on the bank with the others. Leema was careful to only pick the largest shells. She didn't want to harvest all of them. After they left, Fisp would be able to harvest them as they grew.

The young princess smiled as she thought about Fisp. The old woman had changed a lot since they had first met her. She was no longer the frightened half-mad crone. Now, she smiled and often sang while she worked. Leema wondered if it was because she was no longer lonely.

"Oh, Fisp, what will happen to you when we leave?"

Leema straightened and looked out to sea. She wanted to go home, but this was the most freedom she had ever had. Back on Koric, she always had to sneak away from the castle with her friends, most of whom were the village boys. Aritha said they were a bad influence, but she had learned a lot from them. She often wondered if Taus had turned a blind eye to her escapades. There was no way that she had been that stealthy, sneaking in and out.

"He must have known."

She shook her head and bent to harvest the last few mussels that were big enough. She sloshed up out of the pool and sat on the rock near her pile to pull on her shoes. Every time she laced them up, she thought about Ro. Somehow, they had to get her some kind of shoes.

Leema gathered up the small pile of shells and hiked across the rocky beach to the fishing hut. She had made herself at home in Dal's old hut. Since she had been doing almost all the fishing, she didn't think that Fisp minded.

The hut was free from dust now, and the broken chair had been dismantled. Bits from the chair were stacked in the corner next to the shrinking pile of fishing net. The old cup and mouse-eaten blanket had gone up to the cottage. Aritha had washed the blanket, and Brenith had sewn up the holes.

Leema sat down next to the dwindling pile of tattered fishing net in the corner. Most of it had already been reclaimed for other things, like the lacing on their pants. She unraveled more of the knots holding the lines together and looped them into a pile. She wanted to have as much as possible untangled to take with them.

Leema hadn't told anyone about her little projects. She wanted it to be a surprise if they worked and a secret if they failed.

She pulled her sharpening rock out from under the pile and reached for a piece of the broken chair. She scraped at the tip of the chair leg. It was slowly becoming a sharper point. It would never be really pointed using only a rock, but it was better than nothing. At first, a sharpened chair leg was all she could come up with as a weapon for Ro, but then she'd found the tidal pool.

The very first mussel she had tried to pry off the rock had cut the end of her finger. If it's sharp enough for that, then cutting an enemy was just as easy. She had tried a few variations, including tying them to the fish net, but they always fell off. She tried to drill a hole through the shell, but it always shattered into pieces.

A moment of inspiration came last night just as she was falling asleep. Now, she had to try out her idea. She took the other unbroken chair leg outside and wedged it between two rocks. Using Marin's knife, she began to saw a notch into the side of the leg. Sometimes, she had to use the rock to pound the end of the knife like a chisel to get into the wood.

The light faded as she worked away until finally, there was a split down the center of the leg. It was uneven and jagged.

Leema frowned at it, then shrugged. "Close enough."

She set the leg aside and picked up one of the empty mussel shells she had brought back from dinner last night. She carefully wedged a shell into the base of the split so that half of it stuck out the side. Then wedged another shell half into the split so that it stuck out the opposite side. Several more shell halves followed in kind until the split was full.

Leema reached for the cord from the fish net and carefully wove it around the leg and in between the shell halves, binding the split together to hold the shells in place. The princess sat back and gazed at her handiwork. The chair leg now resembled a spiky club.

"Well, *I* wouldn't want to be hit with it."

She gazed around at the darkening beach. A massive black bird sat on one of the rock outcroppings a short distance away. It was watching her. She squinted at it. It was hard to tell in the fading light, but she could almost swear that there was some sort of harness on the bird's breast.

Leema jumped as the bird squawked and flew into the air. It circled once, then disappeared out to sea. The princess frowned as she pulled her new club out of the rocks and returned to the hut. She gathered the new batch of mussels, all of the remaining net cord, the leftover shells, and the sharpened chair leg.

She took one last look around the hut. They would be leaving tomorrow. This would be the last time she was going to be in here. The hut was falling down and smelled funny, but she would miss it.

As she started back toward the cottage, she glanced around, but the bird hadn't returned. Leema shivered. There was something menacing about that bird.

Starting Out

A TORRENT OF RAIN had drenched the cottage overnight, leaving the air saturated in a thick blanket of gray mist.

"Great day for travel," cackled Fisp. She stood next to the rock wall with Ro, watching the swirl of gray.

"I can't keep putting it off." Ro sighed. It had already been nearly two weeks since they had come to Fisp's cottage.

"I know." Fisp didn't look at Ro. "Thank ya for all yer help."

"It was the least we could do," Brenith said from behind them. The old woman turned and smiled fondly at the three princesses. They stood out like a rainbow in the fog. Brenith, in blue, had plaited her dark red hair into two braids that hung down her back. She carried the pack she had made from the mouse-eaten blanket. Aritha, in yellow, stood behind her carrying nothing. Her long, blonde hair also hung in two braids. She had not succumbed to remaking her skirt. Leema, in green, fidgeted with the rabbit-skin satchel that held their food.

"I'll miss ya," Fisp's voice wobbled as she hugged each of the girls. Leema was last. She tugged on Leema's single golden braid. "You remember what I taught ya."

"I will." Leema nodded solemnly. Impulsively, she hugged the old woman again. "I'll miss you! We'll try to come back someday."

Fisp disentangled herself from the young girl and stepped back, rubbing her nose with the back of her hand.

"Ain't never been hugged this much." Fisp chuckled and sniffled. She turned to Ro and stared at her for a long time. "Ya take care of yerself."

"I will, Grandmother." Ro gazed at her sadly, then hugged the old crone for a long moment.

The girls slowly filed past Fisp, each reaching out to touch her shoulder as they left.

"Watch out for each other!" she called as they faded into the fog.

***

The girls made slow progress across the moor. The fog forced them to stay close to each other. Ro set the pace, her bare feet carefully stepping through the wet grass and rocks.

"Funny, isn't it?" Leema's voice sounded subdued in the grayness.

"What?" Brenith glanced back to make sure Aritha was keeping up.

"Fog brought us here, now fog is taking us away."

"I hadn't really thought of it that way." Brenith stepped around a pool of murky water. The rain had filled the depressions, turning the plane into a sopping bog.

"I hate it." Aritha yanked her wet skirt out of a pool that she had failed to step around.

Leema snorted. "You hate everything."

"I do not!" Aritha protested as she sank ankle deep in the wet grass. "There happens to be a great many things that I like."

"Ha!" Leema bounded past her. "Name one."

"I like my own bed." Aritha yanked her foot free and stomped after her sister.

Leema ignored Aritha's answer. "Ro?"

Ro glanced at the young princess but kept moving.

"I made something for you."

"For me?" Ro stopped walking and stared at the girl.

"Yes." Leema stopped Brenith and dug in the pack. She pulled out her sharpened chair leg and mussel-studded club. "I knew you were worried about weapons, so I made these."

Ro stared at the club. Slowly, she reached out and lifted it from the girl's hands. It was only a little longer than her forearm, but the razor-sharp shells protruding from each side looked vicious.

"What is that?" Aritha wrinkled her nose and peered at the club.

"It's a club," Leema tilted her head and stared critically at the weapon she had made, "sort of."

Ro glanced at Leema, then gazed at the club again, turning it for a thorough inspection.

"Where did you learn to do that?" Brenith reached out hesitantly and touched the shells.

"I didn't. It just seemed like it would work, and we needed some sort of weapons, didn't we?" Leema grinned. "I was just being practical. Here." She handed the sharpened chair leg to Brenith.

"I must say, Leema, you have a dark side." Brenith shook her head, staring at the spike.

Leema bristled. "No more than anybody else."

"I couldn't have thought of these." Brenith stared at her sister like she had never seen her before.

Leema shifted from one foot to the other. "I didn't mean anything by it."

"It's remarkable, Highness." Ro bowed solemnly to the young princess. "I am honored."

"Oh," Leema flushed, "you're welcome then."

"Can we keep going now that Leema has scared us all?" Aritha yanked her skirt up as she marched past them. Leema followed her.

Brenith looked down at herself, trying to decide where to put her new weapon. She really wasn't even sure what to do with it, but she wasn't going to turn down even the smallest chance of protection. Finally, she settled on tucking the tiny spear into her belt.

Ro gave the club an experimental swing. It seemed sturdy enough. It even felt balanced.

"I knew I liked her," Ro muttered as she followed the princesses.

They trudged along for hours. Ro's feet were beginning to get sore. She hadn't spent enough time barefoot. The only time she could remember being without shoes was when she had been chained to the wall in the Zatvor mine. Although, she hadn't done any walking there.

"I wish the sun would come out," Aritha whined again.

Brenith sighed, "It's not going to come out any sooner, no matter how many times you say it."

"I'm thirsty," Aritha whined again.

"We all are," Brenith sighed.

Ro sighed. She hadn't been able to come up with anything to carry water in. Fisp had assured her there was plenty of water along the way, but she was beginning to wonder if Fisp had ever been this way.

I hope this isn't the water she meant, Ro thought as she splashed through another puddle.

"I wish the sun would come out."

Ro sighed again. "This is gonna be a long walk."

They walked and walked and walked. The mushy grass plane seemed to go on forever. It was mostly a downhill journey. Ro's feet began to truly ache. She wanted to rest, but there was no way to know how close they were to the forest. She glanced upward. The fog still clung to the ground, but above her, the gray seemed lighter. The sun had to be shining, but she couldn't tell from what direction. It wouldn't be so bad if she could just see where they were. All this grayness was depressing.

"I'm hungry," Aritha whined.

"Should we stop and eat?" Brenith looked at Leema. "Are you hungry?"

Leema shrugged. "A bit."

"Maybe we should stop." Aritha's feet made squishing sounds as she tried to catch up to her sisters.

"Ro?" Brenith looked back through the gray haze.

Leema took one look at Ro's face and then glanced down at her feet. "We stop," Leema commanded.

Ro flashed her a grateful smile.

"Can't we find somewhere dry to sit?" Aritha held her skirts up out of the puddles.

"Unless you keep walking till you find something," Brenith sighed. "We'll stop here."

Leema opened the rabbit satchel and pulled out a piece of dried fish for each girl. She pointedly exchanged a look with Brenith as she handed a piece to her sister. Brenith glanced back at Ro, who was sitting on a mound of grass, examining her left foot.

"You all right?" Brenith asked as she sank down beside Ro.

"Yes, just a little sore."

"We should have waited to leave until we had made shoes for you."

Ro shrugged. "It doesn't matter now."

"We could go back," Brenith offered quietly.

Ro stared at her foot for a while, then sighed. "We can't. The Empress' deadline is almost here. We've already used up nearly two weeks."

"And we have no idea how far it is to the City." Brenith sighed.

Ro glanced at Aritha. "Plus, I wouldn't want to listen to Aritha complain if we came all this way just to turn back."

Brenith watched her older sister balance on a bit of grass while trying to keep her skirt out of the mud and water.

"Nor would I." Brenith shook her head. "We'll just wait until you are ready."

Ro inclined her head. "Thank you, Highness."

"You don't have to call us that, you know," Brenith smiled wryly. "This will be a long enough journey without being overly formal."

Ro shook her head. "You will always be my betters."

"I don't believe that." Brenith chewed on her fish. "Mother knew. You are more than you seem, Rohamina."

Ro stared into the distance for a long time without moving. Finally, she shrugged. "I am what I am thanks to your mother."

"You never talk about it, do you?" Brenith looked at her curiously. "The mine, I mean."

Ro went very still.

"I'm sorry. I guess I shouldn't bring it up, but you must have been someone before the mine."

"Taus and Abeth tried to find my parents, but there wasn't any information at the mine, and I couldn't remember. There was nowhere to look after that."

Brenith kicked at a rock in the pool by her feet as they sat quietly, locked in their own thoughts. The mist was cool against her skin. Her tunic had long sleeves, but it wasn't thick. She shivered and patted Ro on the knee. "Maybe you'll find something on this journey."

"Maybe." Ro stood. "We should keep moving."

"I just got comfortable," Aritha whined.

Watcher

BAZIN LAY FLAT AGAINST the rocky cliff top. The swirling mist would hide him from those below, but he didn't want to take any chances. His body was still not what he would consider combat-ready. Two days crossing the channel from Jardarwa to Ka had not been nearly enough time to tone this cobbler's muscles. And nearly two weeks of hiking along the coastline looking for signs of the shipwreck had not given him much time to train either. Certainly not enough to be ready for a fight where the odds were not in his favor.

In their search along the coast, they hadn't met anyone until today, when they had found an old fishing hut and had heard the old woman's scream. On the off chance that it might have been the girl they were looking for, they had climbed the short cliff.

"Where is she, old woman?"

The old woman cowered on the ground, surrounded by seven rough-looking men. Bazin examined each in turn. They were heavily armed. Scars and battle-worn armor told of experience. A large black bird with a harness across its breast sat on the shoulder of their leader. Something nagged in the back of Bazin's mind about that bird. It was familiar somehow, but he couldn't place it.

"Who?" she cried in terror. "Who?"

Who are they looking for? Bazin felt the feather-light brush of Dinko's mind. He closed his eyes and watched the scene below through his lemur's eyes.

"Please! Please!" Fisp screamed as the leader stepped down hard on her fingers.

"Tell me." He grinned as he ground her fingers into the rocky path.

Porsa shifted on the cliff below him. Bazin broke contact with Dinko and shot a warning glance over his shoulder. The gray-robed apprentice winced and stared back at him in terror. Bazin shook his head. He never should have let the stuttering boy follow him. Bazin had tried to get him to stay on the island, but the boy was adamant that he accompany Bazin to find the girl.

At least he's useful as a pack mule, he thought, eying the supply pack the boy clutched to his chest.

"Black hair. Red uniform!"

Bazin's attention snapped back to the men below. *Black hair, red uniform? They're looking for the girl too? Why?* Bazin narrowed his eyes. If they were looking for her too, his mission just got a lot more complicated.

"Tell me!" the mercenary's voice echoed off the rocky outcropping.

Fisp moaned and cried. She clenched her teeth against the knowledge that threatened to escape.

"Come on, old woman, tell us, and the pain will stop." The leader lifted his foot and then kicked the old woman in the ribs, sending her sprawling in the wet grass. The bird squawked and flapped its wings, trying to keep its perch on his shoulder.

"Krrr." Dinko flattened his ears. The bird cocked its head, listening.

Bazin winced. Between Dinko and Porsa, they were going to get caught. He was not prepared to fight a whole band of mercenaries.

"They were here yesterday." The leader picked her up by a handful of hair and shook her like a rag. "They can't have gotten far, just tell us which way."

Yesterday? Bazin frowned. *How could he know that? At least, we aren't too far behind.*

The mercenary threw her against the wall of her cottage. She cried out as she bounced off the jagged rocks and fell heavily to the ground.

Bazin felt a twinge of guilt. He had applied those very techniques on many a victim in his past. His lips thinned as he recalled the consequences of those actions. The scorched land. The pain and torment. He shifted against the rocks, trying to push those images from his mind.

"Village!" Fisp screamed. Bazin snapped out of his memories and focused on the old woman. The leader had her pinned to the wall by her throat. Her feet were dangling and kicking just out of reach of the ground. Dinko shifted along the wall, allowing Bazin a better view. He could now see the knife in the leader's hand as he pressed it against the woman's belly.

"What village?" Blood trickled down the blade as the knife penetrated deeper. Fisp screamed and clawed at his hand.

"South!" she screeched and pointed. "South!"

The leader drove his blade in up to the hilt. He let go of her neck and held her for a moment, pinned to the wall by his knife, then yanked it free, letting her fall. He turned away and stalked down the path to the rocky wall.

As his connection with Dinko broke, Bazin blinked. The lemur darted for cover as the mercenaries followed their leader away from the cottage. The black bird squawked and launched into the air, disappearing into the gray, shrouded sky.

Bazin counted to twenty, then slowly rose up onto all fours. He peered over the rim of the outcropping. Nothing moved. He counted again, watching carefully. Dinko's head popped out next to the corner of the house.

Bazin glanced over his shoulder and glared at Porsa. "You wanna tell me why there are mercenaries after this girl?"

The apprentice's mouth popped open and closed a few times, finally ending in a confused shrug.

Bazin frowned. "Come on."

Porsa nodded stupidly and climbed up the cliff.

Bazin landed lightly on his feet. *At least some of my skills are usable in this new body.* Softly, he made his way around the rock wall and knelt beside the old woman's crumpled form. She groaned as he turned her over.

"Shh," he warned and glanced around. Porsa ran up the path and squatted beside them.

"I'm d-d-dying?" The old woman trembled.

Bazin only nodded.

"Grandmother?" he asked softly. Fisp's eyes fluttered open. "Was there a dark-haired girl wearing red?"

"Won't let you hurt her," Fisp gurgled. Red spittle dripped from her lips.

"We wish to help her." Bazin shook his head. "Did she go south to the village?"

Fisp tried to cackle but only spewed up more blood and then stilled. Slowly, Bazin lowered her to the ground. He stood abruptly, walked to the door of the cottage, and pushed it open.

Porsa followed him into the gloomy dwelling. "She's d-d-dead."

Bazin searched the room quickly. The old woman's meager belongings were the only items. He stalked past Porsa.

Dinko leapt onto his shoulder from the roof as he cleared the overhang. Porsa scuttled along behind him, wringing his hands. Bazin made a circle of the house, looking for any evidence of the girl's presence. As they passed the body of the old woman, Porsa hesitated and stared down at her.

"What's the matter? Never seen a dead body?" the assassin smirked as he headed for the rock wall surrounding the cottage.

Porsa hurried along behind him. Bazin knelt just outside the wall and searched for signs of passage. Dinko leapt down from his shoulder and roved around on the wet grass with his nose to the ground. Every few steps, he would stop and give his full attention to a particular spot, then hop and step a little way away.

Finally, the little gray lemur stopped, sat back on his hind end, and curled his tail around his front paws. He turned his yellow eyes back to Bazin. An indistinct image of four females shimmered in his mind's eye.

"Four?" Bazin frowned.

"Krrr."

"I'm not doubting your nose." He stepped closer.

"Krrr." Dinko leapt up onto his shoulder, then reached up and tugged his ear.

"All right, all right, I said I believed you." Bazin glanced back at Porsa. "You coming?"

"F-Four what?" Porsa resettled the pack on his back as he trotted to catch up with the assassin.

"Dinko says there're four girls, that way." He pointed into the fog ahead of him. It was in a more east than south direction.

Porsa gestured behind them to the cottage. "But the old w-w-woman s-said s-south."

"Yep." Bazin kept walking.

"S-so how d-d-do—"

"How do I know that she lied? That they're going the wrong way, and we're going the right way?"

"Yes."

"Dinko told me."

"You t-trust a lemur?"

"Krrr." Dinko glared at Porsa with bright yellow eyes.

Porsa shivered.

"This is not just a lemur. He is drugi."

"I d-don't understand."

"It's simple," Bazin spoke as he walked, splashing through puddles and avoiding the biggest mud bogs. "He's a drugi, an other self. He is my eyes and ears."

"Krrr."

"Yes, and nose." He reached up and scratched Dinko's ears.

"How d-do you kn-know what he is s-s-saying?"

"We have a bond. He is drugi."

Bazin glanced at the still fog-covered sky. The light was dimming. It had been late afternoon when they had come across the abandoned fishing hut and heard the men interrogating the old woman. The mercenaries had been convinced their quarry had been at the cottage yesterday. The girls wouldn't have left halfway through the day, so they must have left this morning. They should catch up with them soon. *How fast can girls walk?*

"Do you get to p-pick?" Porsa tripped over his muddy robe.

"What?" Bazin kept walking. The lemur watched the apprentice with sardonic interest.

"Your d-drugi?"

Dinko cocked his head as he watched Porsa trip again.

"No, they pick us," Bazin said absently as he slowed, studying the ground. The farther they came east, the easier it was to find the tracks made by the girls. There were definitely four of them. Three with shoes, one without.

"That's odd," he murmured.

"W-what?"

"Why would she have no shoes?" he asked himself more than Porsa.

"Sh-shipwreck." The apprentice answered just as he tripped and landed on his hands and knees.

"Shipwreck?" Bazin finally turned and looked at him.

"Yes." Slowly, the skinny almost-priest got to his feet and shook his robes out. "The sh-shipwreck and a d-d-dragon."

"This guard you resurrected, what else did he tell your Master Thosin?" Bazin crossed his arms and waited.

"J-just that they w-were attacked by a d-dragon and a sh-ship."

"That's it. Nothing more helpful or detailed." Bazin spread his hands. "Like, why this girl is so important, or who the other three girls are?"

"I w-was just t-told about the one," Porsa moaned.

"Krrr."

"Come on, we're losing the light. I don't really want to be wandering in this fog at night."

Assassin and drugi turned from Porsa and stalked into the fog. Porsa sighed, resettled the pack again, then trudged after Bazin.

Test of the Club

Ro squinted into the gloom. The light that had glowed through the fog was far behind them now. She hoped they were still headed in the right direction.

"I'm tired," Aritha whined again.

Brenith's answering sigh was kinder than what Ro wanted to say to Aritha. The constant grousing of the eldest princess was eroding everyone's patience.

The lack of birds and other animal life had also begun to grate on Ro's nerves. Koric had been so full of life. There were always birds flying over, or sheep bleating, or even a stray dog barking, but here, there was nothing. Even the plant life was somehow diminished here. Flowers covered the meadows on Koric. Ka seemed to only have soggy grass and brown bracken.

"Can't we stop?" Aritha sniffled.

Ro shivered. The air was cooling as the light retreated. Her feet were freezing from constant submersion in the water and mud. They were going to have to stop and make camp, whether it was safe or not. She had hoped to find some kind of shelter before they stopped for the night. Also, the lack of any way to make a fire worried her. Hoping to put off the decision, she trudged on a little farther. But when she felt the small tingle at the back of her neck, Ro stopped short.

Leema walked into her. "Sorry."

Ro didn't answer; she just stared into the growing darkness.

"What is it?" Brenith stopped next to them.

"Shh." Ro held up her hand, listening.

"Are we stopping finally?" Aritha caught up with them.

"Shh!" Ro frowned at the eldest princess.

"There's no need to—" she began, but Leema clamped a hand over Aritha's mouth.

Ro reached for Leema's homemade club, which hung from her belt by a cord. The tingling had spread down her back. Ro stepped forward a single pace. The tingling remained the same. She stepped back and tried a different direction; this time, the tingling spread. She focused on the fog in that direction. Right at the edge of her hearing, she heard a rustling sound.

"There's something out there." Her voice was barely a whisper as she backed toward the princesses.

Brenith pulled her chair leg free from her belt. Leema slipped the rabbit satchel off her shoulder and wrapped it around her wrist, ready to swing it at whatever came. Like a herd of frightened sheep, the girls huddled together while Ro backed them away from the hidden threat. The tingling flared again. It moved. It was in front of them now.

Ro grabbed for Brenith who was the closest. She pulled her back the way they had come. Aritha and Leema followed quickly.

"What is it?" Aritha hissed.

A low growl rumbled from the dark mist to their right. Another joined it from their left. Ro swiveled from right to left, then back to the right. She could barely see anything. The tingling was becoming unbearable. The rustling on their left became a swishing as whatever it was rushed closer through the bracken.

Aritha screamed.

Ro swung just before the thing emerged from the gloom. The club smashed into its head with a crack. One of the mussel shells splintered on impact, but the animal went down with a thud. It was the size of a large dog covered with coarse black hair. She bashed in its head with a second swing, then, brandishing her bloody club, spun to face the second beast.

Leema and Brenith grabbed the still screaming Aritha and pulled her away from the wolf-like carcass. Brenith held her stake out in front of her with a shaking hand.

A second beast launched out of the mist, snarling. Its jaws clamped down on Leema's satchel. Ro swung the club, hitting its shoulder. It yelped and fell sideways, releasing the bag.

It sprang up and lunged at Leema again. She swung the bag at its head just as Ro smashed the club into it again. It rolled sideways, disappearing into the growing darkness. They could hear the grass rustling as it circled them.

It was getting darker all the time. They had to get away from this beast.

"Maybe if we run, it'll feast on its friend!" Leema panted.

Ro glanced toward the last of the retreating light to get her bearings. Then, when the beast was circling to the west, she pushed Leema eastward.

"Start running."

Ro waited until the three princesses were on the move before following. The beast snarled and raced after them.

Aritha held her skirts high above her knees to keep from tripping as they sprinted through the wet grass. Slipping in mud and splashing through puddles, they tried to outdistance the beast. Out of the gloom, a crumpled shadow appeared.

Aritha screamed again.

It was a broken cart. Once she realized what it was, Aritha dashed toward it. She clambered up the side and turned to look for her sisters.

"This way!"

Brenith and Leema emerged from the darkness a moment later. They scrambled up next to her in the bed of the cart.

"Ro!"

"Where is she?" Leema grabbed her sister's arm as they searched the fog.

They heard splashing, and then Ro burst out of the gloom with the wolf creature right behind her.

"Ro! Up here!" Leema screamed. The guard launched herself up onto the wagon barely ahead of the beast.

"No!" Brenith gasped as the beast's jaws snapped closed, almost catching Ro's foot.

Ro hit the bottom of the cart with a thud. She scrambled to her feet and sprang back to the side of the cart. The beast paced the ground below them. If it stood on its hind legs, its nose could reach the top of the sideboard. It snarled at them as it paced. Ro readied her club.

Aritha scrambled back from the side, looking around. Piles of rain-soaked debris littered the bottom of the cart. She searched through the debris with quick, frantic movements.

The beast jumped and snapped at Ro. She swung the club, grazing the animal's nose.

"Go away!" Brenith screamed.

Leema watched it pace. "What if I threw it some fish? You think it would go away?"

"Doubt it." Ro never took her eyes off the beast.

Light flared from behind them. Leema spun around to see her sister holding a torch. It burned bright and hot. Ro spun and grabbed the torch from her.

"Hey!" Aritha fell backward.

Ro swung the fiery brand just as the beast lunged. The smell of singed fur permeated the air as the torch made contact. It yowled in pain and dashed away into the darkness.

Ro stood panting and watching for its return.

"Aritha, where did you get the torch?" Leema crawled over to her sister.

"It was under that pile, and there was flint and a tinder box."

"You saved us." Brenith let out a nervous laugh.

"I did?" Aritha blinked.

"Yes." Leema laughed. "You did."

Slowly at first, but then with more confidence, Aritha smiled.

Ro scanned the scattered bits of home and hearth that littered the ground around the cart. "This was someone's home."

Leema stopped laughing. "What did you say?"

"Look around us."

The laughing faded as the girls moved to look over the side of the cart.

"That's clothing." Ro pointed. "And there are some broken dishes."

"What happened to the owners?" Brenith looked to Ro for an answer, but the guard only shrugged.

"Maybe those things got them," Leema murmured.

"We'll sleep here." Ro's voice sounded odd in the fog.

"We have to sleep here?" Aritha groaned. "In a cart?"

"Would you rather sleep on the soggy grass," Leema looked over her shoulder at her sister, "with the wolf-beast?"

"Leema, perhaps something to eat?" Brenith turned away from the side and began to clear a space in the bottom of the cart. "Aritha, give me a hand, please."

Ro wedged the torch into a bracket on the side of the cart and examined the club. It had held up pretty well, considering it was only shells and cord. Only one of the shells had broken, and the others were still bound tightly into the chair leg.

"Your club proved its worth." Ro held it out for Leema to see.

Leema's eyes glittered in the torchlight as she looked over Ro's shoulder into the darkness.

"You think that thing will come back?"

"Hard to say." Ro scanned the darkness. "It didn't like the fire."

"Let's keep it burning then," Leema whispered as she dug in the rabbit-hide satchel. She poked her finger through one of the holes left from the beast's teeth.

Ro looked at Leema's wagging finger. "I guess it's not water-tight anymore."

"At least it didn't rip it open," Brenith said as she pushed the contents of the cart into a pile. "We could have lost all our food."

Ro turned back again to gaze at the darkness. She didn't want to tell them that the tingling hadn't stopped. There was still something out there. Something dangerous was watching them.

She felt Leema press a piece of fish into her hand. Ro nibbled on it while she tried to see just beyond the ring of firelight. Behind her, the princesses made the cart as comfortable as possible.

"We need to get some sleep," Ro said as they finished their meager meal. "I'll take the first watch."

The cart bounced and shifted as the three girls settled in for sleep.

"Can you move your elbow?"

"I don't have any more room. Why don't you move over?"

"Because Leema is there," Brenith sighed.

"It's fine, I'll sleep down here." Leema crawled over them to the far end of the cart. "Just don't stick your feet in my face."

Night settled over the cart as Ro watched the darkness. She wished the fog would be gone by morning. It was too damp and too dangerous to wander in all this grayness without knowing what else might be out there trying to kill them.

Rustling off to the left snapped Ro's head around. The tingling in her spine had not intensified, but it also hadn't lessened. The rustling stopped. Ro watched the darkness intently. Something was staring back; she could feel it.

Hour after hour crept by, and still, she could feel the eyes in the darkness. Only the back of her neck tingled now. Her eyes fluttered as exhaustion curled its fingers around her awareness. Staring at the unchanging darkness made her eyes even heavier. She shook her head, trying to stay awake.

"Ro?" Brenith tapped her shoulder, making her jump. She must have dozed off. "I'll watch for a while. It's nearly dawn."

Ro nodded and fumbled her way into the bed of the cart. She had just closed her eyes when someone tapped her shoulder again.

"Ro?" Leema shook her a little harder. "Time to wake up."

Rolling onto her back, she opened her eyes to more dim grayness. She heaved a bleak sigh and sat up. Her neck still tingled.

"Look what we found!" Leema held up a pair of ragged boots.

They looked like they had been out in the weather for ages.

"Where did you get those?" Ro scrubbed her face, trying to shake free of her lack of sleep.

"Do you really want to know?" Leema wrinkled her nose and cocked her head. Ro just looked at her. "All right, but don't get upset. When we woke up, we started scavenging, and there was... it was..." Leema's face turned a little green as she struggled to speak.

Ro filled in the words the girl didn't want to say. "A body?"

"Yeah, sorry. He looked like he'd been dead for a while. Well, what was left of him anyway." Leema examined the boot. "They seem to be in good shape. I don't know if they'll fit you, though."

Ro took the boots from her and looked them over. There were only a couple of holes in the upper. They looked like teeth marks.

"I hope you won't mind boots from a dead guy. It really upset Aritha. I said, it's not like he needs them anymore," Leema shrugged, "then she said we're becoming savages."

Ro held the boot sole up to her foot. They were going to be too big. Leema was quick to jump on the problem.

"I saw some spare cloth we could wrap around your feet to make them fit at least until we get to a town or something."

Ro nodded. Leema jumped to her feet, and the cart rocked as she hopped over the side. Ro pushed to her knees and looked around their campsite. Fog still surrounded the cart, although the sun was beginning to glow through. It looked like it might burn off today. She watched Brenith and Aritha wander around the cart, picking through the scattered leftovers of whatever disaster had befallen the previous owners.

The beast that had pulled the cart was still tied to the yoke. It was half-eaten and rotted but no longer smelled of death.

"I found a few helpful things." Brenith deposited her treasures into the cart. "Oh, good morning, Ro."

"Morning." Ro poked through the pile. There were some bits of beads, two rolls of bright colored thread, another cup, and an iron skillet.

"Here." Leema tossed a jumbled tangle of cloth up into the cart. Ro unrolled it and began wrapping her feet with enough cloth to keep the boots from falling off. It wouldn't be the most comfortable thing to wear, but it was better than trying to stay barefoot for the rest of their journey.

"Is Aritha calmer?" Brenith asked Leema as she dropped the beads and thread into her pack.

"No," Leema snorted. "She says we are being uncivilized."

"She is going to have to give in sometime." Brenith pulled a length of cord from her satchel and tied the skillet to the outside of the pack. "This is the time when we do what we must."

"I know," Leema shrugged, "but she doesn't think that way."

"Here." Aritha stomped around the end of the cart and shoved a water skin against Leema's chest as she passed. "I found something useful. Too bad there is no water to fill it."

Brenith watched her sister stomp around the other side of the cart. "She'll come around." She handed Leema and Ro some breakfast. "Eat up. We should get moving."

"Yay, fish!" Leema took a brittle piece and gnawed on it.

Following

BAZIN SLOWLY PICKED HIS way along in the fog. Porsa stumbled along behind him, tripping over his apprentice's robe as it repeatedly caught on the grass. Bazin was already tired of warning the apprentice to be quieter.

Maybe if I cut the bottom off that damn robe, he'll stop tripping on it.

He reached into his jerkin and absently scratched Dinko's ears. The little lemur continued to sleep, curled in a tight ball. He deserved the rest after keeping an eye on the girls all night.

They had heard the girls scream when the beasts attacked at dusk. Bazin had charged into the darkness to help but lost them when they ran. He'd ranged all over in the dark, trying to pick up their trail, when finally, they heard another scream followed by an animal's chilling yowl.

Running toward the sound, they stopped just short of the glowing mist. Porsa wanted to go up and talk to them right away, but instinct made Bazin wait. Rushing in was not his way. He kept the apprentice with him in the dark and sent Dinko to spy.

For a long time, Bazin watched through Dinko's eyes ast he girl in red stared into the darkness. She made eye contact with Dinko several times, although Bazin knew that she couldn't possibly see him.

So, this was the girl he had been hired to kill all those years ago. *What had they called her? Ro?* He remembered the queen screaming her name the night she had skewered him. For a moment, hatred boiled his blood. He wasn't sure which bothered him more, that he had been killed by a girl, or that she had been so unskilled that she only killed him by accident. She was the reason that he had endured months of agonizing torment. He wanted to kill her. He hoped the beast would come back and rip her throat out.

Bazin shook his head and unclenched his fists. He couldn't think like this. His life had been linked to hers, whether he liked it or not.

"She dies. I die," he muttered. He needed to clear his thinking. Assassins who thought with their emotions died by them. Bazin took a calming breath and blew it out. He slowed his heart and cooled his blood, then looked again.

She was older than he remembered. Bazin smiled, appreciating the more mature version. Her hair was shorter too, cut like a man's. He wondered if she had become a better swordswoman than when he had first met her.

As the hours crawled by, he was impressed that she remained on watch for so long. She showed discipline. Finally, her head started to nod, but she kept snapping out of it. She had lasted longer than a lot of guards he had watched over the years. He wondered again why she was so important that someone would want her dead. And then to resurrect him and connect their souls? It seemed like a lot of trouble to go through just to kill a guard. When one of the other girls took over, Bazin stopped watching. He left Dinko to keep watch and hunkered down to catch a few hours' sleep.

Dinko had tugged on his ear as dawn broke. Bazin shook Porsa awake and warned him to be quiet. The fog still hid them, but the girls' conversation drifted easily through the mist. He listened to their chatter, learning as much as possible about the foursome. When they started out again, Bazin, Porsa, and a sleeping lemur followed. He had been careful to stay far enough back to keep them obscured by the fog.

However, as the day wore on, the fog started to burn off.

"Damn!" Bazin hissed. There was no way they could follow undetected if the mist lifted. They were still headed toward the forest. If they were really, really lucky, the girls would reach the trees before the sun burned off the rest of their cover.

More and more of the sky shone through the mist above them.

One of the girls giggled. "I see sky!"

"Are you sure we are going the right way?" It was the angry one.

What had they called her? Aritha? Bazin continued to listen as he slowed his pace a little. He didn't want to catch up to them yet.

"Yes." He heard Ro answer; annoyance was thick in her response. She had a softer voice than he expected. She sounded very young.

"But how do you know?"

"The sun is ahead of us in the east. That is the way the forest lies."

At least she's intelligent, Bazin smiled.

Porsa tripped again and landed with a splash in yet another puddle. The girls stopped.

"What was that?" said the little resourceful one who had found the boots.

Bazin froze and motioned to Porsa not to move.

"Don't know. Bird, maybe."

"You don't think it's that thing again?" the third girl asked.

"I hope not," said the resourceful one again.

"Come on, let's keep moving," Ro commanded quietly.

They started walking again. Bazin waited until they had put a little distance between them before turning to Porsa.

"If you don't stop tripping on that damn robe, I'll cut it off!" he hissed and hauled the skinny boy to his feet. Bazin turned away and followed the girls.

"I-I'm s-sorry," Porsa stammered as he tried to straighten his mud-soaked robe.

As the sun crept higher, Bazin walked slower and slower to increase the distance between the girls and himself. The fog was nearly gone. Only a few stray clumps clung to the lower valleys. So far, he had been lucky. They were more concerned with each other than with looking behind them. Just after the sun reached its zenith, the girls started to giggle and celebrate.

"We found the forest!"

"We made it!"

"'Bout damn time," Bazin muttered as he pulled Porsa down. Dinko crawled out of his jerkin as he crouched low. They lay flattened against the wet grass. He didn't want to risk discovery if they happened to look back. The bracken would allow a little cover but not much.

Aritha reached out to touch a tree. "I can't believe we actually found the forest."

"We would have been here sooner without the fog." Ro looked out at the moor.

"Don't move," Bazin whispered to Porsa. The girl continued to stare toward where they lay hidden. He couldn't see her eyes from this distance, but he could almost swear that she was looking directly at them. She reached up and rubbed the back of her neck.

"Come on. We have a long way to go." She turned and stepped into the shadows of the trees. The others followed her one by one.

Bazin waited, counting to twenty. Dinko turned yellow eyes on him, then sprang through the grass toward the trees. Bazin counted again until he felt Dinko brush against his mind. He closed his eyes and saw the girls threading their way through the dense ground cover beneath the trees.

The assassin opened his eyes and rose up on all fours, cautiously scanning the area around him, then got to his feet. He reached back to pull Porsa up.

"N-now what?" Porsa tried to brush the damp from the front of his robe.

"We follow." Bazin started walking. "It'll be easier to stay close with the cover from the trees."

"W-what if they hear us?"

"Then we'll just say we're travelers."

"Why c-can't we t-t—"

"Tell them the truth?" Bazin finished, and Porsa nodded. "Because truth leads to questions. Questions we can't answer."

"What q-questions?"

Bazin glanced at him. “If a stranger came out of the fog and said, ‘we’re here to bring you back to the Citadel because your soul has been magically linked to mine’, wouldn’t you have questions?”

“Y-yes.”

“Well, I don’t want to deal with the mistrust and disbelief out here in the middle of nowhere. I’d rather give her the impression that we are accidentally traveling in the same direction. Once we get somewhere civilized, we’ll get her on a ship and then tell her.”

“You think they’ll b-believe that?” Porsa tripped again and had to run to catch up.

“You’re a priest from Jardarwa, and I’m escorting you. To Ka-Petra. What’s not to believe?”

“K-Ka-P-Petra?”

“You’ve never heard of Ka-Petra?” Bazin frowned at the boy as they entered the shade of the forest.

Porsa shook his head.

“Don’t they give you an education at the Citadel?” Bazin snorted. “It’s the largest city in Ka Province. Built on a rock in the middle of the Ka River.” He grinned back at the apprentice as Dinko landed on his shoulder. “If we reach it, you’ll be in for a real education.”

Pursued

TWO DAYS. TWO DAYS of misty, cold forest. Two days of shadowing and sneaking. Two days of hauling Porsa around like a two-legged horse. Two days of listening to the most spoiled, bickering, obnoxious girls that ever walked the world.

Bazin wanted to kill something, anything, everything.

He sat in the shadow of a huge oak, watching the idiotic group of girls try to figure out something new to do with dried fish. *Did these girls know nothing?*

He and Porsa had dined steadily on jerky from their pack and a variety of nuts, berries, and roots they had found along the way. The girls, however, never bothered to gather food from the land around them.

It's a wonder they'd made it this far! Bazin ground his teeth and crushed a handful of dirt.

The only high point in the last two days was when the girls had badgered the older blonde one, Aritha, into letting them fix her skirt. She had been complaining non-stop about how the undergrowth was ripping it. The redhead and the young blonde argued with her that they hadn't had a problem with their pants. After an hour of arguing, she finally stripped and let them re-sew her skirt. The view had been entertaining, although she wasn't that enticing.

Bazin dropped the dirt. He shook his head and slowly rose. He faded farther into the shadows, then turned and headed back to his own camp.

He hadn't bothered making a fire. It was too easy to spot and too long to escape with a fire going. He liked being able to move quickly and quietly. His eyes fell on Porsa, snoring against a log.

Bazin frowned. The apprentice was no better than the girls when it came to living off the land. He complained less, but Bazin was pretty sure that was because he was either too scared to, or because it took too long to say anything with his stutter.

In front of him, Dinko hung from a tree branch. His body was upside down, but his head was right side up. "Krrr?"

"Because I can't watch anymore!" Bazin threw his hands up. "I wanna burst into their camp and either take over or kill them. I haven't decided."

"Krrr." Dinko's head swiveled to watch his master pace. The image of Ro shimmered in his mind.

"I only have to keep *her* alive. The others don't really matter."

"Krrr." The image of a burning, desolate landscape shimmered.

Bazin paled and looked at the lemur. "How did you know about that?" He stalked over to the lemur and gently pulled him from the tree, turning him right-side up. He stared into the bright yellow eyes. "You could see?"

"Krrr." The lemur placed gentle paws on Bazin's cheeks.

"Din, I'm sorry! I didn't know..." Guilt for putting his drugi through the torment that he had earned for himself stabbed through him.

"They never told us that you would experience the afterlife with us. By the gods, they never warned us about the afterlife at all."

The lemur rubbed his furry, gray and white-striped face against Bazin's chin and neck.

"I promise. I will keep us out of there. No more assassinations. I'll do whatever it takes."

"Krrr." The lemur bumped his head against Bazin, then jumped back up into the tree. The image of bickering girls shimmered in Bazin's mind.

"All right, your turn."

He glanced again at the sleeping apprentice. Porsa hadn't moved. Bazin unsheathed his sword from its shoulder harness. He needed to get in some practice. He had to get this body into shape.

Bazin had only made it through a few warm-up exercises when instinct stopped him. He froze and listened. All the bird chatter had stopped.

Lightly, he stepped over to Porsa and placed a hand over Porsa's mouth before shaking him. The apprentice came fully awake, staring at Bazin with wide eyes. He signaled Porsa to be silent and watch the trees.

Bazin slipped through the shadowy foliage toward the girls' camp. He expected them to be still arguing, but they were silent. The fire had been doused, and the whiny one and the redhead were quickly shoving things into their pack. The efficient one was watching Ro, who was watching the trees. They both had weapons ready.

From behind the bushes, he squinted at the strange weapons. He'd never seen anything like them. One looked like a chair leg but with jagged razors sticking out of it, and the other looked like a foot-long fat spike.

Where did they get those?

Ro scanned the trees intently. He was finally close enough that he could see her eyes. They were ice blue. She seemed to stare at him for a moment, but then her gaze moved on.

"What's out there?" The efficient one whispered without looking at the other girls.

Ro shook her head. Then slowly took a step forward. She then side-stepped to the left.

What is she doing? Bazin cocked his head. It looked like she was dancing.

Ro stepped back to the right and pointed into the trees across from their camp. Bazin turned to watch where she had pointed. Nothing moved.

He didn't see anything, but the girls thought otherwise. They took one look at the spot that Ro had pointed to and tiptoed in the opposite direction.

What did she know? He was proud of his instincts as an assassin. They had saved his life more than once, but even he couldn't pinpoint the direction the danger would come from. *Just who is this girl?*

Bazin faded away from their camp back to where he had left Porsa. He beckoned the young apprentice to follow. And then they heard it.

Not precisely a crashing, but it was definitely not a quiet passage. Several men were coming this way. Bazin pulled Porsa behind a big oak tree and waited as the men marched past.

It was the mercenaries who had been at the cottage. They must have reached the village the old woman had sent them to and found no trace of their quarry.

The odds were still against him. Seven to one, and he still wasn't confident that his body could handle the fight. Any fight.

A gruff voice drifted through the trees as they found the girls' campsite. "Ashes are still warm."

"Come on, they're close," the leader growled. The black bird on his shoulder squawked its agreement.

Bazin knew he had to take them out. Even with the wicked club the girl had, there was no way she could protect all three girls from seven experienced men. Dinko brushed against his mind. The lemur was keeping pace in the trees above the girls. Bazin turned and slipped silently through the trees.

Porsa started to follow but stumbled to a halt as the assassin disappeared. He hefted the pack to resettle it and started following again but without trying to catch up.

With the noise they were making, it wasn't hard to track them. Bazin closed the distance between him and the last man. Bazin reached out and yanked him off his feet with a hand over his mouth to silence his protest. A quick knife to the throat, and then there were six.

Bazin slid into the trees again and moved parallel to the mercenaries. Once again, he slipped out behind the last man. A few moments later, there were five.

Dinko brushed his mind. The girls had stopped at a river just ahead. It was no tame stream. The water was wide and rushing fast. Dinko's image of the river showed no way across, only white frothing rapids. Bazin cursed silently, but it was too late.

"Look, there!" the leader shouted and rushed forward. The other four followed without hesitation.

Bazin heard a scream from one of the girls. Dinko showed them running along the river. With a roar, Bazin sprinted forward with his sword drawn. The mercenaries turned at his shout and realized they were only five. Two stayed to meet the threat from behind, and the other three crashed through the foliage after the girls.

Ready or not, Bazin was momentarily pleased that he hadn't lost all of his battle skills. It took no more than a couple of breaths to open one man's neck and skewer the other. Without a second thought, he dashed after the others.

A jumble of rocks forced the river to bend away from the trees, forming a sudden clearing. The rushing sound of the river was almost deafening.

There were only two girls, Ro and the efficient one. They stood with their backs to the river, facing down the mercenaries. Bazin gave a quick glance around for the other girls, but he didn't see them.

Ro and Leema watched the leader as he stepped around to their right. The remaining two men circled to their left. All three rushed the girls at the same time. Bazin didn't wait to see what happened; he burst from the trees with a roar. Chaos erupted on the bank.

Ro swung her club at the leader, but she was attacked from behind by his bird. She tried to bat the bird away, and the man tackled her while she was distracted. They landed with a thud. Ro was pinned under the mercenary as they grappled for the club.

Bazin sliced at one mercenary, knocking him into the turbulent water, and turned to strike the other one, but found him holding the young blonde by the hair, using her as a shield. Bazin held his sword in front of him as he circled the man. From behind Bazin, a rustling sound grew louder, then a gray blur shot through the grass. Bazin ducked to the side as Dinko sailed past him straight at the man's face. It was a favorite trick they had used a hundred times. The blonde ducked and twisted with a yelp as Dinko's razor-sharp teeth and claws sank into the man's face. Wasting no time, Bazin plunged his sword into the man's gut. Dinko sprang free as the mercenary crumpled.

Bazin ignored the girl and spun to help Ro. He was just in time to see them roll over the edge of the embankment.

"Ro!" the girl screamed just as Bazin yelled, "No!"

He sprinted forward, but he was too late. The embankment hid a drop-off that plunged into the rapids below. A tangle of red and black bounced off a rock and was swept away around the bend downstream. Bazin slammed his sword into its scabbard and dashed toward the embankment. He heard the girl's protesting scream behind him, but it didn't slow him down.

She dies, I die, was all Bazin could think as he reached the edge and dove into the icy water.

Friend or Foe?

LEEMA WATCHED THE STRANGER who had saved them disappear around the bend in the river. She couldn't believe he had just jumped in like that. Leema spun around, intent on finding her sisters, only to be stopped by the small gray and white furry animal with huge yellow eyes, sitting in the grass. It was the thing that had attacked the man who had grabbed her. It stared at her without blinking. Every time she moved, it shifted to block her path.

"Look, I don't know what you are, but if that guy was your master," she pointed over her shoulder at the river, "then you need to get out of my way so I can find my sisters, and we can go after them."

"Krrr." The lemur stared at her for a moment and then leapt onto her shoulder.

Leema froze. She wasn't sure if this development was good or bad. She had seen the little animal attack the soldier, and it had scared her. She wasn't sure it was safe to let it hitch a ride on her shoulder. Slowly, she took a step. The furry animal didn't move except to tighten its grip on her shoulder. At first, she tried to walk carefully so it wouldn't fall, but it seemed to balance without any trouble, so she dashed toward the trees.

Ro had sent her sisters off on a side trail. She had reasoned that her red uniform would stand out in the foliage, and they would follow her instead of the princesses. It had worked, except they had been outnumbered. At least, until the other man had shown up.

"Who was he?" she asked out loud as she searched for the trail her sisters had taken.

"Krrr." She jumped. She hadn't really expected an answer. Leema eyed the furry body sitting so close to her face. It calmly stared back at her.

"Brenith? Aritha?" she called when she found a slightly familiar clump of berry bushes. She pushed her way past the bush and peered into the gloom. "Brenith?" Cautiously walking a little farther into the trees, she called again, "Bren?"

A shadow dislodged itself from behind a tree. "Leema?"

"Brenith!" The youngest girl threw herself into the arms of her sister. The animal jumped from her shoulder onto a low branch.

"Where's Ro?" Aritha came out from behind another tree and looked past Leema. Her eyes landed on the furry animal just as it leapt back onto Leema's shoulder. "What is that?"

"It-it's a l-lemur."

All three girls spun around and stared at the skinny, mud-covered man standing behind them.

"Who are you?" Leema held up her sharpened chair leg.

"P-please," the man held up his hands, "I'm P-Porsa, ap-p-prentice t-to the Holy M-Mountain."

"Holy Mountain?" Brenith looked him up and down. "What are you doing here?"

"Ah... I—"

"Later," Leema cut him off. "Bren, Ro fell into the river and was sucked downstream through the rapids. This," she glanced at the little animal on her shoulder, "lemur's master dove in after her. We have to find them." Leema tugged on her sister's arm.

"Bazin?" Porsa stumbled forward.

"Leema, what are you talking about? What man dove in after her?" Brenith looked from her sister to the apprentice priest. "And who's Bazin?"

"Come on! We have to go." Leema tugged on Brenith's arm again. "I'll explain as we go, but we have to hurry. That river is so fast." Leema grasped her sister's wrist and pulled her along as she marched back toward the berry bushes.

"Krrr." The lemur bounced on her shoulder as if he wanted her to move faster.

"I'm not going anywhere until you tell us what happened." Aritha crossed her arms and waited, but Brenith and Leema were already past the bushes. She glanced at Porsa, who shrugged and followed the girls.

"Araagghh!" Aritha stamped her foot, clenched her fists, and stomped after them.

Porsa stumbled and hopped over the undergrowth as he hurried to catch up with the sisters. He joined them in time to hear Leema's explanation.

"He just came out of nowhere and killed one, then this lemur attacked the second one, and he finished him off."

"You didn't see him before that?"

"No."

"Are you sure he isn't working with the men who attacked us?"

"Krrr." The lemur stared hard at Brenith and flexed his claws into Leema's shoulder.

Leema eyed the little furry beast. "I think you insulted him."

"Bazin w-wasn't w-working for those m-men." Porsa tripped into their conversation. The lemur turned and stared at him with a look of tolerant suffering.

"Who is this Bazin?" Brenith stopped walking and stared at Porsa.

"He..." Porsa looked everywhere but at Brenith, "he's... um..."

"Never mind." She stalked off.

Aritha pushed past the still stammering apprentice. "They never listen to me either."

Leema led them to the spot at the river where she and Ro had fought the men. She glanced around and then raided the body of the soldier for his pack, his knife, and his sword.

"Leema!" Aritha hissed. "You shouldn't steal from the dead."

"Why not? He won't need this stuff, but we will."

Brenith walked around the body, giving it as much space as she could. She stopped beside Leema and looked over the embankment. It wasn't a long drop, but the rapids just below frothed and churned, making it almost impossible to see the rocks underneath.

"Could she survive that?" Brenith yelled over the roaring of the rapids.

"She's not dead!" Leema glared at her sister.

Brenith looked back at her. "I didn't say she was."

"We have to find a way down." Leema eyed the bend in the river with a scowl.

"D-Dinko c-could show us," Porsa offered from behind them.

"Who's Dinko?" They turned to the nervous apprentice.

He pointed a shaking finger at the lemur.

"Him?" Aritha snorted.

"Krrr." Dinko flexed his claws into Leema's shoulder again.

"I really wish you would stop doing that." Leema winced. "My tunic isn't very thick, and you have sharp claws."

"Krrr." The lemur stopped flexing.

"Thank you."

"Leema, stop talking to that thing. It can't understand you."

"Y-yes, he c-can," Porsa mumbled as he shot a rueful glance at the lemur. Dinko watched him through half-closed eyes.

"You think it can talk?" Aritha crossed her arms, daring Porsa to contradict her.

He shook his head. "N-not t-talk. Underst-tand."

"Krrr."

"What?" Brenith stared at the lemur.

"Krrr." The lemur leaned toward Porsa menacingly.

"I-I'm sorry," Porsa frowned, "b-but d-do you want to f-find B-Bazin or not?"

"Krrr."

Porsa glanced back at the girls who were looking between him and the lemur in confused fascination.

"How does he understand?" Leema craned her neck to try to get a better look at the lemur. Dinko glanced down at her as if he didn't appreciate the examination.

"I-I don't know," Porsa glared meaningfully at the lemur, "b-but they t-tend to have c-c-conversations without m-me."

"Krrr." Dinko stuck his nose in the air at Porsa's last comment.

"Well, whatever he does, can he help us find Ro?" Brenith looked at Porsa questioningly.

"Krrr." Dinko did a little dance on top of Leema's shoulder. She flinched as his bushy tail whacked her in the face.

"I think that's a yes."

"Krrr."

"Alright, fur ball, which way?" Aritha gestured to the forest.

Dinko sat back down and stared at Aritha. "Krrr."

"Don't take it personally," Leema looked up at him, "she's like that to everyone."

"Krrr." The lemur dropped lightly to the ground and cocked his head. Then bounded off into the forest on a path leading away from the river. Brenith and Leema exchanged a look, then trotted after the little furry guide.

"Hey!" Aritha shouted. "We're supposed to be following the river!"

"P-protesting w-won't d-do any g-good." Porsa sighed and walked after the lemur.

Aritha stomped after him. "Your stutter is really annoying."

Waterfall

Ro gasped as they hit the water. She heard Leema scream her name as they were swept around the bend. Ro fought to keep her head above the churning rapids as she and the man careened down the river. Her opponent kicked at her, but she wasn't sure if he was trying to fight with her or if he was just trying to stay above the water.

Flailing her free arm, Ro tried to swim toward shore, but the man had a grip on her club, and his weight was dragging them both down. She tried to free her weapon, but he tightened his grip. She would have let go of the club to escape, but its cord was wrapped around her wrist and was getting tighter all the time.

The raging water tossed them like leaves. They bounced off one rock only to be knocked into another. She felt the undercurrent pull off one of her oversized boots.

The river gushed out into a wide spot, leaving the biggest boulders behind. The water smoothed out. Her opponent jumped at his chance. He spun in the water and grabbed her hair, pushing her under the surface. Ro kicked at him. Her remaining boot made contact with his groin. He let go, and her head broke the surface. She gasped for air.

He sputtered and snarled. She swung her fist as hard as the water would allow and punched him in the face. His head snapped back.

Blood spouted from his nose but was quickly washed away. Ro tried to untangle the cord from her wrist, but it wouldn't give. He roared, spitting water at her as he lunged. He yanked on the club, spinning her in the water so that she faced away from him. He grabbed her hair and shoved her below the surface again.

Ro kicked and punched, trying to reach him. Her lungs began to burn. In desperation, Ro yanked on the club and pulled him under with her. As he fought to reach the air, he lost his hold on her hair. Their heads broke the surface just long enough for Ro to gulp in a short breath before he shoved her under again. Her ears roared as the water pulled at them. The roar became deafening as the current increased, pulling stronger as the river burst through a narrow canyon into nothingness. For a moment, Ro felt weightless, and then she fell.

The man let go just before they smashed into the churning surface and plunged deep into the basin at the base of the waterfall. The currents tore at Ro, keeping her from the surface. Her lungs pleaded for air. She clawed and kicked, but she couldn't reach the surface.

Something touched her arm. She lashed out, thinking it was the mercenary again, but there was only water around her. The touch came again just as blackness was edging in on her vision. It was warm and felt like a hand. Ro stopped fighting. Her lungs couldn't last any longer. She went limp as she was pulled up through the water but blacked out before she reached the surface.

***

Cool water touched her brow. Ro groaned. Her head ached.

"Shh." A voice like a bubbling stream filled her head.

Ro's eyes shot open, then widened at the sight before her. A person, if you could fit that term to a person-shaped pool of water, hovered next to her. Ro tried to move away, but her hand hit the water.

"Stop!" the thing bubbled.

Ro pulled her hand back. Glancing quickly around, she realized she was sprawled on a large moss-covered boulder at the edge of the river and had almost fallen back in. The roar of the waterfall echoed off the canyon walls that bordered the river.

Ro looked back at the watery shape. "What are you?" Her throat felt raw from all the water she had swallowed.

"Sellemeh a Salladeh," the face in the water gurgled. "People of the Water in your tongue."

"People of the Water?" Ro remembered Fisp's warning that they were monsters who snatched travelers.

The water-person shimmered. "What were you doing in Azgin Su's pool, Daughter of Fire?"

"The what?" Ro pushed herself up, trying to focus on the liquid face.

"Azgin Su," the sprite bubbled, indicating another moss-covered rock a few yards away. "You and your friend invaded the pool."

"My friend?" Ro stared at the prone figure sprawled there. His face was turned away. For a horrified moment, she thought that it was the soldier who had tried to kill her, but it was not the man who had attacked her. "I don't know who that is."

"It does not matter," the water-person gurgled. "He jumped in after you."

"What? How do you know that?"

"Azgin Su told us."

"Who is Azgin Su?"

"The river!" The sprite sprayed water into the air as if spluttering in disgust. "You did not know his name?"

"Until I was chased into it... him, I didn't even know there was a river."

"Did not know?" The sprite rippled in agitation. "How could you not know Azgin Su was here? He stretches across most of Ka."

"I'm not from Ka." Ro winced as bruises made themselves known. "We landed on Ka's shores by accident. Our ship was attacked by a dragon."

"Dragon!" The Sellemeh a Salladeh sloshed and gurgled. "Dragons are not of the Azgin Su. Dragons burn life. You stink of dragons!"

Ro watched the light reflecting off the water sprite's surface. "A dragon burned our ship."

The watery figure danced from side to side. "You profane the Azgin Su."

Ro shook her head. "I meant no harm."

"You are not welcome here, Daughter of Fire. You will leave the Azgin Su and not return, or we will extinguish your fire forever!" With that, the Sellemeh a Salladeh was gone with an angry splash.

Ro sat still for a moment, unsure of what to do. The shore was only a few feet away, but it was on the wrong side of the river from where she had started. She wondered if the princesses had survived the attack. Guilt and shame washed over her. She had done a dismal job of protecting them. Ro thought about swimming back across the river to look for them, but she was reluctant to get back in the water after the warning from the Sellemeh a Salladeh.

She pulled her legs up onto the rock and attempted to stand. The boulder was slick, especially with only one boot. Balancing carefully, she jumped the short distance to the shore. She landed heavily on her knees amongst mossy rocks and reeds. Her club was still attached to her wrist by a cord. It banged against the rocks hidden under the grass. She held it up and examined it. Most of the shells were broken now.

Ro struggled to her feet. Every bit of her ached. More and more bruises made themselves known. Gingerly, she felt the side of her head. She could feel uneven, roughened patches of skin. The rocks in the river had left their marks. She looked back up at the waterfall. It towered over a hundred feet above her. Rocky cliffs on each side formed the canyon mouth that she and the man had washed through. Her stomach twisted as she realized that she had fallen from all the way up there.

Ro glanced at the man lying unconscious on the rock a few feet away. She cautiously moved closer to him. Her gait was slightly uneven from wearing only one boot. The wet fabric of her clothes chaffed against her skin. She was sore and tired from fighting her attacker and the river, but she held her club ready in case the stranger was only feigning sleep.

Once she was near enough to see him, but not close enough that he could reach her if he woke, Ro peered at the man. He was young but looked older than her. Closely-cropped sandy brown hair covered his head, and a couple of days' beard growth fringed his jawline. A few bruises discolored his face, but she couldn't tell if they were old and healing or if they were from his trip down the river.

He wore a dark brown tunic with a black jerkin, and his brown pants were tucked into decently made boots. His clothing was not mismatched or worn. It looked nearly new. A sword stuck up over his right shoulder. The straps from the shoulder harness were buckled across his chest. The sword and harness were serviceable and without ornamentation. He didn't seem overly rich, but not shabby either.

"Who are you?" she muttered, wondering why he would jump into a raging river to save a total stranger. *If that was what really happened.* She couldn't very well take the word of a river. And yet, here he was.

She glanced around. The forest was just as thick on this side of the river. She backed away to the tree line and sat down against a tree. Ro pulled her remaining boot off and set it next to her, then unwrapped the soaking wet cloth from around her foot. Her skin was wrinkled from the constant exposure to moisture.

Ro tried to wring most of the water out of the cloth, then hung it on a tree branch. She turned and caught sight of the fair-haired stranger now standing a few feet away. Ro hadn't heard him approach. Her hand instinctively gripped the club. Ro didn't speak; she just stared at him. His bright green eyes returned her gaze.

Camp

BAZIN STUDIED THE GIRL who had killed him. Bruises and scrapes covered the side of her face. Her clothes were torn and soaked from the river. He felt perverse satisfaction that she had suffered until he remembered: *She dies, I die.*

Out of concern for his own hide, he shut off his anger and drew on years of assassin's training to appear friendly. "How did we get out of the river?"

Ro's gaze traveled from his head to his boots and back up. "Sellemeh a Salladeh."

"Ah."

"You know of them?"

"I have traveled extensively and know of many wondrous things," he said, trying for charming, but he couldn't keep the bitterness out of his tone.

"Who are you?"

"I am..." he hesitated. For the last few days, he had debated about using his real name when he finally confronted her. If she had ever heard of Bazin the Assassin, then she would never trust him, and he would never be able to protect her. He could tell her his name was Darin, after all, that was the name of the body he now lived in. However, it finally came down to the fact that he wasn't willing to give up the last bit of his true self. "Bazin."

Ro watched him silently without even blinking. Bazin felt a wash of relief. She didn't know the name. He inclined his head. "And your name?"

"Tell me why you jumped into the river after me," she countered, staring at him with icy blue eyes.

It didn't surprise him that she was not forthcoming with information. Bazin wasn't ready to confess all either. As an assassin, he was no stranger to waiting for the target to relax enough to trust, so he shrugged. "Why not?"

Ro hefted her club. "Generally, people don't jump into raging rivers after strangers."

"Generally, no."

"Then why did you?"

"Seemed like a good idea at the time," he smiled.

"I don't believe you."

He watched her for a long moment. Her eyes looked different than just a few moments ago. The blue color had almost faded completely. They were the eyes that he remembered seeing just before her sword had pierced his gut. His whole body tensed as he felt the steel sliding through him once again. Ro came up onto the balls of her feet, her body suddenly as tense as his.

Bazin took a breath, trying to banish his churning emotions. *She dies, I die*, he reminded himself.

"Believe what you wish," he sighed. He crossed his arms and leaned his shoulder against the nearest tree, then winced and shifted a little when the bark dug into a fresh bruise.

"Where did you come from?"

"Jardarwa."

"Why are you in Ka?"

He cocked his head. "Do you always ask this many questions?"

Ro stared him down silently.

He was beginning to see how she had managed to survive her three traveling companions. It was sheer stubbornness. He watched her relax just a little as he answered, "I was escorting one of the Holy Brothers' apprentices to Ka-Petra."

"Why?"

"Why does it matter?" He watched her watching him. "Why are *you* in Ka?" He gave her the same head-to-toe once-over that she had given him, pointedly staring at her bare feet. "And without shoes? Were you shipwrecked?"

Ro pressed her lips together and glared at him.

Bazin shoved away from the tree. She tensed again. He looked her up and down. "Not very trusting, are you?"

Ro didn't move, so he shrugged and turned back to the river. Hopefully, turning his back wouldn't get him a club to the skull but rather show her that he was not a threat. Slowly, he scanned the banks looking for any sign that the leader of the mercenaries had made it ashore, but he didn't see anything.

Bazin could feel her eyes boring into his back, so he stared up at the waterfall for a long time. "Can you believe we went over that?" He shook his head. "The gods are watching out for us today."

"Then the gods deposited us on the wrong side of the river," she muttered in a monotone.

Bazin stood up straighter and glanced around. He walked a little way downstream, then looked back at Ro. "I suppose we could swim."

"No."

Her blunt refusal surprised him. He wouldn't blame her if she wanted to leave her companions behind. He certainly would've by now, but she didn't seem the type that would.

"Don't you want to get back to your friend?" He was careful to only mention the girl that he had seen. It wouldn't help to make her any more suspicious than she already was.

"Yes, but I was warned not to re-enter the river."

"By whom?"

"Sellemeh a Salladeh."

"Ah, better not risk it then. They aren't known to be forgiving." He looked up at the dimming sky. "Guess we should eat something and make camp before it's completely dark. We can figure out what to do in the morning."

They had very little to make camp with. Porsa was carrying almost all of their supplies, and he knew that the girls hadn't really had supplies to begin with. They would have to make do until Porsa caught up with them. Or rather, he should say, until Dinko brought Porsa with the pack. He wasn't entirely certain that the bungling apprentice would even know to follow him.

"So, shall we have a fire?" When he took a step toward her, she raised her club again. "I'm not going to hurt you, believe me. I'm too damn tired." He held up his hands, taking a moment to really look at her weapon. He squinted at the broken shells and the binding cord. "Did you make that?"

"A friend did."

"It's remarkable. I've never seen anything like it." He moved away from her and gathered a few sticks.

Ro watched him as he cleared a small spot and dug a shallow pit, then meticulously piled sticks and some dry grass together in the depression. "I don't have a tinder box."

Bazin reached into a pocket inside his jerkin and pulled out a little leather drawstring bag. He shook it in front of her eyes for a moment, then turned and sank onto the grass. "Please, have a seat. You look like you're about to fall down."

As he bent over his pile of sticks with the flint, Ro slowly moved back up against the tree. She perched on a knot of roots but remained tense.

After coaxing the spark into a small fire, he sat back. He reached into his jerkin and pulled out a handful of jerky. He tossed some to her. "Here."

She caught it and looked at it. She sniffed it suspiciously, waiting until he took a bite before she tried it.

"It's not poisoned." He gnawed on the jerky as he added a few more sticks to the fire. He had expected some resistance to his presence, but not complete mistrust. He was beginning to respect this runt of a girl.

Ro stuffed the jerky in her mouth, then reached down to grab her remaining boot and move it closer to the fire.

"Why don't you have shoes that fit?"

"That's my business."

Bazin frowned at her hostile tone, but then he felt Dinko brush his thoughts. His face went blank as he connected with his drugi. "They're coming."

"Who?"

"My Holy Apprentice and Dinko and I would imagine your little blonde friend from the riverbank."

"How do you know that?" Ro slowly stood.

"That's my business," Bazin mimicked her tone. He took a bite of jerky and chewed, deliberately holding her gaze.

"Who is Dinko?" she asked after a moment.

"Oh no." He wagged a piece of jerky at her. "No more answers until you at least tell me your name."

It took her longer than he expected to answer, but finally she said, "Ro."

He watched her across the tiny glowing fire. Her eyes seemed more blue again.

"Row? As in, row a boat?"

"No. Rohamina."

That was a shock. He didn't expect the girl who had skewered him and was even now controlling his destiny, his very soul, to be named after that tiny, delicate flower. It made her seem fragile, as if she needed protection. He didn't want to see her in that light.

She had killed him. She had sent him to the Underworld. He hated her. He wanted to kill her not protect her, and he be damned if he would think of her as a flower, especially not that flower. *His flower.*

The memory slammed into him. *Seeing Rohamina, the tiny white, crown-shaped flowers, growing from a crack in the wall just below his window. His desire from a moment earlier to escape the Assassin's Court by leaping to his death being replaced by the terrified will to live. His little fingers clinging to the window ledge as he desperately tried to climb back into his room. His little feet scrabbling against the outside wall of the tower. Finally, clambering back into the safety of his room, falling to the floor, panting as he stared at the ceiling. His child's mind thinking not of his near death, but of the flower growing where no flower should. Thinking that if Rohamina could cling to life at the Assassin's Court, then so could he.*

Bazin snapped out of his memories. He couldn't call her Rohamina. He wouldn't. Things were getting complicated. He never liked complicated.

"Ro." He repeated in an effort to remind himself that she was just a means to an end. She was his ticket to staying alive, and that was all. "I'm going to get some more wood."

She immediately came to her feet when he stood. After only a cursory glance at her, he stalked off into the woods. He reached down and picked up a branch and busted it in two. It eased some of the tension building in his shoulders. He had to get control.

Reunited

THE FURRY LEMUR SPRANG out from behind a tree, startling Aritha.

"What is wrong with you?" Aritha snarled.

"Oh, leave him alone," Leema bent down so that Dinko could jump onto her shoulder. She scratched the lemur's ears as she walked on.

Aritha pushed a branch out of her way. "You are too nice to that fur ball."

Aritha continued to gripe as they pushed through the undergrowth. The path was not a well-trodden one. The forest did not sit on a flat plane. It had been an uphill climb from the moor to the river where they had been attacked. Now, they were slowly making their way downhill again by a long, winding route through the trees.

The lemur led them through the forest and then back to the river a little downstream from where they had started. The banks were still high above the river, and there was no sign of Ro. Dark crept up on them as they searched. Leema wanted to keep going, but Aritha demanded that they stop. Brenith looked to Porsa. The boy looked dead on his feet. She eyed the lemur. He seemed more agitated than before. He wouldn't leave Leema's shoulder since darkness had fallen. If they couldn't follow Dinko, then they had no choice but to stop for the night.

The girls shared their dried fish, and Porsa shared some of his jerky. They slept huddled together under a tree. Brenith didn't feel safe lighting a fire. Sleep was elusive. Leema tried to keep watch for a while, but no one got up to take over, so finally, she just nodded off.

Dinko roused the group at dawn. Exhausted but glad to be moving once again, Dinko led them back into the forest. They continued moving downhill for about two hours, then found their way back to the river.

"Why can't we just walk beside the river?" Aritha complained.

"It would be too easy to fall in." Leema gestured to the jumble of tall, moss-covered rocks along the bank. Once again, they retreated into the forest.

"Are you sure that little hairball knows where he is going?" Aritha asked again, pushing another branch aside.

"Y-yes." Porsa was walking behind her. She let the branch snap back to hit him. He sneered at her back.

"Aritha," Leema sighed, "the lemur knows where his master is."

"I doubt that," Aritha griped.

"Krrr." Dinko turned and watched Aritha with bright yellow eyes.

She pointed directly at his nose. "Stop staring at me."

"Krrr."

"Leema, tell him to stop staring at me."

"Go ahead," Leema whispered, "stare all you want."

"What did you say?" Aritha snapped.

"Nothing," Leema glanced back at her sister, "just passing on your message."

"You're conspiring with it!"

"For the sake of the gods, Aritha!" Brenith snarled.

They marched on, jumping at every sound. Aritha even screamed at one point when a huge black bird flew out of the trees as they passed.

"I miss Ro," Brenith muttered, watching the trees.

The day wore on slowly. The path took them uphill again. The group veered back to the river over and over again, trying to see any sign of Ro or Dinko's master. Each time they saw the river, it was a little more narrow.

"What's that sound?" Brenith paused to listen. Leema stopped beside her, gazing around at the trees.

"Is that the ocean?" Aritha slowed. "It sounds like surf."

"Krrr." Dinko bounced on Leema's shoulder and launched into the air. He hit the ground, running for the river.

"Hey! Where's he going?" She chased after him. The roaring grew louder and louder as they neared the river. The trees parted, and Leema froze in her tracks. They stood at the top of a high canyon that channeled the massive river into a small mouth, spewing the water out over a hundred-foot drop.

"Oh!" Aritha said as she came out of the trees.

"Tell me Ro didn't go over that." Leema stared. "Tell me we missed her somewhere back there."

Porsa and Brenith came out of the trees behind them and stopped.

"Oh," Brenith covered her mouth with both hands, realizing what this could mean.

"Hey," Aritha grabbed Leema's arm and pointed, "your little furball is going crazy."

Dinko ran back and forth, looking over the edge of the waterfall. Leema approached him, then went to all fours to crawl to the edge. She peered over.

"I don't see anyone."

"Is your master down there?" She watched the lemur as he paced the rock ledge.

"Krrr."

"Is that a yes?" she asked. Dinko turned and stared into her eyes for a long time, then bounded away from the edge and back into the trees. Leema scrambled backward from the lip and ran past her sisters. "Come on! I think we're getting close."

One by one, they followed the lemur into the forest. The ground became steeper. The trees were farther apart, and more rocks jutted up from the forest floor. It was near dark before they reached the bottom. The ground suddenly leveled out, and the forest thickened again. Dinko led them through the trees back toward the river. They emerged well below the waterfall. Leema looked back up to where she had peeked over the edge of those massive rocks and shuddered.

"L-look there!" Porsa pointed across the much tamer river. Back in the trees, away from the riverbank, a fire glowed.

"Krrr." Dinko began to bounce in place.

"How are we going to cross that?" Brenith stared at the swirling water.

"Hello!" Aritha yelled.

"Don't!" Brenith hissed. "What if it's more of those men?"

"Oh," Aritha covered her mouth, "I didn't think of that."

"Hello, yourself!" A man's voice echoed across the river.

"B-Bazin!" Porsa shouted and waved.

The sisters glanced at each other and then at the lemur, who was still bouncing.

"I guess that's his master," Leema shrugged. She squinted, trying to see if there was anyone else around the fire. A shorter figure moved toward the river but kept its distance from the man.

"Ro! Ro!" Leema screeched and started bouncing like Dinko.

Tears streamed down Brenith's cheeks. "Ro!"

"Leema!" Ro waved. "Brenith!"

Bazin cupped his hands around his mouth and shouted, "Come across!"

Porsa spread his arms. "How?"

Bazin mimed swimming. "Swim!"

"No." Aritha shook her head and backed up. "I am not swimming across that."

"Is there anywhere to cross downstream?" Brenith yelled.

Ro shook her head. "No way to know!"

"Do you really think we can swim that?" Brenith asked Leema.

"I don't know." She looked downstream, then at Brenith, "Who knows if there is a better place to cross. You saw the terrain on the way down here."

"The longer you wait, the darker it gets!" Bazin shouted, pointing at the sky.

"Well?" Leema looked around at her sisters and Porsa. When no one moved, she shrugged and stalked to the river's edge, settled the mercenary's pack on her back, and jumped.

"Leema!" Brenith ran forward.

Leema bobbed to the surface, and Dinko sprang onto her head. Between Dinko and the pack, she had to work hard to keep her head above water. The current pushed her farther downstream as she slowly worked her way across the river. Bazin and Ro moved farther down the bank to meet up with Leema.

"Stop bouncing!" Leema coughed as Dinko's excited movements knocked her head under the water. As soon as she was close to the opposite bank, Dinko launched into the air, landing softly beside Bazin. He sprang into Bazin's arms, purring. Ro reached down and held a hand out to pull the youngest princess up onto the bank. As soon as Leema was sitting on the grass, she waved to her sisters.

"Come on," she puffed and started to wring the water out of her hair. "It's not that hard."

"I-I'm not that g-g-good of a s-swimmer." Porsa started to back away from the river.

"Oh no, you don't. If I have to swim over there, so do you." Aritha snarled and shoved Porsa forward. He tripped on his robe and landed face-first in the river. He floundered and sank.

"Damn it!" Bazin snarled. He set Dinko lightly on the grass at his feet and dove into the river. He made quick, even strokes out to Porsa, grabbed him by the pack on his back, pulled him to the surface, and then hauled him across to the other bank.

Brenith glared at Aritha. "What is wrong with you?"

"I didn't mean..." Aritha shook her head, but Brenith wasn't listening. She had already slipped into the water. Aritha sighed and followed her sister as the last of the sun's rays dimmed from the sky.

Unhappy Allies

DRIPPING AND SHIVERING, THE group returned to the fire. Leema dropped the mercenary's stolen pack on the ground. The sword she had taken from the dead man was tied to the pack and made a dull thud as it landed. She then huddled next to the glowing heat.

"I'm freezing." Aritha dropped to her knees next to her sister and stretched her hands to the fire. Brenith edged up to the fire, staying as far from Bazin as she could.

Bazin deposited a dripping Porsa next to the fire and pulled the pack from the apprentice's back. He dug through the contents quickly and pulled out two wool blankets. They were only a little damp. The pack had fared relatively well during its time in the river.

"Strip and hang your clothes to dry." He held out the blankets to the girls. They stared back at him with open mouths and indignant eyes.

"Who do you think you are?" Aritha crossed her arms and stared at Bazin.

"I'm sorry, did you want a proper introduction?" He raised his eyebrows. "I'm Bazin and you are?"

"Aritha, Brenith, and Leema." Brenith interrupted before Aritha could speak. Her sister stared at her, but Brenith returned a warning glare, and for once, Aritha stayed silent.

"Nice to meet you." Bazin offered a mocking bow. "Now, if you don't want to sit and shiver, strip."

The girls looked to Ro, who was watching Bazin. She wondered at the impatience that he showed toward Aritha. He hadn't been that hostile when it had just been the two of them.

Bazin glanced at Ro, then dropped the blankets beside the fire with a shrug. She bent and scooped up a blanket, shook it out, and held the blanket up as a shield for the other girls. Leema started to undress, then Brenith. They handed the wet clothes to Ro while wrapping the blanket around their shoulders to maintain their modesty.

Bazin didn't even look. His attention was focused on searching his pack. He dug out a small bundle of cloth and a coil of cord, then stood.

"What's that?" Leema asked as she and Brenith huddled under the blanket.

"Snare," Bazin said over his shoulder as he disappeared into the shadows. Dinko bounded after him.

After he was gone, Porsa crawled over and dug through the pack until he pulled out a dry shirt and pants. Then he squelched over behind a tree and started to strip his wet clothes off.

"Ro? Are you all right?" Brenith asked quietly after the apprentice was out of earshot.

"Yes." Ro glanced back while she hung Leema's clothes on a branch near the fire.

"Did you go over that waterfall?" Brenith whispered.

"Yes," Ro said, spreading out Brenith's clothes.

"What about the soldier?" Leema asked, looking back toward the wall of water.

"I don't know what happened to him. I woke up on that rock over there," Ro said as she turned back to the fire.

"Did that Bazin fellow pull you out?" Aritha wrapped the blanket around her shoulders and tried unsuccessfully to remove her wet clothes. Ro finally took pity on her and reached out to hold the blanket up for her.

"No. The Sellemeh a Salladeh pulled me out and told me never to profane their river again."

Leema's eyes were huge with wonder. "What did they look like?"

"Like a person made of water."

Aritha finally handed her wet clothing to Ro and gasped when she caught a look at the scrapes and bruises on Ro's face. "What happened to your face?"

"I went over a waterfall." Ro turned away and hung up Aritha's wet clothing.

"Let me see." Brenith tucked the edge of the blanket under her arm and motioned Ro closer. Ro obeyed, and Brenith turned her so she could see her face in the firelight. "It seems clean enough, but it doesn't look very pretty."

"I'm not here to look pretty, Highness."

"Don't call us that," Brenith whispered urgently, glancing at the trees where Porsa was changing. "I don't think it's safe."

"Why wouldn't it be safe?" Aritha asked, moving closer.

"We don't know this Bazin fellow, and I don't want to end up being held for ransom." Brenith gave her a sharp look.

"Ransom?" Leema made it sound like an adventure.

"She's right." Ro looked at the three sisters. "I'm not sure we can trust him either, but for right now, until we get dry, eat, and rest, it's best to stay."

At that moment, Porsa tripped out from behind the tree and flopped his sopping robes over a low branch with a splat. Ro turned to look at him. He was too skinny for his height; it made him look unstable.

"Who are you?" she asked.

He cringed under Ro's steady gaze. "P-Porsa, Apprentice t-to the Holy M-Mountain." He shivered and edged closer to the fire, even though it brought him closer to the girls.

"What are you doing here?" Ro wanted to know if he would give the same answer as Bazin had.

"I d-don't kn-now," Porsa moaned pathetically.

"What kind of an answer is that?" Ro stepped toward him.

"The only kind you are likely to get from him," Bazin snorted as he emerged from the trees.

Ro tensed immediately and spun to face him. Bazin dropped a pile of wood next to the fire, then pulled a couple of roots and a wrapped bundle of cloth from inside his jerkin. She watched him as he dug through his pack again.

"Why don't you fill this with water?" he said off-handedly as he thrust a small pot into her hands.

Ro narrowed her eyes, but he ignored her. She pressed her lips together and stalked to the river. Cautiously, she peered at the water. She was a little wary of the Sellemeh a Salladeh reappearing, but nothing jumped out of the water at her. Quickly, she scooped up some water and returned to the fire.

By the time she got back, Bazin had set up a brace of sticks to suspend the pot over the fire. He looked up as she emerged from the darkness and held his hand out for the pot. She watched him efficiently pare off chunks of the roots that he had found and dump them in the water. Brenith and Leema were kneeling together under their blanket, watching him.

"What is that?" Leema asked, peering in the pot.

"Tachoula root," Bazin said without looking up. He pulled a couple of pieces of jerky from his pack, ripped them into smaller pieces, and threw them in as well.

"What is tachoula root?" Brenith asked as he hung it over the fire.

Bazin sat back on his heels and looked over at her. His expression was a mixture of disbelief and curiosity. "You've never heard of tachoula?"

Brenith shook her head. "I am not familiar with the local plant life."

"Hmm," Bazin grunted as he stood and started to unbuckle his sword harness. He gently set the sheathed weapon on the ground near his feet and began to unlace his jerkin. "It is a plant that grows everywhere in Ka. Very filling and doesn't taste too bad raw. It's better in stew. When it's light, I'll show you what it looks like."

He turned his back and hung the wet jerkin on the tree. He pulled his shirt off next, wrung it out, then added it to the growing wall of clothes around the camp.

He caught sight of Porsa's dripping robe. "Porsa! If you want that damned robe to dry, you're going to have to wring the water out of it first."

"Oh!" Porsa scrambled to his feet and rushed to the robe, almost falling over Bazin as he did so.

Bazin growled under his breath as he turned to dig through his pack again. He pulled out a dry shirt and a small wrapped bundle. He pulled on the shirt and then sat down by the fire.

Ro sat down on the grass and watched him. He was still a mystery to her, even though this would be the second night that they shared a fire. In that time, he had made a few attempts to be pleasant but had always turned bitter and growly. He seemed friendly enough, but there was something about him that felt wrong. She'd had no sense of tingling, indicating that he was a danger to them, but still, she couldn't be sure.

He scooped up his sword and set it within easy reach, then pulled off one of his boots. The furry creature that had ridden across the river on Leema's head suddenly appeared out of the trees and leaped onto Bazin's shoulder, breaking the tense silence that had settled over the campsite. Bazin let his boot dangle loosely in one hand while he reached up to scratch the little animal's ears. He seemed genuinely pleased to see the little lemur. He even smiled. As Ro watched the furry critter purr at his master, something nagged in the back of her memory, but it remained elusive.

Bazin dropped his boot by the fire and unwrapped the cloth he had brought back with the roots. Balancing the pile of berries that tried to spill out, he spread the cloth on the ground and re-piled the berries into the center. Dinko dropped down to sit by the pile and started to stuff his furry cheeks with the fruit. Bazin pulled off his other boot and set it next to the other one to dry.

Porsa returned, practically collapsing in a heap by the fire. He rubbed his wet hands on his pant legs and leaned forward to eye the stew. Then he stripped off his sandals and stretched his toes to the heat.

The crackle of the fire seemed overly loud in the tense silence that surrounded the group. Aritha wandered over to shake out her clothes a little more. Brenith and Leema followed the men's lead and removed their wet shoes.

Ro saw Brenith glance from Bazin's boots to her own shoes and then to Ro's bare feet. Her eyes darted around the camp, coming to rest on

Ro's remaining boot sitting alone by the fire. Brenith looked back at her with concern in her eyes, but Ro said nothing. She turned away and caught Bazin watching the two of them. Ro held his gaze until Leema spoke.

"Ro?" The younger girl reached a foot out and shoved the lumpy pack at her feet toward Ro. "It's from one of the men who attacked us."

Bazin reached forward and stirred the stew, filling the air with a delicious smell.

Ro crawled over and knelt beside the princess. Ro glanced at the sword, then opened the pack. There was a bundle of jerky, a few cooking utensils, a blanket, a satchel with oil, a cloth, and whetstone for the sword, and a water skin. She left everything but the satchel and the waterskin in the pack. Turning the pack over, she untied the sword.

For a moment, she just hefted it in her hand, getting the feel of it, then she shifted to sit cross-legged with the blade across her lap. She slowly examined the blade. After reassuring herself that there were no nicks or cracks, she reached for the satchel and unrolled the whetstone and oil. She glanced up at the cooking pot, wondering if she had time before it was done, and found Bazin's eyes on her again.

"You know how to use that?" Bazin asked with an oddly hostile look in his eyes.

Ro said nothing. Instead, she began to sharpen her new blade. He didn't say anything else, but she heard him unsheathe his own sword. He had tried to clean it last night, but without supplies, all he could do was dry it by the fire and polish it with the tail of his shirt. Except for the hiss and pop of the fire and the twin sounds of stones on blades, the campsite was silent.

A Difficult Dinner

PORSA'S STOMACH GROWLED LOUD enough that Bazin put up his sword and leaned forward to check the stew. He nodded and turned to his pack.

"I only have these," he said as he excavated two cups and spooned some stew into them.

"Here." Brenith handed over their scavenged cup, and Ro dug out the cup from the mercenary's pack.

Just as in Fisp's hut, they took turns eating out of the limited number of dishes. However, unlike at Fisp's, this time they ate in silence. Ro and the princesses remained together on one side of the fire. Bazin, Dinko, and Porsa occupied the other. It was not a comfortable meal, but as hot food filled their bellies, the tension eased a bit.

"You're right, tachoula root is rather good," Brenith offered after she had finished her portion.

Bazin nodded. "It's a staple in Ka."

"Thank you for the meal," Brenith added, prompting the other girls to add their thanks.

Bazin grunted in surprise. He was not accustomed to such polite manners around a campfire. He glanced around at the faces of the young women.

Months ago, when he had been sent to kill the only female guard on Koric, he'd had very little information on the family. He knew that Queen Abeth of Koric had three daughters. These girls, then, had to be the Princesses of Koric. Porsa's stuttering pulled him out of his thoughts.

"D-do you m-mind if I eat the r-rest?" He gestured toward the pot hopefully.

Bazin shrugged.

"Go ahead, Porsa, you look like you could use it," Leema said with a grin. Dinko perked up at the sound of her voice and crept around the fire to crawl into her lap.

Bazin felt a little betrayed as his drugi defected to get his ears scratched by the youngest princess. He frowned as Dinko's purr rose in volume. Although after watching the girl fuss over the lemur, he really couldn't blame Dinko. If a beautiful girl was fussing over him like that, he'd probably purr that loud too.

He gathered the empty dishes and walked to the river to wash them out. Without even looking, he knew that Ro was watching him.

That girl never stops watching. She would make a great assassin, he snorted.

He wondered if Ro would sleep tonight. Bazin knew that she hadn't slept more than an hour or so last night. He had let her take the first watch because he knew that she hadn't trusted him enough to let him do it. Bazin had dozed lightly and, partway through the night, he had risen to take his turn keeping watch. Ro hadn't really argued when he told her to sleep, but she didn't really listen either. She had curled up by the fire, pretending to sleep so she could keep an eye on him. Her body had finally given in near dawn, and she'd slept.

Her stamina was impressive. The fight with the mercenary had been exhausting enough without adding the bruising ride in the river to it. If he was tired from their little adventure, then she should be falling-down exhausted. She had taken more of a beating than he had, but she stayed vigilant a lot longer than he had expected.

The grass was cold on his bare feet, and his knees became damp as he knelt to wash the dishes. He scowled, wondering how long it would take this new body to toughen up to the standards of his old one. Cold and heat never bothered him before. He had been trained to withstand any weather or uncomfortable conditions without complaint. The Assassin's Court in Zmajev Doseg was not an easy place to survive, but he had. He had also lived to almost forty years, which was a testament to his level of dedication to the training. Most assassins didn't live more than a few years after finishing their training. Now, he was on his second life.

How long will it last?

He shook most of the water off the cups and set them down on the grass, then looked out across the river. There was just the hint of the moon rising over the trees. He listened carefully to the bird calls and the rhythm of the water. Nothing seemed to be out of place. This might be another calm night. Behind him, he could hear the girls murmuring together. Undoubtedly, they were scheming about what to do next. He picked up the dishes and turned back toward the fire.

Bazin moved silently through the grass, watching the figures around the camp as he approached. Porsa was on his back under a blanket with his bare feet sticking out near the fire. His jaw hung slack, and his snoring almost drowned out the girls' whispering. The princesses had gotten dressed again. Their clothing was made from thin enough material that it hadn't taken long for them to dry. The four of them had their heads together, obviously disagreeing with some decision that had been made.

He stopped far enough back that they couldn't see him and waited. He reached out to Dinko, who was sitting on the blanket that the youngest girl had discarded. He closed his eyes and watched through the lemur's eyes.

"We should stay with them," Aritha hissed.

Brenith shook her head. "I don't trust them."

"What if they don't want us to stay?" Leema asked.

"Some protection is better than none," Aritha argued.

"Ro can protect us just fine," Brenith glared at her sister.

"She barely survived those mercenaries!" Aritha snarled, as if Ro wasn't standing there.

Ro dropped her gaze to the ground.

Leema glared at her sister. "She did everything she could! I didn't see you staying to fight. You hid in the trees!"

Aritha crossed her arms in a pout. "At least I didn't fall over a waterfall!"

"What do you think, Ro?" Brenith looked to the guard.

Ro started to open her mouth but caught sight of the lemur watching them out of the corner of her eye. She stared back at the little animal intently, then slowly turned from the other girls to scan the darkness where Bazin had disappeared.

Bazin broke contact with Dinko. He counted to twenty before noisily sauntering back to the fire. He avoided looking at Ro, acting as if he didn't notice her stare. He looked down at Porsa and shook his head as if surprised to find him snoring. He could feel Ro's stare as he placed the pot and cups into his pack.

"I see your things have dried." He turned to the girls, handing over their cups. He gave them what he hoped was a charming smile. He really hadn't seen his new face enough to tell what his expressions would look like.

"Yes, thank you." Brenith took the cups without looking him in the eye.

He couldn't help it. He had to tease them. "So, what are your plans now?" He looked at each of them. The only one that would hold his gaze was Ro. He almost laughed. They were obviously not good at subterfuge.

Ro crossed her arms. "That's our business."

"Ah." Bazin waited, but Ro didn't even blink. Finally, he gave her the barest of nods and turned away. "Time to sleep then."

"I'll take the first watch." Ro watched him grab a blanket.

"Figured you would," Bazin said as he flopped down next to the fire. He unsheathed his sword, settled it next to him, then closed his eyes. He connected to Dinko again and watched Ro watching him.

She turned away and motioned to the other girls to bed down. Aritha and Brenith shared the blanket from the mercenary's pack and were asleep within a few minutes. Ro picked up her new sword and turned to move out of the firelight, but Leema stopped her.

"Ro?" Leema whispered.

"What?"

"Let me watch."

"Aren't you tired?" Ro asked, glancing back at the other two princesses.

"Not as tired as you are." Leema placed a hand on Ro's arm. When Ro didn't answer, she added, "I can tell you are exhausted. I can see it in your face. You need rest, especially after going over that waterfall." Leema glanced over at Bazin. "I'm guessing you didn't sleep last night either."

Ro looked away toward the waterfall, then back to Leema.

"I'll watch for a few hours, then I'll wake you. I promise." Leema glanced again at Bazin. "I have the feeling that you are going to need all the rest you can get."

Ro looked over at Bazin, then at the sleeping sisters, and finally nodded. "Only for a few hours, then wake me."

"I will." Leema smiled.

Ro stared at her intently. "Do you know what to do?"

"Yes. I've seen you do it a hundred times."

"I doubt that."

"Well," Leema shrugged, "a few."

"Do you want the sword?" Ro offered.

"No. I don't know how to use it." Leema shook her head and held up the club. "This is pretty simple to use, though."

Ro smiled and nodded, whispering, "Goodnight, Highness."

"Sleep well, Ro," Leema grinned and disappeared into the darkness near the river.

As Ro returned to the fire, Bazin turned his head away to keep her from seeing his expression, just in case he wasn't as good as he hoped at feigning sleep. Ro eased down onto the ground near the princesses, wincing as bruised flesh contacted the cold, hard ground. She fell asleep with the sword in her hand.

Bazin broke contact with Dinko and started to relax into sleep. Maybe keeping her alive wasn't going to be as hard as he thought.

Parting Ways

BAZIN WOKE LATER THAN he had planned. He had meant to sleep for a few hours and then take over the watch from the youngest girl, Leema. His body had not automatically awakened when he had wanted it to. Sleep was something his new body was a little too accustomed to. Bazin, the assassin, was used to getting very little sleep; Darin, however, had been a soft cobbler's son who was used to sleeping his fill.

As the pink light of dawn slowly changed into the gray light of day, Dinko stomped up onto Bazin's chest and glared down at him.

"Krrr." An image of Ro waking each princess and quietly slipping into the forest filled his mind's eye.

Bazin shoved up onto an elbow and looked around the camp. The girls were gone. Bazin let out an incredulous laugh. "That was unexpected."

"Krrr." Dinko paced in a small circle, staring down at him.

"Don't blame me." Bazin frowned at the furry creature. "You were watching them. You could have woke me up." He stood and stretched. He still ached from his ride down the waterfall, but a full night's sleep had helped ease the pain a little. He glanced at Porsa, who was still snoring contentedly, and shook his head. Bazin picked up his sword and stalked into the trees to see if his snare had caught anything, but it was empty. He glanced down at Dinko. "Wanna find some berries for our breakfast while I get some practice in? I have the feeling I'm going to need it."

"Krrr." Dinko cocked his head.

"It's not my fault I'm out of shape," he snarled at the lemur. "It's not my body!"

"Krrr," Dinko purred before shooting off into the forest.

Bazin returned to camp, stretched a little, then paced around on the grass, letting the cold morning dew soak his feet. Raising his sword, he worked through rudimentary strokes before slowly advancing into more complicated movements. He concentrated on his muscles, pushing through the stiffness. His new body still didn't take to the exercises naturally, but he imagined that would come in time. Bazin had grown up with a sword in his hand. Darin's body had grown up with a hammer and tacks.

A little while later, Dinko reappeared. He ran over Porsa's stomach. startling the skinny apprentice awake.

"Wh-what!" Porsa sat up, looking around in terror until he saw Bazin, then he relaxed a little. He looked down to see Dinko staring up at him.

"Krrr."

"G-good m-morning to you t-too."

"Krrr." Dinko looked back at Bazin and hopped through the grass to the fireside.

"Wh-what did he s-say?"

"He just said good morning," Bazin chuckled as Dinko dropped the little cloth bundle filled with berries next to the smoldering fire.

"N-no he didn't." Porsa griped as he shoved the blanket off and reached for his sandals.

Bazin grinned and walked over to pick up a few berries. "Breakfast?"

Porsa reached for some too, then noticed that the girls were gone.

"Wh-wh-wh—" He gestured wildly toward where the girls should have been.

"Porsa, take a breath," Bazin ordered as he tucked in his shirt and pulled on his jerkin. The leather was a little stiff from its dunking in the river.

"Wh-where d-did they g-go?" Porsa asked after a couple of deep breaths.

"They left before dawn."

He gaped at Bazin. "Wh-why d-didn't you s-stop them?"

"Krrr." Dinko stared at Bazin accusingly while stuffing berries in his mouth.

Bazin glared at the lemur as he laced up his jerkin. "If they don't want to stay with us, there is nothing that will stop them from going." He sat down and dried his feet with the end of the blanket, then pulled on his boots.

"But wh-what about the g-girl?" Porsa scrambled to his feet and rushed over to retrieve his robe.

"We'll keep following them." He kicked some dirt over the ashes of the fire. "Eventually, they will ask for our help, and then we can escort them wherever we want."

"B-but—"

"Don't worry about it, Porsa." Bazin frowned at him as he buckled on his sword harness. "And don't wear that damned robe."

"I-I have to." Porsa looked pained. "It's d-d-dictated by the Order."

"Well, it's dictated by me that you don't. This is dense forest, and we need to move fast and quiet to keep up with those girls. All you do is trip over that damned thing."

"B-but—"

Bazin glared at him. "Pack it, or I'll leave you behind."

Porsa crumpled. He folded the slightly damp robe, rolled up the blankets, and stowed them all in the pack. Bazin returned to the river and filled the water skins. Then, with Porsa carrying the pack, they set off into the woods to find the girls.

Bazin was perfectly confident that they would catch them in only a few hours. They wouldn't be moving very fast with Ro barefoot. Dinko curled around his neck and dozed as they walked. Porsa was a lot less clumsy without the robe, making the trek almost pleasant for once.

"Are you su-sure they c-came this w-way?"

"Yes," Bazin sighed. He had followed their tracks out of the camp, but as the forest floor grew rocky again, the trail became more difficult to follow. He had expected to catch up with them by now. They should have at least heard them. The constant bickering between the sisters had made it easy to follow them before. A prickling doubt nagged at him. Bazin slowed his pace and watched with more deliberation for the tracks, but they had disappeared. He stopped and scanned the trees.

"Are we resting?" Porsa puffed. For once, his stutter didn't come through because he had to breathe in between each word.

"Sure," Bazin said absently as he reached up to scratch Dinko's ears. The lemur stood, arched his back in a stretch, then settled again on Bazin's shoulder.

"Krrr." Dinko swiveled his head around.

"Maybe," Bazin answered, still scanning the trees. He didn't see any movement, but he did catch a glimpse of a large black bird watching him. He stared at it for a long time until it finally flew away. He looked at Dinko.

"Krrr." Dinko stared down at Bazin intently, leapt off his shoulder, and bounded off into the trees.

"Wh-where is he g-going?" Porsa asked, dumping the pack on the ground and collapsing next to it. He rubbed his legs, watching the trees where the lemur had disappeared.

"Foraging," Bazin replied as he pulled out his water skin and drank deeply. He sat down to wait for Dinko, trying to decide where he had lost track of the girls.

"Is it g-getting d-d-dark already?" Porsa asked, looking around. The light streaming through the trees seemed dimmer than when they had left the waterfall.

"Clouds are building," Bazin grunted. Ka was such a wet climate. So unlike his home in Zmajev Province, where everything was mountains and desert. Ka was all moors, forests, and swamps. It's no wonder that the settlements were few and far between. He had heard stories of frightening things that lived in the wilds of Ka, but as many times as he had been here, he had never seen them with his own eyes.

Bazin shifted impatiently. He wanted to get a little farther before the rain started. He also wanted to know exactly how four ignorant, noisy girls without any survival skills had disappeared on him. He could track anything. He thought about what he had learned about Ro. She was smart even without any practical knowledge of the forest. She was also very suspicious. She obviously didn't trust him enough to stay around, but he didn't think she would just take off and hope they didn't follow. She would have planned something.

"Krrr." Dinko appeared at his elbow. An image of all four girls perched in the trees not far behind them shimmered in his mind.

"That little bitch." Bazin shook his head. She had sent the girls into the trees until he and Porsa had passed by; that way, she could follow and watch him instead of being followed. It gave her control of the situation. It was like something he would have done.

"She definitely would make a good assassin," he muttered under his breath, reaching down to scratch Dinko's ears. "Right, let's play it her way."

"Krrr." Dinko launched up onto Bazin's shoulder as he stood.

"Come on, Porsa." Bazin kicked the bottom of Porsa's foot. "Let's get going before the rain gets here."

The apprentice groaned as he staggered to his feet. He hefted the pack and started after Bazin.

Watching the Watcher

Ro shifted carefully. Her bare feet were aching where the rough bark dug into her skin. She could just see Bazin through the trees. He sat drinking water and watching the forest around him. Thankfully, he hadn't looked up when he had passed underneath their hiding place.

She'd had several hours to think after Leema had woken her for her watch shift. Ro had to make a decision about Bazin. The princesses were her responsibility, and regardless of what Aritha thought, it was ultimately up to Ro to decide their course of action. She agreed that there was safety in numbers, but only if you trusted those in the group. And she didn't.

Bazin was friendly enough, and Porsa seemed a bit dim-witted, but there was something about them that sent her instincts blazing. It wasn't like the tingling she experienced when the dragon had attacked, or when the leviathan had appeared. This was more of a gut feeling. She just didn't believe that he was who he said he was. He was hiding something, and she wasn't about to risk the lives of the princesses on his secret.

Sometime near dawn, she had made the decision. She had filled the water skins and quietly packed what she could. She woke Leema first since the youngest princess had adapted the quickest to their situation.

When Ro had explained her plan, Leema had quickly agreed. Ro used the cloth that she had wrapped her foot in as a sash to hold her sword. She would have preferred a shoulder harness, but she had nothing to make one with. Leema woke Brenith, and then Brenith woke Aritha. They had quietly crept into the forest and had made it almost a hundred yards before Aritha started complaining.

"I don't understand why we can't just stay with them."

"I think it's best to listen to Ro," Brenith whispered, trying to hush her sister.

"What does she know?" Aritha still wasn't whispering. Ro stopped and walked back to her.

"Look, Highness, I know that you don't like me, and that is fine, but I am trying to keep you all safe until we reach the Imperial City." Ro glanced around the faces of the princesses. "We don't know anything about Bazin. He may secretly be a slaver for all we know. However, if he *is* going to Ka-Petra, then it gives us a trail to follow. I would rather follow him and learn what he's up to than let him follow us and never know if he is helping or plotting against us. If he is who he says he is, then fine, we'll rejoin him. If not, then we are well away and safe from whatever he was planning. Either way, this is the safest plan. Do you understand?"

Brenith and Leema agreed, and after a moment, Aritha nodded.

"Thank you," Ro said before marching off into the forest again. They had walked about two hours more before Ro found a couple of trees that looked easy enough to climb and were close together.

"Up there." She pointed and then turned to help Brenith and Aritha into the first tree. "Remember to keep as silent as you can until he's past."

Brenith nodded down to her. She was a bright spot of blue in the green leaves of the tree. Aritha was just as obvious in her yellow clothes. Ro hoped that neither Bazin nor Porsa would notice them shining through the foliage. She turned to Leema, but the girl was already climbing the other tree. Ro hurried up after her and settled in to wait.

It wasn't long before Bazin passed under them. She was glad he wasn't that far behind them; her legs were cramping, and her feet hurt. Unfortunately, her relief didn't last long. Bazin stopped not ten feet past their tree and sat down. Porsa collapsed across from him.

She watched him, trying to figure out what he was doing. Surely, he didn't need to take a break this soon after starting out. Nor did he seem the type to rest for Porsa's sake. Leema tapped her shoulder and pointed to the lemur as he disappeared into the trees. Ro nodded. After a few moments, the fuzzy creature returned. She could hear Bazin talking to him, but she couldn't make out the words. Then they were up and moving again.

She waited several minutes, then slowly climbed down from her perch. Her legs burned, and her feet ached. She flexed her toes, trying to ease the pain. Leema joined her on the forest floor, looking toward the path that Bazin had taken. Ro stepped over to the other tree and motioned Brenith down. She helped both princesses out of the tree, reminding them with gestures to keep as quiet as possible before she turned and followed Bazin through the trees.

She wanted to stay far enough back that he wouldn't hear or see them if he turned, but he was moving at a pretty fast pace, so it was difficult to keep track of him. However, as the day moved on, he seemed to slow his pace more and more. He was also making a lot more noise. Ro narrowed her eyes, wondering at the change.

The trees thinned, revealing rock walls rising above both sides of the path they were following. A little after midday, as they picked their way up the little ravine, the sky opened up and drenched the forest. It was a cold rain. As her tunic became soaked, Ro missed Fisp's little hut with its cozy fire. The red fabric of her uniform clung to her like a second skin as the rain became heavier and heavier. The cliff that formed the right side of the ravine became an endless wall of water, and the ground grew treacherous as the carpet of moss was covered in ankle-deep water.

Ro stopped and looked around, squinting in the rain. She couldn't see Bazin or Porsa. She could barely see the shivering princesses behind her. Ro glanced down to see that the water had risen to mid-calf, flowing faster as it rushed downhill past the girls.

"We need to get out of this." She had to shout to be heard over the deluge.

Leema nodded, searching around them for the best place to go. The ground vibrated with a low rumble, making Ro turn and look up the ravine. A flood of water gushed straight toward them.

"Go!" Ro shouted, pushing Leema and Brenith toward the nearest tree.

Aritha turned from side to side in confusion, not knowing where to go as Leema scrambled up into a sturdy oak tree. Ro boosted Brenith up behind her sister just as the gushing flood reached them. It knocked Ro off her feet. She hit the ground hard and struggled to stand up again in the current. Ahead of her, she saw a flash of yellow disappear into the water.

Ro threw herself after Aritha, slipping and floundering her way forward. The slick moss made it almost impossible to get any traction. Finally, she grasped a handful of Aritha's sleeve. Ro grabbed at a branch above her to keep them from washing farther down the ravine. The eldest princess gasped and cried as Ro hauled her to her feet and shoved her up into the tree.

"Climb!" She ordered as she pushed and prodded Aritha higher into the safety of the branches. Aritha clung to the main trunk as Ro pulled herself out of the water. She stuffed her cold-numbed hands under her armpits to try to warm them.

"I want to go home!" Aritha wailed.

Ro gazed up at the sobbing princess. She could see a red tinge in the rivulets of rain and tears pouring down the side of Aritha's face. Forcing her aching body to move, Ro climbed up behind the princess and reached out to move her hair aside. Aritha flinched and continued to sob. There were cuts near her temple, and a goose egg was forming where she had hit her head. Ro sighed. Until the rain and the flood of water stopped, there really wasn't much she could do except wait.

Shelter

IT SEEMED LIKE HOURS had passed before the rain finally subsided into a drizzle, leaving the ravine eerily quiet after the rage of the storm. Ro helped a shivering Aritha climb out of the tree. With an arm around her waist, she guided her back up the path. Brenith and Leema still clung to the trunk of the oak tree, looking as bedraggled as they had just after the shipwreck. Ro helped Aritha over to sit next to her sisters, then turned to look at the flood-ravaged landscape. Loose timber had been carried down by the floodwaters, blocking the path that they had been following. They were going to have to climb up the rocks or over the debris.

Ro turned back to the princesses. None of the three girls looked capable of climbing anything. All three were shivering. Their skin was tinted slightly blue from the cold. Ro glanced down at her feet. She wasn't much better. They needed to get warm, but everything was soaking wet. There was no way she was going to find anything that would be dry enough to burn in a fire. They had to get out of the ravine first. She looked again at the rocks and the pile of timber. There were no good options. Ro felt a sudden sense of defeat.

"R-Ro, w-we need a f-fire." Brenith's teeth chattered.

"I know, but there is no dry wood." Ro rubbed her head, throwing droplets of water in every direction. "We're going to have to climb out of here first."

Leema wobbled to her feet and turned to help Aritha. Ro reached out to help Brenith stand, then led the princesses up to the pile of timber. The drizzle continued as Ro tried to find a way over the debris. Splinters poked the soles of her feet, making the ascent harder than it should have been, but Ro finally found a path stable enough for them to climb over.

It was nearly dark, and they were all shivering violently by the time Ro led the miserable girls out of the ravine. She had hoped to find some sign of civilization, but the only thing she could see was a dark mist crowding close between the trees. Although she wouldn't admit it, she hoped to see Bazin and Porsa somewhere close by, but there was no sign of them.

Ro walked a little farther along the top of the ridge, searching desperately for anything that could help them. Finally, she noticed a massive shadow in the mist. As they stumbled closer, she saw it was a fallen oak tree. Its branches were sprawled out across the ground, forming a natural hollow. Ro bent down and crawled under the main part of the trunk. She gasped as her fingers touched dry grass.

"What's wrong?" Leema left Aritha with Brenith and came forward.

"Nothing." Ro gave a short laugh. "This is all dry."

She pulled away loose grass and sticks, making a little cave big enough for the four of them to sit comfortably. It was full dark by the time they were sitting in the glow of the fire. Ro took their only blanket and hung it over the branches near the opening of their little tree cave to keep the warmth inside. The princesses shed their wet clothes and huddled together for warmth.

Ro finally joined them after taking a look around the tree's perimeter. The fallen giant was thick enough that she couldn't see the glow of the fire from the outside. She ducked under the blanket and held her hands out to the fire, trying to get some feeling back into them. Aritha was asleep with her head on Brenith's lap, and Leema snuggled next to her with her head on Brenith's shoulder.

Brenith gestured toward Ro. "You better get out of the wet clothes."

Ro nodded and pulled off her soaked tunic. Leema gasped.

"By all the gods, Ro!" Brenith cried softly as her eyes traced the network of scratches and bruises that covered the younger girl's torso. "Is that all from the waterfall?"

Ro shrugged and stripped off her pants. Her legs were in no better shape. There were more purple blotches on her skin than there were flesh tones. Ro turned away and wrung the water out of her clothes as best she could.

"Ro," Brenith whispered, "I'm so sorry."

"Why?" Ro added her red to the rainbow of clothes hanging on the tree.

"You have gone through so much for us."

"It's my duty." Ro shrugged again. She was a House Guard. It was her duty to protect the royal family, no matter what it cost her.

"It's more than that to us," Leema added quietly.

Ro didn't know what to say, so she stayed silent.

"Do we have any food left?" Brenith asked after a while.

"Only the mercenary's jerky." Leema pulled the pack over and rationed out what remained of their food.

Ro chewed slowly. "I'm going to have to go hunting before we go any further."

"Too bad we didn't stay by the river. I could have tried fishing." Leema smiled half-heartedly as she finished off her jerky.

Ro nodded, rubbing her feet.

"What do you think happened to Bazin and Porsa?" Brenith asked.

"I don't know. The rain washed away any sign of their tracks."

"Well, I guess we are just back to where we started then." Leema shrugged. "On our own."

"It's not a bad place to be." Ro gave her a half smile.

Brenith sighed. "It's not a good place either."

"I miss Mother," Leema whispered.

"I know." Brenith put her arm around her little sister and hugged her close.

Ro shifted her gaze to the fire. She also missed the queen. And Taus. They were the only family she had ever known. Silently, she prayed they were still alive somewhere.

"I miss her too." Brenith smiled sadly, then gave a little laugh. "I even miss Sebastian."

"Even though he's always rude?" Leema sounded more like a lost child than the tough girl she'd been so far.

Brenith smiled sadly. "Even though he's always rude."

"Get some sleep, Highness. It won't look so bad once you're rested."

"Just as long as you get some sleep too." Brenith gave Ro her best motherly glare.

"I will try." Ro nodded. Truth be told, she desperately wanted sleep. She could curl up and sleep for a week if she had the chance, but there was no way that she could rest until Queen Abeth's daughters were safe.

Slowly, each princess drifted off to join Aritha in sleep. Ro stayed awake, feeding the fire until her clothes were dry. Quietly, she got dressed and, with her sword, crawled out into the damp night. She climbed onto the fallen tree and scanned the darkness around them. All was still quiet. The storm must have sent everything into hiding. Even the feeling that had plagued her on the moors that they were being watched was gone. Perhaps she *could* get some sleep.

Ro climbed down and poked around the tree, looking for more dry wood. She hauled it into their makeshift shelter. She stacked the wood inside and then settled down with her back against the tree and her feet near the blanketed door. The crackle of the fire was joined by the pattering of raindrops. The monotonous sound lulled Ro into a light slumber.

Ro jerked awake, sword in hand. Soft gray light glowed around the edges of the blanket. It sounded like the rain had stopped. Ro looked around. Their little cave was getting lighter as Leema added a few sticks to the fire before turning to retrieve her clothing. Brenith was already dressed and kneeling over Aritha. The eldest princess was still asleep.

Brenith carefully felt the lump on her sister's head and felt her forehead. She glanced over at Leema, then looked to Ro.

"She has a fever."

"Will she be all right?" Leema crowded close to her sister.

"I don't know." Brenith sat back and put an arm around Leema. "I don't have any medicines. We don't even have anything to make a broth."

They both looked to Ro. She stared back. They wanted her to do something, but she didn't know what to do. "Is there a plant, or tree bark, or fungus that you need. I can look for it."

"I know what I would use at home, but... I don't know if it grows here." Brenith shook her head, staring at Aritha. "We never studied herbs from anywhere but Koric."

"Maybe we should just keep walking and find some help." Leema looked at Ro hopefully.

"But what if there isn't anything?" Brenith looked to Ro again. "If we leave here, there may not be another shelter for days. She could get worse."

Leema looked at her sister. "She could get worse if we stay here too."

Ro looked between the two of them, then at Aritha. After a moment, she sighed.

"What if we start with trying to find your plants? I can look for food too. If we can't find anything, then we'll come up with a new plan."

"All right." Brenith nodded. "Leema, stay with Aritha. Ro, come with me." Ro followed Brenith as she crawled out of the tree cave.

For the better part of the morning, Ro followed Brenith around as she looked for the herbs she needed. Ro kept an eye out for danger as well as for food. After hours of searching, the only thing she had found was a small bush with berries like the one that Bazin had raided when they had camped near the waterfall. It would not last them long, but it was better than nothing. Brenith, however, came up empty-handed.

"Nothing looks familiar." She complained as they made their way back to the tree cave.

Ro didn't have a response, so she just kept walking. When they crawled into their temporary home, Leema looked up from where she sat, stroking Aritha's hair.

"She's getting worse."

"I couldn't find any of the herbs I was looking for." Brenith crawled over to check Aritha herself.

Ro held out a handful of berries to Leema.

"I was thinking," Leema said as she chewed.

"Don't talk with your mouth full," Brenith murmured absently.

Leema rolled her eyes but finished chewing before she spoke again. "What if we looked for Bazin?" Leema gazed at Ro. "He knew local plants. He found that toot toot root."

"Tachoula root," Brenith corrected.

"Yeah, that." Leema nodded. "What if we found him? He could help Aritha."

Brenith sat back. "It might be the best idea."

Ro shook her head. "I don't know where he went."

Brenith looked at Ro. "But if we could find him—"

Ro shook her head. "He might not help us."

"He dove into the river to save you," Leema reminded her.

Ro looked down at Aritha. She moaned in her sleep, and her face was pale. "There is no saying he would know how to help her."

"Even if he doesn't, he obviously knows Ka." Brenith turned to fully face Ro. "He could guide us to someone who could help."

"How are we supposed to find him?" Ro glared at Brenith. "We can't all go, and I can't leave you unprotected while I traipse around the woods looking for him."

"I could go." Leema raised her hand.

"No." Brenith shook her head. "I don't want you out there alone."

"Ro could come with me."

"No. That would leave both of your sisters unprotected." Ro cut the air with her hand. "I won't do it."

Leema looked from Ro to Brenith. "Someone has to go."

"It is my duty to protect you, not leave you alone in the forest."

"Ro, please."

"I will not leave you!"

The two women stared at each other for a long time while Aritha moaned.

Finally, Brenith said, "We don't have a choice, Rohamina."

Ro flinched. Brenith had sounded so much like her mother. She sighed and motioned for Leema to follow her outside. "Come on. I need to show you how to defend your sisters."

Ro gave the youngest princess as much knowledge as she could in the little time she had. She showed her the bush with the berries, and she pointed out a few places that could conceal threats. Ro showed her how to use her club in the most effective way before checking on Brenith and Aritha one last time. She fiddled with the pack and checked the water skin, but there was nothing she could do about their dwindling supplies. Looking at the cloudy sky, she guessed it was nearing mid-afternoon. It didn't give her much time to look for Bazin before dark.

"I'll be back as soon as I can," Ro said as she scanned the trees.

"We'll be waiting for you." Leema tried to smile, but Ro could see the wetness creeping into the younger girl's eyes. Ro nodded, then turned and walked away from them with nothing but her sword.

Help

BAZIN SAT ATOP THE rocky wall all day, watching. After Ro had played her little trick of slipping past him by hiding in the trees, he knew she meant to follow them. He also knew that it wouldn't be easy for the city-dwelling girls to track them in the woods. So, he had made a terrible racket as he walked, making their trail almost impossible for Ro to miss.

However, when they had entered that ravine, he knew the day would end badly. The debris scattered across the bed made it clear it had been the site of repeated flooding. The coming storm would turn it into a death trap. As soon as he could, Bazin found a place where they could climb the rock wall without Porsa falling to his death and sent the boy up the rocks. The rain had started just as they had reached the top.

Unfortunately, the girls either didn't see where they had gone or didn't know to look. They had passed right by and continued on up the ravine. There hadn't been time to warn the girls before the rain funneled into a raging river. He stayed watching for them at the precipice as long as he could, but the downpour was too thick, obscuring the ravine below. When the water began pouring over the rocks where he stood, he finally took shelter with Porsa under the trees.

It was a miserable night. The trees only provided so much shelter. He should have packed better. He had been overconfident in his ability to retrieve Ro and bring her back without a lot of fuss. He hadn't really expected that it would take this long. Truly, he had expected her to sit on the seashore and wait for help. It should have been a quick row to shore, load her up, and be back to Jardarwa to sort out this mess, but oh no, she had to be contrary.

"Krrr." Dinko resettled on his shoulder and gazed down at the ravine below. His fur was fluffed out to ward off the chill of the mist.

"I don't know!" Bazin growled. "I've given up trying to predict their behavior."

"Krrr."

"They are definitely women!" Bazin agreed and reached up to scratch Dinko's ears.

"Krrr."

"Well, my soul hasn't returned to Underworld, so I'm pretty sure she's still alive."

"Sh-sh-shouldn't we g-go look for them?" Porsa asked from where he was huddled under a blanket by their fire.

Bazin grunted. He didn't want to climb all the way back down into the mist-shrouded ravine and wander around, trying to think like a pea-brained girl in order to find them.

"Krrr." Dinko tugged on his ear.

"I know I still have to do it," Bazin hissed, "but that doesn't mean I have to like it."

"Sh-should I pack?"

"Nah," Bazin shook his head and watched the mist swirl, "we'll wait until this mist clears a bit. I don't want to fall off the rocks."

"Krrr," Dinko accused.

"I am not deliberately putting it off." Bazin frowned at the furry creature. "I just don't want to deal with Porsa breaking his neck."

"D-did you c-call me?"

"Nope," Bazin said over his shoulder and grinned at Dinko.

The lemur's head swiveled around, and his body tensed as he came into a half-crouch. He stared down into the grayness below. Bazin followed his gaze. The mist swirled a little, giving him a glimpse of red.

"Ro." Bazin watched for the yellow, green, or blue that would signal the other girls, but he couldn't see them.

"Krrr." Dinko shifted back and forth on Bazin's shoulder in agitation.

The mist obscured her for a moment before parting again. She looked like she was searching for something. *Surely, they hadn't been separated.* She searched the ground for a few moments, then turned around and tried another direction. If she was looking for tracks, she wouldn't find any. The rain had washed away everything. The mist drifted in, obscuring his view again. When it cleared, she was gone.

"Damn." Bazin scrambled to his feet, almost knocking Dinko off his shoulder. He squinted, trying to see through the mist. It was getting harder to see as the last rays of daylight dimmed. He had to get her to come back.

"Krrr." Dinko pranced on his shoulder.

There was no way he could climb down fast enough to catch her. He had to make her come back this way on her own. He did the only thing he could think of.

"Porsa!" Bazin shouted, making the apprentice jump.

Porsa's voice cracked. "Wh-what?"

"Isn't that fire ready?" Bazin shouted, still staring down into the mist.

"Wh-what?" Porsa looked at the fire that had been burning brightly all day.

"I'm hungry!" Bazin shouted loud enough that his voice echoed off the rock walls below him. He stared at the swirling mist, praying for a flicker of red.

"You d-don't have to sh-shout!" Porsa shook his head in confusion.

Finally, Bazin saw her. Ro emerged from the trees, looking around. She hadn't seen him yet.

"Porsa!" Bazin shouted again, watching Ro.

"What!" yelped Porsa, completely confused as to why Bazin kept yelling his name.

Ro, tracing the echo, finally looked up. She glanced around, then glared at him again. "You knew it would flood," she shouted.

"Yes," Bazin shouted and grinned. "Smart girl," he muttered to Dinko.

"Krrr."

"Come on up." Bazin motioned to her.

"Why don't you come down?" she shouted as the mist swirled between them.

"It's going to rain again, and I don't want to be down there." Bazin shrugged.

She remained silent for a long time. He could almost see the defiant expression on her face.

"I need your help," she yelled.

Bazin felt Porsa move up beside him to listen.

"Really?" Bazin couldn't help himself; he indulged his petty side. "Seems to me, you didn't want my help the way you crept off into the night."

"Aritha is sick." He was surprised that Ro didn't rise to the bait. "Brenith and Leema think that you can help her."

"But not you," Bazin muttered under his breath. She was so stubborn. "Where are they?"

Ro pointed. "At the top of the ravine."

Bazin looked in the direction that she was pointing. It was nearly sunset, and the dark clouds were making night come early. Rain would be falling soon, and the landscape would be flooded once more.

"How far?"

"Couple of hours."

"We might make it before the rain." Bazin looked at the clouds again. He didn't really care what happened to the other girls. His only concern was Ro.

"If we h-help them m-maybe they'll st-stay w-w-with us," Porsa said quietly.

"Hmm," Bazin grunted. "All right. Pack up."

Porsa hurried to comply.

"We're coming," he shouted, waving to Ro. The girl nodded and sat down under the nearest tree to wait. Dinko hopped off of Bazin's shoulder and disappeared over the rocky cliff.

"Porsa, you'll follow me down," Bazin grumbled as he helped to douse the fire. "At least that way, I can tell you where to put those big feet of yours."

Porsa nodded miserably as he picked up their pack.

"I'll carry it down." Bazin took the pack from him and slipped it onto his back. "I don't want you losing your balance and falling on me."

Slowly, they made their way down the rock wall. Surprisingly, Porsa only slipped once but regained his footing relatively quickly. Once they reached the bottom, Bazin returned the pack to him.

Ro was still sitting under the tree. Dinko sat next to her ankles with his tail curled over his feet. "Krrr."

Bazin obediently looked to Ro's feet. They were tinged slightly blue from the cold and wet.

"I'm surprised you're not the sick one." He looked up into her eyes and was startled to find their icy blue color shining with defiance.

"I'm fine." Despite her words, Ro stood slowly as if her aches and exhaustion were getting the best of her. "The girls are up there." She pointed toward a pile of timber that blocked the ravine.

The light was fading fast, and thunder rumbled in the distance. Ro kept up a steady but slow pace. Bazin followed her, frowning. He got the impression that she was moving on will power alone. He knew that she was wearing down. She couldn't keep up this pace forever. Stamina could only keep you going for so long.

As they neared the ridge marking the top of the ravine, Ro slowed and then stopped. Bazin froze, and Dinko pricked his ears forward. The forest was dead silent except for the thunder. He scanned the trees as they swayed slowly in the breeze.

He felt nothing. No eyes watching. No presence in the darkness, but something was still wrong.

Ro slipped her sword out and cautiously moved toward a fallen tree. Bazin followed her up to what looked like a cave. The ground around it was torn up, and the remains of a fire were scattered as if something had been dragged through it.

"They're gone!" Ro gasped as she scrambled into what had been their shelter. She spun around and searched the ground, but it was getting too dark to see.

Bazin spun Porsa around and dug in the pack for his oil. He grabbed a thick branch that was broken and split at the end. He knelt to stuff it with dry grass. Quickly, he poured oil on the grass and then struck his flint to it. The makeshift torch blazed brightly for a moment. He handed the torch to Porsa and repacked his oil. Ro snatched the torch from Porsa and swung it back and forth near the ground.

"The tracks go that way." She pointed as Bazin crouched down to examine them.

"It wasn't a large group." Bazin reached out to touch the footprints.

"Krrr." Dinko pranced over the track and looked up at Bazin.

"Damn." He stared into the darkness.

"What?" Ro demanded.

"I really did not want to run across them."

"Who?"

"Wenzake." Bazin sighed as he stood. "Cannibals."

Ro's eyes grew huge. She whipped her head around and stared off into the darkness.

"C-c-c-c—" Porsa grabbed Bazin's arm.

Ro didn't wait for Porsa to get his words out. "We have to go after them."

"No way." Bazin shook off Porsa's hand. "They're as good as dead already."

"No." Ro shook her head. "I won't accept that."

"Well, you better." Bazin snorted.

"I'm going." Ro gazed at him. "With or without you."

"No, you're not!"

She turned and started following the tracks. "I won't let them die."

"I am not going to get myself skinned alive to save those spoiled brats!" Bazin stepped in front of her and grabbed the torch.

"Then don't," she snarled and stepped around him, stalking off into the darkness.

"Krrr." Dinko followed her a few steps, then looked back at Bazin.

"Son of a bloody bitch!" Bazin yelled after her, "You're gonna get yourself killed!"

When Ro didn't respond or slow down, Bazin snarled a few more curses and then stomped after her.

Porsa stood frozen, afraid to go toward the cannibals but afraid to be left behind in the darkness. Finally, he hurried after them.

Rescue

THE WIND PICKED UP as the storm arrived. Bazin's torch spluttered and hissed as the rain began. He elbowed his way around Ro to take the lead and light the way. The trees began to thin, and he knew that they would have to ditch the light soon. Lightning flashed across the sky, illuminating the forest and something ahead. Bazin stopped and waited for another flash. The sky lit up, and he saw it again. He mashed the torch into the ground to douse it, then pulled Ro and Porsa down to crouch behind the nearest tree.

"W-why d-d-did—" Porsa began, but Bazin cut him off.

"There's a village."

"C-c-c—"

"Yes, it's the cannibals."

The poor boy was shaking in fear. Bazin looked to Ro. "You sure you want to do this?"

Ro shrugged, trying to see the village. "You can stay here if you're afraid."

"Afraid has nothing to do with it. I just have no desire to be strung up and flayed."

"F-flayed?" Porsa whispered hoarsely.

"Yeah, see Wenzake don't just kill you and cook you. They string you up and flay bits of your skin off, then carve chunks out of you. It's part of a great big ceremonial feast where you get to watch them eat you bit by bit."

Porsa tugged Bazin back the way they'd come. "M-maybe w-we should g-go."

"We will. Right after I get them out." Ro's voice was quiet but steadier than he expected.

"You're really stubborn, you know that?"

"Krrr." Dinko launched off of Bazin's shoulder and headed for the village.

"Where's he going?" Ro whispered.

"To take a look." Bazin pulled them off into the trees. He eyed Porsa, wondering if the apprentice would be able to keep up once the fighting started. Then he looked at Ro's bare feet and wondered the same thing.

"This is suicide," he muttered.

"I didn't ask you to come," Ro hissed, wiping the rain from her face.

"No, you didn't," Bazin grumbled, then lapsed into silence as Dinko brushed against his thoughts. He closed his eyes, and the image of the village appeared in his mind. He described the images as he saw them.

"Village is sitting on a lake. There are seven wooden huts on stilts, presumably to avoid the flooding from the lake. They're connected by rope bridges. Those will make it difficult to sneak in quietly, but maybe the storm will cover the noise. Several torches are burning at intervals around the village."

"You see what he sees?" Ro asked.

"Hmm." Bazin barely answered. He was too busy concentrating on Dinko's progress. The image changed as Dinko crept closer. It was quiet. The rain must have driven the Wenzake inside. Dinko darted from hut to hut until he found the one that contained the three girls. Bazin concentrated on the route that Dinko used as he left them.

"All right," Bazin whispered. "Dinko's found them."

"Then let's go." Ro moved to stand.

"Wait." Bazin grabbed her arm and pulled her back down beside him. Her arm was thinner than he expected. "We need to find a way out of the village first. Once we steal their dinner, they're not going to be happy. We'll need an escape route."

Ro nodded and brushed the water from her face. Bazin closed his eyes to reconnect with Dinko.

"If we are really lucky, this storm will keep them inside. We can sneak in, grab the girls, and be gone without a fight," he muttered. "But once we leave, there will be no stopping. Even if we have to run all night. If we stop, they'll catch us."

"I understand," Ro sighed, but said no more.

"Dinko's found a trail leading east around the lake." Bazin reached back and drew his sword quietly. "There's no cover, though." He opened his eyes and looked at Ro.

She nodded and drew her sword.

"Follow me and keep quiet." He glanced at Porsa. "I mean it. Quiet. Or it'll be our deaths."

Porsa didn't bother trying to speak. He just nodded bleakly.

Bazin stepped out from the shelter of the tree and crept forward. Ro followed a few steps behind him. They moved slowly, trying to keep to the remaining trees. The lightning increased, making it easier to see their way. Suddenly, Bazin felt Ro grab his arm.

She pulled him back a step and pointed to a clump of bushes. As the lightning flashed again, he saw one of the Wenzake standing guard. Bazin motioned for Ro and Porsa to wait. He crept back the way they had come. He slowly made his way around behind the sentry, pulling his dagger out. He waited for the lightning to flash, then stepped forward and slit the man's throat. He lowered him to the ground quietly and pushed his body under the bushes to delay discovery.

Bazin motioned for Ro to move forward. Once again, they crept toward the village. Bazin led them past the first rope bridge that served as the main entrance to the village from the forest side. The rain hammered on the wooden planks above them as they slowly made their way under the village. Light from the torches flickered, sending shadows dancing through the cracks in the walkways above them.

The tiny rocks that made up the beach crunched under each step. He glanced back at Ro. She grimaced as the rocks bit into the soles of her feet, but she didn't stop moving. Bazin continued forward but froze when he heard hurried footsteps approaching. Rain poured down through the cracks as the three of them looked up. Someone hurried by overhead. Bazin prayed they were just trying to get out of the rain.

Silence returned, and Bazin led them out into the water under the huts. When Dinko swung down from one of the walkways and landed on Bazin's shoulder, he turned to Ro and pointed up. They were directly under where the girls were being kept. He pointed to himself and then to the hut above. Then he pointed to Porsa and Ro and gestured for them to stay put. Ro shook her head and gestured that she would go up. He pointed to her red shirt and, with hand signs, made it clear that she would be easy to spot in her bright colors. Finally, she frowned at him but nodded. He motioned for her to give him a boost.

She handed her sword to Porsa, then cupped her hands, waiting. He stepped up on her folded hands, grabbed the edge of the walkway, and pulled himself up. Dinko slithered up onto the planks. Hanging still for a moment, Bazin checked for Wenzake before quietly climbing the rest of the way up.

Slowly, he crept forward, keeping to the shadows as much as possible. As he moved to the door of the hut, the boards creaked under him. He froze, waiting to see if he'd been heard. When nothing moved, he stepped closer to the door.

He lifted the hook holding the door shut and eased it open. Dinko peeked around the edge and then disappeared inside, assuring him it was safe. Bazin slipped in after him and closed the door.

The room was dark, but he could hear the girls breathing near the middle of the room. He stepped forward, and the floor creaked loudly.

"Who's there?" Brenith gasped.

"Shh!" Bazin hurried forward as they started to shift around.

"Krrr." Dinko's little claws made a ticking sound as he did a nervous little dance.

"Bazin?" Leema whispered.

"Yes. Be quiet." The room lit up for a moment as lightning blazed across the sky. He could see Aritha huddled beside Brenith. Leema was tied on the other side of the pole in the center of the room. He felt around for the ropes tying their hands. Working quickly, he sliced through their bonds.

"Aritha." Brenith grabbed his arm.

Bazin sighed but bent to pick up the limp sister. Aritha moaned as she roused, and he shushed her.

"Now move! And stay quiet." He led them to the door. Slowly, he opened it a crack to let Dinko out.

"Krrr." Came the all clear. He opened the door farther and crept out, half-carrying Aritha. He knelt at the edge of the planks and lowered her down to Ro, then motioned Brenith and Leema to climb down. He heard faint splashes as they landed in the water. Bazin swung over the side of the walkway and dropped silently to the ground.

"Krrr!" Dinko chittered a warning as he leapt from the boards above them to land on Bazin's shoulder just as Ro grabbed his arm and pointed toward the bridge.

The Wenzake were coming.

"Damn," he swore under his breath.

They could either run or try to sneak away. Neither option held good odds. He glanced at the girls. Ro had one hand on Leema, but her attention was focused on the Wenzake who were milling around above them. Brenith was trying to hold Aritha up and keep her from making a sound. Porsa just stared at Bazin. Ro looked at Bazin and pointed to the east.

Good, he nodded, *she's smart enough to want to try a quiet retreat.*

The arguing from the Wenzake covered some of the noise they were making as their retreat disturbed the water and rocks. Ro led them toward the end of the village, staying under the huts as much as possible. Shouts of alarm confirmed that the tribesmen had just realized their dinner was gone.

We are running out of time, Bazin thought. He knew the chances of getting spotted were growing exponentially with every minute.

They paused under the last hut, and another cry went up as the Wenzake found their dead sentry.

Ro looked back at Bazin for a moment, then whispered to Brenith and Leema, "We have to run now. No stopping."

Escape

BAZIN WATCHED THE TERRIFIED girls nod in agreement, putting their complete trust in Ro. It surprised him. He expected them to be more hysterical.

"Follow Dinko," Bazin whispered. "He'll lead us somewhere safe."

Dinko bounded out from under the hut. Porsa shot out after the lemur. Leema and Brenith carried Aritha between them as they followed as quickly as they could. Ro and Bazin took up rear guard positions. They had only made it a few yards when lightning flashed, illuminating the entire lake. Shouts from the Wenzake sounded as their luck finally deserted them. They had been spotted.

The rocks of the beach gave way to slick mud as they ran after Dinko. The dark and the rain made it nearly impossible to see the little lemur. Bazin splashed and slipped in the slimy mud. He glanced over his shoulder to see how close the pursuers were. There were eight Wenzake, and they were gaining. He would prefer to get them into the trees and pick them off one by one, but they would never make it to the trees before the Wenzake caught them. They would have to stand and fight.

"Keep going!" Bazin shouted to the others as he turned to fight. Ro stayed with him. "What are you doing?"

Ro said nothing. She just drew her sword and took up a ready stance beside him.

"Do you have a death wish or something?" He snarled as the first Wenzake warrior arrived. He cut down the angry cannibal quickly.

Then there was no time for conversation as the rest of the Wenzake caught up. Lightning flashed, and thunder rumbled as Bazin fought for his life. He could hear the clang of Ro's steel as she fought only a few feet away from him, but he couldn't afford to look her way. He only hoped that her sword skills had improved since the day she'd killed him.

He sliced and stabbed anything within reach. Two more warriors went down under his blade before the first Wenzake short spear found its mark in his side. He grunted with pain but fought on. He could feel his strength oozing out of the wound near his hip.

Ro snarled to his left, followed by a grunt from her enemy. His muscles were tiring. His body was not up to this level of fighting yet. As he turned to meet another attack, his foot slipped in the mud. The Wenzake's spear that had been aimed at his head shot past his face, slicing his cheek just as another came from the side, stabbing his right leg just above his knee. In that moment, he knew they weren't going to win. It was only a matter of time, but he would go down.

A screeching snarl sounded behind him, and the Wenzake in front of him flinched. A rock flew past Bazin's head and smacked the warrior right in the forehead. He grabbed his head and collapsed to his knees. Bazin took the opportunity and lunged at the warrior to his right, gutting him before turning to meet the next threat.

Behind him, Leema screeched again, and another rock flew past him. In moments, Bazin was in a storm of projectiles. A few of Leema's rocks hit him in the back and arms.

"Watch it!" He snarled over his shoulder.

Wenzake warriors were trying to simultaneously dodge the rocks and press their attack. Ro and Bazin seized their advantage and fought harder. Lightning flashed, showing the fight was tipping in their favor. After what seemed like years to his aching muscles, the last warrior lay bleeding in the mud at his feet.

Ro stood to his left with her hands braced on her knees and her sword tip resting in the mud.

"You all right?"

She nodded at him, blinking the rain from her eyes and panting. He couldn't tell in the dark how many injuries she had.

"We need to go." His breath came in puffs as he put a hand on his hip and winced.

Ro nodded and staggered toward Leema. She patted the girl on the shoulder as she passed. Leema waited for Bazin before turning to follow Ro.

Bazin nodded to her as he limped by. They would never have survived if she hadn't come back to help with her rocks.

"Thank you," Leema kept pace with him as they caught up to where Ro was waiting, "for coming to get us."

Bazin grunted. He was too focused on ignoring the pain in his hip to spare energy for conversation.

"I don't know where to go," Ro said when they joined her.

Leema led them through the darkness as the rain and lightning continued. They hadn't made it very far when they heard Dinko chittering. Brenith and Porsa were crouched behind a copse of bushes, trying to shelter Aritha from the rain.

Bazin looked down at the lemur. "I thought I said no stopping."

"Krrr."

"Let's go." Ro staggered forward and tried to help Brenith lift Aritha but nearly fell instead.

Bazin pressed against the wound on his hip and felt the hot blood oozing out around his fingers as he waited for the girls to get Aritha moving. They were going to have to stop sooner than he wanted to. Sooner than it was safe. They may have left some of the Wenzake warriors dead or injured, but the others would eventually come looking for vengeance.

"Krrr." Dinko peered at him with concern.

"I'll live," Bazin growled. "We need shelter."

"Krrr." The lemur sprang forward, then returned a few moments later.

"We're coming." Leema sighed at the lemur's impatience.

They tried to keep up a quick pace, but as the night wore on, they moved slower and slower. Bazin couldn't seem to walk in a straight line, and he felt dizzy. He repeatedly glanced behind them, just waiting for more Wenzake to appear. But so far, there was no sign of them. Hours wore on, and the rain slowed to a drizzle. The landscape got brighter as dawn tried to push through the clouds. They had made it most of the way around the lake. Ahead of them lay another stretch of forest.

They lost sight of Dinko as he disappeared into the trees. Bazin tripped and landed hard on his knees with a grunt. Ro looked back at him and frowned. She staggered back to where he knelt, huffing and puffing. He looked up at her and blinked as his vision blurred. Ro sighed and leaned down to help him up. Normally, he would never have accepted help, but blood loss does funny things to a man. She pulled his arm over her shoulders to help him, and once again, he was amazed at how thin she was.

"Krrr!" Dinko shot out of the trees and leapt onto Leema's shoulder.

"Shelter," Bazin translated.

Field Medicine

RO TRIED TO STEADY Bazin as they staggered the last few yards to the tree line. He was heavy, and she was exhausted. She couldn't remember the last time she had eaten or even slept.

"Wait." Bazin stumbled to a stop, staring at the ground and blinking to clear his vision. He pointed to a patch of weeds at his feet. "Pick that."

When Ro bent to retrieve the plant, she noticed his leg was covered in blood. She glanced back at his face to see it etched in pain. Under the dirt and blood, he was very pale, and it wasn't just from the cold.

"Listen carefully," Bazin panted as they started walking again. "Find more of that plant. Boil the leaves and make a poultice." He blinked again and rubbed his eyes. "It'll pull infections out and help with pain."

He staggered a few more steps, leaning more and more on Ro as they went. Dinko bounced up and down in front of a dark patch in the forest next to a fallen tree.

"It's a cave," Brenith said as she hauled Aritha closer. "Porsa, clear away those branches."

"Put... on wound before... you close it," Bazin hissed. "Hide... tracks..."

Ro could hardly hear him. Ro stopped just outside the cave's entrance and waited for the way to be cleared. Bazin was leaning almost all of his weight on her now.

"Don't pass out on me," she muttered, breathing hard with the effort of holding him upright.

"I don't think I have a choi..." He hissed as his legs gave out and he dropped to the ground, taking her with him.

"Bazin?" Ro snarled as she extricated herself, but he was out cold. Panting, Ro stayed on her knees beside him because she was too tired to stand up again.

Ro watched as Leema helped Porsa and Brenith move Aritha inside. Leema and Porsa came out to lift Bazin and carry him in too. Brenith returned for Ro.

"Here." She held the plant out to Brenith. "Bazin said to boil the leaves for a poultice to draw out infections and help with the pain. Said to put it on before closing the wounds."

Brenith took the plant and looked at it closely, then nodded.

"He has a bad gash on his hip and another on his knee. And his face," Ro continued in a monotone. She was too tired for anything else.

"Are you hurt?" Brenith asked, looking her over.

"A few scratches, I think. I'm just really tired. The Wenzake..." Ro began, gesturing back the way they'd come.

Brenith shook her head. "We've left them behind."

"Bazin said to hide our tracks."

"Go inside and rest. I'll get more of this," Brenith said, holding up the weed. "Leema and Porsa can take care of our tracks."

Ro nodded and staggered forward. She dropped to the ground right inside the mouth of the cave. Leema hastily gathered a pile of sticks for a fire, and Porsa began digging through Bazin's pack. Whatever supplies Bazin and Porsa had were all that were left now. The mercenary's pack and their meager supplies from Fisp were gone, left behind in the Wenzake village.

As the fire's glow filled the little cave, she looked around. A jumble of boulders and packed dirt formed the walls and roof of the cave. A fallen tree covered most of the cave's mouth, and a tangle of vines spilled over the rest of the opening like a curtain, obscuring the cave's entrance.

Her gaze fell to Bazin and Aritha, both were unconscious. She could forgive Bazin for passing out. He had lost a lot of blood, but not Aritha. She just had a fever. Ro sneered at her weakness but then felt guilty for thinking of Abeth's daughter in such a way.

"Here." Leema shoved the water skin under Ro's nose. "Drink."

Ro nodded and gulped down the cold water.

"We don't have much for food. Porsa still has some jerky, but it is only enough for right now." Leema sighed. Ro was trying to listen, but her eyes were closing before she could respond. She barely heard Leema say, "I'll see if I can catch something with Bazin's snare."

Something cold was touching her face.

Ro jerked awake and winced. Her whole body felt like a single agonizing bruise. Leema knelt in front of her... still or again? The youngest princess dabbed at a cut on Ro's face with a cold cloth. Ro blinked at the water as it trickled into her eye.

"How long?" Ro rasped out. She felt so weak.

"A few hours," Leema answered quietly.

Ro looked out through the mouth of the cave. Dim gray light seeped in here and there between the tree branches and vines. A steady rain was falling. "Did you cover our tracks?"

"We tried to." Leema shrugged. "I'm sure the rain will do the rest. I haven't had a chance to check you for other wounds." Leema dabbed at the cut above Ro's eye again. "Are you hurt anywhere else?"

"I don't know." Last night, she had been running on fear. She hadn't felt a thing except the intense tingling that always warned her of danger.

"Bazin is in pretty bad shape." Leema nodded toward the back of the cave. "We're gonna need your help."

Ro tried to sit up but groaned.

"Are you all right?" Leema laid a hand on Ro's arm.

Ro started to shrug but winced and stopped halfway through. "I'll live."

Leema nodded but didn't say anything as Ro crawled farther into the cave. Bazin's pot was sitting near the fire. The steam curling out of it let off a pungent odor. Next to it, sitting in the fire, was a knife. Its blade glowed orange. Across the fire, Ro could see Aritha wrapped in one of Bazin's blankets.

Brenith looked up as Ro stopped beside her. "Are you all right?"

Ro gave her a half-hearted smile.

"Here." Brenith reached behind her, then turned back to hand Ro a piece of jerky. "That's the last of our food."

Ro tried to give it back. "Then you eat it."

"I've already had mine." Brenith smiled sadly and looked down at Bazin, tucking the blanket around him a little more.

He was too still to be merely sleeping. A green glob covered the cut on his cheek. Bruises covered the skin of his chest and arms. His hip and leg were outside the blanket, giving access to his wounds. Porsa poked at a glob of green goo on Bazin's hip. Blood trickled out from under the blob. Another green glob was just above his knee.

"We are going to have to seal the wounds on his hip and leg." Brenith's voice shook a little.

Ro glanced back at the knife in the fire as Brenith reached out with a wet cloth and cleaned away the green goo from above Bazin's knee.

"It won't stop bleeding." She wiped away the poultice from his hip, letting a fresh spout of blood loose.

Ro watched the blood ooze out. Suddenly, she was back in the queen's chamber, watching the assassin bleed to death at her feet. Why had she thought of that now? She shook her head and tried to concentrate on what Brenith was saying.

"I can't tell if there is damage to the muscle. I can't... I have nothing to sew it up with. I don't know what else to do. All I can do is seal it and hope that it heals."

"What do you need me to do?" Ro asked, dragging her eyes from the red blotch.

"I'll need you, Leema, and Porsa to hold him while I cauterize." Brenith shuddered. "If one of you holds his legs and the others his arms, I should be able to do it quickly."

"All right." Ro swallowed and looked at Porsa. "Which end do you want?"

The apprentice looked at Bazin, then immediately said, "L-legs."

"It's going to hurt a lot, so he may come to." Brenith crawled over to the fire. Using a bit of cloth to shield her hand from the heat, she picked up the knife. "You might want to put your full weight on him."

Porsa turned and knelt on Bazin's shins, bracing his hands just above his knees.

"Hold here." Brenith moved his hands to just below Bazin's knees. "I can get both wounds at once then. All right, Ro, take this side. Leema, hold his arm on that side."

Leema knelt at his head and leaned on his right arm. Ro stopped watching Brenith and turned her attention to Bazin's face. If he came awake, she wanted a little warning. She took a few moments to study him. His beard had grown shaggy. New bruises from the waterfall overlapped some old ones. His eagerness to jump into the river after her and to help rescue the princesses confused her. He looked so much younger than he acted. His confidence and knowledge seemed to belong to an older man, not to a youth only a couple of years older than she was.

"Ready?" Brenith warned but didn't wait for an answer. The sound of sizzling and the smell of burning flesh filled the tiny space. Bazin's body thrashed as he cried out in pain, nearly throwing Porsa off his legs.

"Hold him!" Brenith gasped as a second sizzling sound filled the cave.

Ro scrambled to hold him down. Bazin's eyes popped open, filled with delirious rage. His pain-fueled strength was no match for her weight. He ripped out of Leema's grasp with a roar and took a swing at Ro. His fist connected with her jaw, snapping her head back. She was out cold before the pain even registered.

Respite

"COULDN'T WAIT TO GET my clothes off, huh?" Bazin murmured to the woman bending over him. He wasn't sure who she was, but he was naked and a woman seemed like a good idea at the moment.

"Hardly." Brenith smiled down at him.

Bazin sucked in through his teeth as she probed the tender area around his hip, reminding him exactly who she was and what had happened. His hand shot out and grabbed her. "I wish you'd stop that!"

"I'm just checking." Brenith gently loosened his iron grip from around her wrist. "I'm sorry, Bazin, but I had nothing to stitch them up with, so we had to cauterize your wounds."

"Bad?" Fire burned along his leg.

"You wouldn't stop bleeding." Brenith sat back on her heels and pulled the blanket back over his leg. "The one just above your knee was small but deep. The one by your hip was a bad slice." She shuddered as she spoke. "I used the plant you gave Ro, so I hope there won't be any infection."

"It's a painkiller too." Bazin tried to shift his leg but winced, and that hurt his cheek.

"I know. I have some more brewing." Brenith leaned forward and felt his forehead. "You've managed to avoid a fever so far."

She bent close to examine his cheek. He stared up into her face. Brenith was a beautiful woman. The braids of her dark red hair were a bit frazzled, her face was covered in dirt, and her gown was barely blue anymore. She had a few bruises and her lip was split, but she remained regal and graceful, every bit a princess.

He licked his parched lips. "Is there water?"

"Yes." She held the skin for him to drink.

"The others?"

"Aritha is still asleep." Brenith sat back and folded her hands in her lap. "Her fever is almost gone. I think she is weak from a lack of food. Ro took Leema and Porsa foraging."

"How long have we been here?" Bazin asked, glancing around. Roots dangled from the ceiling and poked through the dirt walls.

She sighed. "This is our second day in this cave."

"Isn't anyone watching for the Wenzake?" Bazin tried to sit up. They couldn't just sit here so close to the cannibals' village. "Where's my sword?"

"Rest easy." Brenith pushed against his chest, trying to get him to lie back down. "The rain has washed away our tracks."

Bazin closed his eyes and connected to Dinko. He was sitting in a tree watching the lake.

"Dinko is watching."

"Leema thought that's what he was doing." She smiled and shook her head. "I never... he is a remarkable animal."

"Yes, he is." He shifted and gritted his teeth against the pain in his leg as he felt his hip.

"Where did you get him?" she asked as she turned to the fire.

"I didn't." Bazin groaned, hating his weakness. "He chose me."

"Then I think you are both lucky."

"Why is that?" Bazin watched her as she leaned over the fire to check on the boiling pot.

"You just are." Brenith shrugged, then turned to Aritha.

Bazin watched as she checked her sister and tucked the blanket around her.

"When the flood came down the valley, she slipped and fell." Brenith watched her sister. "She hit her head. Then, after we made it out of the valley, she was on fire. We sent Ro to find you when I couldn't find anything to help her fever. It was after dark when the Wenzake came."

He wasn't sure why she was telling him all this, but he let her talk. Brenith sat back and drew her knees up, wrapping her arms around them. She stared at her sister, then smiled. "Leema was so fierce. Her and that ridiculous club she made."

Bazin's eyebrows rose at that. *The littlest princess made that club?*

"We were completely defenseless. I should never have sent Ro away." She turned and looked at Bazin, "She didn't want to go, but I made her."

"It's done now." Comforting distraught women was not really his strong suit. He wasn't even sure why he was trying.

"Thank you for coming to get us." She smiled sadly. "I'm sure that it wasn't your first choice and now look at you."

Bazin stared back at her. He didn't know what to say. He couldn't very well tell her that he had only gone to keep Ro alive. Fortunately, he was saved from answering by a rustling at the cave's entrance. Pain radiated from his hip as he groped around, trying to find his sword, but his searching hands felt nothing.

"Where's my sword?" he hissed at Brenith, but she ignored him.

The branches moved aside to reveal Porsa with an armful of wood. He tripped as he stepped over the foliage, dropping most of his burden.

"Porsa," Leema sighed loudly from behind him.

Bazin smirked. Her tone was the same one that kept coming out of his own mouth whenever he dealt with the clumsy boy.

"You're awake!" The youngest princess caught sight of him and smiled. She hopped lithely over Porsa's mess and landed on her knees between him and the fire. She reached out and poked his cheek, peering at the cut.

"Ow."

She wasn't nearly as gentle as her sister, but still, he could get used to all this female attention.

"Where's Ro?" Brenith glanced at the cave entrance.

Her question brought Bazin to attention. *She dies, I die.* He struggled to sit up again, but this time Leema pushed him back.

"I'm here," Ro said quietly as she stepped into the gloom.

Bazin strained to see around Leema. Ro was holding the tails of her shirt up in front of her as a basket. She crouched slowly until she was kneeling by the fire and lowered her shirt, letting a load of berries spill onto the dirt. She was wearing his sword harness, and that irked him. His jaw clenched involuntarily as he saw the molted color of her swollen jaw.

"What happened to your face?" he snapped.

"You punched me."

They glared at each other. "I don't remember that."

Leema interrupted, "What does that toot toot root look like?"

"What?" Bazin blinked in confusion.

"Tachoula root," Brenith corrected.

"Oh, it's about this big..." Bazin measured out with his hands. "Has broad leaves, dark green with five points."

"Right." Leema shot up and was out of the cave before he could say another word.

"Wait!" he called, but she was gone. He lowered himself back down with a groan and closed his eyes to make contact with Dinko. Leema would be searching for ages without help. He didn't think about how involved he was getting with these girls. He just thought about how hungry he was.

Porsa finished stacking his kindling, then reached for some berries.

"Here." Brenith placed a few of the berries that Ro had found into Bazin's hand, then turned away to try and get Aritha to eat.

Ro sat down across the fire from him and started to rub her feet. He could tell they were blue from the cold, even through the caked-on mud.

"You borrowed my sword but not my boots?"

She didn't even look at him. "I didn't borrow your sword, only your harness."

"You're going to be as sick as that one," he nodded toward Aritha, "if you don't keep your feet warmer."

Ro grunted, "I'm fine."

“If anything happens to you—”

“I said, I’m fine!” she snarled, turning her icy blue eyes on him. A second later, she shoved to her feet and left the cave.

“Don’t be offended, Bazin,” Brenith said quietly. “Ro is just frustrated.”

“I know the feeling.” He shook his head. “Where’re my clothes?”

A Stroll in the Rain

Another day passed. The rain continued to fall, making their little cave damp and muddy. In Ro's opinion, it was a small price to pay. They needed time to rest, and the rain would continue to hide their tracks from the Wenzake.

Aritha had recovered enough to complain incessantly about the dirt. And the cold. And the damp. Every time Leema came in from foraging with Dinko, Aritha complained about the draft.

"D-d-do y-you th-think i-it'll s-stop r-raining s-soon?" Porsa asked Brenith for the hundredth time, making her sigh. His stutter seemed to get worse the longer they huddled in the cave.

Ro knew it wasn't his fault that he had a stutter, but she still wanted to shake him until he stopped. And she wasn't the only one. Ro noticed Bazin watching Porsa with narrowed eyes. His hand crushed a handful of dirt beside his leg. His jaw clenched and unclenched. Finally, he grabbed his harness and limped his way to the front of the cave.

"Where are you going?"

He didn't answer, so Ro waited until he had disappeared through the makeshift foliage door and then followed him. The drizzle felt cold against her face as she emerged from the warmth of the cave. She winced as the freezing mud covered her bare feet. Carefully, she picked her way into the forest to look for Bazin.

A bird squawked in a nearby tree. Ro turned to find it. It was a large black bird with a harness. Bazin stood looking up at it. He stepped closer, staring hard at the bird just as Dinko shot out of the undergrowth. The bird squawked and took to the air. Dinko landed on Bazin's shoulder, chattering at him.

Ro slipped behind a tree and watched as the lemur continued to chatter.

"I know we need to go." Bazin scratched the little animal's ears. "We'll be on the move soon enough."

"Krrr." The lemur tugged on Bazin's ear, chittering excitedly. Bazin snapped his head around and stared into the forest.

"How soon?"

"Krrr." Dinko danced around on his shoulder.

Bazin spun on his heel, wincing as it pulled at his hip. "Ro?"

She jumped at the sound of her name, chagrined to think that he knew she was there the whole time.

"We have to leave. Now." He walked straight toward the tree where Ro crouched. He rounded the tree and stared down at her. "The Wenzake are coming."

"How soon?" Ro shivered more from the thought of fighting the cannibals again than from the cold. They had survived one fight, but how much of that had been luck, she couldn't say.

"Three, maybe four hours. No more resting." He propelled her back toward the cave.

"The rain has hidden us so far." Ro wasn't exactly against his decision; deep down, she was aware that he had much more experience than she did in the wild, and they were on their own deadline. But she didn't like the way he was trying to take charge.

"I'm not willing to chance it." His face was grim. "I don't want to be cornered in that cave if they find us. We'll be outnumbered."

She sighed and hurried back to the cave, but Dinko beat her there.

"Krrr!" The lemur burst through the entrance and jumped into Leema's lap.

"What's wrong?" She looked up as Bazin and Ro ducked in through the entrance.

"Wenzake," Ro answered. "Pack up."

Leema jumped up, dumping Dinko on the floor. She gathered the pots and cups. Brenith packed the herbs and roots she had collected into Bazin's pack. Porsa folded the blankets quickly and stuffed them into the pack as well. Aritha, as usual, just watched with fear in her eyes. Bazin kicked dirt over the fire while Ro wrapped her make-shift sword belt around her waist.

"Do we know where we're going?" Brenith asked as she helped Aritha with her shoes.

"Ka-Petra," Bazin grunted, rubbing his hip absently as he watched the forest.

Ro wondered if his leg was up to this.

"How far is that?" Leema asked as she helped Porsa shoulder the pack.

"A few days." Bazin ushered them out into the dim gray light. "If we keep up a steady pace."

Ro was the last out of the cave. She glanced back to make sure they hadn't left anything. When she turned back, Bazin's face was tight with pain, prompting her to ask, "Can you?"

He looked at her. "What?"

"Keep up a steady pace." She wasn't trying to be mean, but it still sounded like an accusation.

His jaw worked rhythmically. He looked like he was debating what answer to give her.

He finally said, "No."

Ro nodded. She appreciated his honesty.

She shrugged, returning the favor. "Me neither."

"We'll make a great pair then." His lips twitched like he wanted to smile. "Let's go."

"Krrr!" Dinko stared back at them as he danced around on Leema's shoulder.

"We're coming!" Bazin snarled and limped between the girls.

Bazin set the pace, leading them into the forest. The princesses stayed in the center of the group with Porsa and Ro bringing up the rear.

Tension hovered around them as they moved farther into the trees. Even though she expected the tingling to warn her when the danger of their pursuers became imminent, Ro couldn't help glancing behind them every few yards, just in case. The drizzle turned to rain after about an hour, and the temperature began to drop once again.

"How much farther?" Aritha called ahead to Bazin.

"We've only been walking a few hours." Leema glanced over her shoulder at her sister.

"I know," Aritha moaned. "It's just that it's so cold."

Bazin didn't look back. He just resettled his sword harness and kept walking.

"D-do you w-w-want m-my robe?" Porsa trotted up next to Aritha.

She stopped walking and gazed at him. "Could I?"

The hopeful look that she gave him completely destroyed what little power of speech he possessed. Finally, he managed to nod and slid the pack off his back. It landed in the mud with a splat. Ro stopped to wait for them as he started to dig. She glanced ahead at the others as they continued on. Porsa found his robe and shook it out, then helped Aritha pull it over her head.

"Thank you, Porsa," Aritha whispered as she snuggled into the thick gray material.

Porsa's mouth tried a few times to form words but nothing came out. Ro picked up the pack and shoved it into his arms, then motioned for him to move on. He trotted after the others, tripping only once.

"That was so kind," Aritha said, gazing after him.

"Come on," Ro sighed, pushing Aritha in the right direction. Ro followed more slowly as Aritha hurried to catch up with her sisters.

"Why do you think Porsa is going to Ka-Petra?" Aritha asked Leema as they walked.

"I don't know." Leema puffed as the ground began to slope upward again. "Why?"

"Ka Province hates the High Priests of Jardarwa. Remember? Fisp said they don't believe the afterlife should be tampered with. They find it blasphemous."

Leema brushed the wet hair from her eyes and squinted through the rain at the apprentice. "Does seem odd."

"Do you think Bazin knows that?"

"I'm sure he does." Leema looked to the man leading them. "Surely he wouldn't be oblivious to such an important detail."

"Maybe he's some sort of ambassador," Aritha mused.

"I doubt they would send an apprentice for that."

"Maybe they have a secret mission," Aritha said, making it sound romantic.

Leema stopped for a moment, staring after Aritha. She shook her head and followed her sister.

Hours passed. The rain lessened to just mist, then it poured again. Ro squinted through the downpour. Sunset was happening somewhere beyond the clouds. The waning light made it hard to see. The climb became steeper, and loose rocks instead of mud covered the ground. Her legs burned from the exertion, and her feet were aching. She could just make out Bazin walking ahead of the princesses. He was limping badly now. She watched the shuffling movements of the princesses. They were all moving slower and slower. Everyone was tired. They needed to stop for the night.

Ro returned her gaze to the ground, hoping to avoid most of the sharp rocks. She was so focused on her feet that she jumped when Dinko dropped out of the tree and landed on her shoulder. She walked stiffly for a few paces, unsure of what the little animal would do.

"Krrr." Dinko curled his tail around her neck, keeping it dry just for a moment. "Krrr."

"I don't know what you're saying," Ro muttered, watching where she stepped.

"He's saying that we can stop for the night." Bazin stood right in front of her. His face was pale and drawn. His breathing was heavy, and he stood with all his weight on his good leg.

"Where?" Ro glanced at the princesses who stood huddled together like lost sheep.

Bazin gestured around. "Pick a tree."

"No fire?" Aritha whined.

"No." Bazin glared at her. "It's too wet for one, and I don't want to make it easy for the Wenzake to find us."

"Oh." Aritha's shoulders slumped as she turned away. Brenith wrapped her arm around Aritha's waist and guided her to a nearby tree. Porsa dug in his pack, pulling out some of their roots. He silently handed them around.

"Do you think they're still following us?" Ro asked, looking back the way they'd come.

"Yes." Bazin sighed. "Wenzake are like dogs with a bone. They'll want revenge. We might be able to lose them when we reach Ka-Petra."

She thought she heard him say *I hope* under his breath, but it may have been her own muttering. She was too tired to tell anymore.

***

Two more days of walking, and two more nights spent sleeping in trees finally saw them clear of the forest. Patches of scrub brush covered the ground ahead. Ro was both glad and sorry. They could finally see where they were, but so could their pursuers. There would be no shelter at all from the rain now, either. Bazin stopped at the edge of the trees and waited for them to catch up.

"Does it ever stop raining in this cursed place?" Aritha sighed.

Leema shrugged. "It was nice yesterday."

"On the other side of those mountains is Ka-Petra." He pointed to the towering sentinels of white rock standing only a few miles away. Their tops were lost in the black clouds that hovered overhead.

"How far?" Brenith brushed at her running nose as she stepped up beside them.

"A day, maybe two."

"Our destination always seems to be a day or two away." Aritha gazed out at the chalk colored mountains. Ro glanced over, noticing her face was thinner, and her eyes were sunken. In the last week, her comments had lost most of their aristocratic bite.

Bazin looked down at Ro's feet, then out at the rocky shale that covered the lower half of the mountain. He met her eyes. Ro gazed up at him without expression. His jaw started working again, but he said nothing.

He pointed. "We'll have to head more to the south. There is only one way into Ka-Petra. Mayoth's Bridge."

Ka-Petra

BAZIN SANK ONTO THE knee-high boulder that stood next to the trail. He massaged his hip and knee as they throbbed in time with his heart. His lungs burned from the climb, and he was sweating despite the cold, thin air at the top of the pass. The sun had finally come out, but its blazing heat had baked the side of the mountain as they climbed.

He took a long drink from the water skin and glanced back to watch the girls slowly climb. The old goat trail may not have been the easiest way to get over the mountain, but it was the quickest. It was also a better trail for Ro's bare feet to handle, unlike the shale rocks that had slowed their progress to a near-crawling pace. Her feet were toughening up after nearly a month without shoes, but she still struggled.

Not that she would admit it.

His growing concern for Ro didn't sit very comfortably with him. He still harbored a grumbling of hatred towards her for skewering him and sending him to the Underworld, but the situation was forcing him to alter his feelings. Bazin told himself that it was self-preservation driving him, not concern for Ro as a person. Assassins didn't become concerned with others. Assassins were only concerned with the assignment.

He handed the water to Leema as she and Dinko made it to the top first. She stood puffing beside Bazin as Brenith and Aritha climbed over the crest. They collapsed on the ground together, gasping for air. He glanced down the trail, looking for Ro. She was helping Porsa with his footing. It was pathetic how clumsy that boy was. He looked past them, trying to see if the Wenzake were any closer, but he couldn't see them. Ro and Porsa finally gained the summit and stood panting. He waited for them to catch their breath and get a drink before pointing down the mountain ahead of them.

"At the bottom of that gorge is the Ka River."

Leema turned to look as Ro came forward. Brenith climbed to her feet and moved to stand beside them as they stared down the mountain. Aritha didn't even try to stand; she just turned where she sat.

Splayed out at the base of the mountain was a wide expanse of rolling hills dotted with little farms. The hills ended abruptly at the lip of a canyon and seemed to pour off into the gorge.

"Taus told me one day I would see the Ka," Ro muttered. Bazin glanced at her. She sounded sad and a little bitter.

"Over there is Ka-Petra." He pointed to the center of the canyon, where a tall column of rock stood with a jumble of buildings perched on top. It was connected to each side of the canyon by massive stone bridges.

"Finally, civilization!" Aritha sighed, climbing to her feet.

Bazin looked at her and snorted, "You've obviously never been there."

All four girls turned at the same time and looked at him. Their expressions were a rainbow of emotions. Brenith looked worried. Aritha looked insulted and hurt. Leema watched him with a speculative gleam, and Ro was suspicious.

"Is that the only way across the river?" Ro asked, pointing at the bridge.

"No." Bazin pointed farther south. "There is a crossing near the Southern Ocean, but it's better to cross here."

"Why?" Ro demanded.

Bazin sighed. If there was one thing that he had learned about her, it was that she was stubborn and wouldn't just listen to his experience. He stood and reached for her shoulders. She took a step back and narrowed her eyes. Frowning at her continued suspicion, he took her by the shoulders and turned her around so he could show her.

"To the north is the Arazi Sea, only accessible by scaling the cliffs, and there are no harbors there." He turned her again. "To the west, cannibals." He turned her again and pointed down the mountain. "To the east, the Ka River and southeast is nothing but swampland until you reach the Southern Ocean." He dropped his hands from her shoulders. "The forest we just left is tame compared to what lives in that swamp. Understand?"

Ro pointed. "And that road on the far side, does that lead to the Imperial City?"

"Eventually." Bazin nodded and saw the look of worried relief that Brenith shared with Aritha.

As Bazin turned around so he could sit back down, he caught a glimpse of movement on the trail behind them. He squinted at the tree line at the base of the mountain. More than a dozen men were moving out from the edge of the forest.

"Damn." Bazin reached out and tapped Ro's arm. She followed his gaze. The Wenzake had made it to the base of the mountain.

Ro sighed. "Are they ever going to stop?"

"No."

Leema stepped up beside them and looked down. "Will we be safe once we reach the settlements?"

"No." Bazin sighed. "They pretty much do what they want. I've even seen them inside Ka-Petra."

"Maybe we should make a stand here." Ro eyed the rocks around them. "The pass isn't very wide."

"Air's pretty thin, and I'm not in the best shape." Bazin hated to admit that he would rather retreat, but he knew they couldn't win this one. He glanced at her feet. "And neither are you."

Ro nodded slowly.

Leema tugged on his sleeve. "We should go."

"Yeah." Bazin watched them for a moment longer, then turned back to the girls. "Time to move."

"Why?" Aritha whined. "We need a rest."

He jabbed a thumb over his shoulder. "They're gaining."

Aritha scrambled to her feet and headed down the goat trail without any further prompting. The others followed as quickly as they could. Bazin limped after them. Each step jarred his hip. He worried over the damage that his muscles may have taken, but it was too late to do anything about it now.

By midday, he was sweating and dizzy. They were nearly halfway down the mountain. His hip throbbed, and his knee threatened to give out.

"Let's stop for a rest," he snarled, hating his own weakness and thinking, *I never would have been this worn down in my old body!*

Aritha and Brenith gratefully collapsed where they were.

"Why is going down harder than climbing?" Brenith panted. "You'd think it would be easier."

"Just keep reminding yourself that there is a bed at the end of this trail. That's what I'm doing," Leema said as she slid on some loose rocks and landed on her backside next to Brenith.

"Fresh b-bread," Porsa sighed dreamily, flopping onto the path.

"Roast beef," Brenith added.

Aritha brushed at her clothes. "A hot bath."

"Krrr." Dinko purred, jumping up on Leema's shoulder.

"What did he say?" Leema glanced back at Bazin.

Her relationship with Dinko still surprised him. "Ale."

She grinned. "He did not!"

"Krrr."

"He says he likes his ale, thank you very much."

"Do lemurs get drunk?"

"Leema!" Brenith scolded.

Bazin grinned.

"I just wondered," Leema huffed, scratching Dinko's ears.

"Yes." Bazin tried not to groan as he eased down onto a rock and stretched his leg out.

"Really?" Leema stared at him with wonder.

"Krrr," Dinko growled at Bazin and narrowed his eyes.

"There was this one time," Bazin began, "Dinko was really—"

"Krrr." Dinko stood up on Leema's shoulder and glared at him.

"What? You were!" Bazin shrugged but took the warning. "Anyway, let's just say that he wasn't his usual graceful self and that brothel will never be the same."

"Krrr." Dinko danced around on Leema's shoulder a little and settled with his back to Bazin.

"I think you hurt his feelings."

"Nah," Bazin reached out and scratched Dinko's back, making him purr. "He's seen me do worse."

"In a brothel?" Leema sent him a mischievous look.

Behind him, he heard Ro snort, but she tried to cover it with a cough when Brenith twisted around.

"Leema!" Brenith glared at Bazin instead of her sister.

"Why are you glaring at me?" He frowned. He couldn't tell if Brenith was blushing or just sunburnt.

"That is not an appropriate conversation for a sixteen-year-old!"

"She's the one who asked."

"I would appreciate it if you didn't corrupt my little sister." Brenith stared him down with her best royal glare.

Bazin shrugged, thinking that if he was any judge of character, Leema was probably already a lot more corrupted than her sister imagined.

"Bren," Leema rolled her eyes, "it's not like I don't know what a brothel is."

Brenith glared at her, but Leema shrugged. She turned to Bazin. "Why don't you tell us about Ka-Petra instead. What's its history?"

Bazin glanced up the trail behind them, wondering if they had the time for a story, but he ached and was glad of an excuse to sit for a little longer. "Long time ago, there was a warlord who thought he could conquer Ka."

"What was his name?" Leema interrupted.

"Mayoth." Bazin rubbed his hip. "He had no idea what he was taking on with Ka. She was too wild. So he did what all good warlords do when they can't conquer."

"Get themselves killed?" Aritha smirked.

"No. He turned to making money," Bazin explained. "He enslaved the few inhabitants of Ka that he could catch and built his bridge. He knew that it would be the only way for hundreds of miles to cross the Ka, so he built his city in the middle of the Ka and took advantage of every traveler that came by."

"Sounds like a horrid man." Aritha threw a rock into the brush, frightening a lizard.

"Sounds pretty smart to me!" Leema snorted.

"What is it like now?" Brenith asked.

"About the same." Bazin gazed down at the city and shrugged. "Anything is for sale. Lots of goods from the Southern Ocean. Slave trade is booming."

"Slavery?" Aritha gasped. "That's disgraceful."

"Like I said, everything is for sale." Bazin shrugged. "Commerce is the only real law in Ka-Petra."

"Isn't there a king or council or something?" Leema asked.

"There are five main families in Ka-Petra. Any one of them could be in power at any given time. It's best if you're associated with one of the House families if you're going to be staying there."

"Are you?" Brenith asked.

Bazin stretched and winced. "I was once."

"What are you going to do when we get there?" Leema asked.

She seemed a little too eager for his answer. He wondered if she was suspicious or hopeful. He hadn't really had time to form a plan of action for when they reached the city. He'd been too busy staying alive.

If he'd had his way, they would have gone right back the way they'd come to the beach and rowed across the channel to Jardarwa, but that plan had crumbled after the waterfall. He knew that he had to get Ro back to Jardarwa, but beyond that, he hadn't given much thought to the fate of the princesses. He had no intention of escorting them to wherever they were bound. Evasion tactics would have to do for now.

"I'm going to sleep for a week."

"And after that?" Leema asked, still fishing for the answer she wanted.

She's just as stubborn as Ro, he thought. Then he noticed Brenith and Aritha were looking at him expectantly. He had no idea what Ro was thinking behind him. Porsa had a somewhat panicked expression on his face. Bazin was beginning to feel cornered himself.

"I'm going to take Porsa to a brothel and try to cure his stutter." He grinned as Porsa squeaked in shock and Leema giggled, but his amusement faded as he caught the disapproving scowl on Brenith's face. He cleared his throat and shoved to his feet. "We better get moving."

Locked Out

"WHERE ARE WE?" Ro stopped just outside the glow of torches near the cluster of buildings. The evening air felt deliciously cool after their sunbaked trek across the fields. The roar from the Ka echoed up from the canyon, nearly drowning out the laughter and music coming from the town.

"Southgate." Bazin limped up beside her and rested his weight on his good leg.

"What do we do now?" Brenith asked as she peeked around his shoulder.

"Personally, I'm going to get across the bridge, find an inn, and pass out." He started to limp forward. He was looking forward to reacquainting himself with the ale and women of Caith Quadrant.

He only made it a few steps before he realized they weren't following him.

"Now what?" he muttered, closing his eyes. He just wanted to lie down. They had kept up a punishing pace to stay ahead of the Wenzake. His hip ached, his knee ached, and he was starving.

"What's the problem?" Bazin snapped as he turned around. Pain was making his temper sharp.

The four girls were exchanging unhappy looks.

Finally, Brenith stepped forward. "We have no money."

"That's not my problem," he snorted. He didn't want to spend his money on them. He eyed Ro for a moment. He could just take Ro and leave the rest. She was the only one he had come for anyway.

"You can't just leave us!" Aritha shrieked only to be hushed by Brenith.

Porsa stood behind them with the most mutinous expression Bazin had ever seen on the boy's face. Maybe the boy would grow a backbone yet.

"Krrr." Dinko sat on Leema's shoulder and glared. He had obviously defected to their side too.

"Fine," Bazin snarled. "I'll take care of it."

He made a sweepingly sarcastic 'after you' gesture. Aritha passed by him with her head held high and a haughty expression. Porsa followed with Brenith muttering a thank you. Ro gave him a suspicious glance as she walked by, gripping the hilt of her sword.

Leema paused and scanned the trees behind them for any sign of the Wenzake. They were still a few hours ahead of the cannibals before the sun set, but now that it was dark, there was no way to know how close they were.

"They're still coming," Bazin assured her as he also gazed at the trees. "Come on." He turned to limp after the others, and a moment later, Leema followed him.

The little town had popped up around the road leading to the South Gate. The opportunistic residents of Ka-Petra realized a long time ago that they stood to make a fortune off weary travelers who wanted to rest before braving the city. Taverns and inns lined the road. Music and laughter filtered out into the night.

Bazin was so tired he almost wanted to stop here for the night, but with the Wenzake so close, it wouldn't be safe. It would be too easy for the cannibals to find them. The people of Southgate wouldn't stick their necks out for anyone against the Wenzake. It would be easier to just disappear into the crowds of the city itself.

As they walked, he could feel Leema watching him. Something was on her mind, and he got the impression that either she was too scared to ask him or she was not sure what it was she wanted to say. So, he kept walking and ignored her.

They passed through the town and approached the gate. The closer they got, the thicker the crowd of people and wagons. The gate was wide enough for two loaded wagons to pass side-by-side through it. It was well lit on either side by torches. Guards armed with crossbows paced along the top of the gate, watching the traffic. There were others on the ground near the gate itself, keeping an eye on things.

Off to the side were the Affiliation Kiosks. They were small wooden offices with an open counter at the front. Each one was draped with a colored banner corresponding to one of the ruling families of Ka-Petra. Travelers waited in lines at each kiosk to register with a House. After registering, they would receive a sash declaring their affiliation.

The last time he had been here, Caith House had hired him to dispose of a troublesome advisor. He could still technically be on their payroll, making his affiliation with that house still valid, but they would still have to register. He needed to catch the others before they entered the city. Aritha and Porsa had already reached the gate.

"Why are you taking Porsa to Ka-Petra?" Leema pulled on his elbow.

"Krrr." Dinko leaped from her shoulder to his.

"What do you mean?" Bazin didn't stop. Brenith and Ro were nearing the gate. He had to stop them before they crossed through.

"Ro!" He shouted, trying to catch her attention, but she didn't turn.

"The Holy Mountain is shunned in Ka. It's dangerous for him to be here," she accused, keeping pace with him.

He didn't want to get separated. They had no idea how to act in Ka-Petra. Entering without affiliation was dangerous.

"Ro!" He called again. He could see Porsa and Aritha waiting just inside the gate near the wall. They were motioning Brenith and Ro to join them.

"It can't be because he's some sort of delegate. He's only an apprentice. And you treat him more like a servant than an employer. Why are you really coming here?"

Leema tugged on his sleeve, but Bazin's attention was on the rider approaching the gate from the city's side. Rider and horse skidded to a stop just as Ro passed through the gate. The rider shouted to the gatehouse.

"Krrr." Dinko sat up straight with all his attention focused on the rider.

"Hey!" Leema grabbed him again. "I said, why are you really here?"

"Damn! Damn! Damn!" The gate was closing, and Ro was on the inside. Bazin shook Leema's hand off and hobbled forward as fast as he could. "No! No! No! No! No!"

The bridge gate was closing faster than he could run with an injured leg. It thudded shut with a bang. Several guards stepped forward to manage the angry crowd. "Back up! No one goes in until the new chancellor is chosen."

Bazin was arguing with the guard when Leema caught up with him.

"Half of our party is on the bridge already." Bazin started forward again, only to be stopped by an older guard. "They didn't have a chance to register."

The guard shrugged. "They shouldn't have passed through, then."

"They didn't know."

"Sorry, son, nothing we can do." The guard shook his head. "You'd best find a good spot to sit and wait it out."

"Leema!" He could hear Ro shouting from the other side of the massive gate.

"Ro!" Leema's voice was full of panic. "Wait!" Leema grabbed the guard's arm. "We have to get in there. My sisters—"

"You'll just have to wait!" The guard shook her hand off and turned to manage the rest of the crowd.

"Damn!" Bazin spat and turned away from the gate, trying to get through the mob of shouting travelers.

"What do they mean we'll have to wait?" Leema pushed her way through the crowd, trying to follow Bazin.

He grabbed her arm and dragged her to the edge of the cliff where the stone wall ended. In the glow from the torches, he could see the crowd on the other side of the gate. As soon as the rider arrived with his news, everyone on the bridge had reversed course and had tried to get back to Southgate. He caught a glimpse of Ro as she was shoved and jostled. He cupped his hands and shouted, trying to be heard above the roar of the Ka and the shouts from the angry crowd.

"Ro!" He waved his arm until she saw him and signaled back. "Find Caith Quadrant! Tell them my name!" Ro leaned forward over the stone balustrade, squinting as she tried to hear. "Find Caith Quadrant! Tell them my name!" Ro nodded. He lifted Dinko off his shoulder and set him on the grass. "Go. Hurry."

Dinko chittered at him and then sprang across the grass toward the gate. The little lemur wove his way through the crowd. Bazin lost sight of him for a moment but then found him again as the furry drugi scaled the side of the gate. He reached the top of the stone structure within minutes. A guard spotted him and lunged forward. Dinko dodged him easily. Another guard tried to grab his tail but missed. Dinko ran a few circles around the shouting guards and then disappeared over the far wall.

Left Behind

BAZIN TURNED AND LIMPED back toward town.

"Wait." Leema's attention swiveled back and forth between the bridge and Bazin's retreating form. "Wait!" She hurried after him. "What's going on?"

"Someone must have disliked the current chancellor's politics and decided they wanted a change."

"I don't understand."

"Look," Bazin stopped and turned back, "Ka-Petra is in the middle of a power coup right now. They'll open the gate when they've decided who wins."

"My sisters are walking into a civil war?"

"They're walking into a lot more than that," he muttered as he turned away.

"What?" Leema squeaked. "Can't you do something!"

"Like what? The gates are closed."

"I don't know, find a way in! Can't you sneak in?"

Bazin grabbed Leema and pulled her behind the corner of the closest building. "Keep your voice down, damn it!" He glanced around to see if anyone had heard. "You can't just sneak into Ka-Petra!"

"Why not?" She shoved his hands away. "There are always ways in and out of a city."

He shook his head. "Not Ka-Petra."

"There's always a back way."

"How would you know?"

Leema raised her chin. "I know a lot about cities!"

"Really?" Bazin glared at her. "Then what do you know about Ka-Petra?"

"It's a trade city."

"And...?"

"And... everything is for sale."

"And...?"

"And that's it." She waved her arms in frustration. "I just know what you told us."

"There's a lot more to it than that, honey. It's a fortress."

"So?"

"So, that means that you don't just sneak in!" Bazin snarled. "Mayoth's Bridge is the only way in or out of Ka-Petra."

Leema crossed her arms. "Rulers always have bolt holes."

He stared at her a moment. She was right. There was another way into Ka-Petra, but it wasn't one that he wanted to try ever again, especially not with a bad leg. He'd barely survived it the last time.

"What was that look?" Leema peered at him. "Do you know another way in?"

"No." Bazin turned away from her perceptive gaze. "We'll just have to wait until they open the gates."

"How long will that be?"

"I don't know. Could be a day or could be weeks."

"What's going to happen to my sisters in the meantime?"

Bazin's gut clenched. *She dies, I die.*

"Bazin!" Leema grabbed his arm, trying to spin him around. "Will you answer me?

"What do you want me to say?" He turned on her. "You want me to say they'll be fine and safe? I can't. During a coup, all bets are off. Anyone not registered with a House is fair game."

"Fair game for what?"

"I told you. Slave trade is booming."

"You're not suggesting that they would just take people off the streets?"

"That's exactly what I'm saying. No one is in charge during a coup. All laws are null until the new chancellor is in power." Bazin gestured toward the gate. "That's why they close the gate."

Leema stared at him wide-eyed. "And this Caith Quadrant you told Ro about, is it safe?"

"No." Bazin shook his head. "No more than anywhere else."

"Then why did you send them there?" Leema shoved at his chest.

"They didn't register with Caith House before passing the gate, but if they can make it there, there's a slim chance that they'll be safe. I was affiliated with Caith, and if Ro tells them my name, they might let them in." Bazin looked away. "It's better than nothing."

She shoved him again. "That's not good enough!"

"Hey! I'm doing my best, all right?" Bazin grabbed her arm. "I've had nothing but trouble since I met you, and if it was my choice, I'd drop the lot of you and walk away. But it doesn't work that way, so don't yell at me for trying to help!"

"What do you mean 'it doesn't work that way?'" She shook her arm free. "Why exactly are you helping us if you're so against it?"

Bazin stared at her and wished he had kept his mouth shut. He scrubbed his head with his hands, ruffling his hair.

"Look," he chose his words carefully, "right now, there's nothing I can do about what is happening to Ro, Brenith, Aritha, and Porsa. I'm hoping that Dinko will be of some help in getting them somewhere safe, but I doubt they'll make it past the first street without being captured."

Leema tried to digest this news.

"What happens if they are taken?"

"They'll be sold at auction."

"No! They are daughters of the Queen of Koric!" She blurted, forgetting that Bazin wasn't supposed to know their true identities. Leema clamped her hands over her mouth, realizing too late what she had said. When he didn't react, she frowned at him.

"Wait, you're not surprised." She dropped her hands. "Did you know we were Princesses of Koric?"

"Yes," he said, watching the confusion, betrayal, and finally suspicion cloud her face.

"How long have you known?"

"A while."

"Is that why you brought us here? To ransom my sisters?"

"What?" Bazin frowned at her. "I don't give a damn about your sisters!"

"Then why did you bring us here?"

Bazin gestured to the forest behind him in exasperation. "It's the only city for miles!"

Leema stared at him for a long time, blinking against the tears that clouded her eyes before she turned away.

Bazin sighed and tried to get his temper under control. He didn't need a crying girl on his hands. He gazed across the clearing at the mass of people around the gate. If they didn't get a room quickly, there wouldn't be any left. He didn't want to be left without some kind of shelter when the Wenzake caught up with them.

"Come on." He limped toward the nearest inn. Reluctantly, she followed him.

"Once the gate opens, we go get them, right?" Her voice held all the fears of a child left behind.

Bazin scrubbed a hand across his face. "We can try."

"But?"

"But it won't be safe for you."

"But it will be for *you*?"

"Yes! No!" Bazin stopped walking. He was getting frustrated trying to explain all this, and his leg was aching more and more the longer he stood arguing with her. "Well, saf*er*."

"I can fight."

Bazin sighed and started limping forward again. "It's not always about fighting."

"Then what is it? Bazin, please." Leema tugged on his arm until he stopped and looked at her. "You're not leaving me behind."

As she gazed at him with her big, teary brown eyes filled with barely controlled terror, she looked younger than her sixteen years. She looked just like what she was, a lost child. Her chin quivered.

He suddenly felt uncomfortable. Three months in the Underworld must have changed him a lot more than he would have admitted. He was getting soft-hearted. No more than an hour ago, he was willing to leave all three princesses behind without a second thought. Taking her into the city shouldn't bother him. If she wanted to go, that was her problem; and Ro was his.

"Come on," he snarled. He didn't like feeling soft. "There's nothing we can do about your sisters right now. When the gates open, we'll find them, but for right now, we have to look after ourselves."

Cut Off

Ro saw the rider approaching just as she passed through the gate. She moved to the side.

"Close it!" the rider shouted at the guards. "Close it!"

His voice echoed off the stone, and people all along the bridge stopped and turned. They began rushing back toward Southgate in a panic. Ro pushed her way to the edge of the crowd, looking for Brenith or Aritha. She couldn't see either sister or Porsa. She turned back, seeking Leema and Bazin. They had been right behind her.

"Leema!" she shouted as loud as she could.

"Ro!" Leema shouted back, but it was from the other side of the gate.

"Oh no." Ro pushed against the crowd. She was shoved and jostled until she was up against the thick stone parapet that made up the edge of the bridge. She glanced out over the wall to see the sheer cliffs standing nearly a hundred yards high on either side with the Ka River raging at the bottom. She looked down. The Ka was a massive, rushing, foaming river that was nearly three miles across. The color shifted from light blue and white, where the most dangerous rapids were, to deep dark blue, where the river ran deepest. She suddenly felt very small.

"Ro!" She heard Bazin shout. She scanned the crowd along the cliff edge. Finally, she spotted him waving. He shouted something. She leaned out as far as she could to hear what he was saying. The roar of the Ka from below and the shouts of the crowd behind her were deafening.

"Go to Caith Quadrant! Tell them my name!"

She waved to show that she heard, even though she didn't have any idea what he was talking about. Then, he turned away and disappeared into the crowd.

Ro left the side of the bridge and moved through the chaos, searching for the others. She tried to discern from the shouts and arguing what exactly had happened but could make no sense of anything. She alternated searching the crowd and gazing up at the monstrosity that was Ka-Petra. The city was a jumbled mess of buildings piled on top of the rock column. It looked as if they were climbing on top of each other, trying to get away from the river. Some of the buildings looked like they were sliding off the rock and had been braced up from underneath by huge stone supports.

Ro pushed her way past the crowd, then wove her way down the row of wagons and abandoned horses. Wind and wet mist whipped across the bridge as she spotted Brenith, Aritha, and Porsa huddled against the other side of the bridge.

"Are you all right?" she asked when she got close enough.

"No," Aritha answered without looking away from the city.

"What is happening?" Brenith pointed back toward the gate.

"W-where's Bazin and L-leema?" Porsa grabbed her shoulder.

"They were on the other side of the gate when it closed." Ro shook off his hand. "I can't figure out what happened."

Some of the people had returned to their wagons and had started toward the city again.

"Hey!" Ro stopped a young boy with a golden sash hanging from his shoulder, riding a white horse. "What's going on? Why did they close the gate?"

"Chancellor Villeah's been assassinated," he said as his horse danced sideways. It could feel the tension and fear in the crowd.

"What does that mean?" Brenith pushed forward, trying to lay a hand on the nervous horse while looking up at the boy. "Did they close the bridge to stop the assassin from escaping?"

"No, who did it don't matter." The boy glanced around nervously at the tide of people trickling along the bridge. "There'll be fighting now between the Houses. Mostly Mayoth and Villeah. It's been brewin' for a while now. You better get indoors. The slavers'll be out lookin' to fill their pens." The boy pulled his horse back from Brenith's hand and held out his sash for her to see. "If you're with a House, you should be safe."

"We're not!" Aritha shook her head and looked at her sister.

"You'd better hide, then. Good luck." The boy kicked the horse into motion, nearly mowing down the people in front of him.

"What are we going to do?" Brenith looked to Ro. "If they are taking people..."

"Why didn't Bazin tell us?" Aritha backed away from a wagon that had veered toward them.

"I don't know. Bazin said to get to Caith Quadrant. I have no idea where that is." Ro glanced around. "We'll have to ask someone and hope we don't come across any of those slavers."

"I d-don't w-w-w-want to be s-s-sold again." Porsa's face was pale, and he was shaking.

"Were you sold before?" Brenith reached out and grabbed his hand.

"Y-yes," Porsa started to shake. "F-f-father s-s-sold m-m-m-m-m—"

"Take a breath." Brenith patted his arm and waited.

"M-my s-s-sister and I."

"I'm so sorry, Porsa."

Ro pulled them back against the stone as another wagon rolled past. More and more people were heading for the city.

Brenith watched the crowd. "Maybe we should stay on the bridge."

"Wouldn't do that if I were you." A man with a heavy pack stopped next to them as a herd of goats swarmed around them. "You'll be easy pickins out here."

"We should get moving." Ro turned toward the city as the man moved on, following the goats.

"We should stay with the group as much as possible." Aritha stepped closer and slid her arm through Porsa's as if he were going to protect her. "Safety in numbers."

"Good idea." Brenith nodded.

They turned and followed the crowd. Ro tried to keep as close to the wall as possible. It would have been easier to protect the princesses if they weren't completely surrounded. The torches spaced out along the bridge danced wildly, and the massive stones below their feet vibrated. Ro wasn't sure if it was from the river crashing into the rocks below or from the traffic that was crossing it.

As they approached the end of the bridge, they could hear the shouts and screams of the city as it changed hands. But as they passed under the arch into the city, there was no clear view of the fighting. As soon as they were off the bridge, the wagons whipped up their teams and disappeared into the city. However, any travelers who were on foot were left to seek shelter anywhere they could. Unfortunately, shop doors slammed closed faster than they could reach them. Even the taverns closed and barred their doors.

Ro looked around the square at the frightened travelers. "We can't stay here. We're too exposed."

"Street or alley?" Brenith crowded close to Ro.

Ro looked up the street the wagons had taken. She didn't like the idea of taking a main thoroughfare. She looked for other exits. Some were nothing but stairwells between buildings, and others looked like alleys leading to other streets. She shrugged and picked a quiet-looking alley. Ro led the girls and Porsa through and came out in a square where the buildings were crowded so close together that they leaned on top of one another, arching over the streets. It was hard to tell where one building stopped and another started.

"The builders must have been drunk." Aritha breathed as they moved under a hat shop whose upper story was hanging out far enough to touch the building on the opposite side of the street.

"They just tried to fit too much into a small space." Brenith shook her head and hurried past the leaning shop.

The screams were getting closer.

"Maybe we should go back to the bridge and just wait it out," Aritha suggested just as the tingling started. Ro wasted no time drawing her sword.

"Brenith! Aritha!" The sisters hurried back to where Ro stood, watching the streets and alleys. "Get behind me."

She backed them up against the hat shop and scanned the street. Porsa tried to be brave and placed himself between Ro and the girls. Aritha grabbed a handful of his shirt. Brenith turned and started to bang on the door of the hat shop.

Men carrying torches, ropes, and nets came down the street. They pulled people from the alleys and stairwells where they had sought shelter. Some were released who were wearing a colored sash; others were not so lucky. Each new acquisition was lashed to a rope by their hands.

A few men surrounded Ro's little group and taunted them. Ro moved from left to right, trying to cover the half circle of enemies. They came at her all at once from two sides. She swiped and stabbed, killing one and wounding another. They swung their ropes at her, trying to throw her off balance.

"Ro!" Brenith cried out as one man tried to rush past Ro, intent on grabbing Aritha. Ro stabbed him as he passed, then retreated until she was closer to the hat shop again. The men stayed back, circling, waiting for her to make a mistake.

One lunged at her from the left. She parried the blow, but it was only a distraction. Aritha shrieked as the net hit Ro from behind. She struggled to free herself from the quickly tangling mesh. Her sword was stuck in the weave of the net. She tried to rip it free, but it wouldn't come loose. The men jerked on the net's ropes, and she toppled over. She hit the ground with a grunt. Behind her, Brenith and Aritha screamed. Porsa shouted something unintelligible.

"No!" Ro screamed, fighting like a crazed animal to get loose.

"Quiet!" One of the slavers snarled and hit her over the head with a club.

Her vision swam. She still tried to struggle, but her body didn't want to work right. She caught a glimpse of Porsa on the ground as they tied his hands behind his back just before the slaver hit her again, and the world went black.

Gambling

BAZIN FINALLY FOUND A room at the fourth inn they tried. It cost him more than he wanted to pay, but in true Ka-Petra style, the demand made the costs rise. Bazin ordered hot water and two meals to be sent up, then ushered Leema up the narrow stairs to their room on the third floor.

"Strange," she said, looking around at the small dingy room.

There was one bed with a little table beside it and a chair by the door. No fire burned in the small fireplace, but it was full of ashes and old wood.

"What is?" Bazin crossed to the single window and looked out. It overlooked the roof of the next building. Just beyond it, he could see the edge of the forest. Not ideal, but as escape routes went, he had seen a lot worse. He bent to get a fire started.

"Being in a building," Leema said as she poked at the pillows on the bed. "So, what do we do now?"

"We are going to eat, rest, and gamble." He stood slowly as the fire crackled to life and turned back to her.

"What?" Leema frowned.

"Aren't you hungry?" Bazin grinned at the confusion on her face.

"Of course I'm hungry! That's not what I was asking, and you know it."

He started to say something, but was cut off by a knock at the door. Leema moved to open it, but Bazin stopped her and drew his sword. He pushed her behind him.

"Yes?" Bazin stepped up to the door.

"Yer meal," A woman's voice called from the hallway.

"All right." Bazin slid the bolt back and opened the door. A short, harassed-looking woman shouldered her way into the room and set the tray filled with steaming food on the table beside the bed. She turned and caught a glimpse of the naked blade in his hand and hurried out of the room.

Bazin checked the hall, closed the door, and locked it. He turned to find Leema stuffing her face.

"Slow down," Bazin warned, sheathing his sword. "You haven't eaten real food in a long time. If you eat too fast or too much, you'll be sick."

Leema obediently chewed more slowly as he moved over beside her. Looking down, he saw meat from an unidentifiable animal swimming with some vegetables in a pool of greasy gravy. A chunk of bread teetered on the side of the plate, and two mugs of ale sat waiting. The ale was a welcome sight. He took his plate and eased himself down onto the chair next to the door. His hip throbbed, but he ignored it. He leaned his sword against the wall beside him and started to eat.

Leema finally took her plate and sat on the floor across from him.

"What did you mean by gamble?" she asked between bites.

Bazin finished three mouthfuls before he answered. "I intend to increase my small holding of coins."

"Water," came a call from the hallway, then a foot tapped against the door.

Although Bazin had recognized the woman's voice, he still picked up his sword before reaching up and unbolting the door. She staggered through the door with two steaming buckets. A rag hung on the side of each bucket. She plunked them down just inside the door and fled.

Leema stared at the steaming buckets and then down at her half-empty plate, torn between two luxuries.

"Eat first," Bazin smirked and gestured with his bread. "Water will still be warm, but I doubt this will be edible when it's cold."

Leema dabbed up some more of the greasy gravy and looked up at him expectantly. "Finish telling me."

"Telling you what?"

Leema wiped her mouth with the back of her hand. "What your plan is."

"Oh." He wasn't used to sharing his plans. He ate a little more before answering.

"We have a lot to do before those gates open," Bazin said when he had finished his food. "I intend on making a bit of coin at the game tables. We will need provisions, and if worse comes to worst, we might have to buy your sisters back." He washed down his meal with the ale.

It's worse than the food, he grimaced, trying to swallow.

He stood and limped over to the buckets. He removed his shirt. Bazin picked up a rag from one of the buckets and started to wash the dirt off his face and arms.

"I can help," Leema said as she chewed.

"Help with what?" Bazin asked as he stripped so he could wash the rest of him.

Leema's face turned red, and she turned her back toward him. *She saw me nearly naked in the cave, and it didn't bother her,* Bazin mused, *but now that we're in an actual building, it's embarrassing?*

"I can help gamble."

"I don't think so," he said as he examined his hip and knee. They looked awful, but they were healing.

"Please, Bazin!" Leema pleaded as she set her empty plate aside. "I can do it."

When he was as clean as he was going to get, he reached past her and grabbed the blanket off the bed. Shaking it out to make sure there were no bugs, he wrapped it around his waist, then dunked his clothes into the bucket. Leema turned slightly, and seeing that he was mostly decent, she scooted around the rest of the way.

"I used to play dice with some of the village boys, and I played Peril with Mother every day." She watched while he washed and wrung out his clothes. "I want to help."

Bazin sighed and looked down at her. Her face was glowing in the warmth from the fire. He had to get her to stay out of sight until the gate opened. Even through the dirt, her hair shimmered gold. He stared at her hair for a long time, then shook his head. He started to hang his clothes along the mantle. "I want you to stay in the room."

"I'm not staying in here by myself. I'm going to help you get enough money to get my sisters back." Leema scrambled to her feet.

"You are not leaving this room unless we do something about your looks."

"What's wrong with my looks?"

"With that hair of yours, you'll stick out like a gold piece in the gutter."

Leema stared at him with her mouth open.

"Don't look at me like that. Golden hair isn't native to Ka. We don't know how long it'll be before the gate is open, and the Wenzake are still out there."

"You weren't worried about it before." Leema accused, running her hand across her hair self-consciously. "Why is it a problem now?"

"Well, that was before the coup. Now, I want to keep a low profile." Bazin braced his hands on his hips. "Slavers would love to get their hands on a golden-haired girl." Bazin rubbed his fingers together. "Would make them a lot of money."

"But I'm with you."

"So?" he scoffed. Although it flattered his ego that she thought associating with him would bring her that much protection, he didn't understand her logic.

"Couldn't you just pretend that we are brother and sister? Wouldn't that discourage them?" Leema cocked her head.

"That won't stop anyone from trying to make a profit."

"Husband and wife then."

"Husband!" Bazin gaped at her. "I'm old enough to be your father!"

"No, you're not. What are you, twenty years? Twenty-five?" Leema frowned at him.

Bazin blinked. He had forgotten that he was in a different body. He reached up and felt behind his ear. There was no tattoo there to mark him as an assassin anymore. There was no way to prove he was Bazin once they finally got into the city. He shook his head. He would worry about that later. "It wouldn't work. Besides, the Wenzake saw your hair when they took you. All they have to do is ask if anyone's seen a golden-haired girl, and they'll lead them straight to us."

"Then what?" Leema crossed her arms and glared. "Because you're not just leaving me behind."

He turned back and watched her, trying to decide if she would explode at the suggestion forming in his mind. "How attached are you to your hair?"

"Very attached. It grows on my head." She put a hand up to her braid and eyed him warily. "Why? What do you have in mind?"

"I have a couple of ideas. We muddy your hair and face and hope that no one looks twice at you, but I doubt that will be enough to keep you from being noticed." He looked meaningfully at her.

Leema snorted. "Or?"

"Or we chop your hair off."

"What!" Leema scrambled to her feet.

"If we chop your hair off and slap a hat on you, we may get away without you being noticed." Bazin shrugged.

Leema stared at him in disbelief. The muffled sounds of the common room floated up from downstairs, and the fire crackled quietly. She fingered the end of her waist-length braid with one hand. She sighed and sank down on the bed. "Fine. I'll stay in the room."

He was surprised that she gave up that easily. "I'm only trying to—"

"I know," she interrupted, "keep me safe." She got up, grabbed the rag off the side of the second bucket, and started washing her face with a vengeance.

Bazin turned back to the fire so she wouldn't see his smile and jiggled his clothes, trying to get them to dry faster.

"Don't turn around," Leema commanded.

"You sound like your sister," Bazin smirked, listening to the water splashing behind him.

"Which one?"

"Brenith."

"Oh, good. If you'd have said Aritha, I would've hit you."

"And I wouldn't have blamed you," Bazin chuckled. He heard some more splashing and rustling behind him, then she appeared at his elbow with the sheet from the bed wrapped around her. She tried to hang her clothes next to his but was having trouble untangling the wet material one-handed.

"Here." Bazin took the bundle of green from her hands and spread it out near the fire.

"Thank you." She held her hands out to the fire to dry them.

He glanced at her. "You gonna throw a fit about sharing the bed too?"

She thought for a moment, then shook her head. "I know that I should because I'm a princess and you're..." she gestured toward him at a loss for what to call him.

Bazin grinned. "A man?"

"Yeah, but really, I'm too tired to care."

"Good, because I intended to sleep in the bed no matter what you said."

She yawned. "So did I."

A New Plan

"I MEAN IT. DON'T leave the room." Bazin jabbed a finger at her.

"I won't. Go." Leema waved him away. "Win money."

"Bolt the door after I leave," Bazin reminded her. He shut the door and waited until he heard the bolt before trotting down the stairs.

He paused at the foot of the stairs and surveyed the room. It was crowded with displaced travelers and merchants. Smoke hung heavily in the air, mixing with the smell of that nasty ale. He eased into the crowd and listened to the conversations as he went.

The gossip from Ka-Petra had finally reached Southgate. Apparently, Chancellor Villeah had been sitting at dinner with his family when an arrow pierced his throat. Most were speculating that Utsa Mayoth, the vicious woman who ruled House Mayoth, was behind it. A few thought it might be House Caith, but Bazin knew that an arrow through the throat wasn't Annorah Caith's style. When she had contracted Bazin last time, she insisted that the assassination look like an accident. If it had been Caith, she wouldn't have wanted any undue upset in the city while she took over.

However, there wasn't much optimism about House Mayoth taking control. The general consensus was that she was too much like her ancestor, power hungry and vindictive. Most expected martial law or worse. They whispered that Utsa was probably the one to loose the arrow herself.

Bazin tucked all this information away for later and moved on to the table where a game of dice was taking place. He watched for a few moments, then moved on. He had never liked the odds in dice games. He moved to a table where they were playing Peril. Leema would like that. She had insisted that she could beat anyone except Taus, and she was certain that was only because he'd cheated.

Bazin moved on until he came to the card table. Eight men ringed the tiny table. They were playing Havran. Bazin smiled a little and watched them play for a while as he studied each player. After about an hour of playing, two of the consistent losers got up and left.

"May I join you?" Bazin stepped forward when another player tossed his cards down and left.

"Sure." The man who had been winning all night looked up and grinned. "I'd love to take your money."

Bazin pulled the chair out and sat down carefully, trying not to wince. His leg had been throbbing continuously while he had stood watching, but he wasn't about to let it show. The grinning man dealt the cards and threw a few coppers into the center of the table. Bazin picked up his cards and added his coppers to the pile.

This is going to be easy, Bazin thought, glancing around the table. He had worked out each player's habits already. Now, all he had to do was sit back and gather the winnings.

Hand after hand, Bazin raked the pile of coins out of the center of the table. Several players had left and been replaced by others. The grinning man wasn't grinning anymore.

Time to lose a few, Bazin thought as he noticed the dangerous gleam in his opponent's eye.

Once the grinning man's smile was back in place, Bazin won another hand.

A buzz in the conversation near the door drew the attention of the entire tavern. Bazin looked up but couldn't see through the crowd. The subject of the conversation traveled through the tavern like fire through a dry field: Wenzake.

Bazin sat up and strained to hear what was being said. He scooped his winnings off the table into his coin pouch and stood.

The grinning man stopped him with a hand on his arm. "You're not going to give me the chance to win that back?"

"Maybe tomorrow night." Bazin glanced down absently. He headed for the bar. A pale-faced man stood in the center of the crowd, guzzling down ale as fast as he could.

"Where are they?" someone asked.

"Just up the street," the terrified man said between swallows. "They're looking for someone. They're searching each building."

"Who are they after?" another asked.

"Don't know," the man turned around and looked through the crowd as if he expected the cannibals to be in the room already. "I gotta get out of here!" He pushed his way through the crowd, knocking into Bazin as he ran up the stairs. A few people followed his example and retreated upstairs to pack. Bazin looked around the room for a moment. It had fallen eerily quiet. Everyone was watching the door.

Bazin scratched at the scab on his cheek, then disappeared up the stairs. They wouldn't have long. If the Wenzake were already coming this way, going out the front was not safe. He knocked quietly on the door.

"Yes?" Leema called out.

"It's me." He heard her slide the bolt, and the door opened slightly. Leema peeked out at him, then opened it the rest of the way.

"How was gambling?" she asked as he ducked into the room and quickly locked the door behind him.

"Profitable," Bazin answered as he moved to the window. He scanned the trees outside, looking for any sign of more Wenzake warriors.

"Then why are you acting like a guilty child? Make someone angry, did you?" Leema settled back on the bed and hugged her knees.

"No." Bazin opened the window and poked his head out. He looked around, then ducked back inside. "Wenzake are searching the town."

"What!" Leema shot off the bed but stumbled to a stop in the middle of the room. "What do we do?"

"No one is going to stop them from looking in each and every room if they want to. I don't plan on being here if the innkeeper decides that he wants to be helpful and suddenly remembers a blonde girl."

"Do you think they'll know it's us?"

"Blonde hair isn't native to Ka, remember? Face it, Princess, you're the only blonde girl in town. Told you we should do something about your looks." He grinned back at her as he crawled through the window.

"Yeah, yeah," Leema growled and hurried to the window. Bazin held on to the sill and braced his feet against the wall below the window. He looked around and then glanced back in at Leema.

"All right, no one around. Come out the window and then onto the next building's roof. Got it?"

Leema nodded.

He hung from the windowsill for a moment, wincing as the scab on his hip pulled. He swung his foot toward the next roof.

They heard the innkeeper's voice in the hall. "It's just up here." Even through the door, the tremor in his voice was clear.

"Hurry up!" Leema squeaked, motioning him to get out of the way.

His foot found the edge of the roof. The buildings were close, but not close enough to make it easy. Leema didn't wait for him to move and climbed out, nearly stepping on his fingers. Bazin shoved away from the inn and teetered precariously on the edge of the next building. Once he caught his balance, he motioned to her. Leema hung from the sill with one hand and stretched the other back to Bazin. He reached out and grabbed Leema's arm and pulled her over the gap between the buildings.

The door of their room banged open.

"Where are they?" The Wenzake warrior's voice was harsh.

"I swear to you," the innkeeper stammered, "this is the room they rented."

Bazin hauled Leema along behind him as he scrambled for the ridgepole. His wounds ached and pulled as they rolled over the peak of the roof to the other side. He froze and pushed Leema back against the roof. The ridgepole would hide them from sight if the Wenzake looked out the window.

"If they come back, you will tell me." It sounded like the Wenzake was standing just above them.

Bazin motioned for Leema to stay quiet.

"Of... of course." They heard the innkeeper agree as the door slammed again.

"They're gone," Leema barely whispered. "Do we go back?"

Bazin shook his head and motioned her to follow him. He led her across roof after roof until they were at least half the town away from the inn. He crouched near the edge of the last building and surveyed the street below. There weren't many people out now that the Wenzake were around. He shifted his weight a little to ease the pain in his leg.

There weren't many options now. They couldn't just leisurely wait at an inn for the gate to open. They would have to be constantly on the move if they were going to avoid the Wenzake.

"Should we go back to the forest?" Leema whispered as she crouched beside him.

"No, I want to be close when the gate opens." Bazin gazed around, looking for inspiration. Worst-case scenario, he would take Leema down the cliff and take the back way into the city. They'd probably die going that way, but they were walking a fine edge staying in the town too.

Further to the east side of town near the cliff edge, some of the traveling merchants had made camp with their wagons. Sitting amongst them was a brightly colored Vardo. Bazin smiled; the Free Folk had long been friends of the Zmajev Assassin's Court. They often gave shelter and transportation to assassins in exchange for protection.

"Come on." Bazin motioned for her to follow him to the lower end of the roof. He glanced over the edge. Below them was a narrow alley. No one was around, so he dropped down and landed with a grunt. Quickly, he looked around to see if he'd been heard. Nothing moved, so he motioned for Leema to jump down. She slowly slid off the edge of the roof, hung for a moment, then dropped down next to him, landing less gracefully than he had. She recovered quickly enough and scooted close to him as he edged toward the alley's opening.

He peeked around the corner. Torches burned along the main street of Southgate. To the right, two Wenzake warriors stood in the middle of the street. They gestured toward various buildings, obviously arguing about what to do next.

"Where are the rest?" Bazin muttered.

To the left, the gate stood glowing in the darkness. The guards who were stationed on the ground in front of the gate watched the Wenzake with keen interest. There was no good way to cross the street without being seen by the Wenzake. Bazin leaned back from the corner and cursed silently. Leema tugged on his sleeve questioningly.

He frowned and pointed to the street, easing back so she could look.

"So what now?" she asked when she'd seen the dilemma.

"We have to cross somehow. See that wagon with all the bright colors on it?" He pointed to the Vardo. She nodded. "That's where we're headed. It's the Free Folk."

"Aren't they dangerous?" Leema's eyes were huge again.

"Yeah. Dangerous enough, but," Bazin peeked around the corner again, "the Wenzake are superstitious about them and usually leave them alone. Usually."

The Wenzake were walking toward one of the taverns. Bazin turned back to Leema and caught the glint of gold from her hair. Reaching out, he grabbed her braid and stuffed it down the back of her shirt. She fought him for a moment until she understood what he was trying to do.

"Now keep your head down and follow my lead." Bazin looked for the Wenzake again.

They were facing the far end of town. Bazin wrapped his arm around Leema's shoulders and pulled her head down against his chest. If Bazin kept himself between her and the Wenzake, maybe they wouldn't notice right away that their golden-haired dinner was crossing the street. He took a deep breath, then wandered out into the torchlight. He staggered in a somewhat straight line, trying to look like he'd had too good a time and was heading home with a woman. Leema looped her arm around his waist for balance and tried her best to stagger alongside him.

It took years to cross the street, but finally, they staggered into the shadows between the buildings on the far side. Bazin immediately released Leema and moved to the edge of the alley.

"Damn," Bazin hissed. The Wenzake were coming this way.

"Come on." He spun away from the alley entrance and grabbed her arm, pulling her along behind him. He led her out the other end of the alley and into the cluster of merchant wagons. Weaving through the camps, he found his way to the Vardo. Glancing behind him, he rapped on the door at the end of the Free Folk's wagon.

"Go away!" An old voice creaked. It was hard to tell whether it was male or female.

"Kaleh-po tat-meh Sellemeh!" Bazin said in a rush.

"What does that mean?" Leema whispered, glancing around for the Wenzake.

"It means," a creaky voice said from the suddenly open door above them, making Leema gasp, "those who wander are free. What do you want?"

Bazin gazed up at the face in the shadows. "Wenzake are looking for us."

"Better hurry, then." A gnarled hand motioned them inside.

Bazin wasted no time. He shoved Leema up the wooded steps into the wagon and followed just as quickly. The door slammed shut behind them just as the Wenzake entered the camp.

Sold

"LOT SEVENTEEN!" THE AUCTIONEER called as the girl who had been lot sixteen was led off the raised stand.

"That's you, sweetheart." Scratches looked down at her.

Ro had no idea what his real name was. She had started calling him Scratches after raking her nails down his face. For that little outburst, they had chained her hands to a short wooden beam. Her second guard, Broken Nose, held his broken and bleeding nose from when she had hit him in the face with that very same beam after they'd chained her to it. After that, they had added a chain that ran from the beam to her ankles and chains on her neck that looped down through rings set into the support braces of the auction stage. The two men holding the ends of those chains had so far escaped injury, but Ro intended to change that. Every once in a while, she would pull against the chains just to watch them flinch.

"This is the one you've been waiting for!" the auctioneer teased.

A murmur of anticipation rolled through the crowd. The slaver reached down to pull Ro to her feet. Ro bucked and strained against the bonds that held her.

"Settle down, damn it!" Scratches grabbed a fistful of her hair and yanked her head back until they could get the chains free of the rings.

"This one is a fighter!" The auctioneer worked the crowd with his best sales techniques. "She killed three men when they took her and has been trying to kill the rest ever since!"

The two men tugged on the chains attached to her neck as they tried to get her up the stairs to the auctioneer. Ro couldn't take a full step. Her ankles barely had a foot of space between them. Despite that, she took every opportunity to make things difficult as they hauled her up the stairs.

"You all saw the havoc she created when they unloaded her this morning! If you can tame her, imagine the power you could wield! Imagine the entertainment she could provide!" the auctioneer continued.

Scratches climbed up the side of the platform, beating her to the top. He grabbed her arm and tugged. She pulled back from him, forcing Broken Nose to prod her from behind. The two holding the chains tried to keep them tight as best they could.

The chains at her neck grew slack just for a moment as Scratches let go and moved to the side so the crowd could get a good look at her. She took the opportunity and reared back against the chains, surprising the two men holding them.

They tried to compensate by throwing their weight toward the front of the stage. Their combined weight pulling in one direction was way more than what Ro could resist, causing her to stumble toward the front of the stage. She couldn't stop her forward motion, so she did the only thing she could and tucked into a lopsided forward roll. The men weren't prepared for it, and she dragged them with her as she rolled right off the edge.

The people standing just in front of the platform were unlucky enough to break her fall. The rest of them screamed and shouted as they scrambled backward, trying to avoid being hit by the crazed woman. She snarled as she threw her shoulders against anything that came close. Her two handlers finally regained their feet and pulled on the chains. Scratches appeared in front of her and tried to punch her in the face. She saw it coming and ducked.

"See what I mean, folks! A fighter!" The auctioneer was happy to capitalize on her escape attempt.

Broken Nose tackled her from behind and sat on her, crushing her into the stones with her arms pinned painfully by the chunk of wood. Ro struggled a little more but finally subsided. She hadn't really thought she could get away, but that didn't mean she was going to go tamely. She remembered all too well being chained to the wall of the mine, and she had no desire to ever be in that position again. She would fight every step of the way.

The auctioneer grinned. "Bring her back up, boys!"

Ro was lifted and carried back up to the platform. She bucked against her captors, keeping them twitchy. Finally, she was forced to her knees beside the auctioneer. Scratches and Broken Nose braced another beam across her legs, right behind her knees and held it there to keep her still. She tried to ignore the pain it caused.

Ro raised her head and stared out across the square. Tented merchant stalls lined the sides of the market, and the center of the square was filled with people. Everyone wore colored sashes that marked which house they belonged to. Some wore purple sashes or white, others had black or red, and there were some gold sashes here and there. Curtained sedan chairs were mixed in amongst the pedestrians, each sporting a house color. Black-clad Mayoth guards patrolled through the crowd.

"All right! A fighter," the auctioneer grabbed her chin and held it up, "and a looker!" Ro twisted her face away from his grasp. "A lot of pleasure either way! Let's start the bidding!"

Ro stopped listening. She didn't really care what she sold for. She wouldn't stay a slave long. She had to escape and find Brenith, Aritha, and Porsa. They were sold earlier in the day. Porsa had been sold to the stables of House Delaet. Aritha was going to the same House. She hadn't heard where Brenith had been sold to. Ro hoped that as soon as Bazin and Leema got through the gate, they would find her. Although deep down, she was certain that it would never be that easy.

The coup had lasted a week. Ro was almost glad that she had been safely tucked away in a cell during the worst of it. Her fellow captives had whispered that Chancellor Mayoth had taken over with an iron fist. The tension in the city was like a muggy fog. Everyone was keeping one eye ahead and one behind. Ro returned her attention to the bidders, hoping she would end up in the same house as one of the princesses.

"Fourteen gold pieces." An older woman dressed completely in white, sitting in a white sedan chair, raised her hand gracefully.

"Fourteen gold pieces to my Lady Caith!" The auctioneer beamed. He was making more for the sale of Ro than he had for all the others sold that morning combined.

"Fifteen," an oozing sort of voice echoed out from under the purple-curtained sedan chair.

The auctioneer bowed in that direction. "Fifteen to House Villeah."

"Sixteen." The lady in white bid again.

"Seventeen." A fat, bejeweled hand waved from the shadows under the purple canopy.

"Eighteen." The lady in white didn't wait for the auctioneer. She leaned forward and stared intently at the man in the purple chair. "What do you want her for, Villeah?"

"That's my business, Annorah." Ludlow Villeah leaned forward out of the shadows. "I say twenty gold pieces."

Annorah Caith stared at him for a long while with shrewd blue eyes.

Villeah returned her gaze without blinking. "You would do well to let me have her."

"Twenty gold pieces. Going once." The auctioneer's head swiveled between the two sedan chairs. "Going twice."

Slowly, Annorah Caith nodded, acknowledging something to Villeah.

"Sold to House Villeah." The auctioneer clapped his hands and gestured to the guards to remove Ro from the platform. "She's all yours, my lord. Good luck to you!" he added, causing a ripple of laughter through the crowd.

The guards pulled Ro along. She was going to a completely different house than any of the others. It would make it nearly impossible for her to help the princesses, but she promised herself that she would. They stopped at a wagon with an iron cage in the back. It was filled with men, women, and even a few children. They all stared at the ground, trying to come to terms with their new life as slaves for House Villeah.

"Up you go." Scratches opened the gate and shoved her forward. Broken Nose and Scratches bodily threw her into the cage.

"Good riddance," Broken Nose muttered as he turned away from the wagon.

Ro looked around. The slaves sitting closest to her scooted as far away from her as they could. They had seen the damage she had done to her guards earlier. They avoided looking her in the eye in case she decided to take her anger out on them too.

No help from them, Ro scowled.

They sat in the cage baking in the sun for another hour or so until the auction had concluded. No other slaves were bought for House Villeah. Finally, the wagon lurched and rattled forward through the crowd. She felt as helpless as she had all those years ago in the mine, chained to a wall and forgotten. The chains on her wrists rattled as she began to tremble.

"Krrr." A familiar chitter made her look up. Dinko dropped down onto the top of the cage with a thud. His yellow eyes gazed at her intently. Ro felt relieved beyond words. She tried to reach up to the little lemur but was brought up short by the chains.

"Krrr," Dinko purred. Ro looked around. Everyone in the wagon was looking at the lemur. She stared up at him, suddenly afraid that he would be noticed by the guards.

"Krrr." He purred once more and sprang off the wagon onto the canopy that shaded the nearest stall and was gone.

Transformation

"ARE YOU SURE I have to do this?" Leema asked again, looking up at the woman who had sheltered them in her colorful little wagon-house for the last week.

"How many times do I have to say it?" Bazin sighed. They had argued this point more than a dozen times. "You're the only blonde around, and I want to keep a low profile."

"What if it doesn't change back?" she protested.

"Would you rather cut it all off?" Bazin threatened again, tempted to do just that.

Leema blinked up at him. "Maybe."

Grandmother Taree held up a small clay jar. It was about the size of her palm.

Bazin reached for the jar, uncorked the top, and poured a few drops onto her scalp. Leema screwed her eyes shut and let out a whimper as he scrubbed the dark liquid into her golden hair.

"It's all right. It'll last for a few weeks if you don't get it wet, but it'll come out in days once you start washing it." Grandmother Taree patted Leema on the knee.

Leema grabbed her hand and held on tight.

Honestly, Bazin didn't understand why she was so upset. It was just dye. He had never colored a woman's hair before, but he had dyed his own hair once or twice, and it hadn't upset him. As he rubbed the long strands of her hair between his fingers to spread out the color, Leema made more and more distressed noises.

Bazin shook his head. *Women.*

Taree handed him a comb, and he slowly pulled it through her tresses to spread the color evenly. After a while, her hair was an all-over deep brown.

"Well," He stepped back and examined her critically. "I guess that's it."

The delicate green tunic and improvised pants she'd been wearing for a month had been replaced with a pair of brown nondescript pants and a linen tunic. There was no ornamentation except the leather belt. Her slippers had been replaced with a pair of sandals.

"Transformation complete." Taree squeezed her hand. "You don't look like a princess anymore." The old woman grunted as she dug through a drawer of the cabinet built into the outer wall of the Vardo. When she turned back, she held a small mirror up for Leema to see her new hair.

Leema's jaw dropped open, and her eyebrows rose as she turned her head from side to side. "Oh my." She peered at herself and tried out some facial expressions.

Bazin snorted and turned to wash the dye off his hands. He felt the light brush of Dinko in his mind and closed his eyes. He could see Ro sitting in some sort of cage in a wagon. She was sporting enough chain to start her own dungeon. "Damn."

"What?" Leema turned away from the mirror, self-consciously tugging at her hair.

"Ro's been sold."

"What!" Leema jumped to her feet. "What about my sisters?"

"Dinko only showed me Ro."

"Can't he find the others?" Leema handed the mirror back to Taree.

Bazin frowned at her. "Do you know how big Ka-Petra is? He's only one lemur!"

"But he's the only one *in* Ka-Petra!" Leema flung her hand toward the city. "It's been a week! I know we have to sit here, but—"

"He's doing the best that he can!" Bazin threw the towel down. "I don't want him to get caught and cooked for someone's dinner!"

"Eww!" Leema blanched. "People eat lemurs?"

"In Ka, people eat a lot of stuff, including other people! Or have you forgotten?"

"I haven't forgotten," Leema whispered, "but they are my sisters. They are all I have."

Bazin felt a twinge of guilt as she glared at him, trying to look tough. Sometimes it was easy to forget that Leema was only sixteen. She had always been so bubbly, despite all that she and her sisters had been through. He didn't want to see that light go out of her eyes.

Bazin shook himself. *I can't afford to go all soft about her. She is not my responsibility. I have to get Ro and get back to the Citadel. I've already wasted over a month with these girls. I'm running out of time.*

Taree handed the towel to Leema. "Dry yer hair. You can only do what you can do."

As the princess tousled her hair dry, Bazin thought about what Dinko had shown him. Ro wouldn't have been sporting that much chain unless she was being difficult. And if she was giving her new masters that much trouble, they might decide they don't need the hassle. *If she isn't careful, she'll get us both killed.*

Bazin paced to the door. "When are they going to open that damned gate?"

"Gossip says maybe this morning, maybe tomorrow," Taree replied as she cleaned up from Leema's transformation.

"What else does the gossip say?" Bazin pulled the curtain aside a little and peered out the window toward the gate. The Wenzake had taken to sitting in front of it. There were four squatting there at the moment.

"Said Mayoth is in charge, but people don't like it. Black guards are everywhere. There's been arrests, and it's making people nervous." Taree rinsed out the rag and wrung it out. "I'm all for driving straight through town and out the other side."

"I wish we could." Bazin let the curtain fall closed again.

Leema's head shot up. "We can't leave my sisters!"

"I know, I know." Bazin rubbed a hand over his beard.

"What are you going to do?" Taree stretched her aching back and stared curiously at Bazin.

"Ride with you into the city, then head for Caith, I guess."

"Caith isn't known for her kindness."

"I know."

"Well, I guess you know what you're doing." Taree hobbled forward, edging past Bazin to the door. "I'll take you to the Caith Quadrant, but then I'm heading straight for Northgate."

Bazin bowed solemnly. "Thank you, Taree."

"Yes, thank you." Leema gave the old woman a hug.

"I just hope you live long enough to see me again someday." The old woman shook her head as she left the wagon.

Bazin watched as she hobbled across the grass to the gate and spoke to the guards.

"Do you really think this Annorah Caith will help us?" Leema asked as she peeked through the curtain beside him.

"I hope so." Bazin was more than a little concerned that she wouldn't. He was in a different body and had no way to prove who he was. He let the curtain fall and sat down to sharpen his sword. There had been no chance to go back to the gaming tables to make more coin since the Wenzake were prowling around. Fighting might be the only way he was going to get Ro back.

"The gate is opening," Leema said from her position at the window. "Taree is coming back."

Bazin grunted as he heard Taree whistling a tuneless song as she began to harness the horses.

"Shouldn't we help her?" Leema asked over her shoulder.

"Only if you want to dine with the Wenzake."

"But they shouldn't recognize me now, right?" She put a hand up to her hair uncertainly.

"You willing to take that chance with the gate finally opened?"

"I guess not." Leema folded into a heap on the floor of the wagon. "I just feel useless."

"We'll be on the move soon enough."

Nearly half an hour went by before the wagon lurched into motion. Leema scrambled to her feet and pulled the curtain aside. She wanted to see what was happening. The Vardo rumbled and creaked as it shifted into line with the other merchants eager to get into the city. The line moved slowly as each wagon passed under the arch of the gatehouse. The Wenzake were pacing around the wagons, peering into each one as it passed.

"You might want to sit down until we are through the gate." Bazin reached up and pulled the curtain down over the window. Leema sat down with a huff and started to braid her new brown hair. Bazin sheathed his sword and leaned back.

The journey across Mayoth's Bridge took nearly an hour, but finally the wagon tilted as it angled up a street into the city itself. Noise from the markets they passed drew Leema to the window once more.

"You weren't joking," she said in awe as she ate up the sights of Ka-Petra. "Everything really is for sale."

Bazin chuckled and closed his eyes, leaning his head back against the side of the rocking wagon. After another hour of creaking along the twisting roads of Ka-Petra, the Vardo finally stopped. Taree banged on the front wall of the wagon, signaling Bazin that they had arrived at Caith House.

Bazin ushered Leema out into the glaring light of the afternoon. Heat reflected off the stone streets and buildings, making it feel like an oven. Breezes never made it to the streets of Ka-Petra, so there was never relief from the heat.

Bazin shouldered his pack, which held the few supplies that Taree had found for them, and led Leema along the side of the wagon.

"Last chance." Grandmother Taree gazed down at him. "You can still come with me."

"Another time, perhaps." He held a hand up in salute to the old woman.

She nodded, then slapped the reins to urge her horses forward. Leema watched her go, then gazed around them. The street was crowded with merchant stalls and people rushing about their business. Most wore the white sash of House Caith, but other colors were intermingled in the crowd as well. Guards garbed in Mayoth black snaked their way through the streets, watching everyone. A couple of eager merchants pushed their wares into Leema's hands.

"Come on." Bazin reached out and yanked her away from them by the arm. "Stick close."

Caith House

Bazin and Leema crossed the street toward an imposing white marble house with a massive white stone wall encircling it. Vines crept over the top, hinting at the lush garden within. A few trees stretched their branches over as well, shading the street and providing a little respite from the searing heat. Bazin led Leema off the street and down the alley between the garden wall and the building next to it, stopping at an iron gate that was recessed into the wall.

A guard dressed in white from head to toe glanced out at him without interest and waved his hand in a dismissive gesture. "Move on."

Bazin shook his head. "I'm here to see Lady Caith."

"But does Lady Caith want to see you?" the guard snorted.

"Tell her Bazin requests an audience."

"And who is Bazin?"

Bazin clenched his jaw. He wished he could just flash his assassin's mark like he used to. He shot a glance at Leema, but she was watching the activity on the street. "Just tell her I'm here."

The guard sighed as though Bazin's request would take too much effort but motioned to a servant who stood behind him near the door of the marble house. The servant boy quickly ran over to the gate.

"Go ask Lady Caith if she wants to see someone named Bazin."

The boy nodded and ran for the house.

"Thank you." Bazin smiled pleasantly and leaned against the cool stone of the wall. Leema fidgeted and peered through the gate, trying to see the garden.

Just as Bazin began to wonder if Caith even remembered him, the panting boy ran back up to the gate and nodded. "She says bring him in."

The guard sighed again and, with effort, found his keys, then slowly searched for the right key.

Bazin watched the guard's slow movements. "Need some help there?"

The guard stopped, looked at Bazin with a blank expression, then continued looking through his keys. Bazin was ready to grab the key ring and open the gate himself by the time the man finally unlocked it and swung it open.

They followed the servant boy through the garden and into the house itself. The change from the heat outside to the shaded interior almost felt like walking into a wall of ice. Their footsteps echoed on the white marble floors as they moved down the hallway. Elegant white carved doors blocked their view of each room they passed, but colorful paintings and beautiful statues lined the hall, showing off the wealth of House Caith.

"I never knew there were so many colors of white," Leema whispered to Bazin as she gazed around her.

Bazin looked around. He had been intent on the dangers that being in this house posed, not the furnishings. But now that he looked, it occurred to him that the color of House Caith was a prominent decorating tool. The walls, the floors, the upholstery, even the woodworks were all in shades of white.

The servant led them up a wide open stairway to the fourth floor and down another white hallway. Leema moved closer to Bazin as the boy stopped at a door and opened it.

The boy indicated that they should enter the room. "Lady Caith asks that you enjoy her hospitality until she can speak to you."

The suite of rooms was laid out in luxurious white. The massive, canopied bed, the elegant sofa and chairs, even the soft fur rug sprawled across the center of the room, were all brilliantly white.

"Thank her for me and please express that my visit is of some urgency," Bazin said as he guided Leema into the room.

As Bazin looked the room over, the servant closed the door behind them and locked it. Leema rushed back to the door and tried the handle. She spun around to stare at Bazin. "Why did they lock us in?"

"Wouldn't you?" He shrugged as he crossed to the window and looked out. No ledge, no balcony, and a four-story sheer drop. He frowned. There were disadvantages to people knowing your profession.

"No!" Leema protested as she tried the door again. "We never locked our guests in their rooms!"

"We're not just guests," Bazin said as he continued to explore. The adjacent room on the left was a beautiful marble bathroom, and one on the right was a dressing room. Neither had a second exit. "Everything in this house is white, but underneath, there is red."

"What do you mean?" Leema turned from the door.

"This city was built by blood. Don't forget that. Everyone wants something here." Bazin looked at her pointedly, then turned and sat down on the bed. "Don't expect help from Annorah without a very bloody price tag." He flopped back and stretched out with his ankles crossed.

"You should have told me that before we came in here," Leema accused.

"It wouldn't have made a difference."

"Yes, it would have." Leema scowled. "You should have given me the choice."

"A choice to do what?" Bazin laughed. "This is Ka-Petra. Without help, we would be rattling around the city for weeks looking for them. This way is faster, even if you don't like it."

Leema stared at him, digesting what he said. Her eyes narrowed with concern. "What do you think she'll want?"

"Hard to say." Bazin shrugged, staring at the canopy draped above him. "Probably wants me to kill someone."

"What?" Leema came forward a few steps. "You can't do that!"

"Why not?" He watched the surprise, disgust, and anger flit across her face.

"Be—because!" Leema gestured wildly.

"You sound like Porsa."

"No, I don't!" she sputtered. "How can you be so casual about being asked to kill someone?"

"Occupational hazard," Bazin muttered, thinking of the fiery pit of torment he had been in not so long ago and shivering at the memory. He didn't want to go back there. He had promised Dinko no more assassinations, and yet here he was. Anger at his situation boiled through his system.

"What?" Leema asked, stepping closer.

"What?" He snapped as he fought to control his temper.

"You muttered something. I didn't hear you." She leaned against the bedpost and frowned down at him.

"It was nothing." Bazin waved her question away. "Look, you want to find Ro and your sisters, right?"

"Yes."

"Then we will do whatever it takes." Something in his voice must have frightened her because her knuckles turned white where she was holding the bedpost. "Leema, you've trusted me this far. Trust me a little longer."

Leema shook her head. "I'm just not sure."

"What choice do you have?"

Leema backed away from him, walked to the window, and stared out across the haphazard jumble of buildings. "I wonder where they are?"

Bazin sighed. She sounded so dejected. He was getting too attached to Leema. She was such a feisty little thing, and Dinko liked her. Dinko had good taste. He just hoped he could find Ro, the other princesses, and Porsa, and get them out of the city alive. Anger flared again as he realized he was making himself responsible for all of them. He shouldn't be responsible for anyone. He was a Zmajev Assassin. They didn't get attached.

He glanced over at the sixteen-year-old girl, standing at the window with her head pressed against the glass, and sighed. *Who am I kidding? Like it or not, I am attached by my soul.*

Maybe he wasn't really an assassin anymore. He had died and been reborn. This was his second life. *Is it possible to start over?*

Maybe staying out of the Underworld wasn't just about not killing anyone. Maybe it was about killing for the right reasons. Perhaps he could tip the balance by helping these girls. He would do whatever it took to stay out of the Underworld. If that meant championing the three princesses of Koric as well as saving Ro, then so be it.

Bound

RO WAS TRANSPORTED TO what looked like a walled fortress on the north side of Ka-Petra. She had tried desperately to study the route they had taken, but the city streets twisted and backtracked onto each other so much that she wondered how anyone ever found their way around. The caged wagon rumbled through a set of iron gates into a courtyard surrounded by stone and purple-clad guards.

The man driving the wagon warned the guards about Ro, so they opened the gate with caution, but there was no need. Ro was too hot and tired to try anything. She was weak from lack of water or food, and she felt defeated. She allowed them to help her out and stood quietly while the rest of the slaves were unloaded.

The sun blazed down, baking the courtyard. Ro shifted to keep her bare feet from making contact with the hot stones any more than necessary. Sweat poured into her eyes as she squinted at the bare stone wall that surrounded House Villeah. It was roughly ten feet high and smooth. There was no way she could scale it without equipment or help.

She turned her gaze to the house. It was four stories tall and made from dusty, pink-tinted stone. A long balcony overlooked the courtyard with a wide veranda underneath. Heavy wooden double doors led to the interior of the house. She glanced around once more, checking for exits when, just for a moment, she caught sight of a furry form running along the top of the wall.

"Dinko," she whispered.

"What?" One of the guards looked at her sharply.

Ro only stared back at him.

"Come on." He grabbed her by the arm and tugged her toward the doors of the house.

Eager to get off the hot paving stones, she followed willingly. She didn't get the chance to look around the interior before he led her down a curving stairway into the dark pits under the house. One or two of the others were brought along behind her. The rest were led off in a different direction. The sound of her chains rattling with each step echoed loudly as they descended into the chilly depths.

The stairs opened into a large, cavernous room lit by torches. Cells lined the walls on two sides. Some were occupied; some were not. A third wall contained four heavy wooden doors with iron bars set across them. Through the center of the room was a long table with benches and a few strange metal objects that she couldn't define the purpose of, but she was sure she didn't want anything to do with them.

The men and women behind her were escorted into one of the cells and locked in. Then the guards turned to Ro.

"You gonna behave?" The head guard asked, watching her closely.

Ro said nothing. She looked him over, gauging her chances against him. He was a burly man about three times her size. He looked like he could crush her with one hand.

He frowned at her appraisal. "Let me rephrase. You behave, and I won't club you over the head."

Ro merely continued to watch him as he and another guard stepped forward to unlock her chains. They removed the ones on her neck first, then released her hands from the wooden beam. She curled her toes back to avoid the chains as they fell one by one into a heap at her feet. However, they didn't remove her ankle or wrist manacles.

He grabbed her elbow and turned her away from the cells. She shuffled along beside him until he came to one of the heavy wooden doors. One of the other guards opened the door to reveal a roughly furnished room.

A sturdy wooden table and chair occupied one corner, and an equally sturdy bunk stood against the opposite corner. There was a small square grid in the wall above the door to allow light and air into the tiny cell. The hole was barely bigger than her hand if she spread her fingers out wide.

Ro planted her feet. She didn't want to be locked in that tiny, dark room.

"Come now." The burly guard hauled her forward. He ignored her squirming efforts to stay out of the room. She felt like a fly trying to stop an ox. "You'll be out again soon enough."

He deposited her on the bed and bent to unlock her ankles. She thought for a moment about hitting him over the head, but he was already unlocking her wrists before she could make the decision. The other guard brought in a pile of clothes and a jug and deposited them on the table.

"Better clean up and get changed. Lord Villeah will want to see you as soon as he returns."

Without another word, they left her alone and locked the door. The room dimmed as soon as the door shut, leaving only the light from the vent shaft.

She wasted no time. She yanked on the ring that served as a handle, but the door didn't budge. She examined every inch of the door, but there were no locks to pick, nor could she access the hinges.

Ro turned and leaned against the door, watching the dust motes float in the light from the shaft. The air felt damp, and she could hear the faint roaring of the Ka. She wondered how far down they had come. It hadn't occurred to her that Ka-Petra was built down into the rock as well as on top of it.

Ro shuddered. Realization set in. She was locked away under tons of rock, again. She was no better off now than when Abeth had first found her in the mine. Ro snarled. She spun around and beat on the door with her fist. Pounding against the wood until her hands were nearly numb, Ro couldn't even make the door rattle.

She pressed her face against the wood. She was never going to get out of here on her own. Her breath came short and quick as despair tried to suffocate her. Ro slid to the floor. For long minutes, she just sat there, breathing hard. Her temples throbbed.

"Oh, Abeth. I've failed you." Tears dripped onto the front of her tattered and filthy uniform. "I'm so sorry."

She had vowed to give her life to protect Koric and the royal family. And yet, here she was, alive, but the royal family was lost. Koric was lost. Anguish washed over her. She had failed. Failed to protect Abeth. Failed to protect Abeth's daughters. Failed to protect Koric. She hid her face in her hands.

Pity never built a city. Taus' voice sounded loud in her mind.

She sat up straighter. He was right. Feeling sorry for herself wasn't going to save Abeth's daughters. She couldn't give in. She banged on the door again. She hadn't given up in the mine. She wouldn't give up now. She had to pull herself together.

Pushing to her feet and staggering to the table, Ro picked up the jug and sniffed the contents. Water. Hoping it wasn't drugged, she gulped down swallow after swallow. The cool liquid restored some clarity to her fuzzy mind. She poured some of the water into her hands and rubbed it over her face.

Ro looked at the pile of clothing. It was just a rough tunic and pants, but it was in better shape than what she was wearing. Her red uniform was barely hanging together, and yet she was reluctant to take it off. She was a House Guard of Koric. Her uniform was a symbol of her purpose in life.

She fingered one of the many holes in her tunic and sighed. Whether she wore the uniform of a House Guard of Koric or not, Koric was no more. The Empress' deadline had come and passed while they had trekked across Ka. In all likelihood, the Empress had deemed Koric a traitor province by now. She sat down abruptly on the bed as all of her strength drained away.

Long ago, when she had only been eight years old and had first seen the Guard practicing, she had asked Taus if she could have a uniform like theirs. *It's not the uniform that makes you a House Guard!* He had tapped her chest and then her head. *It's what's in here. And here.*

Ro sighed. Whether she was a House Guard of Koric or just plain Ro, she had a debt to pay. She sniffled as she stripped off the ragged material and laid it aside carefully. She turned back to the water jug and began to scrub at the dirt that covered every inch of her.

She checked the scratches and bruises that marked her progress across Ka. Some were almost gone. The scrapes on her foot were nearly healed, although they would probably scar. The bruises from the waterfall were fading, but the scrapes down her face were still bumpy scabs.

The wounds from tangling with the Wenzake were fully visible. She hadn't received as many injuries as Bazin had. She thanked her special gift for that. The tingling always seemed to help her anticipate where the next blow would come from. Time and again, she wondered why she had this gift, but there were never any answers. Not about that and not about her past. Sighing, she dressed again, this time in the clothes provided for her. However, there were no shoes.

"I'm destined to be barefoot the rest of my life," she muttered as she crawled onto the bunk to rest while she waited for this Lord Villeah to show up. Exhaustion and the silence of her dark cell finally lulled her into the first real sleep she'd had in over a month.

Bait and Bargains

"This is ridiculous." Bazin paced the length of the room again. "Two days! Two days we've been sitting here."

"I know." Leema rested her chin in her hand and stared out the window. "I've been here the whole time, remember?"

"What in Vunkah is taking so long?" Bazin paced again.

"What's Vunhak?" Leema frowned.

Bazin stopped and stared at her in disbelief. "The Uscar deity? Odd little runt that perpetuates disasters?"

Leema raised an eyebrow. "That's a dumb god."

Bazin threw up his hands and started pacing again. "Two days!"

"Say it again, maybe it'll help." Leema rolled her eyes.

By his calculations, more than half of the sixty-day time limit had already passed. At this rate, he might not make it back to the Holy Mountain. *What will happen to my soul then? If Ro is still alive, does the time limit matter? Will my soul just shoot back to the Underworld?* Bazin sighed. Either way, he had to get back to Jardarwa and persuade the Holy Brothers to keep him alive. "I'm running out of time."

Leema frowned at him. "Time for what?"

Bazin ignored her. "Don't you realize, sitting around all this time will make it hard to find your sisters?"

"I know exactly how hard it will be," Leema muttered.

Bazin stopped pacing and glanced at her. He knew his temper was getting out of control, and he shouldn't be so emotional, but it was hard not to be impatient. He felt so cut off. Dinko had followed Ro to House Villeah, but the lemur couldn't get in to find Ro. There was no saying what had happened to the others. Bazin growled and started to pace again.

He stopped as he heard the click of the door lock. It wasn't near any of the mealtimes, so it couldn't be a servant with food. Leema jumped to her feet and moved over beside Bazin. They stared at the door as it opened to reveal an old man dressed as a servant.

"Lady Caith will see you now." The servant bowed slightly. "Leave your weapons here."

Bazin frowned but didn't pick up his sword from where it leaned against the bed.

"If you would like to follow me, please." The servant beckoned them with one hand.

"About time," Bazin muttered and followed the man into the hall with Leema close on his heels.

They returned to the main floor of the house and trekked down another long hall to a set of double doors. The servant stopped at the doors and opened them wide. "My Lady Caith? Bazin to see you, as requested."

Bazin moved into the room and glanced around, passing a cursory glance over the three white-clad guards placed strategically around the room. Except for the large desk in the center of the room, there were no other pieces of furniture. A man dressed in gold stood off to the side with a book under his arm. He looked like he was maybe in his fifties. He was short and studious-looking. Bazin knew him by reputation. Caelan Pohle. He was the head of House Pohle and had a reputation for finance and architecture. He was one of the few House rulers of Ka-Petra who could be considered mentally stable. Pohle watched Bazin and Leema with interest, especially Leema.

Bazin turned away to look at Lady Annorah Caith, matriarch of House Caith. She looked just the same as she had thirteen years ago. She sat behind the desk, dressed in a simple white silk dress. Even at the age of sixty-seven, she had lost none of her beauty. She was a striking vision with her snow-white hair curling gracefully around her shoulders. Her shrewd blue eyes glowed brightly as they examined Bazin.

"I thought you said this was Bazin?"

"I am Bazin," he answered before the servant could speak.

Caith narrowed her eyes. "You're not the Bazin I know."

"But I am." Bazin could feel Leema staring at him, but he ignored her.

Caith ran her gaze from Bazin's head down to his toes and then back up again before standing and rounding the desk. She sauntered toward Bazin with an assurance that she would be proved right. Bazin held her gaze as she reached out and felt behind his right ear. She smiled when she didn't feel the raised bumps of the assassin's tattoo that should have been there. "I think you are not."

"I *am* Bazin." He assured her.

"Ha!" She laughed. "You aren't old enough!"

Bazin's eyes glinted. "I can prove it."

She thrust her chin upward and looked down her nose at him. "Then do so!"

"Very well." Bazin suppressed his smile and leaned forward to whisper in her ear. "You liked the way my mustache tickled."

Caith reared back and stared at him.

"How did you know that?" she hissed.

"I was there." Bazin smiled and winked. His intimate relations with her thirteen years ago were a very dangerous secret. He could see her calculating the threat he posed to her power now.

She peered at him. "What happened to you?"

"I would rather not discuss that." He glanced meaningfully at Leema.

She turned her shrewd gaze on Leema and examined her from head to toe just as she had Bazin. Leema lifted her chin and waited, refusing to look away.

"Hmm." Caith turned back to Bazin. "Why are you here?"

"I am searching for three women and one boy who were taken during the coup."

"If they were taken by the slavers," Caith shrugged as she returned to her seat behind the desk, "they would have been sold by now."

Caelan Pohle cleared his throat and shifted uneasily.

"I am aware of that possibility." Bazin nodded, glancing at Pohle. He was staring intently at Leema.

"So, what do you want from me?" Caith asked.

"I was hoping for your help in locating them."

"Ah." Caith sat back and eyed him. "In exchange for what?"

He hated playing these games. "I'm willing to negotiate."

Caith braced her elbows on the arms of her chair and tapped her fingers together, considering. She flicked a glance at Leema, who stood just behind Bazin.

"Who is that?"

Bazin tensed. He had no idea what Caith would ask for in return for her assistance, but he hoped it wouldn't cost him Leema's freedom. "She is the sister of the women I'm looking for."

Caith watched them silently for several long breaths.

Pohle cleared his throat again. "Annorah, you know that I never liked the slavers filling their pens unlawfully." Pohle turned toward her. "If these women have been taken because of the chaos that Mayoth caused, then it is our duty to find them and send them on their way."

"All in good time, my dear Caelan." Caith waved him to silence. She was still staring at Bazin. "Caelan, perhaps you could escort this young lady back to her room while I discuss things with Bazin."

"Of course." Pohle bowed slightly and stepped around the desk. His expression barely showed his disapproval as he stopped by Leema. "If you'd like to come with me." He gestured toward the door, but Leema looked at Bazin.

Bazin nodded to Leema. "It's all right, go ahead."

Reluctantly, she allowed Pohle to lead her from the room. Caith gestured for the guards to leave as well. As soon as the door closed, Annorah stood and walked to the window. Bazin waited for her to start the conversation. He had no intention of giving her any more information than he had to.

"So?" She finally turned to watch him. "How is it that you are Bazin, but not Bazin?"

"I died." He shrugged. "I was brought back in a different body."

"Interesting way to continue living."

"It takes some getting used to."

"Finally, a use for those ridiculous monks from Jardarwa." Caith smiled. "Perhaps I should look into the Holy Mountain's practices a bit more."

"I wouldn't bother." He smiled. "I'm a fluke."

"Hmm." Caith wandered around the room, watching him. "Why are you looking for these girls?"

"We were traveling together. They are my responsibility." Bazin crossed his arms. "When the gate closed, we got separated. I just want to continue our journey."

"Journey to where?"

"I don't believe that is relevant."

"Hmm." She sat down at the desk again. "What will you offer me in return?"

"Why are you asking?" He swaggered up to the desk and perched on the corner. "We both know you already have something in mind."

"Now, that is the Bazin I knew." She smiled. "Very well. I want you to kill Mayoth. In exchange, I will find your companions."

"She must have really pissed you off." Bazin snorted. "She's only been in power a couple of weeks."

"She is bad for business." Caith shrugged. "We all want her out."

"Like last time? You want it to look like an accident?"

"No. This time I don't care." Caith sat forward and stared at him intently. "I just want her dead. And I want it soon."

Bazin thought for a moment about his 'no more assassinations' vow to Dinko. This would definitely be breaking it, but it wouldn't be wise to refuse Annorah Caith. It may also be his only shot at finding all the girls and getting out of Ka-Petra as quickly as possible. Sending a silent apology to Dinko, he nodded.

"We have a deal then?" She raised an eyebrow. "Do you wish to sign a contract?"

"No." Bazin shook his head and ran a finger over the spot behind his ear where the assassin's tattoo should have been. "I am not officially part of the court right now. I have no desire to insult them as a pretender."

"I understand." Annorah inclined her head. "There is going to be an event at House Villeah tomorrow night. All the Houses will be represented. It is supposed to be a feast welcoming Mayoth as the chancellor."

"Isn't Villeah the House she usurped?" Bazin frowned.

"Yes. This is Ludlow's way of showing her he bears her no ill will."

"And does he?"

"Of course he does! She killed his father and arrested his uncle." Annorah scoffed. "I expect he has something in mind as a special surprise. There are rumors that he intends to put on some sort of fighting exhibition. I expect something disastrous to come of it. I think it would be an excellent opportunity for you to remove Mayoth from this life."

"Nothing like a murder to make a party memorable."

Doubt

When Bazin returned to their room, he found Leema sitting in the middle of the bed waiting for him.

"You want to tell me what that was all about?" She glared at him.

"What?" Bazin shut the door and wandered over to stare out the window.

"Don't do that! Don't treat me like I'm an idiot!" Leema bounced off the bed and stomped toward him. "She knows you, but she doesn't? You're too young to be Bazin? Just what in Vunkah is going on?"

"You shouldn't swear like that," he said without turning around. "Brenith wouldn't approve."

"I'll swear if I want to!" She punched him in the arm. "I want to know what is going on. Who are you really?"

He barely glanced at her. "I'm Bazin."

"That's not an answer."

"It's all the answer you're going to get."

"No!" Leema shoved him. "That's not good enough. You asked me to trust you. How can I when you're hiding things from me?"

He turned around. "You kept things from me too."

"I did not!"

"You never told me that you were the Princesses of Koric."

"You already knew!"

"Ah," he held a finger up, "but you didn't know that."

Leema ignored his twisted logic and crossed her arms. "If I'm going to put the safety of my sisters in your hands, I think I deserve to know who you are."

"Trust me," Bazin turned back to the window, "you'll not like what you hear."

Leema went quiet behind him. Finally, he heard her sigh. "Very well. If you refuse to tell me, then I withdraw my request for help finding my sisters."

"What?" Bazin spun around, wincing as his leg twinged.

"I have no desire to put their fate in the hands of a stranger with dubious goals. I no longer require your help. I have other options."

"I am not a stranger!"

Leema gazed up at him sadly. "You are now."

The pain in her eyes needled at his heart. "I've been traveling with you for almost a month."

"And we know nothing about you."

Bazin growled in frustration and scrubbed his head with both hands. Then he stopped and stared at Leema. "What did you mean you had other options?"

"Lord Pohle has agreed to help me."

"What! Why would he help you?"

"He knows who I am."

"Why did you tell him?" Bazin grabbed her by the shoulders and shook her slightly. "Do you have any idea how dangerous it is for anyone in Ka-Petra to know you are unguarded royalty?"

"I didn't tell him." Leema shoved his hands away. "When he brought me back to the room, he said he thought that I looked familiar. He said he knew my mother. They met when he was in the Imperial City. He doesn't want to cause animosity with Koric. He's going to make arrangements to find my sisters."

"And you think he'll come through and not just ransom you back to Koric?"

"Yes." Leema stared up at him in defiance and jabbed him in the chest. "It's not like I have anyone else I can trust."

"Dammit, Leema! You can trust me!"

"Not if you won't tell me who you are!"

Bazin scrubbed his head again and began to pace. If he didn't tell her, then she was going to run off somewhere with Lord Pohle and get into who knows what kind of trouble. If he told her the truth, she might never trust him again. Maybe he could get away with half-truths.

Bazin turned to face her. "I worked for Annorah Caith once, thirteen years ago."

"Why didn't she recognize you?" Leema's voice was barely a whisper.

"I've changed a lot." Bazin ran a hand over his beard.

"Why did she say you weren't old enough?" Her eyes narrowed with suspicion.

"Like I said, I've changed a lot. I've been through some things that have altered me permanently."

"You're still not telling me anything." Leema crossed her arms. "Did you come across us by accident in the forest?"

Bazin sighed, "No."

"Were you looking for my sisters?"

Bazin looked her directly in the eyes. "No."

"Are you going to hurt my sisters in any way?"

"No."

"Are you here to hurt Ro?"

"No." Bazin walked over to her and took her shoulders again. "I promise you. I have no intention of hurting any of you. On the contrary, your safety is my highest priority."

"Swear it." Leema peered at him. "Swear it on Dinko's life."

Bazin suppressed a smile at her choice of assurances. "I swear on Dinko's life."

Leema gazed into his eyes for the longest time before she nodded.

"I still don't entirely trust you because I know there's more you're not telling me, but I will believe, for now, that you don't want to hurt us. But know this, if you betray us, I will find a way to hunt you down."

Bazin gazed down at the young girl who barely reached his shoulder. Her expression was as hard as any mercenary he had ever met. She was finally showing her royal blood. He had no doubt she would carry out her promise. For some strange reason, he felt pride in her declaration.

"Good." He nodded. "I would expect nothing less."

Leema blinked in confusion and opened her mouth, but he didn't allow her time to question his response. Instead, he moved forward with the business at hand.

"What exactly did Pohle say he was going to do?"

"He said he would find them and then send me a message as to how we could leave."

Bazin scowled. "That's it?"

"At least it's a plan." Leema shrugged. "What's yours?"

"It's not much better." Bazin snorted. "Annorah promises to reunite me with my companions."

"In exchange for what?"

"Killing Chancellor Mayoth."

Leema stood very still, watching him. Her expression was a mixture of fear and revulsion. Slowly, her arms came up to hug her waist.

"I warned you that killing would probably be her price," Bazin said quietly.

"I know," she whispered.

Leema looked like she wanted to take a step away from him, but she didn't move. He admired her for it.

"Are you going to do it?"

"If I have to." Bazin ran a hand over his beard. "Look, we're going to have a hard time leaving this city either way. So, I suggest we get you prepared."

"Prepared?"

"You need to learn to fight. I'm not saying you'll have to, but I'd rather you know what to do and not need it than need it and not know."

"Ro taught me a few things already."

"You're going to need a lot more." Bazin shook his head and crossed the room to where his sword leaned against the bed. "Do you know how to fight with a knife?"

"A little. I'm better with a bow."

"You know archery?" Bazin turned around. He eyed her arms, surprised that she would be strong enough to pull a bow.

"Yes." Leema's chin went up. "I used to practice with Taus." She choked to a stop.

"Taus?"

"He was... the head of my mother's..." Leema sniffled. "Mother made him the High Marshal. He was rough and crass and..." She broke off, trying to stop the tears from flowing.

Bazin pressed his lips together. He wasn't sure how to comfort her, but he wanted to try. "I'm sure you'll see him again."

"No, I won't," Leema croaked and swiped at her nose with her knuckle. "He was on the ship with my mother and brother when the dragon attacked. I'll never see any of them again."

"You don't know that. You made it out alive, maybe they did too." Bazin stepped closer. "But you need to worry about yourself right now. So, go wash your face, and let's show you how to fight."

Leema sniffled and walked to the bathroom. Bazin turned toward the window, absently rubbing his hip. He gazed out at the city, wondering again how he had ended up in this position.

He stretched to the side carefully, feeling the pull of scar tissue in his hip. His leg was healing, but not fast. He hoped that it would hold up against whatever was coming tomorrow night.

Just as he started to turn away from the view, a movement on the roof across from the window caught his eye. A huge black bird flapped its wings and then settled down again. Bazin stepped closer to the window and peered out at the bird. It was wearing a harness. It was the same bird he had seen in the forest after the Wenzake came after them. It was also the same bird that had been at the old woman's cottage that first day.

"Damn." Bazin clenched his jaw as he realized the mercenary was still alive. The waterfall hadn't killed him after all.

As he watched the bird, that nagging feeling of familiarity tugged at him again. Bazin scratched his beard, trying to remember. Finally, it came to him. If that bird was sitting up here watching when his master couldn't, then that meant the bird was a drugi just like Dinko. He hadn't met anyone with a drugi except a few of his fellow assassins. *Had the mercenary been trained at Zmajev?*

Why would the Drugi Moc go to the trouble of resurrecting me and then send another assassin after Ro? Bazin scowled at the bird. *Did they know that Porsa bungled the spell? Or was there someone else after her?*

"What are you looking at?" Leema asked as she walked up behind him.

"Nothing," Bazin growled as he turned away from the window.

Leema glanced out the window. "That bird is still following us."

Bazin looked at her sharply. "You know about the bird?"

"Yes." Leema snorted. "I'm not blind. I think it belongs to that mercenary who attacked Ro. The one who fell into the river with her. It's been following us for weeks. I imagine that means the mercenary is still alive."

Bazin shook his head. "I've underestimated you, Leema."

"Yes, you have." She took the sword out of his hand. "Now, teach me."

Entertainment

RO WAITED. SHE WAS now well fed and well rested. It had been two days since she had been locked in the tiny room. She had seen no one but her jailer when he brought food and water. There was nothing to do but sleep and wait, neither of which got her any closer to escape, but at least she was healing.

She sat up when she heard voices. Ro moved quickly to the door and pressed her ear against it. The muffled sound got louder. They were coming closer. She backed away and put her back to the wall across from the door.

The locks rattled and clacked. The door swung open. Light flooded the room, making her blink. Her burly jailer came in first and stopped about halfway across the room. Behind him, another man stepped through the door. He looked to be in his mid-thirties, although his dark hair had flecks of gray in it. He was dressed in purple and was very round in the belly.

"So, how is my little troublemaker?" His eyes roved over Ro. "I have to say, that was one of the most entertaining slave auctions that I've been to in years."

Lord Villeah watched her for a reaction, but Ro remained silent.

"I should think that you would thank me for buying you. Others would have beaten you until you broke. Whereas I have greater plans for you in mind."

The burly jailer glared down at Ro. "Say thank you, Lord Villeah."

Ro stared back at him, saying nothing. He stepped forward only to be stopped by Villeah.

"It's all right." Villeah gave Ro an oily smile. "I like your spirit. I don't want it broken just yet." Villeah stepped closer to Ro, examining her. "I wonder... what are your politics, girl?"

Ro looked him up and down, wondering what he was talking about.

"I said, what are your politics?"

"Answer him," the jailer growled.

Ro shrugged. "I don't have any."

Villeah's eyebrows rose. "You don't favor any one House?"

"I don't know what you're talking about." Ro scowled. "I'm not from Ka."

"Ah," Villeah leaned back, patting his belly with bejeweled fingers. "That explains it. I'm sure you'll not have any objections then."

"Objections to what?"

"I assume from the chaos you caused at the slave market that you know how to fight?" Villeah peered at her closely.

Ro nodded slowly, unsure of where this was leading.

"Good. When I saw the way you knocked your handlers around, I knew that you had some skill." Villeah smiled. "I am putting on a little celebration for the new Chancellor Mayoth. I plan to have a fighting exhibition as the entertainment. You will be one of my fighters. Does that please you?"

Ro said nothing. She had no desire to fight for the entertainment of others, but at least it would give her a chance to get above ground. With a weapon in her hand, maybe she could escape.

"Well, I was hoping for a little more enthusiasm but..." Villeah gestured with mock helplessness, "ah well. Although I will demand that you show some enthusiasm in the courtyard when you fight. I want all eyes on you. Do you understand? All eyes on you."

Ro nodded slowly.

"I want no mistakes about this. All eyes must be on *you*."

Ro eyed him suspiciously. Instinct told her something was wrong. He was planning something, and it wasn't just about entertainment. She wondered if she would be able to shift it to her advantage.

"Good." Villeah patted his belly again and smiled his oily smile. "I will send you some appropriate clothing for tomorrow night." He glanced down at Ro's feet. "And some shoes."

***

The next day, the burly jailer brought Ro the 'appropriate clothing' that Villeah had promised.

"Appropriate for what?" Ro held up the short tunic that only came to mid-thigh. It was bright purple. There was also a gaudy silver belt that was more shiny than useful. There were no pants.

"All eyes will be on me all right," she muttered in disgust.

She wondered idly what they would do if she didn't wear it. She picked up the shoes that Villeah had sent and rolled her eyes. There was no way she could fight in dainty sandals with a raised heel. She dropped them on the bed and sighed.

Ro jumped at the sound of the door locks. The burly jailer swung the door open and stopped with a frown.

"Why aren't you dressed?"

"How am I supposed to fight in these?" She picked up the sandals and waved them at the jailer.

"You will wear what you're told."

"If Villeah wants a decent fight out of me, then he needs to give me decent equipment. In these shoes, I'll break an ankle and be dead in less than a minute."

The jailer sighed, but she could see that he agreed with her assessment of the shoes. He stepped into the room and held his hand out. Ro slapped the sandals into his palm.

"I'll see what I can do, but there's no arguing about the rest of it. Lord Villeah was very specific that you—"

"Catch the eye?"

"If you don't wear it, I'm authorized to strip you and send you out naked."

Ro's lip curled. "You can try."

"Don't tempt me!" he growled as he turned away. "Just get dressed. I'll try to find you some different shoes."

The door slammed behind him, and Ro looked down at the purple tunic. It was going to be embarrassing to wear something so revealing, but she didn't want to end up fighting naked either. She changed quickly. As she waited, she kept self-consciously pulling down the tunic. The splits in the side seams allowed her freedom of movement, but it also made her feel naked. She fiddled with the belt and pulled on the hem of the tunic again, trying to make it longer.

The door swung open, and the jailer handed over a new set of sandals. They were still dainty, but at least the heel was flat. She quickly slipped them on and fastened the buckles. She settled into a fighting stance and shifted her weight, trying to get used to the feel of shoes.

She looked up at him. "How long until I fight?"

"Don't know."

"Do you know who I'm fighting?"

"Nope."

"Do you know what I'm fighting with?"

"Nope."

"You're a lot of help," she muttered as he closed the door.

Ro began to stretch her muscles. She was stiff from doing nothing for two days, and she didn't want to get herself killed if her muscles cramped. Her heart was already pounding from nerves. She had spent a lot of time on the practice field, but she didn't have much real experience. She had been in more fights since being shipwrecked than she had in all of her years in the Guard combined.

"Relax," Ro breathed, trying to calm her nerves. She paced a little and then took a few practice swipes with an imaginary sword. She laid it out in her mind with each swipe. She would perform for Villeah, and somehow, she would find an opening and escape. She would go to House Delaet for Aritha and Porsa and somehow find Brenith. They would find their way out of the city and hopefully meet Leema and Bazin along the way. It sounded so easy in her head, but she felt a moment of despair as she realized how impossible it was going to be in reality. *What if they don't give me a sword?*

Hours crept by as she paced the tiny room. She stretched again. Ro worked through another drill with her imaginary sword and then paced some more. She pulled her hem down and checked the buckles on her sandals. Her mind swayed from imagined success back to imagined failure over and over again.

Finally, she heard the thud and clank of the door being unlocked. It swung open. Her jailer stared in at her.

"Ready?" the guard asked.

Ro nodded and followed him out of the room.

"You *will* behave tonight. None of those antics that you pulled at the slave market, or I'll smash you over the head and throw you back in your cell. Understand?"

Ro said nothing until he grabbed her by the arm. "Say you understand."

Ro glared up at him. "I understand."

Escape Plans

PORSA FLUNG ANOTHER SHOVEL full of manure into the cart sitting outside the stall. He wiped the sweat from his forehead with the back of his wrist and bent to scoop up another shovel full.

"Porsa?" A woman's voice echoed through the stable.

"Y-yes?" Porsa straightened and looked around. No one had called him by name since he had been sold to House Delaet. They simply told him his duty and then ignored him. He didn't really mind. It was a very peaceful existence.

"Porsa?" The woman came closer.

He could hear her dress sweeping against the straw that littered the aisle as she approached. Porsa set his shovel aside. Opening the gate, he stepped out to see what she wanted.

"Hello, Porsa." The woman stopped in front of him and gazed at him with a smile. "It's good to see you again."

Porsa blinked in confusion, trying to remember if he knew any beautiful women besides Aritha, Brenith, and Leema. The woman smiling at him was nearly as tall as he was, and as thin, but in an elegant, graceful way.

He shook his head. "I-I'm s-sorry."

"You're still stuttering?" She frowned. "I thought for sure you would outgrow that."

"I-I-I—"

"Don't you recognize me?" She stepped forward and covered his hand with hers. "Porsa, it's me, Paila."

"P-Paila?" He felt faint for a moment. "B-but I th-thought f-father sold you t-to the C-C-Consort G-Guild."

"He did." Paila smiled as she hugged him. "I was there for three months, and then Lord Pohle found me. He bought my contract and brought me here."

"P-P-P—" he tried to ask as he stepped back.

"Pohle," Paila said for him. "He is a kind man. He sent me to find you."

"M-Me?" He looked around the stable, wondering if there had been a mistake, but there was no one else.

"Yes. He said that you were traveling with a girl named Leema and her sisters."

"Y-yes! And B-Bazin. And Ro."

"He wants to help you all escape."

Porsa gaped at her. "Wh-why?"

"I told you, he is a kind man," Paila smiled a sweet smile, "and slavery doesn't sit well with him."

"Wh-what d-do we d-d-do?"

"Well, first..." She reached into her bodice and produced a gold-colored sash. She pulled the red sash from around Porsa's waist and quickly tied the gold one in its place.

"W-won't s-s-someone n-notice?" Porsa didn't want to get into more trouble.

"You were taken from the streets unlawfully, so I don't really see the problem with stealing you again." Paila waded up the red sash and shoved it under the manure in the cart.

"-" Porsa couldn't even form a word.

Paila grabbed Porsa's hand and pulled him toward the door of the stable. She glanced around the small courtyard. A few grooms lazed under the shade of a tree in the far corner.

"Follow me." Holding her head high, she swept out into the blazing sun and crossed the courtyard as if she owned it. Porsa trailed along behind her, glancing at the grooms and praying that they didn't care enough to stop them. So far, he had found that the servants of House Delaet cared more about their own comfort than about anything else. He hoped that included him.

Outside the gate, Paila shoved him toward the waiting coach. "Get in."

She climbed in after him and slid onto the cushioned bench. Paila blew out an excited breath and raised her eyebrows. Her eyes sparkled. "How exciting!"

Porsa couldn't believe that they had just walked out without anyone challenging them. If he had known it was that easy, he would have left a lot sooner. "W-what now?"

"Well," Paila sighed as the coach started forward, "now, we wait."

"W-wait?" Porsa shook his head. He thought of Bazin's deadline. "W-we c-can't!"

"Porsa, don't worry, I'm following Lord Pohle's instructions." Paila sat back and smoothed out her skirts. "Our spies have been searching for the girls. We know who they are. Unfortunately, the one called Brenith is out of reach. She's already out of the city."

"How?" Porsa sat forward.

"I don't know."

Porsa looked down at his dirty hands and worried about Brenith. She had been so kind. He wasn't sure that she would survive the life of a slave. He looked up at his sister, almost afraid to ask. "The others?"

"Don't worry. We know where they all are. It might be a bit tricky to get to them, but we have a plan." Paila smiled. "There is a celebration at House Villeah tonight. It is shaping up to be an interesting party."

Porsa groaned. He didn't want to go to a party. He didn't want to be in Ka-Petra anymore.

Paila laughed. "We're not going *to* the party, silly, we're using it as a cover."

Porsa nodded as if he knew what she meant.

His sister took pity and explained, “Lord Delaet left for House Villeah earlier, taking the one called Aritha with him.” Her tone was brisk and businesslike. “The black-haired one, Ro, was bought by Villeah, so she will already be at the house. All we have to do is bring them out to the coach.”

“W-what about B-Bazin?”

“Lord Pohle will attend to Leema and that Bazin fellow.”

“Wh-what if someone c-comes after us?”

“Lord Pohle believes there will be sufficient distractions to keep anyone from noticing our escape.”

“H-how do w-we g-get out of the c-city?”

“The coach will take you to Northgate. Pohle has horses waiting for you. As soon as you are mounted, run.” Paila’s eyes flashed in the shadows. “Even if they come looking for you, you should be able to outrun them across the plains. If you head straight north, you’ll come to the Sinir River. There will be a ship waiting to take you to the Imperial City.”

“Are y-you c-coming with us?”

“No.” Paila shook her head and smiled sweetly again. “I will stay with Lord Pohle.”

Porsa nodded and sat back against the seat but then looked up again. “Wh-why is L-Lord Pohle d-doing this?”

“He is the real leader in Ka-Petra,” Paila answered passionately. “He has a higher understanding of the world than those other fools who just bicker amongst themselves for power.”

Porsa stared at his sister as the coach bounced and rattled through the city. The Paila he remembered had been a shy and dreamy child. This Paila was a very confident and passionate young woman. “Y-you’ve changed.”

“I had to.” Paila smiled. “The Consort Guild was a harsh place, but Caelan saved me. I owe him everything.”

Porsa tried to smile. “I’m g-glad you’re happy.”

“And what about you? Are you happy at the Holy Mountain?”

Porsa grimaced.

“I can’t imagine how you ended up here traveling with a group of girls.”

"I-it's a l-long s-story." Porsa sighed. Slowly and with a great deal of starting and stopping, Porsa told his sister about Bazin and the botched spell.

Paila frowned at him as the coach slowed. "What will happen to Bazin and Ro once you are back in Jardarwa?"

"I d-don't kn-know." Porsa shook his head as the coach rocked to a stop.

Paila peeked out of the curtained window. "We're here."

"Wh-what d-do I d-do?" Porsa sat forward.

"Follow me and don't say anything. I don't know the girls we're looking for, so you'll have to be my eyes. If you see one of them, let me know." Paila reached forward and gave her brother a quick hug. "I'm so glad I could see you."

Porsa couldn't speak. He only nodded and hugged her back.

"Come on." Paila released him and stepped out of the coach.

The Celebration

BAZIN MOVED SLOWLY THROUGH the party with Leema trailing behind him. He periodically felt her hand on the small of his back. He wasn't sure if she was trying to reassure herself or if she was just trying not to lose him in the crowd.

Villeah's celebration was no small affair. The main and second floors of the house were packed with citizens of Ka-Petra. Every House color was represented. There was plenty of drinking and laughing, but the laughter rang hollow. Palatable tension simmered just below the sparkling joviality. Bazin could see it in their eyes as they passed through the crowd. Something was going to happen.

Bazin didn't like it.

A crowd this jittery was liable to panic at the slightest provocation. It would either make their escape easier or more difficult. He expected disaster. Ever since his life had become entangled with Ro, everything seemed like it was more difficult.

Leema tugged on the sword harness that hung empty on his back. The black-clad guards at the gates had insisted that he leave his weapon outside.

"What?" Bazin turned to Leema.

She pointed toward the balcony. He looked up. Aritha stood in a crowd of people dressed completely in red. They swarmed like drunken bees around a scruffy man who had a drink in each hand and laughed too loudly. He had one red-clad arm flung over Aritha's shoulders. Her face was pale and tight, but she stood regally as she tolerated the man showing her off as a trophy. Aritha's red dress emphasized her golden hair. Bazin was glad they had dyed Leema's hair, or she would be catching as much attention as Aritha.

Bazin leaned down so he could speak directly into Leema's ear. "Pohle said that he would take care of getting Aritha out."

"I haven't seen Brenith or Ro."

"Keep looking." Bazin shook his head as he looked around. "We need to find Mayoth."

Leema grabbed the front of his jerkin and pulled him back when he tried to walk away. "You're still going through with it even though Pohle is getting us out?"

He stared down into her big brown eyes. They were filled with fear. Bazin spoke into her ear again. "I may have to. If we need a distraction, then that is the best we'll get."

Leema nodded and let go of his jerkin. Bazin turned and wove his way through the crowd again. He found the wide, curving stairs that led to the second floor and started up. He threaded his way toward the balcony, looking for the telltale black of House Mayoth. Finally, he spotted Chancellor Utsa Mayoth.

She was hard to miss. Her hair had been dyed black, and she had painted her face with black geometric accents that contrasted with her deathly white skin. She looked every bit as vicious as her reputation said she was. She sat near the edge of the balcony, glaring at anyone who came near her. Several guards dressed entirely in black ringed her chair. It would be hard to get close enough to Mayoth to kill her with that many guards, but it wasn't impossible.

Bazin could see Annorah Caith. She stood on the far side of the Chancellor, glaring at the back of Mayoth's head. She glanced up and caught Bazin's eye. She gave him a slight nod. Behind him, he heard Lord Delaet laughing again as he approached, dragging Aritha along beside him. As Bazin turned, he shifted Leema behind him, shielding her with his body so that Aritha didn't see her. He had no faith in Aritha's ability to keep her head if she saw her sister.

"Utsa! Wonderful party, isn't it?" Delaet laughed and stumbled, nearly spilling what was left of his wine onto Mayoth's lap. One of her men stepped forward to move him back.

"No harm done!" He smiled at the guard. "Wine! More wine!" he shouted.

"Quit your braying, Delaet!" Mayoth snarled and waved the guard back, dismissing Delaet as any kind of a threat.

"You should learn to relax, Utsa," Delaet chided. "Life isn't all about killing and power!"

"What are you implying?" Mayoth turned an icy stare on Delaet.

"Nothing!" Delaet smiled as he shoved his frowzy brown hair out of his face. "I'm just saying it's a party, you should enjoy yourself!"

"More wine, my lord?" Aritha took the empty glass from his hand and turned to go.

"Oh no. You stay here, my beauty." Delaet hugged her close and buried his face in her neck. Aritha looked like she wanted to be sick. He lifted his head and smiled again. "Isn't my new girl a beauty, Utsa?"

"Hmm." Mayoth gave Aritha a cursory glance and looked away again.

As Bazin watched them, he caught a glimpse of a familiar face. Porsa stood next to a tall, thin girl who looked a lot like him. The girl stepped up and poured more wine into Delaet's glass as she whispered something to Aritha.

Aritha flinched and glanced at the girl but noticed Porsa. She looked back at the girl again and nodded slightly, then turned back to Delaet. Her expression remained rigid. Her composure surprised Bazin. He thought for sure she would give the game away.

Bazin leaned down and whispered to Leema, "Aritha's taken care of."

The youngest princess nodded as she watched Porsa and the girl fade back into the crowd. They didn't leave, but they stayed far enough back that they wouldn't draw attention to themselves.

Leema stretched up on her tiptoes to speak into Bazin's ear. "We still need to find Ro and Brenith."

"My Lords and Ladies! Distinguished members of all the Houses of Ka-Petra!" Lord Villeah called out from the balcony just a few feet away from Bazin and Leema.

"Your attention," he raised his hands and his voice to gain the attention of the crowd, "please!" Slowly, the noise faded into an excited hush. Light from the crackling torches danced and glinted off countless jewels, making the crowd glitter as all eyes turned to Lord Villeah.

"I offer entertainment tonight like no other!" Lord Villeah shouted. "I was going to offer just a fighting exhibition, but then fate stepped in. I know many of you were at the slave market recently when a feisty young woman tried to tear apart half the square!"

A murmur of anticipation raced through the crowd. The people standing below the balcony started to point and whisper to each other. Dread tensed Bazin's spine.

"I bought that young woman so that she may fight for you tonight!" Lord Villeah gestured toward the courtyard. Applause greeted his proclamation. "A tribute to Chancellor Mayoth."

Bazin peered over the balcony, but he couldn't see what they were looking at. He scanned the courtyard looking for Dinko. Earlier, he had been on the wall near the gate. The lemur now sat on the wall across from the balcony, watching the proceedings. He would have the perfect view. Bazin closed his eyes and reached out to Dinko. The image of Ro emerging from the depths of a dark stairway shimmered into his mind.

Bazin frowned as he assessed her skimpy attire and very impractical shoes. *How in Vunkah is she supposed to fight in that?*

Bazin's eyes popped open, breaking his connection with Dinko as a burly man guided Ro out onto the veranda. People stopped talking as Ro and the jailer passed through the crowd. A few even reached out to touch and pinch her arms as if trying to decide if she would make a good fighter. Ro shook them off and glared, bringing a murmur of delighted anticipation from the spectators. The jailer stopped her near the center of the courtyard and turned her to face the house.

Dozens of torches ringed the courtyard, making the space glow. The center had been cleared to leave a large open space for her to fight in, but spectators crowded onto the benches that lined the walls.

"Now for the real surprise!" Villeah rubbed his hands together. "I have another treat for you! This will be no ordinary fight! This will be a fight for revenge!"

Bazin glanced at Villeah, trying to figure out his game. Beyond him, Bazin could see Mayoth glaring at Villeah. It was written all over her face that she thought he was speaking about her. Annorah Caith also glared at Villeah. Only Delaet seemed unconcerned with the political tension surrounding him. He continued to drink and giggle into Aritha's hair.

"Recently, I was approached by a few men. They were looking for someone who had murdered their brothers. They wanted revenge." Bazin watched Mayoth's expression change from anger to suspicion.

"Here is the woman who wronged them!" Villeah gestured toward Ro. She cocked her head and frowned up at Villeah. "Tonight they will have their revenge! Tonight, for your pleasure, I give you the fight to end all fights!"

"Oh no." Bazin had a very bad feeling about who those men were. He shoved his way to the front of the crowd and looked down. Leema hurried after him.

Below the balcony, an excited murmur flared up. Bazin leaned out over the balcony, trying to see what caused the commotion. Bazin looked to Ro. She shifted away as if she would run, but the guard held her elbow to keep her in place. Every muscle in her body tensed as all her attention centered on something below the balcony that Bazin couldn't see. Her chest rose and fell in quick, short breaths. Her face paled. Bazin could see her eyes from where he stood. They were no longer blue. They were ice white.

"Here are your opponents, my dear! The Wenzake!"

Bazin's gut twisted. *She dies, I die.*

The excited crowd surged forward to get a better look, pressing Bazin and Leema against the stone balustrade. Six tribe members walked out into the courtyard. Their faces were lined with ritual scars, and their hair had been painted muddy red. Matted braids from previous victims hung from the back of their hardened leather jerkins. Each held a Wenzake short spear and a long knife.

"Bazin?" Leema's voice trembled as she grabbed his arm.

"Damn!" Bazin glanced around, looking for a way to help Ro.

The odds were given, and bets were shouted.

"Give her a weapon," Bazin muttered, wishing he hadn't given up his sword. "Give her a weapon!"

A few of the less-brave spectators vacated the benches that lined the walls, only to be replaced by other, more bloodthirsty watchers. The crowd began to clap and demand that the fight begin. The Wenzake spread out in a semicircle around Ro and the guard.

"It's six against one!" Leema tugged on Bazin's sleeve as if he could change it.

The burly man looked up at Lord Villeah. Bazin looked too. Lord Villeah glanced at Mayoth. She was watching the Wenzake warriors with vicious anticipation. Villeah then looked down at the courtyard and nodded.

The jailer turned to the side and motioned to a servant. The young boy hurried forward, carrying two swords. He held them out to Ro.

"Choose."

Ro glanced at the Wenzake and then at the two swords. She reached out, hefting one and then the other. Then took the first one again. The guard took the spare sword and ushered the servant out of the courtyard.

Bazin's glance darted from Ro to Mayoth, to Villeah, to Caith, to Dinko. *How in Vunkah do we get out of this one?*

Entertainment

"BEGIN!" LORD VILLEAH SHOUTED.

Ro took up a ready stance and watched the Wenzake as they circled. They taunted and jabbed their spears at her, but no one made any real moves. The tip of Ro's sword swayed back and forth, trying to keep all six in her view. The crowd began to cheer and shout.

"Do something!" Leema tugged on Bazin's sleeve.

Bazin tried to back away from the balustrade, but the crowd was pressing too close. He could barely move. All he could do was watch.

The first Wenzake lunged at Ro from her left. She parried the blow easily. A second warrior lunged, and again she parried with ease. The Wenzake started to test her in pairs, feigning and lunging from two sides at a time, but she continued to avoid their blows. Despite her feminine appearance in the ridiculously short tunic and sandals, she was proving a worthy opponent. Her skill began to shift the odds in her favor. The crowd shouted, placing more wagers.

Again and again, they danced around. The sound of steel on steel reverberated off the stone walls of the courtyard, only to be drowned out by the restless crowd. They had expected more of a bloody massacre with the Wenzake involved. They wanted more. They wanted carnage.

"Something's not right," Bazin muttered, watching her fight. He watched her dodge each blow seconds before she should have known where it would be. Somehow, she knew where each swipe and jab was coming from before it happened.

"She's anticipating," Bazin whispered.

The Wenzake were getting frustrated. They couldn't seem to land a blow. Ro feigned and sliced at one warrior and then spun to block another. Bazin watched her in fascination. No wonder she hadn't received as many injuries as he had when they fought the Wenzake before. It also explained how she had managed to skewer him too. It wasn't that she was a better swordswoman; it was because she had the ability to predict her opponent's move.

Clanging and grunting filled the air as she fought for her life. Ro swiped to the left, turned, and sliced open the leg of the nearest warrior on her right. The crowd cheered as blood splattered the stones. The Wenzake pressed her back, shouting and feigning strikes. Their frustration grew with each injury. She twisted and turned. She sliced the neck of one of the warriors. He fell heavily, clutching his wound. She circled to the right to avoid the growing pool of blood on the ground.

"Don't!" Bazin growled as he watched her turn her back on the wounded Wenzake.

"No!" Bazin shouted as the wounded man swung his long knife at her hamstring.

In one motion, she sidestepped and turned, jamming her sword through the man's face. The crowd cheered as she jerked her weapon free. The remaining four Wenzake screamed in anger and charged her.

"No! No! No!" Bazin shoved at people crowding against him. *She dies, I die*, was all he could think.

Suddenly, the crowd on the balcony burst into chaos and surged away from the balustrade. Their screams drowned out the cheering of the people below. Finally free to move, Bazin glanced around, trying to see what had caused the sudden panic.

Utsa Mayoth struggled to get out of her chair. Red blood stood out brightly against her pale neck. Delaet stood over her with a broken bloody glass in one hand, grinning triumphantly. Blood covered his wrist. Several men in red fought with Mayoth's black-clad guards.

"No!" Villeah screamed, moving toward Delaet. "She was mine!"

Annorah Caith glared at Delaet, jealousy of his move to power written clearly on her face. She swung around to glare at Bazin. It was clear that Caith believed he had failed her. In that moment, Bazin knew he had gained an enemy.

Bazin glanced back at Ro. She was still fighting against four of the Wenzake. They cared nothing for the commotion happening above them. They only wanted revenge. He had to get down there.

"Come with me!" Caelan Pohle appeared beside Bazin. "This way!"

Bazin and Leema pushed their way through the crowd after Pohle. He led them to a secondary stairway away from the panicked exodus of guests rushing to get away from the massacre on the balcony. They thumped down the stairs and around the corner. Pohle held his arm out to stop them as a group of purple-clad guards ran past, shoving panicked citizens out of their way. Pohle glanced around and spotted Paila waiting near a small door in the hallway.

"Hurry!" Paila held the door. "Aritha's in the coach with Porsa."

Pohle pulled Leema forward, but she jerked her arm out of Pohle's grasp. "We have to get Ro!"

"Leema, go!" Bazin shouted as he turned and ran back into the panicked crowd. By the time Bazin had reached the courtyard, Ro was backed into the wall. Sweat poured down her face. The tunic was now dark purple, discolored by sweat and blood splatters. Blood ran down her left leg from a gash across her thigh. There were only three Wenzake left.

Bazin glanced around. He needed a sword. Without a weapon, his chances would be slim. The Wenzake lunged at Ro. Realizing he had no time, he charged forward and tackled the closest warrior. His momentum carried them both into the second Wenzake. They rolled to the ground in a heap of flailing limbs, crashing into the torch stand near the wall.

The pole holding the torch toppled onto Ro just as she took a swing at the last Wenzake. She hissed as the flames washed over her arm, but the fire hadn't burned her. The warrior she had been fighting jabbed his spear at her. She ducked and dodged to the side.

Bazin wrestled with the warrior that he had tackled, while the second cannibal scrambled to get out from under them both. Bazin reared up and punched the Wenzake warrior in the face and then smashed his head into the stone-covered ground.

Ro leapt over the wrestling men. The warrior Ro had been fighting lunged for Bazin. Ro spun back and, using the warrior's momentum against him, skewered him on her sword.

Bazin scrambled to his feet and kicked the remaining Wenzake in the jaw.

"Run!" Bazin grabbed Ro's arm and pulled her away from the courtyard toward the back hallway.

"Krrr." Dinko shot past them, zig-zagging through people's legs.

"Where are we going?" Ro panted.

Pohle waited for them at the door. "The coach will take you to Northgate. I have horses waiting for you."

"What about the girls?" Ro asked as they ran down the hallway.

"Aritha, Leema, and Porsa are already there," Pohle answered as he opened another door. This one led to the alley.

"What about Brenith?" Ro stopped. "We can't leave without her!"

Pohle shook his head. "Brenith is gone."

"Gone? Gone where?"

"She was sold before I could find her," Pohle answered as he tried to push Ro forward again. "Please, there's no time!"

Ro's sandals slid on the loose dirt in the alley as she tried to resist. "We have to find her!" Ro turned to Bazin as he grabbed her arm and propelled her forward. "Bazin, please!"

Bazin stared at her in surprise. He had never seen her frantic before. Her desperate eyes pleaded for his help. Behind him, they could hear shouting.

"Ro, we have to go. Now." The shouting was getting closer. "I promise we will find Brenith. But right now, we have to get the others to safety."

Ro hesitated as though she meant to argue but then nodded.

"I will make inquiries," Pohle promised as they hurried Ro around the corner to the waiting coach. Leema was hanging out of the door, watching for them.

"Hurry!" She waved excitedly as they rounded the corner. Dinko shot past them and disappeared between Leema's legs into the dark interior of the coach.

"Move!" Bazin shouted at Leema. She scrambled backward as he tried to help Ro up. Bazin glanced at Pohle. "Thank you."

Pohle nodded and glanced over his shoulder. "Go!"

Bazin climbed in. The coach was moving before he closed the door.

He didn't bother trying to find a seat in the already crowded space. He just squatted down next to the door and held on, wincing as his leg throbbed. The interior was in complete shadow with all the window shades drawn.

"We'll be at the gate in a few minutes," Paila said from the shadows to his left.

"Who are you?" Aritha asked in a strained voice.

"Sh-she's m-my s-sister," Porsa said. His bony knees knocked into Bazin's back as the coach bounced and swayed. Thinking of knees, Bazin turned, searching for Ro in the darkness.

"Ro? How's your leg?"

"It's fine." She sat behind him next to Porsa.

"We need to bind it," Bazin warned. "It's going to be a hard ride."

"Do you need a bandage?" Paila asked. He heard movement, and then she shoved something into his hand.

He turned to find Ro in the darkness. He reached out until he felt the warm, bare skin of her leg. She jerked away from him.

"Hold still," he snapped.

She grabbed his hands and took the bandage from him. He gave up and let her tend to her own wound.

The coach rocked to a halt. Bazin peeked past the leather shade covering the door's window.

"It's clear." He stood, opening the door. Stiffly, he climbed out. Bazin rubbed his hip and scanned the area. Torches burned along the street, illuminating the way to the North Gate. News of the attack on Mayoth would reach the gate soon. If she died, they would be closing the gates again.

Dinko leapt out and vanished under the coach. Bazin turned back to help the others. Leema came first, then Porsa, Paila, and Ro. Aritha was last.

"You're his sister?" Aritha blurted as she stared at the beautiful Paila.

"Yes," Paila answered absently. Her mind was on business. "This way. This stable belongs to Caelan." The girls followed her as she led the way around the coach. "Supplies are already packed on each horse. Just leave the horses with the harbor master at Sinir. He'll get them back to us."

"Thank you." Leema hugged Paila.

Paila returned the hug and then pushed her toward the waiting horses. "You better hurry."

They each thanked her as they moved to mount up. Porsa stood, awkwardly gazing at his sister.

"Don't worry," she hugged him tight, "I'll see you again soon."

Porsa only nodded and turned away to mount the last horse. He struggled clumsily, but finally, with a boost from the coach driver, he was sitting up straight on his horse.

"Krrr." Dinko launched into the air and landed on the pommel of Bazin's saddle.

"Let's go." Bazin reined his horse around and started for the gate.

"Close the gate!" A shout echoed off the buildings.

"Shit!" Bazin spurred his horse into a run, thundering through the opening, nearly trampling the guards. The others followed as quickly as they could.

Night Race

"HURRY!" BAZIN SHOUTED OVER the roaring of the Ka.

The five fugitives raced across the North Gate Bridge. The sound of the raging river almost drowned out the echo of the horse's hooves as they pounded across the stones. The first few travelers they met on the bridge scrambled to the side. Behind them, they could hear their pursuers shouting.

Chaos erupted as merchants and residents of Ka-Petra suddenly recognized the significance of approaching riders when coupled with the cry of "Close the gate!" Many tried to turn around. They didn't want to be trapped on the bridge if another coup was starting.

Horses snorted and screeched as riders pulled roughly on their reins. Wagon drivers tried to turn their unwieldy vehicles around but only succeeded in running into each other and blocking the bridge. The drivers yelled at one another. The noise on the bridge was deafening.

"What do we do?" Aritha shouted as they tried to avoid the tangle.

Bazin didn't answer. He nudged his horse forward and pushed past Aritha and Porsa's mounts. They followed him as he guided his horse between two wagons and around a herd of bleating goats.

"Krrr." Dinko danced around in Bazin's lap, glaring down at the goats.

Once they were past the worst of it, Ro called out, "Bazin!"

"What?" He turned around, and she pointed at the troop of mounted guards approaching from the city.

"Damn!" They wore the white of Caith House. "Quick! Get moving!"

Aritha wasted no time in spurring her horse on again, but Porsa was having trouble. Bazin reached over and slapped the flank of the boy's horse. It shot out forward with the apprentice barely hanging on as Bazin, Ro, and Leema raced to catch up with them.

The glow of the torches illuminated the stone arch that led to Northgate like a beacon ahead of them. As they raced closer, the guard standing on top of the arch shouted something to the men below and pointed back toward the city. The guards in front of the gate started to yell and pull on the massive wooden doors that would close off the bridge from the town.

"Wait!" Aritha screamed as she urged her horse to go faster.

The guards looked back at the approaching riders and tried to wave them off. They didn't want to get crushed between the horses and the gate. The torchlight reflected off Aritha's golden hair, making it glow as she raced under the arch. The guards dove away from her horse's hooves. Porsa and Leema dashed through next. Ro and Bazin thundered through last, forcing the guards to jump back again to avoid being trampled.

Bazin glanced back. Their pursuers were caught up in the chaos of wagons and goats. He faced forward again only to find Aritha reining in her horse. "Don't stop!"

"Why?" Aritha glanced back. "We made it out."

"Caith sent men after us. They might get past the gate." Bazin shouted as he rode past her. "We need to keep our head start."

Aritha whimpered, but she spurred her horse back into motion. They thundered through Northgate, zipping past taverns and inns. The few pedestrians in the street scurried to the side as they passed.

They raced into the darkness beyond the town. Faint moonlight showed the road that would take them to Sinir. Soon, the glow of the town was far behind them, and Bazin slowed their pace. Bazin twisted around in the saddle, scanning the road behind them.

"Krrr." Dinko climbed up onto his shoulder and stared into the darkness. Neither man nor lemur could see any sign of pursuit. It was too dark.

"Why are we slowing?" Aritha's voice was shrill, making her horse toss its head. "I thought you wanted to keep our head start!"

"I don't want to kill our horses by pushing them too hard either!" Bazin said over his shoulder.

Leema sighed from the darkness to his left. "And it's too dark to safely ride fast."

"And it's too dark," he agreed.

"Krrr." Dinko shuffled a little, then jumped. The sudden gasp from the youngest princess showed that Dinko had hit his mark.

Bazin glanced at Ro. Her bare leg reflected the dim moonlight. "Nice outfit."

"It's completely ridiculous." Ro pulled the too-short hem of her tunic down.

"At least you have some shoes now."

Ro snorted. "Now that I'm riding."

Bazin laughed.

They rode in silence until Ro glanced at him. "Thank you."

"For what?"

"Getting them out." She nodded toward Leema and Aritha. "We wouldn't be here if not for you."

Bazin shook his head. "Don't thank me. Thank Pohle."

She tried to pull her tunic down again. Her self-conscious gesture drew his eye to her bare leg again. A shadow was spreading across her thigh.

"You all right?" He edged his horse closer to hers.

"I'm fine."

"Liar." Bazin reached out and poked the shadow.

Ro hissed and slapped his hand away. "I said I'm fine."

"You're not going to pass out, are you?"

"You mean like you did?"

Bazin scowled into the darkness.

"I'm not going to pass out." She reached down, pressing her hand against her leg where the Wenzake had stabbed her.

"Well, you're not doing us any favors by letting it bleed."

"What do you mean?"

He could feel her glaring at him, but it was too dark to see her expression. "You're leaving a blood trail for Caith's men."

"We don't have time to stop."

Bazin grunted. He turned again and searched the horizon behind them but saw no sign of pursuit. Turning back, he squinted at the road ahead.

"I think we have enough of a lead. They might have gotten stopped at the gate."

"Or maybe they didn't." Ro turned to look behind them.

"Risk worth taking." He turned his horse toward what looked like a little grove of trees. He led them a little way into the trees away from the road, then dismounted.

"Why are we stopping?" Aritha asked Porsa as they stopped next to Bazin's horse.

"Ro is injured," Leema answered as she and Ro rode over to a second tree.

Bazin tied his horse to a low branch on the far side of the tree. He quickly began to dig through his saddlebags.

Leema dismounted, leaving Dinko in the saddle. She tied her horse to the tree and then moved over next to Ro. The young guard tried to dismount, but her injured leg buckled. She would have hit the ground if Leema hadn't been there.

"Thanks," Ro grunted through clenched teeth.

"Lean on me." Leema pulled Ro's arm across her shoulder and walked her away from the horses.

"I'm fine," Ro insisted.

Leema lowered her to the ground. "Yeah, I know."

Bazin crouched beside them and organized a very small fire. Light flared suddenly as he struck his flint to the bits of dry grass and branches. He glanced up to search the horizon again as he tried to shield the light so it wouldn't be seen from the road.

"I wish Brenith were here," Leema muttered as she carefully unwrapped the sodden bandage. Leema squinted in the dim light, trying to see the wound. It wasn't big, but it was still bleeding.

Bazin picked up a burning branch and turned away. He walked in a large circle, squinting at the ground, searching for the plant that he had shown Ro when he was injured. Finally, he found some. He reached down and yanked it from the soil. He turned and stalked toward Porsa and Aritha, where they stood huddled next to the horses. "Porsa?"

Porsa jumped. "W-what?"

"I need you to dig through our supplies and find water, a pot, and see if there are any clothes for Ro."

"I'll look for the clothes." Aritha stepped forward, smoothing down her dress.

"Look for another bandage too," he called over his shoulder as he stalked back toward the fire.

Porsa hurried up to the fire with a small pot and a water skin he'd found draped over the saddle horn of Leema's horse. Bazin splashed a bit of the water into the pot and set it on the fire.

"What is that called?" Leema asked as he ripped the weed into little pieces and threw them into the pot.

"I can't remember the name." Bazin shrugged. "I just remember what it looks like."

"I found a shirt and pants," Aritha said as she moved up to the fire.

"Thank you." Ro tried to reach for them, but Aritha held them back. "You can wait until they fix your leg. No sense getting blood on these too."

"Porsa, go keep a lookout." Bazin glanced at the fidgeting apprentice. Porsa stood and walked off. "Porsa?" Bazin stopped him and pointed in the opposite direction. "That way."

Porsa nodded and sheepishly disappeared into the darkness. Aritha folded the clothes into a pile and left them by the fire before following Porsa.

Silence descended while they waited tensely for the water to boil the plant. Bazin kept glancing back toward Ka-Petra and muttering at the slow-boiling pot as Leema washed as much blood off Ro's leg as she could. Finally, Bazin could wait no longer. He mashed the soggy weed into a pulp and turned to Ro.

"This is going to hurt," Bazin muttered as he scooped out a glob of green goop.

Ro's eyes glittered in the firelight. "Don't worry, it's not like I would punch you or anything."

Bazin stopped and glared at her. Then, without breaking eye contact, he slathered the goop all over her leg. Ro hissed and reared back. She clenched her teeth and her fists, but she didn't say a word. She only glared at him. He grinned wolfishly at her.

"Will that stop the bleeding?" Leema interrupted their silent battle.

"It should. You can wrap it now." Bazin moved out of Leema's way and carried the pot out into the darkness to empty it.

Hidden Truths

Ro winced as Leema wound the bandage around her thigh. The green glob that Bazin had smeared into the gash was still boiling hot. Her leg tingled, and she had to resist the urge to scratch it. Leema tied the bandage, making Ro hiss again.

Leema paused. "Did I hurt you?"

"Just get it done."

Leema nodded and finished quickly.

"Best get it all done at once." Leema scooped up the clothes from where Aritha had left them by the fire. "Let's get you changed."

The pain was starting to subside, and Ro wanted nothing more than to sit still for a little while, but Leema was right. The youngest princess reached out to help her up. Ro grabbed her hand and struggled to her feet. The cut on her leg roared to life.

Wincing, Ro sidled around the tree into the shadows and leaned against the rough bark while Leema helped her into the clean clothing. The pants drooped from her waist, threatening to fall. Ro used the belt from Villeah's costume to keep them up, but they still bagged around her ankles.

"You ready to go?" Bazin asked from near the fire. He dragged dirt over the spot where Ro's blood darkened the ground.

"Almost," Leema said over her shoulder as she rolled up the cuffs on the oversized shirt.

"We've stayed here too long already." Bazin glanced toward the city, then started to kick dirt over the fire.

"Are we going?" Aritha's voice floated out of the darkness.

"Yes." Bazin scattered the ashes and embers to hide the fact that they had stopped there.

"Do you need help mounting?" Leema asked Ro, but she shook her head.

"Don't forget that." Bazin pointed at Ro's blood-soaked tunic.

Leema nodded, reached down, and scooped it up along with the used bandages. She rolled them into a bundle, carried them to her horse, and stuffed them into her saddlebag.

"Do we stay on the road?" Leema shifted Dinko out of the way so she could mount.

"Yeah. Our tracks will be harder to pick out from what's already there," Bazin answered as he mounted.

Ro limped toward her horse and tried to get her foot in the stirrup, but the horse kept sidling away from her.

"Here." Aritha rode over beside Ro's horse and grabbed the bridle using her own horse to keep Ro's steady. Ro glanced at her in surprise. Aritha didn't say anything more; she just held the horse still until Ro managed to get mounted.

"Thank you, Highness."

"You're welcome." The princess's voice was subdued. She let go of the bridle, turned, and rode past Bazin toward the road.

"Never thought I'd see that," Bazin mused, watching the princess by the dim glow of the moon.

"What?" Ro asked as they turned their horses onto the road.

"In all the time I've been with you ladies, never once have I seen her do anything nice for any of you." Bazin glanced over his shoulder.

Ro shrugged. "Caring just doesn't come naturally to her."

"I noticed."

"She's better suited to other things."

He snorted. "Uh-huh."

Ro felt obligated to defend Abeth's daughter. "She's actually quite knowledgeable when it comes to court politics and histories."

Bazin's horse danced a little but then settled again. "That's really useful trekking through the wilderness."

"We didn't choose to go trekking."

"I know," Bazin said, causing Ro to peer at him. He smiled. "Leema told me."

"Hmm." Ro looked ahead to where Aritha rode. "It hasn't been easy for them, you know."

"For you either." Bazin reached down and patted the neck of his horse. "You're all a long way from home."

Home.

She put a hand up to Marin's locket that still hung around her neck. She felt a pang of guilt for not thinking more about Abeth and Taus or the good men who had died that day on the Arazi Sea. But survival only allowed for thinking about survival, not for sentimental musings.

She wondered if anyone else had survived the dragon attack that day. Perhaps some of the others had escaped and made it to shore. She watched the two girls riding in front of her. The thought that no one knew where they were, or that they were even alive, twisted her gut. *And what of Brenith? How will we ever find her?*

"I just hope someone's looking for them." Silently, she counted the days. They had been gone from Koric for a little over a month. Well past the Empress' deadline. If anyone were to look for them, it would be to arrest them. Ro shifted uncomfortably.

"Someone is."

She looked at him sharply. "What do you mean?"

"Those men at the river, they were looking for you."

"Why do you think that?" she asked carefully.

Bazin seemed reluctant to answer. Finally, he sighed. "Porsa and I first came across them at a cottage near the sea. They were questioning an old woman about a group of girls."

"Woman?" Something clenched in Ro's gut. She didn't want to hear what he was going to say.

"An old fisherman's wife. They beat her, but she refused to tell them anything." Bazin scratched at his beard thoughtfully. "She actually sent them in the opposite direction. Though it didn't do her much good in the end."

Ro squeezed her eyes shut. "Fisp."

"It was a quick death," Bazin assured her quietly.

Ro opened her eyes and stared straight ahead. "Have you mentioned this to the others?" Ro couldn't get the image of Fisp out of her head. She had been so happy while they stayed with her. Anger and grief boiled deep in her heart.

"No."

"Don't," Ro rasped. "They don't need to hear any more bad news."

They rode on in silence. Ro kept turning the events of their journey around in her head. The attack on the ship, followed by a dragon attack, and a group of mercenaries tracking the princesses. It was too much to be a coincidence. They couldn't have been a search party looking for survivors. Search parties don't attack the people they're looking for. Perhaps they were linked to the original ship that attacked the *Maiden's Crown.* Ro glanced at Bazin. His intervention at the river suddenly seemed a little too convenient as well.

"Why were you at the cottage?"

"That's where we were put ashore."

"Why?" Ro watched him in the dim light.

"Why?" Bazin glanced at her.

"Yes, why?" Ro rubbed her leg absently. "If you were going to Ka-Petra, wouldn't it be easier to sail to Sinir rather than land in the wilderness and walk?"

"Maybe." Bazin shrugged.

"Then why? Why choose to walk, especially with someone like Porsa?" Ro reached up and scratched the back of her neck. It was tingling. She eyed him. "Why were you at the river, Bazin?"

"Krrr!" Dinko bounced on Leema's shoulder, watching the road behind them.

Leema turned to see what the lemur was looking at. She pointed down the road behind them. "Ro!"

Bazin and Ro turned at the same time to see the light of several torches glowing in the night behind them. They bobbed in the darkness.

"Men on horses," Bazin snarled.

"Caith's men?" Leema was still watching the lights.

"Probably." Bazin's horse danced around, sensing his agitation. "We have to get to Sinir. Get moving."

Even though they rode hard, the miles crawled by slowly. The sound of hooves pounding and the huffing of the horses' labored breathing filled their ears. Ro's leg throbbed as she bounced around on the saddle. She'd never had much training on horseback, and it was beginning to take its toll.

By the time the sky began to lighten, Ro was clinging to her saddle and shaking with exhaustion from just trying to stay on her horse. Just ahead, the golden light of dawn reflected off the smooth surface of the Sinir River. They could see the harbor town of Sinir nestled into a bend.

"We have to find the Harbor Master!" Bazin shouted, and Ro realized that he had never answered her question. *Why* had *he been at the river?*

Sinir

THEY RODE QUICKLY THROUGH the town. Sinir seemed almost idyllic after the chaos of Ka-Petra. Streets fanned out from the river, lined with houses and shops in neat little rows. Bazin followed his nose to the docks and guided his horse through the busy market. The air reeked of fish and sweat. A few men glanced up as the group passed, but Bazin glared at them until they resumed their work. Aritha covered her nose with her sleeve but said nothing as they passed the bins of fish.

Several ships were moored against the quays. Dock workers transferred goods on and off several of the ships. Bazin glanced at the rows of ships then at the river. The Sinir was wide enough and deep enough for the larger ships that sailed the Arazi Sea and the Southern Ocean to pass through easily. Despite that, the Sinir River looked like a trickle compared to the wildness of the raging Ka.

The Harbor Master's office was inside the huge wooden warehouse that sat in the middle of the docks. Bazin stopped outside the main door and dismounted.

"Stay here. Stay ready." Bazin glanced back at Ro, then looked around the docks before turning toward the warehouse. He gazed up at the building. The windows were dirty, and the walls were weather-beaten.

Two massive doors faced the quay like an open mouth ready to devour the merchandise coming from the ships.

"Krrr." Dinko sprang from Leema's saddle onto Bazin's shoulder as he moved past the line of horses and into the building.

"You Bazin?" a man called.

Bazin turned to find a man, who was almost as wide as the table he was sitting behind, staring up at him. His cap sat at an angle on his graying hair. His shirt was stained with food, and the end of his nose was red. But for all that, his eyes were sharp and saw everything.

"Krrr." Dinko flexed his claws into Bazin's shoulder.

"You know me?" Bazin reached up to scratch Dinko's ear.

"Pohle sent word you were coming." The man heaved himself up and hobbled from behind the worktable. "Said you needed passage to the City."

"That's right." Bazin followed the Harbor Master out into the yard, wondering if they could trust this man. He could easily hold them for Caith's men instead.

"I'm Master Prim." The old man looked over the line of horses, nodding to himself. "You're being followed."

Ro narrowed her eyes. "How did you know?"

Prim smiled and pointed. "Your horses are lathered up pretty good, so either you're stupid, or you've been running hard." Prim crossed his arms and stared up at Ro. "I doubt you're stupid, so they must be hunting you."

"Best to get out of sight then?" Bazin prodded.

"Hmm," Prim grunted and pointed toward a ship on the far left end of the dock. "That's the *Dawn Runner*. She's loaded and waiting for you." He glanced at Bazin. "Captain is Darnell."

Bazin's eyebrow twitched as he glanced toward the ship, then back at Ro.

"Cade!" Prim shouted at a boy just rounding the corner of the warehouse. The boy started like a rabbit but ran over to the Harbor Master.

Prim threw an arm around his shoulder and leaned down. "Take care of these horses. And do it quick and quiet like."

The boy nodded and ran over to grab the reins, waiting as the girls and Porsa dismounted.

"Good boy. My sister's youngest." Prim smiled fondly, watching the boy lead the horses into the warehouse. "Don't forget to walk 'em out a bit!" Prim shouted after the boy, then turned back to Bazin. "Now, you best get on board."

"What about the men following us?" Aritha asked.

Prim smiled. "They won't be a problem. This is my harbor. Nothing happens without my say so."

"But does that mean you won't turn us in?" Aritha glared at him.

His smile turned predatory. "Pohle has deeper pockets than Caith. I'll not betray him."

"Come on." Leema grabbed Aritha's arm and pulled her toward the *Dawn Runner*. She called back to Prim over her shoulder. "Thank you!"

"Krrr." Dinko bounded off Bazin's shoulder and scampered after the girls.

Ro and Porsa followed the princesses, but Bazin lagged behind. "Won't there be problems if Caith finds out you helped us escape?"

"Nah," Prim shook his head. "She needs me too much. Here." Prim pulled a sealed envelope out of his vest. "Pohle sent this too. Said it was for the Arazi."

"You know what it says?" Bazin turned the letter over.

"Probably an explanation for all this." Prim gestured toward the princesses as they boarded the *Dawn Runner*. "Pohle likes to keep things on the level with the Emperor. It's better that way."

"I hope that's what it is." Bazin stuffed the letter into his jerkin and extended his hand to Prim. "Thank you."

Prim shook it as the clatter of hooves echoed from the direction of the town. "Better run."

"Right." Bazin took off across the docks. He dodged around workers and cargo, then dashed up the gangplank.

"You the last one?" asked a short, stocky man as he reached the deck.

"Yeah." Bazin glanced back to see Caith's riders enter the docks.

"Cast off!" the stocky man hollered, creating a flurry of activity throughout the ship. He glanced back at the dock where the riders were pointing toward the ship. "Get your people below. I'll be down shortly to sort you out."

He turned away from Bazin, shouting orders. Bazin looked around for the girls. They stood in a cluster, trying to avoid the ordered chaos of the crew. Bazin limped his way across the deck.

"Come on. We need to get out of sight." He led them to the companionway and motioned them down into the darkness of the ship's hold.

Ro and Bazin stayed at the top of the stairs, watching the dock as the *Dawn Runner* slowly moved away. Bazin frowned. "We cut it close."

"Do you think they'll follow?" Ro watched the riders circling Master Prim.

"I don't know." Bazin sighed. "Caith can be a real bitch when she doesn't get her way."

Ro eyed him. "And what did she want that she didn't get?"

Leema saved Bazin from answering by shouting up the stairs. "Where are we supposed to go?"

Bazin glanced down at the youngest princess. "Captain said he'd sort us out as soon as we were safely away."

The ship lurched as it was caught in the Sinir's current, and Ro groaned. Bazin watched her holding her stomach and wondered if she had an injury that he didn't know about from her fight with the Wenzake.

Captain Darnell appeared next to Bazin and tipped his hat. "Welcome aboard the *Dawn Runner*. Let me squeeze by, and I'll show you to your cabins."

He moved down the stairs and motioned for them to follow him. The *Dawn Runner* wasn't very big. It was only a few feet down the corridor before they were at the passenger accommodations.

"There's one here." He opened the door to a small room with two bunks and a small table built into the wall with a chair under it. He opened another door on the opposite side of the corridor, "And one here."

Ro grimaced and reached out an unsteady hand toward the wall.

Darnell peered into her face. "You all right?"

"I don't like sailing." Ro braced herself against the door frame and held her stomach.

Darnell pointed. "Bucket's under the bunk."

Ro nodded and stumbled into the cabin. Leema and Aritha followed her.

"She gonna be all right?" Darnell asked, watching Ro sit carefully on the side of the bunk. Leema sat down and put an arm around Ro.

"I hope so." Bazin had no idea that Ro suffered from seasickness. At least it would delay her asking him any more questions.

"Right." Darnell tipped his hat and started back toward the stairs. "Call if you need anything."

Porsa stood awkwardly until Bazin prodded him toward the other cabin. The apprentice shot Bazin a significant look and then nodded toward the girls. The boy's expression was a mixture of impatience and apprehension. Bazin nodded his understanding; it was time to tell the girls the truth. But first, he had to make some arrangements. Bazin motioned Porsa into the cabin and then turned to follow the captain up the stairs.

"Captain Darnell?"

"Aye?" The captain stopped and looked down at Bazin.

"May I have a word?"

A Friend in Need

Darnell led Bazin up on deck, through the flurry of activity as the sailors brought the *Dawn Runner* down the Sinir, and finally to the captain's cabin. He motioned for Bazin to enter. Leaving the door open behind him, Darnell crossed over to the desk that stood in front of the window. He gestured to the chair in front of the desk. "What can I do for you?"

"You don't remember me, do you?"

"No, should I?"

"Name's Bazin."

Darnell squinted at him. "Yer not Bazin."

"Body's different, but it's still me."

Darnell's face flushed in anger. "What are you playin' at?"

Dinko chose that moment to dart into the cabin. The lemur leapt onto Bazin's shoulder and then down onto the pile of papers on the desk. He stared at Darnell. "Krrr."

"Dinko?" Darnell stared at the lemur, then at Bazin. "By all the gods..." His face turned from red to white in the blink of an eye.

Bazin jumped up and hurried to the cabinet near the captain's bunk, where he remembered Darnell kept his liquor. He quickly opened it, poured a generous amount of brandy into a mug, and brought it back to

Darnell. The captain was still staring at Dinko. His mouth kept moving but no words came forth. Bazin pressed the mug into his limp hand.

"Drink."

The captain obediently downed the entire mug and then handed it back to Bazin. "Another."

After the third mug, Darnell finally managed to speak. "By the gods, I'm glad to hear you're alive." Darnell engulfed Bazin in a bear hug. Bazin stood stunned as Darnell slapped Bazin on the back a few times and then stepped back. "I must say it grieved us to hear of your passin' after all you did for me and the missus," he shook his head, "but here you are."

A slow smile tugged at Bazin's lips. He'd had no idea anyone would mourn his death.

"Stanis said you were dead!"

"Stanis?" Bazin cocked an eyebrow, wondering what Darnell was doing talking to the bookkeeper at the Assassin's Court.

"We delivered his," Darnell coughed and sent Bazin a wink, "medicine."

Bazin's lips twitched. Stanis loved his spiced kerris nuts, and Darnell was a good smuggler.

"How?" Darnell interrupted his thoughts. "How are you alive? And in a different body!"

Bazin propped his hip on the edge of the desk and crossed his arms. "It's a long story."

"Krrr." Dinko agreed, twitching his tail.

Darnell shoved his chair back and went to refill his glass. He brought one back for Bazin too. "We have time. What in Vunkah is going on? What are you doing on the run in Ka with a bunch of girls?"

Bazin sipped at his drink, deciding how much to tell Darnell. The captain was the closest person Bazin had to a real friend. If it hadn't been for Hans Darnell and his wife, Bazin would have died.

Bazin snorted, *Not that I didn't die, I just would have died sooner.*

"Krrr." Dinko cocked his head and stared up at Bazin. He reached out and scratched the lemur's ears.

"That girl, the black-haired one?" Bazin glanced at Darnell. "A few months ago, I was sent to Koric to kill her."

"Why?"

"I don't know." Bazin shrugged. "They never tell us why, they just tell us who."

"Never did like that assassin business." Darnell shook his head. "Smuggling, I see the need for. Assassins, not so much. Damned silly idea, legal murder. You're better than that."

"Am I?" Bazin's throat closed as he thought about the tortures that he had endured in the Underworld as recompense for his actions. Every assassination. Every forceful intimidation. Had he deserved to suffer through each pain he had inflicted? Maybe, but he had carried out the assignments given to him. *How was that my choice?*

"Krrr." Dinko scooted toward the edge of the desk, watching Bazin.

Bazin looked back at the lemur. *Dinko's right. I could have chosen not to. It would have meant my death, but...*

"So, what happened?" Darnell prodded. "You obviously didn't kill her since she's here."

Bazin stood and paced to the window. "She killed me instead."

"What's it like? Death, I mean," Darnell whispered.

"Krrr."

Bazin shuddered. "Let's just say, I would rather not return."

"Is that a possibility?" Darnell reached out to scratch Dinko's ears.

"That is the problem I need to talk to you about." Bazin turned from the window and proceeded to recount his situation to the captain while Darnell sat with open-mouthed disbelief written all over his face.

When Bazin had finished, Darnell whistled softly. He sipped his drink as he mulled over Bazin's story. "Does the girl know all this?"

"I haven't told her yet." Bazin leaned against the window. "I couldn't guarantee that she'd come with me, so I just let her believe that we'd met by accident."

Darnell snorted. "She didn't seem that oblivious."

"She's been rather suspicious." Bazin nodded and stared down into his brandy. "She barely trusts me."

Darnell stood and walked to the window where he quietly stared out across the river. The faint sound of sailors at work buzzed in the background, mingling with the soft roar of the river. Dinko launched off the desk and landed on Bazin's shoulder, wrapping his tail around Bazin's neck. Bazin sipped his drink and waited. It was a lot to take in.

"You certainly got yourself into a pickle." Darnell slid his cap back and scratched his balding head. "So, what is it you want me to do?"

"Would you mind a detour?" Bazin pointed toward the west. "I have to get Ro to Jardarwa."

"Pohle paid us to take you to the Imperial City."

"I know, but my time is running out. We wasted a lot of time crossing Ka." Bazin sighed. "It takes nearly three weeks to get from the Imperial City to Jardarwa. If we go to the City first, I may not make it back to Jardarwa within the sixty days. I need to get to the Holy Mountain first."

"Krrr."

"Tide's right, but the *Dawn Runner* is not exactly fast." Darnell rocked back on his heels. "As long as we don't meet anything along the way," Darnell shrugged, "we might make good time."

Bazin looked at him sharply. "What do you mean 'meet anything'?"

"Been a lot of nasties out this past month." Darnell leaned against the windowsill.

"What kind of nasties?"

"Arazi warships. Dragons. Mostly on the north side of the sea, but there's been leviathans coming in from the Southern Ocean too. Getting a bit crowded in the Arazi Sea these days."

"We could hug the southern coastline."

"We could." Darnell crossed his arms. "As long as we don't run into Arazi blockades."

"Blockades?"

"Warships have taken up stopping merchant vessels left and right in the last few weeks. They say it's for protection from the dragons. That it's 'defensive inspections' to make sure the merchants are well protected, but they are searching every ship. Started right after the Empress declared Koric a traitor province."

Bazin was pretty sure that it all had to do with the wayward princesses.

"I got a lot of men on this ship. I've no desire to run afoul of the Arazi. I'm not risking them just for fun."

"I'll pay you. You know I'm good for it."

Darnell chuckled. "You had money once, but you've been dead. You think the Court kept it around for you?"

"I still have money." Bazin scratched Dinko's ear. "The Court didn't know about all of it."

Darnell glanced at him. "You take some jobs on the side or something?"

Bazin's lips twitched. "Or something."

"Well," Darnell sighed.

"I'd be in your debt." Bazin gazed solemnly at the captain.

"Yeah, you would be!" Darnell scratched his head again, then nodded. "All right, but I don't guarantee our safety."

Bazin shook his head. "I'm not asking you to."

"West we go then." Darnell sighed, looking out to sea. "But, Bazin?"

"Yeah?"

"You better tell your companions."

Duty

RO SAT ON THE bunk and tried not to think. Her stomach rolled and heaved.

"Are you all right?" Leema started to rub her back. "You look a little green."

"I hate sailing," Ro muttered as her stomach rolled again.

"I'm not sure I like it myself after the last one," Leema chuckled.

Ro glanced at her and scowled. "What happened to your hair?"

"Long story." Leema touched her braid self-consciously.

Ro groaned and dove for the bucket. Her body convulsed as she threw up. Leema held her shoulders and stroked her hair as she dry heaved.

She heard Leema say something to Aritha, but she couldn't make it out past the pounding in her head. Her stomach rolled, and she started dry heaving again and again until she didn't know what was worse, vomiting or not having anything to vomit up. Her leg throbbed. Her head hurt. Her throat felt like she'd swallowed glass. She hated herself for being so weak. *How can I protect them if I can't keep my head out of a bucket?*

The thought was pushed from her mind as the *Dawn Runner* bounced and bobbed. Ro bent over the bucket and started the whole process over again.

Leema pushed something into her hands, forcing her to drink it. Her stomach began to settle a little, then everything faded away, and she slept.

***

"Krrr."

Ro opened one eye and stared at the furry face that was only inches from hers.

"Krr." Dinko flexed his claws into her chest.

Ro groaned. The room smelled faintly of vomit, making the bile rise in her throat again.

"Good evening." Leema appeared beside the bunk. She reached out to scratch the lemur's back.

Ro pushed Dinko off her chest. He growled and disappeared out the cabin door. She rolled over and let her feet drop to the floor. She held a hand to her head and groaned again.

"How long did I sleep?" Ro massaged her temples, trying to get the fuzziness to go away.

"About two days."

Ro peered at Leema through gritty eyes. "Two days?"

"Sorry." Leema shrugged. "We had the cook make up a sleeping tonic. We thought it would help."

Ro nodded, although she didn't like the idea that they had gone unprotected during that time. She tried to swallow and winced. Her throat felt raw.

"Here." Leema pressed a jug of water into Ro's hand. "Drink."

Ro obeyed, hoping that the water wouldn't make her throw up again. It tasted faintly herbal.

"What's in this one?" She held the jug out and eyed Leema suspiciously.

"Nothing bad." Leema shrugged. "The cook said it would help your stomach."

"Hmm." Ro tasted the water again and nodded. "The cook on the *Maidens Crown* gave me something similar when we left Koric."

"Do you want something to eat?" Leema asked.

"Not just yet." Ro took another drink. "Let's see if this stays down first."

Leema bent and scooped up Ro's shoes and held them out. "Come up on deck and get some air. It might help."

Ro fumbled with the sandals. Her brain felt like mush. She finally got the shoes on and tried to stand. Leema steadied her when she swayed. She picked up the jug and then guided Ro out the door and up the stairs. They staggered across the deck to the stern.

Ro groaned again as she leaned on the railing. The fresh sea breeze helped her nausea, but only a little.

"We need to have a chat." Leema leaned on the railing beside her.

Ro didn't like the sound of that.

"Aritha and I were talking." Leema picked at a splinter on the railing. "We are long past the deadline for the summons."

"I know." Ro nodded and fiddled with the jug. "I failed you, Highness."

"No!" Leema shot upright. "It's not your fault! You kept us alive. We never would have made it this far without you. You have never failed us!"

"Thank you, Highness."

"And you can drop the Highness." Leema snorted. "We've been through too much. You're my sister. Always have been. Always will be."

Ro's eyes misted over as she reached out a hand to the youngest princess. Leema grasped it and held on.

"That being said, the Empress is not going to be pleased to see us."

"Right." Ro squeezed her hand and let go. "So, what do we do?"

"That's what Aritha and I wanted to talk to you about. It is very likely that the Empress will have declared Koric a traitor province already, so we will probably be arrested as soon as we enter the palace."

"I won't let them." Ro glared at Leema.

"I don't think you'll have a choice." Leema smiled sadly. "The Arazi is just, but if he isn't there..."

Ro shook her head. "Abeth said that the Emperor was in the east with the Border War. She also said that the Empress didn't share his temperament."

"So, the Empress won't listen like he would have," Leema looked grim, "and will go through with her threats."

"Very likely." Ro nodded. "I can't say that I liked the Empress."

Leema's eyebrows shot up. "You met her?"

Ro nodded. "When Abeth found me in Zatvor, she questioned why a seven-year-old was in the prison mine. When they couldn't find any records, they took me to the palace until they could figure out what to do with me. That's when I met the Empress."

Leema stared at her in awe. "What was she like?"

Ro's lip curled. "Insulting, rude, arrogant. She makes Aritha look kind." She glanced at Leema. "Doesn't bode well for lenience in this situation."

"No, it doesn't." Leema sighed. "That's why we, Aritha and I, want you to leave us."

"What!" Ro shot away from the railing and grabbed the princess' shoulders. "I will never leave you! I made a promise to Abeth to guard you with my life. I will not go back on that promise!"

"Ro, if they arrest us, there is nothing you can do to protect us." Leema's face paled. "We want you to live."

"No!" Ro felt like she was back at the King's Tower, arguing with Abeth. The queen had been resigned to her fate too. Ro couldn't stand it. "There must be another way. We could run!"

Tears dripped down Leema's cheeks. "Oh, Ro, there's nowhere to run to."

"What about to the Arazi himself?"

"There's no saying we could make it that far." Leema shook her head. "We must accept our fate. It is our duty as the ruling family of Koric to obey. Don't you see? If we run or fight, then we really *are* traitors."

Ro shook her head. "I can't accept that."

"Mother always said that being royal had its glory, but it also had its pain." Leema fiddled with her braid. "I don't like it. I don't want it. But it is our responsibility. So, when we go to the palace, we are asking you not to interfere. Stay free. Go find Brenith. Go look for survivors from the *Seabird* or the *Maidens Crown*, but don't fight for us. Promise me."

"I can't promise that." Ro thought back to that small cell in Villeah's house where she had shed her uniform but had renewed her vow to protect the family. "I swore my life to the House Guard to protect the family."

"And if the family is no more?"

"As long as you are alive, I serve."

Leema's face grew hard. "Then serve us by obeying our wishes in this."

Ro studied the set expression on Leema's face and knew that they would never agree on this. It would be better for them all if she agreed to Leema's request, for now. But in her heart, there was no question of leaving. She would protect them until her dying breath. Her debt to Abeth demanded it. *And I will pay that debt.*

"Very well." Ro nodded, and more tears slid down Leema's cheeks before she turned and leaned on the railing again.

They stood quietly looking across the blackness of the sea as the last light of the day faded. One by one, the stars winked into existence.

"Look." Leema pointed at the sky. "The King's Spear." The young princess turned and smiled sadly at Ro. "It watched over us before; maybe it will bring a better fate again."

"Maybe." Ro looked at the sky and frowned. She rubbed her forehead to clear her thoughts. She turned, looking around at the rest of the stars.

Leema watched her. "What's wrong?"

"The King's Spear." Ro looked back at the constellation. It was riding right above the bow of the ship.

"What about it?" Leema turned to look.

"It's always in the west." Ro looked around the ship.

"So?"

"So, we're sailing toward it. The Imperial City is in the east." Ro shoved the jug of water into Leema's surprised hands. "We're going the wrong way!"

Betrayals

RO TURNED AND STALKED off unsteadily across the deck. Leema hurried after her. Grabbing the first sailor she found, Ro demanded to speak to the captain. The sailor took one look at her face and led her to Darnell.

"Just where are we going?" Ro glared at the little square man.

"Pardon?" Captain Darnell lifted his cap and scratched his head.

"We're sailing west." Ro gestured toward the front of the ship. "We're supposed to be sailing east!"

"Umm..." Darnell looked around desperately.

"What's going on?" Aritha asked as she emerged from the shadows near the starboard railing. Porsa followed her.

"Seems we're sailing the wrong way." Leema glanced at her, then back to the captain.

"I'm just doing what I was paid for." Darnell held up his hands and tried to smile.

"And what exactly is that?" Ro glared at him, not realizing her eyes were turning ice blue.

Darnell flinched. Without taking his eyes off her, he roared, "Bazin!"

"What?" Bazin was sitting above them on the lowest yard arm with his back braced against the main mast. He sat with his good leg dangling off the side and his bad leg stretched out along the beam. Dinko was curled in his lap.

Darnell scowled up at him. "You were supposed to tell them about the change in plans."

"Oops." Bazin shrugged and grinned, scratching Dinko's ears.

"Oops, my eye!" Darnell grumbled.

"What change in plans?" Ro stalked over until she was standing under him. Looking up made her feel a little dizzy. She staggered slightly as the ship rolled.

"Ah..." Bazin looked out to sea, then back down at her. "We have to take a little detour before going to the Imperial City."

"What detour?" Leema moved up beside Ro.

"We need to make a stop at Jardarwa."

"What!" Aritha stomped over. "That is unacceptable. We can't just run off to the other end of the Arazi Sea! We need to get to the Imperial City!"

"Well, we," Bazin gestured between himself and Ro, "need to get to Jardarwa."

"What are you talking about?" Ro frowned up at him, grimacing when her stomach rolled as the ship swayed. "I have no business on that island."

"That's where you're wrong." Bazin shook his head, then smirked. "It's a funny story, really." Bazin gazed down at Porsa, suddenly serious. "Isn't it, Porsa?"

The girls turned toward the apprentice.

Porsa's face flushed bright red. "Wh-what?"

"Why don't you tell them what you did?"

"B-but..." Porsa started to shake his head.

"You're the one who landed us in this mess." Bazin crossed his arms.

Porsa gazed pathetically at Aritha. "I-it w-wasn't m-my f-f-f-fault!"

"Krrr." Dinko hung off of Bazin's lap and leered at Porsa.

"Stop picking on him." Aritha turned and shouted up at Bazin. "If you have something to say, just say it and leave poor Porsa alone."

"Oh yeah," Bazin rolled his eyes, "poor Porsa."

"Look, why don't you come down, and we can discuss this without shouting?" Leema looked up at Bazin.

"Krrr." Dinko turned to Bazin.

"Fine." Bazin sighed. He climbed down the ratlines to the deck. He limped slowly over to the indignant girls and a scowling Porsa.

"All right, spill it." Ro glared at him. "Why are we detouring?"

"You want the long version," Bazin returned her glare, "or the short?"

"The true one."

Bazin searched her face and then nodded. "Porsa worked a spell that connected our souls, only he screwed it up." Bazin glanced at the apprentice. "Now, we need to get to the Holy Mountain so that they can separate us."

Aritha turned to Porsa. "Why would you do that?"

"I-I j-just d-d-did what m-my m-m-master t-told m-me!" Porsa shook his head. "I-I d-d-didn't want t-t-to re-resurrect anyone!"

"Resurrect?" Leema looked from Porsa to Bazin. Dinko sprang up onto his shoulder.

"Yeah," Bazin snorted and hooked a thumb at Porsa. "He pulled me out of the Underworld."

"Why?" Ro stared at him.

Bazin stared back at her for a long time. Dinko shifted his weight from paw to paw. "Originally?" He reached up and scratched Dinko's ears to settle the little animal, then looked Ro in the eye and sighed. "To kill you."

Everyone began talking at once. Aritha nagged Porsa for information. Porsa tried to defend himself. Ro stared at Bazin, wondering why the tingling hadn't warned her that he was dangerous. It had never failed her before. Her hand flexed, and she wished she hadn't left her sword in the cabin.

Leema shoved Bazin. "You said you weren't here to hurt anyone!"

"I'm not!"

"Please!" Captain Darnell stepped in between them with his hands up. "Please!"

"I trusted you!" Leema ignored the captain and lunged at Bazin, punching him in the chest. Dinko jumped down and chittered at everyone.

"Damn it, Leema!" Bazin grabbed Leema's wrists. "Stop!"

"Leema!" Ro snapped, pulling Leema back and shoving her toward Aritha. She glared at Bazin. "Explain!"

"You're the one who sent me to the Underworld." Bazin glared at her.

"I sent you?" Ro shook her head, trying to understand.

"I assume I was resurrected to kill you because I had the best reason for wanting you dead! Porsa's spell was supposed to bind my soul to yours for two moon cycles. If I killed you in that time, then my soul would get to stay in its new body. If I failed, I'd go straight back to the Underworld." Bazin's jaw clenched and unclenched. He threw an arm toward Porsa. "But he got the spell wrong. I'm now bound to you for sixty days, and if you die, I die."

Leema gaped at him. "That's why you jumped into the river after her?"

"Yeah." Bazin glanced at Leema, then back at Ro. "I have to keep you alive. And I will. Believe me, I have no desire to return to the Underworld."

"Krrr." Dinko shifted nervously in a little circle at his feet, glancing from face to face.

Ro looked down at the lemur. Suddenly, she knew what had been nagging her since meeting Bazin and Dinko. In her mind's eye, she could see that day so long ago. She'd chased a yellow-eyed animal in the courtyard, then she'd seen a furry ringed tail disappearing out the window in the hallway. It had been Dinko's tail. Her gaze shot to Bazin.

"It was you!" she accused. "That night in the Queen's chamber. That was you."

Bazin nodded. "That was me."

"You were going to kill the Queen!" Ro snarled.

"Kill Mother?" Aritha gasped in disbelief.

Ro reached for her sword, but it wasn't there.

"Wait!" Bazin held his hands up, but he didn't move away. "I wasn't there to kill the queen." Bazin shook his head, but his eyes never left Ro's. "I was there to kill you, not the queen."

"Ro?" Leema edged away from Bazin toward her sister.

"Why me?" Ro took a step towards him.

"Ship Ho!" The shout froze her mid-step.

Company

Captain Darnell cupped his hands around his mouth and shouted up at the crow's nest. "Where?"

The lookout pointed. "Dead ahead!"

"All this?" Darnell glanced between Ro and Bazin. "You need to stow it." He turned and headed for the bow.

"This isn't over!" Ro poked Bazin in the chest.

Bazin nodded before following the captain.

"Please, let it be a friendly ship!" Leema whispered as they dashed after Darnell.

They joined the captain just as one of the sailors appeared and handed him a spyglass. Darnell put it to his eye.

"Who is it?" Aritha asked, searching the darkness for the lights from the other ship.

"Arazi warship." Darnell breathed.

"A warship?" Bazin frowned, gazing toward the bow.

"There's been more since they declared Koric outlaw." Darnell watched the ship approaching. "Told you this might happen."

"What?" Aritha grabbed his arm and yanked him around to face her.

Darnell spluttered, "Leave off, girl!"

"What do you know about Koric?" Aritha demanded.

"Koric delegation didn't show up for the swearing ceremony, and no one's heard a peep from 'em. Empress declared the island outlaw."

"Aritha?" Leema looked to Aritha for some kind of reassurance. "Can't we just tell them what happened?" Leema looked from Aritha to Ro and back again.

"We could try," Aritha nodded grimly, "but ultimately what happens to us is up to the Empress. They declared Koric outlaw, Leema." Aritha's voice sounded hollow. "We talked about this already. If they catch us, they will arrest us."

"You're from Koric?" Darnell looked from Aritha to Leema to Ro.

"Meet the Princesses of Koric." Bazin sighed, gesturing to Leema and Aritha.

"Princesses?" Darnell lifted his cap and scratched his head, then grinned and elbowed Bazin. "You cheeky bastard."

Bazin rolled his eyes and glanced back at the ship. "We're headed straight for them."

"Yep." Darnell turned back to the bow and raised the spyglass again.

"Can you outrun them?" Bazin looked at the captain.

"Not a chance." Darnell shook his head. "*Dawn Runner*'s not fast, not like a warship. They'll be on us in a heartbeat and hang us for running.

A sailor shouted from the helm, "Orders, Captain?"

"Stand ready ta heave to," Darnell shouted back. "Run or continue, either way, they'll catch us."

"Couldn't you just hide us?" Leema latched onto Darnell's arm.

Darnell stared at her. "If they search us and find you, they'll hang us for conspiring against the Arazi. No, thank you!"

"Wait!" Leema grabbed at the captain's arm again. "You can't just hand us over!"

"Look," Darnell snarled. "I'm not sacrificing this entire crew for you girls, princesses or not. You'll have to sort out your own problems. I want no quarrels with the Arazi."

"Coward!" Leema snapped.

"Leema!" Aritha gasped. "The captain is right. This is not his fight, and it would be wrong for us to risk the lives of these men. This is our business, not theirs."

Leema deflated. "Sorry."

"That's all right, girl." Darnell nodded and thumped her on the back. "You've got spirit. You'll learn ta temper it in time."

Aritha watched the sailors scramble up the ratlines to take in the sails, then turned back to study the steadily approaching ship. "Captain, what's going to happen now?"

"Well," Darnell lifted his cap and scratched his head, "they'll come alongside, and we'll have a little meeting with their captain. Then I imagine they'll take custody of you lot," he gestured at Aritha and Leema, "and send the rest of us on our merry way." He turned to Bazin. "Doesn't help *your* problem though."

Ro glanced at Bazin and then at Darnell. "I'm not letting them separate us." Ro glared at the warship. It was only a couple of ship lengths away from the *Dawn Runner*.

"Vunkah moh fana!" Bazin turned on her scowling. "You're coming to the Holy Mountain with me. We haven't got time for a jaunt to the Imperial dungeons."

"Dungeons?" Leema squeaked.

"You may be a princess and get to have a nice room while you wait for trial, but we won't." Bazin gestured between himself and Ro. "We won't get the royal treatment."

"So just who are you, Bazin?" Ro's voice cut into him like a knife. "I want the truth this time. All of it."

"Krrr." Dinko sprang up onto Bazin's shoulder as he turned to face Ro.

Darnell held up his hands. "Before you all go at it again, we best get you out of sight. If we can, I'd rather get by without them searching us. But if you're up here yelling and fighting, there'll be no stopping them from arresting all of us."

Ro pressed her lips together and nodded. Darnell ushered the princesses, Bazin, Porsa, and Ro into his cabin. Dinko left Bazin's shoulder and climbed up onto the yard arm once more.

"You stay in here and keep the shouting to a minimum," Darnell said before shutting the door behind them.

Ro turned on Bazin. "Why did you try to kill me that day on Koric?"

"I was a Zmajev Assassin." Bazin watched her carefully. She looked more scared than angry now. "I was given the assignment of killing the only female in the Koric House Guard."

"As simple as that?" Leema accused.

"Yes." Bazin turned his head to acknowledge Leema's question, but didn't take his eyes off Ro. "As simple as that."

"That's stupid!" Leema snorted. "Don't you question it when they send you off to kill someone?"

"I was trained not to question my assignments," Bazin said bitterly, thinking about the beatings that solidified that lesson in him.

"Then who resurrected you?" Aritha asked. "Surely not the Assassins' Court."

"Th-the D-D-D-" Porsa tried to spit out the words, but as they all turned to the shaking apprentice, their glares made him too nervous.

"You know who did this?" Aritha asked.

Porsa tried again but couldn't get more than a hissing "Th" out.

"Porsa, it's all right." Aritha patted his arm. Outside, they could hear shouting from the warship as it pulled up alongside the *Dawn Runner.*

"D-D-Drugi M-M-Moc." Porsa finally blurted.

"The what?" Leema stared at him.

"Drugi Moc." Bazin explained. They didn't have time for Porsa's stutter. "They're a small group of fanatics obsessed with dragons."

Leema frowned. "Why would they want to kill Ro?"

All eyes turned to Ro. She shrugged and shook her head.

"No one knows where you came from, Ro," Aritha said quietly.

"What does she mean?" Bazin turned back to Ro.

Before Ro could answer, he felt the flutter of Dinko brushing against his thoughts. He closed his eyes and saw what Dinko saw.

"What's happening?" Leema grabbed his arm. "Tell us."

Bazin relayed what he was seeing.

The warship pulled up alongside the *Dawn Runner*. The Imperial sailors lashed the ships together just before the soldiers from the warship flooded onto the *Dawn Runner*. Darnell wandered over to meet the Arazi captain. It seemed to be a congenial conversation at first. The captain of the Arazi ship glanced around but then continued to speak to Captain Darnell. After a few moments, the Arazi captain shook his head, then pointed to the east. Darnell gestured toward the west.

"That doesn't sound good," Leema muttered.

The Arazi captain said something, pushed past Darnell, and stalked toward the captain's cabin.

"Leema! Aritha!" Ro whispered. "Something's wrong."

The edge to her voice made Bazin break the link with Dinko. Her face was tight, and her eyes had turned completely white except for the tiny black pupil in the center. It was a frightening effect. She no longer seemed like a frightened girl, trying to get her charges to safety. Now, she was something else entirely.

"What is it?" Leema took one look at Ro and ran to the window, looking left and right.

Ro started toward the door.

"Wait." Bazin grabbed her arm. "What are you doing?"

"Let go!" Ro jerked away from him.

"What's coming, Ro?" Aritha huddled close to Porsa.

"What are you talking about?" Bazin frowned at the three of them.

Ro muttered, "Get ready."

"Ready for what?" Bazin still couldn't see what she was reacting to.

"Dragon!" The shout penetrated the cabin as the air outside the windows glowed orange.

"That." Ro's breath shot out all in a rush as she ran for the door.

"Not again!" Aritha cried out, clinging to Porsa. "Please, not again!"

Dragonfire

As Bazin rushed out of the cabin after Ro, fire engulfed the warship's crow's nest. Both captains bellowed orders as sailors shouted and ran for weapons. The men from the Arazi ship piled back over the railing to their own ship, dodging the chunks of burning mast that fell to the deck. Some of the burning debris spilled over onto the *Dawn Runner*. Sailors from both ships scrambled for buckets of water to douse the fires.

Arazi sailors rushed to the massive ballistae mounted on swiveling platforms along the sides of the warship. The huge crossbows sported bolts as long as a man. The dragon swooped back across the ship, roaring. Its powerful wings sent gusts of air downward, fanning the flames and pushing clouds of smoke down onto the deck.

Darnell's men armed themselves as best they could with bows and swords. A couple of sailors emerged from below deck carrying harpoons. They turned, watching the dragon, ready to throw at a moment's notice.

Ro and Bazin stood shoulder to shoulder, watching the dragon's flight path. They turned with it, keeping the girls behind them.

The Arazi sailors worked quickly, swinging the ballistae around to aim at the dragon. One after another, the weapons launched bolts at the beast. Some missed their mark, but the few that struck the dragon only made it roar in anger. Aritha sank to her knees and covered her ears to block out the sound.

The beast banked to the side and blasted a gob of fire at a ballista on the far side of the warship. The men aiming it screamed and convulsed as they were engulfed in flames. The ballista spun wildly to the side, shooting its bolt across the decks of the two ships.

"Down!" Bazin yanked Ro and Leema down on the deck as the bolt flashed overhead. He looked back at the warship just in time to see the melted weapon fall into the sea, taking the burning men with it. The smell of charred flesh permeated the air.

Leema tugged on the back of Ro's shirt. "We need to get off this ship."

"Where you gonna go?" Bazin snorted. "We're in the middle of the sea!"

"I don't care!" Aritha shrieked. "Anywhere is better than here with that thing!" She jabbed a finger at the dragon, which, at that moment, dipped low as it flew past and snatched a sailor from the rigging on the warship.

"We need to get off the deck!" Bazin grabbed Leema's arm and propelled her toward the companionway entrance.

Leema scooped up Dinko and ran. Aritha squeaked and ducked as the beast flew low around the *Dawn Runner*. Porsa scrambled forward on all fours, wrapped an arm around Aritha, and yanked her to her feet. He practically dragged her toward the companionway. Bazin turned back to Ro, expecting her to follow, but she wasn't paying any attention.

"What are you doing?" he snarled, taking a few steps after her. "Come on!"

"Voto fora mantha," Ro muttered under her breath, watching the dragon circle back.

"What?" Bazin stared at her. He had no idea what she was saying.

"Voto fora mantha." She moved with the dragon as she repeated the phrase over and over again, finally shouting, "Voto fora mantha!"

The beast dipped suddenly in the air as if something had struck it in the nose. It shook its powerful head and roared. The snapping of its leathery wings echoed across the decks of the two ships as it hovered just off the port side of the *Dawn Runner.* Darnell's men took advantage of the beast's distraction and aimed their harpoons.

Bazin dashed forward and grabbed her arm, but she shook him off absently. He caught a glimpse of her eyes as she stared at the dragon. They were completely white except for the tiniest pinpoint in the center. A chill of primal fear shot down his spine, freezing him to the spot. He could only stare as she stepped toward the dragon.

"Voto fora mantha," Ro repeated.

Bazin stared up at the dragon as it hovered only a few yards away. The fire from the sails reflected off the beast's eyes as it searched the deck. Finally, it focused on Ro. It pumped its wings, sending it backwards from the ships. She stepped forward, matching its retreat, moving ever closer to the port side rail.

Bazin looked from the dragon to Ro. She was too close. If the dragon sent another blast of fire at the ships, Ro would be right in the middle of it. He wanted to run forward and pull her back, but his feet seemed rooted to the deck.

The dragon opened its mouth, then closed it again. It shook its head as if it were being worried by insects. Its eyes seemed to lose focus.

"Voto fora mantha!" Ro roared. There was something otherworldly in her tone. Bazin shuddered. The dragon's roar mingled with Ro's as a harpoon pierced the soft tissue where its wing attached. The dragon's eyes snapped into focus, and a blast of fire erupted from its gaping maw, engulfing Ro.

"Nooo!" Bazin shouted, stumbling forward, finally free from his paralysis, but the blast of heat forced him backwards again. He flung his hands up to ward off the inferno. Smoke and flames filled the air, obscuring Ro from view.

The twang of multiple bolts being fired filled the air as the ballistae pelted the dragon. Bolts punctured its wings and pierced its underbelly. The dragon screeched and thrashed in the air before plunging into the sea.

Ro screamed.

The sailors cheered as the beast sank out of sight, but Bazin barely noticed. He staggered forward in a vain attempt to reach Ro, but the fire was too intense. Heat seared his eyes, making them water as he searched the flames for her. There was no way she could have survived. He fell to his knees with a cry of anguish.

Darnell's men threw bucket after bucket of water at the fire. Clouds of smoke wafted across the deck. He waited for the smell of her burning flesh, but all he could smell was the burning timber.

Around him, the sailors rushed to get the flames under control. The shouts from both ships mingled into one massive cacophony. He stared at the fire with a growing sense of doom.

He waited for the sight of her charred corpse.

He waited for the jarring sense of his soul being ripped from his body.

He thought of Dinko, wishing that this time he could have said goodbye.

Bazin raised his stinging eyes to the smoldering fire. It was taking so long. *She must be dying slowly*, he thought, squeezing his eyes shut.

When he opened his eyes again, the smoke had begun to clear. Bazin squinted through the haze. He could just make out a shape on the deck. He slowly staggered to his feet and started forward. He expected to see a charred hunk of meat instead of a girl and was glad the smoke was hiding it. Suddenly, a breeze pushed the remaining haze aside. Bazin gaped. All the sailors who had been trying to douse the flames stopped dead and stood staring. Silence punctuated by the crackle of the remaining fires gripped the men of the *Dawn Runner*.

"What in the—?" Bazin stepped forward again, unsure if what he was seeing was real. "Ro?" he whispered.

Darnell shoved through the crowd of frozen sailors, trying to see what had caused his men to stop fighting the fires. "By all the gods!"

Slumped in the center of the scorched section of deck, surrounded by glowing embers, was Ro. Her clothes had been burned away, and her skin was reddened and starting to blister. Blood trickled from her nose, and her hair was burnt away, but she was whole.

The captain crept forward and carefully knelt beside her, trying to avoid the hot timbers around her. He reached out a shaking hand and felt for a pulse, then turned wide-eyed to Bazin. "She lives."

Bazin shook his head in denial. "No one can survive dragonfire."

"Well, she has." Darnell shoved to his feet and turned quickly to Bazin. "Get her below deck!"

"What?" Bazin stared at him in bewilderment.

Darnell snapped his fingers in Bazin's face. "Snap out of it! We haven't much time!" He glanced over Bazin's shoulder at the Arazi warship. "If those boys from the Arazi find out that she can withstand dragonfire, they'll snap her up in a heartbeat and take her back to the Imperial palace. You'll never see her again!" He shoved Bazin forward as he glanced at the Arazi ship again. "You've got to get her outta sight." He looked around at the stunned faces of the sailors. "And as far as anyone knows, she's dead. Got it?"

They all slowly nodded as discipline overrode the awe of what they had just witnessed. Bazin stepped forward haltingly, afraid to touch her. Afraid to find out she was actually dead. He took a deep breath and knelt beside her. The air around her smelled faintly of burnt hair.

He reached down carefully and slid his hands beneath her. Ashes fluttered to the deck as he slowly lifted her. Her skin radiated searing heat as he carried her away from the ring of sailors.

Parting Ways Again

"Ro!" Leema exclaimed as Bazin neared the companionway entrance. She stood at the top of the stairs, peering out. Dinko clung to her neck, chittering at them both.

"Move!" Bazin hissed, sending her scuttling back down the stairs.

"What happened?" Aritha stared in horror at the limp, naked form in Bazin's arms.

Bazin carried her into the princesses' cabin. "Leema, move that blanket!"

Leema jumped forward and yanked the blanket off the bed. Bazin carefully laid Ro on the bunk, then turned to take the blanket from Leema.

"Lock the door!" he said, glancing at Porsa as he gently spread the blanket out over Ro.

Leema dropped to her knees beside the bunk. "Is she all right?"

"I don't know." Bazin stood, looking down at Ro uncertainly.

"What happened?" Leema gazed up at him with tears in her eyes.

"She... the..." Bazin stammered, trying to understand what he had seen. "She was... speaking to the dragon, it was like she was putting it into a trance, but..." He frowned as he tried to explain. "When they hit it with harpoons, it broke the spell and blasted her with fire."

"Fire?" Leema gasped, looking back at Ro. "She's barely burnt. Did the dragon miss?"

"It didn't miss," Bazin choked out. He stared at the reddening skin on Ro's face.

"Krrr." Dinko stared up at his master from Leema's shoulder. Bazin held his arms out, and Dinko sprang into them.

"Is the dragon still out there?" Aritha asked, clinging to Porsa's arm.

"No." Bazin shook his head as Dinko climbed to his shoulder. "Can you do anything for her?" he asked Leema.

"I don't know." She reached out and felt Ro's forehead. "Brenith is the healer, not me."

"But you must know something?"

"I'm sorry, Bazin," Leema looked up at him with tears in her eyes, "but I've never heard of anyone surviving a blast of dragonfire. She should be burnt to a crisp but look at her! She just looks like she's gotten a bad sunburn!"

A knock on the door made them all freeze.

"Krrr." Dinko stared at the door.

"It's me," Darnell said from the other side.

Porsa moved over to the door and fumbled with the lock until it opened. Captain Darnell slid in and closed the door behind him. He looked around at the worried faces, then moved over to the bunk where Ro lay.

"How is she?"

"Unconscious." Bazin scratched at his beard.

Darnell tapped Bazin on the arm. "We found this on the deck. The cord's been burnt, though." In his hand was a small metal locket that was covered in soot.

Bazin took the locket and shoved it into a pocket inside his jerkin.

Sighing heavily, Darnell shook his head. "The Arazi Captain wants everyone on deck."

"No!" Leema jumped to her feet.

"You don't have a say in this. You're princesses from an outlawed province. He has every right to arrest you. We're lucky they aren't arresting my whole crew for harboring fugitives."

"But we can't leave Ro like this!" Leema was near panic.

Darnell lifted his cap and scratched his head. "If you throw a fit about leaving your friend, there'll be questions. Questions you don't want to answer."

"Like how she survived a direct blast of dragonfire," Bazin muttered.

"Exactly." Darnell nodded. "If they find out, the gods only know what they'll do with her." He looked at Leema and Aritha. "If you have any hope of keeping her safe, you need to keep your mouths shut. This never happened." Darnell looked pointedly at the girls. "If their captain asks, then we say she died. Got it? The dragon got her."

"I don't want to leave." Leema stared at Bazin, appearing once again every inch the lost child.

"Don't worry." Bazin rallied every bit of reassurance he could and nodded at Leema. "We'll get to the Mountain, sort out this mess, then come back for you."

"Um, Bazin?" Darnell interrupted. "You're going with them. You and Porsa."

"What?" Bazin turned to Darnell. The captain's face was filled with worry.

Darnell swallowed hard. "Their captain is taking all of you into custody. There's nothing I can do."

Bazin's face turned gray as he realized what this meant. There wasn't enough time to get to the Imperial City and then back to Jardarwa. And if he was arrested, there was definitely no way that he would get to the Citadel in time.

Aritha turned toward Darnell. "Take care of Ro for us."

"No!" Leema shook her head. "We are not leaving her here!"

Darnell took the youngest princess by the shoulders. "I will take care of her. I promise." He turned her toward the door. "Now, go on."

Aritha put her arm around Leema and walked out the door with her head held high.

As the girls left, Bazin flicked a glance at the bunk. Everything in him screamed to stay with Ro, that there was some way they could escape and reach Jardarwa in time, but he knew it was impossible.

"I'll follow you to the City." Darnell stepped up beside Bazin and stared down at Ro. "If you get free, find me, and we'll make a run for the Mountain."

Bazin couldn't summon up his voice. He simply nodded, took one last look at Ro, then shooed Porsa out the door and up the stairs.

On deck, the Arazi sailors were already conducting Leema and Aritha onto the warship. Others waited to escort Porsa and Bazin. After they had climbed over, the sailors began loosening lines to separate the ships.

"Krr." Dinko tugged on his ear, staring toward the *Dawn Runner* as the ships drifted apart.

"I know," Bazin muttered. He didn't want to leave Ro either.

As the warship came about to sail back toward the Imperial City, the sailors led the princesses, Bazin, and Porsa below deck to the brig. They were searched for weapons and then locked in a small cell where the only light came from the small portal placed head-high on the back wall.

Bazin sat down in the corner. In his mind, he kept replaying the fire swirling around Ro. *How did she survive dragonfire? What does 'Voto fora mantha' mean? Was she controlling the dragon? Putting it under a spell? What have I gotten into?*

"This is your fault, you know." Leema glared at him.

"Krr." Dinko stood between Bazin and Leema, looking back and forth as if torn in his loyalties.

Bazin shook his head. "I didn't do this."

Leema crossed her arms. "You wanted to kill Ro. If you hadn't, none of this would have happened!"

"I didn't *want* to kill her. I was *sent* to kill her." Bazin wasn't sure if the youngest princess understood the distinction. "If it wasn't me, then it would have been someone else."

"Why?" Aritha stepped forward and glared down at him. "Why should anyone want to kill her?"

"You tell me!" Bazin shrugged. "You know more about her than I do. To me, it was just another assignment."

Leema and Aritha exchanged a look, the meaning of which Bazin could only guess at.

He sighed. "Look, I received the assignment to go to Koric and kill the only woman in the House Guard. I didn't know a thing about her until I got the assignment."

The betrayal in Leema's eyes made him angry. She wasn't the one whose life had been usurped by everyone. Her life wasn't the one hanging by a very small thread. He scrambled to his feet.

"I didn't sign up for any of this!" He flung a hand out. "Ro killed me!" Bazin pointed at Porsa. "And then he resurrected me into this..." he gestured wildly at himself, "...body of a cobbler and told me I had to go back and kill the same woman! Then, he changes his mind and tells me I have to keep her alive. Now, she can talk to dragons!" He flung his hands up and paced from one end of the cell to the other. "But it's all my fault! What does it matter? I'll be dead again in a few days!"

"No!" Leema squeaked, stopping Bazin's pacing.

He turned to look at her. She looked scared and lost again. It evaporated his anger. *Damn it, how did I get into this mess?*

Journey's End

The Imperial warship slid through the glistening waters of Mirath Bay. The last rays of sunlight reflected off each wave, gilding the sea. Sea birds screeched overhead as they swooped looking for tidbits.

But the beauty was lost on Bazin as he gazed out the portal in their cell at the approaching Imperial City. As the bustling dock came ever closer, he could see torches flickering along the quays, reflecting off the dockside buildings. People were everywhere. It seemed a thousand times busier than he remembered it. The wooden quays were crammed with ships and more were anchored just outside the harbor.

"Why are there so many ships?" Leema stood on her tiptoes in front of Bazin to see out the portal.

"Don't know." Bazin let his eyes roam over the fleet of ships. "But I don't like it."

"Krrr." Dinko sat on Leema's shoulder with his tail curled around her neck. She reached up and scratched his ear.

"What's going to happen now?" Leema sank back down and turned to Aritha.

"I don't know." Aritha pushed herself up from the floor near Leema's feet. She shook out her skirts. "We will have to see the Arazi." Aritha came to stand next to Leema. "I'm afraid we won't be welcomed with open arms." She stared at the approaching city.

Porsa picked at a splinter in the floor. "It w-wasn't your f-fault your sh-sh-ship was attacked."

Aritha sighed. "The Empress may not see it that way."

Shouts went up from the crew as the warship eased up to the pier. Lines were tossed out to secure the ship.

Aritha swallowed, then she squared her shoulders and looked at Bazin. Her face was grim.

"Bazin, thank you for your aid. I appreciate that you stepped up to help us when we were lost, even though you lied," Aritha gave him an accusatory glare, "a lot. Despite that, I hope that they deal fairly with you."

"Highness." Bazin bowed slightly.

"Leema." Aritha took her sister by the shoulders and gazed intently at her. "This is a time for court etiquette and politics. This is about appeasing the Empress. If we are not careful, it will mean our deaths."

"I know." Leema looked from Aritha to Bazin. "I'm not stupid."

"I'm very serious, Leema." Aritha sighed. "You must be on your best royal behavior. No outbursts. We don't know what the Arazi's son is like, but Mother warned me that the Empress is difficult. We must tread carefully."

Leema nodded. "All right."

A key jangled in the door, and metal scraped on metal. The door swung open, and a guard poked his head in. "Well, we've arrived. Been good to meet you. I don't envy the next stage of your journey."

"What do you mean?" Leema stroked Dinko's tail.

"Someone knew you were coming." The guard shrugged. "There is a troop of the Arazi's guards on the dock waiting for you."

"Who would have known?" Leema looked at Aritha.

Aritha shrugged and shook her head.

"Shall we?" The guard gestured for the girls to come out.

"Come along." Aritha pulled herself up to her full height and moved regally out of the cell.

Leema followed with her head high. Dinko sprang from Leema's shoulder over to Bazin's as they filed up the companionway into the fresh sea air. The lemur dug his claws into Bazin's shoulder as their guard stepped up to the waiting Imperial officer. Bazin didn't hear what he said, but the officer turned and shouted for a wagon to be brought over.

Noise and smells surrounded them as they rode through the city to the palace. Darkness had fallen, and bright spots of torchlight glared as they wove through the streets. Soon, the wagon rumbled through the gate of the Imperial Palace, revealing a bustling hive of color and light. Bazin watched Leema's face light up in awe. He wished he could share her enthusiasm, but he had a bad feeling about this meeting. The silence of the Imperial officer as he reached up to help the princesses out of the wagon increased Bazin's anxiety.

The Imperial guard took up an escort formation: two in front, two behind, and two on the left and right as they marched the princesses, Bazin, and Porsa through the palace. His assassin training kicked in. He took note of the footmen who stood near every door and the maids who scurried about, tending to household duties. He marked every possible exit and began to plan. He had hoped they would be taken to a waiting area until they could have a private audience, but the Imperial officer took them through the main door, straight to the dining hall. It didn't bode well that he had no qualms about interrupting the evening meal. In his experience, the ruling class never liked to have their meals interrupted.

Bazin wondered if the sailor had been right, *Are they expecting us? Who could have warned them?* Bazin pushed his speculation aside. He needed to focus on not getting locked up in the Arazi's prison. He needed to get back to Ro.

The guards stopped just inside the door while the Imperial officer spoke to the steward. Bazin surveyed the room. Nearly a hundred members of the Court had gathered for the formal evening meal and were sitting at tables arranged in a giant square, leaving the center of the room empty for entertainment. Minor members lined the walls, ready to serve the more prominent figures of the Court. Standing against the wall amongst the sycophants were several hooded figures in brown robes.

Drugi Moc? What are the dragon priests doing at Court? To Bazin's knowledge, they had never been welcomed by the Arazi. One of the priests had his hood pulled forward, shrouding his face. Bazin's gut twisted as he felt the man watching him. The Drugi Moc had paid to have him resurrected. Were they also the ones who commissioned Ro's assassination? It couldn't be a coincidence that they were here now.

"Krrr," Dinko chittered quietly into Bazin's ear.

"Oh n-no!" Porsa muttered.

Bazin glanced at him. The apprentice's face had lost all color. Bazin followed Porsa's gaze to the opposite side of the room, where several white-robed priests waited. The Holy Brothers were alternating between watching Bazin and glaring at the dragon priests.

This is going to get interesting, Bazin thought as he watched the two sets of priests.

The officer returned and led them to the center of the room. Suddenly, Bazin had a bad feeling that they were about to become the entertainment. Conversations stopped as they passed by, leaving a pregnant silence. The middle section of the table at the far end was raised above the others on a dais.

The Empress Neila Arazi sat at the center of the dais. Beside her, the prince slouched in his chair. Although he had reached the age of majority, he looked younger than Leema's sixteen years. Bazin's eyebrow lifted just a bit as he studied the Empress' son. He looked like his mother with dark hair and cruel eyes. However, that is where the similarity ended.

"What is this interruption?" Prince Vayle Arazi moaned in a bored voice.

The officer bowed. "Princess Aritha and Princess Leema of Koric, Your Majesty."

Aritha and Leema sank into perfect curtsies and stared at the floor. Bazin tugged Porsa down to his knees.

The Reckoning

"SO, YOU'VE FINALLY COME crawling in?" Empress Neila stared down her nose at the group. "You seem to be missing a few family members."

"My Empress," Aritha remained bowed, "forgive our late arrival, but I fear that disasters have kept us from reaching the celebration of Prince Vayle's majority."

"Really?" Empress Neila raised delicate eyebrows, then smiled slowly, but her voice was like a whip when she finally spoke. "By all means, Lady. Explain."

Bazin's knees were aching by the time Aritha had finished telling their story. He couldn't help but hate the Empress for forcing them to continue kneeling throughout the entire explanation. He was relieved that Aritha left out his reason for joining them and his connection to Ro, explaining his presence as a 'lucky circumstance'. However, he was surprised by Aritha's praise of Ro and her tireless efforts that had kept them all alive.

Empress Neila leaned forward. "And where is this guard with such ferocious loyalty?"

The Court snickered at the venom in the Empress' words. Bazin clenched his jaw. He wasn't sure why it bothered him that she was asking about Ro, but it did. Leema shifted nervously, and out of the corner of his eye, Bazin noticed Porsa was shaking. Bazin flicked a glance at Aritha, hoping that she would lie, that she *could* lie.

"Unfortunately, she fell to the dragon that attacked Your Majesty's warship."

Bazin was impressed. Aritha's voice held no sign of deception. He glanced up at the Empress. She didn't look convinced.

"Unfortunate indeed." The Empress leaned back and tapped her fingers on the table in front of her. "An interesting story, Princess. However, I am appalled that you would make up such fantastic lies."

"I know that our tale seems outlandish, Your Majesty," Aritha continued carefully, "but it is all true."

"Why should we believe you? For all we know, this is some elaborate plot against the throne!" The Court gasped at the Empress' words. "Koric has already been declared outlaw for its defiance of the Arazi's authority." Neila glanced around, playing to the shocked Court. "How can we trust the words of those from Koric?"

"No!" Leema's protest burst out of her before she could stop herself.

"Leema!" Aritha's hissed warning silenced her sister. Aritha looked back up to the dais. "Your Majesty, Koric has been loyal to the Arazi for centuries. Our failure to attend the swearing was not an act of defiance. It was an accident. We tried to reach the Imperial City as quickly as possible. Surely sending a message to Koric would sort out this misunderstanding."

"Don't patronize me. We have sent messages to Koric. Our messengers never returned. Koric has refused all communication." Empress Neila glared down at Aritha. "That is a pretty clear answer."

"Has there been no word from the queen or our brother Sebastian, then?" Aritha glanced at Leema. The worry was plain on her face.

"We haven't heard a thing!" Prince Vayle snorted.

"And now just two of you appear and say that you were lost, with not a shred of proof! I find that a bit suspicious." Empress Neila spoke to the Court, encouraging their agreement.

Prince Vayle sat forward eagerly. "*Do* you have proof?"

Aritha shook her head. "Just the evidence of our bodies and our missing sister."

"Well," Empress Neila sat back and smiled, "that isn't good enough, is it?" Silence stretched as she waited for Aritha to come up with a response. "Nothing to say?" She glared at each princess. "I have half a mind to throw you all in Zatvor as enemies of the Arazi!"

Bazin's gut clenched. There was no way he was going to rot in that mine for the few remaining days he had. "Your Majesty?" Bazin's voice echoed in the silence. "I believe that I have the proof you are looking for."

His declaration sent a buzz of whispering through the hall. Leema glanced at him, but he kept his eyes on the Empress.

"Who addresses the Empress?" A steward stepped forward from the end of the Empress's table. He eyed Dinko. "What business have you with these proceedings?"

The Empress' eyes drifted over Bazin, pausing on Dinko. "Speak."

"I have been traveling with these lovely ladies for nearly a month."

"Ah," the Empress pursed her lips, "you must be the 'lucky circumstance'. And what proof do you offer?"

Bazin reached into his jerkin. Several guards stepped forward, then paused as he pulled out a packet of papers. "I was given a sealed missive from the wise and noble Lord Caelan Pohle in Ka-Petra that will, I hope, corroborate our adventures in that fair city."

Out of the corner of his eye, he saw Aritha flinch as his eloquence surprised her. He was secretly pleased to shock her with his ability to use court flattery. She regained control of her expression as the steward came forward and retrieved the packet from Bazin. He could feel Leema's gaze as the Empress opened the packet and silently began to read.

"Well, well, well." Empress Neila glanced down at Aritha. "Lord Pohle confirms at least part of your story. It seems that you will be spared the mine."

Bazin winced as Leema's sigh of relief sounded overly loud.

"However, I still need to be convinced that your island is not mounting a rebellion, and until I am, you will not leave this palace." Empress Neila motioned for two guards. "You will be placed under house arrest until we can obtain some information about what is happening on Koric."

"You can't do that!" Leema blurted as a guard wrapped his hand around her upper arm, pulling her to her feet. "We have to find our sister!"

The Empress glared at Leema. "Young lady, I have had enough of your outbursts!" She flicked a glance at the Imperial officer and nodded at Aritha. "Place that one in confinement," Empress Neila turned angry eyes on Leema, "and put that one in the mine."

"No!" Aritha's face turned white as a guard took her arm and pulled her toward the door. "Leema!"

Leema threw a desperate glance at Bazin as she struggled against the guard.

He tensed, wanting to jump up and fight. He held Leema's gaze, hating the terror he saw there as she was hauled away. The Court had gone very quiet as if they were desperate not to be noticed.

"What of these two?" The Imperial guard gestured to Porsa and Bazin.

The officer's questions forced Bazin to push aside his anger over Leema. He glared at the Empress.

"Confine them as well." The Empress waved a hand dismissively. The Court began to chatter as the Imperial guards encouraged Porsa and Bazin to stand.

"Krrr." Dinko danced nervously on his shoulder.

Desperation bloomed in Bazin's chest. He couldn't allow them to lock him away.

"I'm sorry, Your Majesty," Bazin's voice rang out over the din, "but that will not be possible."

His declaration shocked the Court into silence again.

"Excuse me?" Empress Neila turned to glare at him.

Bazin smiled and bowed slightly. "I have a prior obligation that won't wait."

The Empress sat forward. "Your obligations do not matter one whit to me!"

"I'm afraid that this one does," one of the Holy Brothers stepped forward.

All eyes turned. The owner of the voice shuffled forward until he was standing between Bazin and Porsa. The silver-haired monk inclined his head but did not kneel. Behind him, five more white-robed monks drifted forward, forming a semi-circle behind Bazin and Porsa.

"Master Farin." The Empress eyed the monk with barely concealed loathing.

"You are a long way from your mountain, Brother." The Prince glared at the monk.

"Indeed." Master Farin crossed his arms and tucked his hands into his sleeves. "A long way for one so old as I, but I am afraid that it was a necessary journey."

Empress Neila lifted her chin slightly. "State your business, monk."

Bazin narrowed his eyes. *Since when has there been animosity between the Arazi and the Brothers?*

"I have come to retrieve these two souls." Master Farin reached out and placed a hand on both Porsa's and Bazin's shoulders. "Through Holy Edict, we assert our claim."

"You deal with the dead, Brother." Prince Vayle snorted. "Those two are still alive. You should leave us to deal with the problems of the living."

"Hush!" Empress Neila hissed at her son. The sullen prince sat back and crossed his arms.

Empress Neila flicked a glance at the left-hand side of the dining hall. Bazin followed her gaze. The hooded dragon priest had stepped forward. He turned from Bazin to the Empress and inclined his head as if granting permission. Bazin looked back at the Empress. She nodded slightly. Bazin narrowed his eyes.

The Empress's smile was all teeth as she gazed down at the Holy Brothers. "If this is the purpose of your visit, then take them and go with all haste. For you are not welcome here."

A surprised murmur rippled through the Court. The Empress openly favoring the Drugi Moc over the Holy Brothers did not bode well. It put her in direct conflict with the Emperor's ideologies.

Bazin's eyes widened as his mind began to race. *If the Empress is dealing with the Drugi Moc, and if they were the ones who had me resurrected, is the Empress involved?* He glanced back at the dragon priests. *This can't be just coincidence. Why would she want Ro dead? What does this have to do with Koric? Just what am I in the middle of?* Bazin had the feeling that whatever it was, he might not live to find out.

Master Farin's lips tightened as he bowed to the Empress. With some urgency and more than a little anger, Master Farin turned to Porsa and Bazin. "Come. It is time to repay your debts, and we are nearly out of time."

About the Author

Adriana Pridemore has loved reading and writing all of her life. She has been a journalist, freelance editor/proofreader, and teacher. She currently lives in Montana with her wonderful husband and family, a fuzzy feline queen, a judgmental but cuddly Schnauzer, and a moose-sized St. Bernard.

Also by Adriana Pridemore

Council of Races Series

This Job Sucks!

Your Job Bites!

Worst Job Ever!

Short Stories

(Available on Amazon KDP)

Just a Little Nap

The Apple's Bite

Flaming Fang

Bonus!

If you like the works of Adriana Pridemore,
please scan the QR code and sign up for my newsletter.
You'll get a free short story!

Also, follow Adriana Pridemore on social media:
On Facebook at Adriana Pridemore Author
On Instagram at @adrianapridemore

www.ingramcontent.com/pod-product-compliance
Lightning Source LLC
LaVergne TN
LVHW041142150826
845673LV00001B/56